The Confessions of Sherlock Holmes

THE THEOLOGICAL ODYSSEY OF THE GREAT DETECTIVE
Volume 5

The Estates of Sherlock Holmes

Thomas Mengert

Blue Forge Press
Port Orchard, Washington

The Estates of Sherlock Holmes
Copyright 2024
by Thomas Mengert

First eBook Edition August 2024
First Print Edition August 2024

ISBN 979-8-89439-015-4

For information about film, reprint or other subsidiary rights, contact: blueforgegroup@gmail.com

Blue Forge Press is the print division of the volunteer-run, federal 501(c)3 nonprofit company, Blue Forge Group, founded in 1989 and dedicated to bringing light to the shadows and voice to the silence. We strive to empower storytellers across all walks of life with our four divisions: Blue Forge Press, Blue Forge Films, Blue Forge Gaming, and Blue Forge Records. Find out more at www.BlueForgeGroup.org

Blue Forge Press
7419 Ebbert Drive Southeast
Port Orchard, Washington 98367
blueforgepress@gmail.com
360-550-2071 ph.txt

Acknowledgements

The Confessions of Sherlock Holmes has, for all of its primary theological intent, a subtext that emerged in the course of the writing. That subtext is the decline and fall of the British Empire and of the imperial family structures that once supported it. The three Holmes brothers each manifest the end result of the system of primogeniture and the conflict present between art and reason in their blood. Each brother in his own way manifests the conflict entailed in finding a place and an identity in opposition to their father and his estate.

The character of the Holmes father remains distant and perhaps finally indecipherable. As the reader will discover in the course of reading the book the parental figure looks beyond his own sons in order to find an image of a substitute son that would meet the requirements and the pattern that the father needed each of them to represent. Unfortunately, each son manifested instead a diluted solution of traits that drew more from their artistic mother and her French heritage than from their stern father and his code. The individuality and character of the brothers manifests a freedom from convention that the father perhaps wished that he could have claimed for himself, but to see it present in his sons seemed both indulgent and a betrayal of his own strict principles. He valued rebellion, but not within his own house and among his own progeny. For this reason both Mycroft and Sherlock are comparative exiles, while Sherringford is saddled with maintaining Sigerside, the Holmes estate. If the Christian religion can be seen as the process of overcoming exile from God as Father through the sacrifice of a Son, the parallels will be immediately apparent.

I doubt that I would have been able to compose this book if it were not present as a reflection of the dynamics of my own family. So for this reason I dedicate this book as with all my efforts in life to my parents and grandparents and especially to my two grandmothers who each nurtured my early love for literature with their deep love and affirmation.

The support of my parents made my life possible in every way imaginable.

To my Father's mother, Tilly, who read me Longfellow's poetry on sunny afternoons.

To My Mother's mother, Gerda, who gave me the Doubleday Edition of The Complete Sherlock Holmes.

To my Father's father, Otto, who shared his library with me and taught me the value of family heritage.

To my Mother's father, Fred, who instilled in me a love of the sea and for his humor and love of stories.

To all of these my everlasting thanks.

"What is the meaning of it, Watson?" said Holmes, solemnly, as he laid down the paper. "What object is served by this circle of misery and violence and fear? It must tend to some end, or else our universe is ruled by chance, which is unthinkable. But what end? There is the great standing perennial problem to which human reason is as far from an answer as ever."

—From The Adventure of the Cardboard Box

"There is nothing in which deduction is as necessary as in religion," said he, leaning with his back against the shutters. "It can be built up as an exact science by the reasoner. Our highest assurance of the goodness of providence seems to me to rest in the flowers. All other things, our powers, our desires, our food, are really necessary for our existence in the first instance. But this rose is an extra. Its smell and its color are an embellishment of life, not a condition of it. It is only goodness which gives such extras, and so I say again that we have much to hope from the flowers."

—From The Adventure of the Naval Treaty

"The greatest schemer of all time, the organizer of every deviltry, the controlling brain of the underworld, a brain which might have made or marred the destiny of nations – that's the man!"

"Barker beat his head with his clenched fist in his impotent anger. 'Do not tell me that we have to sit down under this? Do you say that no one can ever get level with this king devil?' 'No, I don't say that,' said Holmes, and his eyes seemed to be looking far into the future. 'I don't say that he can't be beat. But you must give me time—you must give me time.' We all sat in silence for some minutes while those fateful eyes still strained to pierce the veil."

—From The Valley of Fear

Preface

Readers of the previous volumes of The Confessions of Sherlock Holmes will notice an altered preface for this present volume in the series. The initial preface that was included in the first three volumes was designed to act as a base and to prepare the reader for the unique style and methodology employed in this multi-volume retelling of the final decades of the life of the great detective, Sherlock Holmes. Many avid Sherlockians have awaited a synthesis where many loosely connected threads in the original tales of Sir Arthur Conan Doyle begged for a comprehensive solution. It was this need that The Confessions of Sherlock Holmes was written to fulfill.

When the series was initially written it was composed sequentially so that even in its formation the twin narratives could not anticipate what would happen next. In this sense the entire series was dictated by Holmes and Watson rather than being imposed upon them by an outside voice. The overriding intent was to write the ultimate Sherlock Holmes adventure while simultaneously answering some of the most challenging questions posed by theology and philosophy, while addressing the deeper questions raised by human beings during the course of their lives.

Such an ambitious project had not been attempted since the writing of two major works by the modernist literary figures

Marcel Proust and Robert Musil who together served as models for the present work. Each of these authors envisioned a multi-volume work that would contain every aspect of human life during a significant historical period, one that was very close to the time period chosen for The Confessions of Sherlock Holmes—the end of the 19th century and the period after the *fin de siècle* leading up to what is now called World War One.

When the entire series was completed and initially published in 2014 in a separate edition its length was just over 830,000 words. The present edition with its extensive revisions now includes an eighth volume sequel and contains over one million words in 20 Books printed in 7 volumes (plus the 8th volume sequel). This places the series among the longest fictional narratives written in any language. Its length was in keeping with the complexity of the subject and the example set by *In Search of Time Lost* (formerly translated as *Remembrance of Things Past*) by Marcel Proust and *The Man without Qualities* by Robert Musil that was left incomplete by the author's untimely death. Both of the latter works belong to the tradition of the philosophical novel that includes Thomas Mann's, *The Magic Mountain* and two novels by Herman Broch: *The Sleepwalkers* and *The Death of Virgil.*

The ultimate dream of every author committed to the great treasury of literature is to devise a new form to communicate the deepest human truths. Recent parallels in this effort embrace musical composition as the inspiration. The Confessions of Sherlock Holmes with its sequel may together be thought of as analogous to a symphony. The first volume forms an overture to the whole symphony. The second and third volumes form the 1st movement of the symphony. The fourth and fifth volumes represent the 2d movement of the symphony. The sixth and seventh volumes represent the 3d movement of the symphony, and finally the eighth volume represents the climatic 4th movement of the symphony.

The astute reader will notice that a resolution is sought to many of the institutional problems confronting the Catholic Church, and theology in general today, as anticipated in the debates of Holmes and Moriarty. Various echoes of Kierkegaard, Nietzsche, Feuerbach, Sartre, Heidegger, the post-modernists, and various textual and linguistic theorists such as Jacques Derrida and Ferdinand de Saussure will appear. Sherlock Holmes and Professor Moriarty are about to meet in volumes 5 through 7, face to face, and to begin their long-awaited battle of wits over the nature of human existence and the quest for a solution to what philosophers refer to as "the problem of evil."

In the remaining volumes of the series other characters are introduced to expand the scope of the debate. Sherlock Holmes, Doctor Watson, and the woman who accompanies them face an expanding circle of challenges as they review their lives and examine the events and relationships that have defined their separate identities and set the stage for all their hopes and dreams. Finally, the eighth volume sequel, entitled *The Testament of Sherlock Holmes,* alters the format of the series while being an uninterrupted continuation of the previous seven volumes. There the saga reaches the 20th century and the haunting omnipresence of the Great War of 1914-1918 as well as the peace settlement that followed its termination. The final volume of the series embraces the retirement years of the great detective as he assumes a greater role in the overarching events that still cast their shadow over the present world.

The Estates of Sherlock Holmes

THOMAS MENGERT

Book Eleven

The Eternal Questions that Lie Before Us

Preface by Dr. Watson

I have entitled Book 11 of this extended narrative covering the last years of my association with Sherlock Holmes, *The Eternal Questions that Lie Before Us*. It recounts the beginning of the series of encounters that eventually led Professor Moriarty to cast in his lot with us and to agree to help us in our efforts to bring to bay the redoubtable Baron Maupertuis.

Some of my readers may have initially wondered why I required four previous volumes in this epic work in order to reach the point where I could record this decisive battle of wits between these two intellectual gladiators, Sherlock Holmes and Professor Moriarty; but a moment of reflection will reveal the reasons for my choice of this unique method of narration.

The first is that the form of this literary work differs radically from that of the ordinary mystery story where the surprise revelation at the end provides the mainspring of the reader's interest and the final reward for the persevering reader. I could hardly count on the patience of the average sensation seeker to avoid jumping ahead to read the outcome at once and perhaps then dismissing most of the remainder of the book as a superfluous journey. The truth is that this book is not as much about the defeat of Professor Moriarty as it is about the means by which he was defeated, or rather not defeated but liberated from a course of thought that had led him to defeat himself by forfeiting his chance of obtaining eternal happiness in heaven. It has always astonished me how often men of great wit and intellect such as that possessed by Professor Moriarty will use every means at their disposal to undermine the dignity that is implied by having an eternal destiny in a life of intimate communion with God. What can be the reward for compromising or calling in question the deepest instinct of human life that our thoughts and actions have a meaning deeper than any that may be encompassed by the merely material and temporal order? From whence comes this desire to limit the full prospect of human life by confining our horizon to the brevity of an average lifespan that no matter how long it may appear from the perspective of our youth seems all too short as we suddenly find that we have unaccountably grown old.

Who is that strange specter gazing back at us each day from our looking-glass? Who traced, seemingly overnight, those furrows of care or dulled that once sparkling eye? Is the prospect of error in this one regard, the hope for eternal life really so fearful, particularly when one considers that if there is no life after death we shall never know that our trust was misplaced? Should the many comforts of religion particularly in times of adversity be denied to the many people who may profit by its comforts simply in order to placate the few sour stoic philosophers whose only joy appears to lie in reminding poor suffering mortals like us that life often has few joys or assurances and even these most uncertain and rare? Why should we be urged to welcome death as an end of our troubles rather than a termination of all our hopes?

So it is that I have written this great tome of many volumes even in this most dreadful period of our collective European history, the Great War that still rages on the battlefields of France. It has been written so as to celebrate the struggle for faith of those who have not found that quest to be an easy one. My intention has not been to awaken doubts and discouragement in simpler souls for whom a gentle and unquestioning faith has never been in question, but rather to reach those souls who have a perverse instinct for discontent, for doubt, and for the diminishment of the residual glory of the human race possessed even after the fall of our first parents, Adam and Eve in the Garden of Eden. I also desired to humble those who in the pride of technological conquest have forgotten the final frailty of our human nature, so that they could substitute for the vision of some future grand triumph of mankind's own engineering and design the hope that religion offers in the patient waiting of the Christian for the promised return of the Savior of the World Jesus Christ and the final revelation of the renewed stature of the sons and daughters of God.

Another reason for my choice of form in this final literary effort of mine is due to my own doubts that I would ever live to finish it. Even now the end of my labors, though it is already in sight, is by no means guaranteed at the time that I write these words. It is in the nature of man to always live in advance of himself and I am no exception to this general rule. Still my health seems sound and my walks at home by the sea keep me fit and trim, even if not as strong and hearty as I once was as the man who once stood side by side with Sherlock Holmes fighting crime and solving mysteries.

As regards the search for an entirely earthly happiness, which of us does not entertain some private notion of individual bliss, one in many cases that is divorced from the only true happiness that justifies an irrevocable hope that it will finally be attained? The early and imperfect views we might display in pursuit of private happiness is that of a version of the world that would most perfectly correspond to the dictates of our own will. Sometimes we actually manage to achieve some fragment of this mélange of earthly desires. We hold that life to be most fortunate that combines pleasure with longevity. We envy those persons who have been spared most of life's humiliations at the hands of ignorant or stupid men and women. We bestow our admiration on those who are gifted with wealth and beauty and feel ourselves ill-used by an unkind fate if our circumstances have denied us these same advantages to obtaining security and a happy life.

Others ask less of fate and account it sufficient if the body they were given by God has been free of constant pain or deformation. Among the various candidates for what constitutes life's blessings few of us covet crosses, trials, or tribulations. Yet we must admit that misfortunes and sorrows, although they may do little else, seem to perfect our character and strengthen our endurance and to open us to helping others who are similarly afflicted.

Good fortune in contrast often leads to a sense of the complete sufficiency of this life's joys, so that when the inevitable end of life comes at last to those who have been spared most of life's miseries, they must face in a single moment a loss that others have managed to spread out over a lifetime by facing the little deaths implied by pain, disappointment, and frustration. How great must be that discontent of spirit among the mighty of the earth when in an instant they are brought down to the common fate of mortality only to be buried in that same earth from which the majority of their fellows have through suffering learned not to spurn but to value as the path of sacrifice and the redemption of this present order of things by the grace of God. The life, death, and resurrection of Jesus Christ is thus the model for all humanity because it promises us our only lasting dignity and remembrance.

I must be honest and admit certain private reasons for writing as I have done here. Not the least of my motives was my desire to finally meet the challenge that Sherlock Holmes once posed to me that I could not write a simple textbook of detection without appealing to that desire for sensation and melodrama that so often animates the British reading public. All too many readers are addicted to what were once called penny-dreadfuls and forever return again and again to the shallow blandishments of romance. By allowing Holmes' own journal to tell half of the tale in this extended account of his life, while I in my own fashion endeavor to be as informative as I can be about the history and circumstances of our most intricate case together I hope that I might deserve his praise, but without the usual reservations that he was wont to apply towards my earlier efforts to celebrate his extraordinary gifts both as a detective and as man.

Lastly I desired to create something that would stand secure against the eroding agencies of time. I am not immune to the vanity that many men feel that leads them to compose some everlasting testimony to the days and nights of their lives that seem to be falling away like those last leaves of summer when the autumn is well advanced. In these last years of what I trust will soon be the end of the Great European War that began in 1914 I have used my pen as the only weapon of an old soldier. I have consumed my days and nights sketching together this combined tale in the form of two interwoven texts that cover the years from 1891 to 1900. I do not know if I shall live long enough to record the years of what might euphemistically be termed the retirement years of Sherlock Holmes that began in 1903. I will only say here that this period was more a change of vocation than a proper retirement. Much of its activities remain secrets of state and have not been revealed even to me. At the present time I am sworn to secrecy regarding those years. It may be that a final sequel will need to be composed by the man himself to complete the saga begun here. I will be content if I live to complete these last volumes of The Confessions of Sherlock Holmes. The story in this volume opens with an entry in his journal written in Copenhagen, his embarkation point for his long anticipated return to England and to the home of his youth at the estate of Sigerside in Yorkshire. Onward then dear reader, for the game is afoot!

From the Journal of Sherlock Holmes

April 22, 1893
Copenhagen

I have arrived in Denmark. Today I booked passage on a small inter-coastal merchant steamer for my passage cross channel to Whitby. How hungry I am being this close to home for my first glimpse of my beloved England. After leaving Paris I traveled northwards across Belgium and into Holland. I spent the night in Amsterdam and before leaving by train was able to visit the site of the former home of the great Jewish Philosopher, Baruch Spinoza. Though our disagreement, theologically speaking, is fundamental, I honor the man for his extraordinary sincerity and courage. His image of God as the mere totality of all things still has about it a sense of wonder and even of worship. Men like him, though in error, may be closer to the truth than they suppose. Which is better after all, to seek to approach God in Himself or to confine theology to the content of divine revelation? If God, as He truly is, exceeds all of our concepts, then he must exceed revelation even as embodied in Sacred Scripture as well. Insofar as any revealed truth is adaptable to our limited minds and capable of formulation in words it must be changed in the translation process from what, in itself, it is. God must then be to that extent lost in translation. Can Spinoza be justly blamed much less justifiably excommunicated by his own Jewish community, as he in fact was, if he attempted to invigorate the concept of the deity through direct observation of the furthest parameters of God's creation? Is his category error any more egregious than the absurd strictness of an orthodoxy that has bequeathed to so many ardent believers the sanguinary image of God depicted in the early books of the Bible? Which is better, to seek God with a sincere heart, or to blandly accept an inadequate image stitched together from carefully abstracted phrases drawn from, scripture?

As an author I can see that any revelation of character is a continuous process. This is true even of my gradual revelation of my own thoughts and observations as presented in my accounts supposedly written by this fabulous if fictional Norwegian explorer, one Knut Sigerson.

It would appear that this explorer, Sigerson, is well known now outside of Norway and that even the Danes consider him to be a national hero. I had barely signed into my hotel under my false passport in his name when either the desk clerk or one of the staff noticed my still bronzed complexion and noting the name Sigerson drew the inevitable conclusion that I was the very man who has been called recently, the Nordic Marco Polo.

This morning a small crowd of journalists surrounded me in the lobby after I had finished my breakfast of kippers and eggs and requested an interview. I told them that I would give the interview on the condition that it must not appear in print until I had departed their fair city. I explained that I was about to begin a book length summary of my travels and that I had rented a cottage in England where I might complete this labor in peace and isolation. Though I appreciated the esteem of the public, I required time and a private retreat to add to the glory of the Nordic nations by continuing the labors that had made me famous.

They readily agreed to my conditions. Thank heaven that journalists in Europe have yet to descend into the maelstrom of the intrusive and convoluted creations of the American newspapers. I made no mention to them of Colonel Moran, since it was part of the persona that I have assumed that I am a lone explorer. Besides, the Colonel has known enough of notoriety in India and I knew that he would prefer that no mention should be made of his part in my recent adventures in the Far East.

The reporters remarked at my excellent English and I explained that it had been my habit to practice the tongue of the next place on my itinerary as preparation. I tossed out a few phrases of Tibetan, Farsi, and Hindustani which satisfied them that I was indeed an accomplished linguist though my brief expostulations represented the sum total of my knowledge of those languages. I was fortunately not asked to converse in Norwegian as a courtesy to me since I know not a word of it. The reporters were soon satisfied with a few colorful stories which I related and I was left to spend a quiet day in Copenhagen with my general anonymity still intact.

We shall cross the channel in a few days to Whitby and I shall be in England again at last. I shall spend some time in Whitby simply to enjoy the novel sensation of homecoming and to enjoy again the pleasure of smelling the heather, of eating cockles and whelks by the harbor, and wandering about on the sea cliffs that overlook the channel from the ruined abbey above the town. I am still at times troubled by a persistent cough and there can be no doubt that I have used myself up too freely in these last two years.

I do not have a delicate constitution, but my habits have been irregular over much of my career. Watson has often needed to take me in hand and I have wanted the benefit of his reproachful eye and general supervision of my health during my travels. Sun and wind have had their effects as well as the ghastly foods I have had to endure. Often dreamed of steak and kidney pie and the thought of fish and chips has been enough to induce a sort of trance-like state in me. Oh for a pint of Guinness in a local pub and the friendly talk of Englishmen!

To travel is to know that only one nation can ever truly be ours. Even the mists of English fields and the smell of new mown hay are dear to me. The sight of a white and well-kept English cottage with crocuses crowding the path to the door, the pale beauty of English women, the hale and honest laborers, a brace of spaniels with an elderly gentlemen, partridges rising from a field;

these and a thousand other images suggest themselves to me and all cry out to me, "England!" I think often of the great lines by Robert Louis Stevenson that he desired for his epitaph, "Here he lies, where he longed to be; home is the sailor, home from the sea, and the hunter home from the hill."

April 23, 1893
Copenhagen

The habit of recording my daily reflections here has now become habitual. The question of how one is to approach religion appears to me to be both central and at the same time not immediately apparent. For much of the history of Christianity theology was dedicated to applying the philosophy of the day to texts that still bore the primary imprint of the original Hebrew mindset, rooted as it was in the particular fate of the Jewish people for whom all other nations and people were a threat and an impediment to the final triumph of Jerusalem.

The early spread of Christianity took over this sense of difference and of exclusivity but now applied it to the church centered on Rome where it was to eventually emerge supreme. The ocean of conflicting mystery cults present at the time of Jesus Christ lacked both the appeal and the institutional efficiency of the Roman Church after the time of Constantine so that after the fall of the western empire Roman Catholicism emerged as the sole center of literacy and civilization in Europe as Christianity spread throughout Gaul and among the scattered German tribes and into Ireland and England.

This cultural supremacy remained unchallenged until the age of the French Enlightenment in the late 18th century after which industrialism and the secular and pragmatic scientific outlook it fostered dared to turn a skeptical and critical stance towards religion as a social institution and began to question the historical and cultural roots of religion. Even the texts of the Bible that had through the centuries become severed from critical inquiry as the sovereign word of God began to be approached less as iconic and simply as a carrier of information. This meant that textual study was less hesitant and reverential and more thoughtful and critical, seeking to discover precisely what was being communicated and to whom. The fractured Christianity that was the result of the Protestant Reformation could not bring forward a univocal voice to oppose incipient rationalism and even atheism. Even the Roman Church, stripped of its control over the empires through the royal families of France and Austria, could not oppose the rising tide of intellectual thought that was willing to see religion in a diminished capacity. Gibbon's massive book, *The Rise and Fall of the Roman Empire,* had already in elegant prose managed to encase Christianity in a gentle but firm denial that anything supernatural was in play and that Christianity was as historically conditioned and limited as any other period in the blundering and unsavory course of human existence.

Once stripped of its privileged and unquestioned status it was only a matter of time before theology, particularly when applied to Christianity, lost its aspect of joyous proclamation of the good news of salvation and took on instead an embattled stance, one that could claim venerable status in the history of the various branches of the inquisition that had vanquished heresies and stamped out folk-religion, superstition, and witchcraft over the course of the centuries. The devil who had once played a diminutive role in the Hebrew Scriptures had grown in status over the ages until by the present century and under threat of free inquiry had grown to hitherto unsurpassed status as a rival to God for world supremacy. The loss of the Papal States plunged Catholicism into a deep depression where even the Pope now fashioned himself as a prisoner of the Vatican. History now proceeds unhindered by fear of divine retribution, at least on this side of the grave. It is in this diminished posture that any appeal to theism must proceed in order to ground ethical thought in something more than commandments backed up by the threats of a supreme institution. The only other alternatives at the present moment are to ground ethics in reason, the categorical imperative of Immanuel Kant, or alternatively to ground ethics in either aesthetic preferences or in "the will to power" as suggested in *The Genealogy of Morals* by Friedrich Nietzsche. However, a third choice also beckons at this beleaguered time and from a decidedly Protestant source in the Danish writer, Soren Kierkegaard. Over the course of his short lifetime this extraordinary man returned Christianity to its stance of being a scandal to reason and foolishness to the wise. He managed to restore the element of risk to a complacent Christianity.

In this city of the great philosopher, Soren Kierkegaard, and before leaving the continent it may be helpful for me to comment on what it is to actually be a Christian as opposed to being counted among those who fall pre-reflectively into an automatic profession of one's being a Christian as a mere political act, an act of social cohesion rather than one of radical differentiation. To be a Christian is to rest one's entire being in life and after death upon a great contradiction: God became man in the person of Jesus of Nazareth, an actual living man with a particular life history, a life that is of universal significance because of why Jesus died and what He said while He was alive – who He claimed to be.

The proclamation that Jesus was and is today the expected one, the Christ, the messiah, was a radical proclamation even within Judaism when Jesus taught in the synagogues; how much more radical must this proclamation be when it is applied two millennia later long after the tumults of that vanished era are over. For Kierkegaard God's intervention begins with what he calls "the teleological suspension of the ethical" in his book, *Fear and Trembling.* Abraham is asked to take the supreme risk entailed in sacrificing his own son if God should command it. That God does not exact such a sacrifice after all and instead later sacrifices God's own Son Jesus is the fundamental paradox of Christianity, a paradox that can give us some insight into the efficacy of the atonement for sin worked by the crucifixion of Christ. God asks of God what God does not ask of humanity. It is we who demand strict justice for offenses; it is we who demand retribution and not God. It is our demand for punishment that keeps the wheel of revenge turning in age after age, even after the redemption wrought by Jesus.

To lose a sense of paradox and of vertigo when confronted by Jesus is to miss Jesus altogether. When theology is reduced to a science or to simple affirmation of a series of unconnected truths, each insular and discrete, Christianity ceases to be the fundamental ground on which one can base an entire life and becomes instead something cold and lifeless no matter how infused by passion and prejudice it may be.

The idea that Christianity should ever become the normative position of any society ignores the difficulty that Kierkegaard perceived in affirming a religion beset by various contradictions and improbabilities. A fierce and strident Christianity is a sign of doubt and insincerity rather than of firm faith and ardent charity. The command to preach the gospel to all creatures, baptizing them in the name of the Father, the Son, and the Holy Spirit is directly attributed to Jesus rather than simply being a commission to those who would carry out that mission from the church and at its command. Once any idea, no matter how exalted it may be, is assimilated into a human structure it ceases to be divine.

The idea that a sacred narrative cannot contain interpolated dialogue in order to reinforce a point seems a startling oversight in Biblical interpretation. To reject out of hand the possibility that the Jesus of Holy Scripture is as likely to be a creation of the documents in which Jesus is embodied for us would seem to deny the universal human tendency for any institution to justify its own existence by assembling a set of statements that inverts cause and effect. The Catholic Church traces its existence and mandate back to Jesus as cause, while it can at least be alternatively proposed and considered that the scriptural Jesus is a creation of the church, representing a gradual discernment of the nature of Jesus, who he was and what his life means for us.

The need and expression in the New Testament of a parallel accord with prophesies is as likely to be a product of editorial skill as it based upon the actual life of Jesus. The centrality and unique character afforded to Jesus by various proof texts such as the voice from heaven at the Jordan proclaiming the identity of Jesus as the Son of God, when the sound was heard by many as only the sound of thunder, is an example of this possible literary device of mysterious affirmation shared by a few but incomprehensible to the uninitiated. The effect is to flatter the believer and to denigrate the skeptical. The text alone cannot resolve this editorial possibility.

To be blind towards or in denial of human agency in religion is to deny the effort demanded by faith in what is in many respects a human project. Even the forceful sanctions imposed by the church against heretics through history, sanctions that did not stop short of violence, indicate the delicacy of even posing questions such as these. The history of Christianity would be entirely different if it was animated by the Holy Spirit in all of its aspects rather than simply using the event of Pentecost as a commission to enforce faith and compliance less by example than by injunctions backed up by force and by fear.

If these social powers were taken away Christianity would probably not have been the dominant force in European culture that it has been for the past two thousand years. The circular validation of ecclesiology is its most salient feature. Christianity and even our view of Jesus in His own subjectivity are best served by assuming that the self-deprecating statements of Jesus when He refers to Himself as the Son of Man and His re-directing to the Father alone the Kingship that the followers of Jesus would have impressed upon Him shows the solidarity of Jesus with our perplexity in the face of human pain and death as well as His submission to the will of the Father in all things. Occasionally theology appears to be in advance of itself. When we consider that The New Testament appears to be in many ways a desultory anthology we can appreciate that much of our certainty in later theology may be more a reflection of our own suppositions rather than a definitive last word on God. Not until the gospel of St. John do we have an elaborated theology of Jesus as the logos, the Eternal Word of God. The humanity of Jesus is too easily eclipsed.

A comprehensive Christology is as likely to be a self-serving human construction as the fulfillment of a Divine commission resulting in a guarantee of absolute truth.

By self-serving I do not mean in a purely selfish manner, although those who are money-changers in the temple are not confined to those who were present in the temple at Jerusalem. Self-serving behavior is more likely to be found among those who make an idol of certainty. If our salvation was best assured by obtaining comprehensive knowledge, Jesus would have included men drawn from other walks of life than simple fishermen and other common people. Elaborate liturgies, great basilicas, and other testimonials to the glory of God were later accretions that although not impious would have been viewed as of only secondary importance to those who shared the unmediated presence of Jesus among the people of Judea during His life. Not that Christianity needs to be frozen in place and time or confined to the early practices at Jerusalem, but it is essential to recognize that human ingenuity has played a role in the increasing complexity of doctrine and worship that grow up around any religion over time. Jesus left no encyclopedia behind at his ascension or even a definitive hymnal. There were no monasteries, hermitages, convents, or abbeys. The crusades were a millennium away and St. Thomas has yet to create his great *Summa* or St. Augustine his great treatise *The City of God,* yet souls were saved. Even most of the books of The New Testament had yet to be written. Where and to what then did Christianity refer its faith but to the indwelling Holy Spirit that initiated the Church at Pentecost.

April 24, 1893
Copenhagen

I was up early today to explore this lovely city located on two islands, Zealand and Amager. Copenhagen is a seaport with access by the Oresund to the North Sea and the Baltic nations. I am sitting in a café on the Magstraede with my journal before me. I had kippers for breakfast with an omelet and coffee and a small aperitif glass of Aquavit to set my wits aflame. To continue with my discussion here yesterday I would like to address the question of whether religion and ethics are two names for the same thing. Certainly if I plan to influence Professor Moriarty I should have at my disposal an alternative if he does not find the theistic option convincing.

By adopting a critical stance yesterday in my review of the approach to Christianity taken my Soren Kierkegaard I may have drifted from the Catholic position. Catholicism as its name implies is both authoritative and universal in scope. Nothing in Catholic belief implies that any sort of disunity is compatible with the single Mystical Body of Christ governed by the Pope and the Bishops as conservators of the fundamental truths leading to the salvation of the world. Metaphysics and ethics from this viewpoint of the faith lead in a straight line to affirmation and consent to follow the doctrines of the Church so as to merit heaven. The idea that any discipline, whether it be philosophy or science or even the arts, might call into question theology or have anything of substance to contribute as an added incentive to belief would seem to subtract from the strictly linear plan of God from creation to redemption to final judgment and the advent of the New Jerusalem.

Already there is suspicion that the human arts and sciences have moved from adornments to the faith to being the lens to focus on all things while setting up the criteria for what is acceptable in theology. For Catholicism the supposed risk implied by faith in the thought of Kierkegaard is the direct result of the drift from authority manifested ever since the time of Martin Luther. The overemphasis in Protestantism upon the individual and the centrality of the act of belief rather than living a virtuous life in hope of salvation (but without certainty) within the Catholic Church as the way to sainthood would appear to be the fundamental error leading to humanism. For a Catholic the act of faith is a necessary prerequisite of being a Christian, but is in itself insufficient to attain the end without the aid of the sacraments and the intercession of the entire body of believers in union with Christ as the head of the Church. The entire process of faith in

Catholicism then is communitarian rather than individualistic.

From this point of view intellectual temptation may be seen as a greater source of evil than the everyday human passions that beset us all and are part of the fallen nature of mankind. Part of the definitive nature of Catholicism is its view that this world is passing away. St. Ignatius of Loyola the founder of the Jesuits dared to address the world of great achievements manifested in the Renaissance while at the same time surrendering all things to God so that one should be ready to accept whatever may come our way in life without protest while seeking only the greater glory of God in everything that we do. So great was his ardor and that of his associates that in his lifetime members of the original tiny band in the Society of Jesus (the official name of the Jesuit order) had reached India under St. Francis Xavier and were soon to reach China and the American colonies.

Father Ignatius in his rules for thinking with the church would have provided an immediate answer, not only to Professor Moriarty but to me as well, since his entire approach to life was to ground our thinking in the direct experience of the love of God and of our love for God in return. Doubt, let alone systemic skepticism, would have been as absurd for Ignatius as to doubt his own existence – such was his commitment to the mission and the loyalty that he felt towards God. From this stance my effort to find God by traveling all about the world and entertaining alternative beliefs would have appeared a sheer waste of valuable time that might have been better spent feeding the hungry and clothing the naked and instructing the ignorant. To my protest that I thought I was doing the latter by asking such difficult questions he would have answered that such open intellectual queries are the fruit of idleness and lack of commitment. What would a universe without God care if I was mistaken and trusted and loved a God that did not exist? Even from a human point of view who can quarrel with the millions of selfless souls who have spent their lives joyfully serving others from within the heart of the Catholic faith for two thousand years?

Have I made too many concessions then in the initial wager

at the Reichenbach Falls that grants Moriarty equal standing in our contest as though it is to be waged between the two of us rather than between Moriarty and two millennia of European culture and ultimately with God. Do I need to do God's work for Him? Is the salvation of Moriarty up to me as the agent of God or is it Sherlock Holmes that I am trying to convince and was this true all along?

Who has standing to call God to account? Was that not the message of the Book of Job? Is that not the one aspect of Islam that should most motivate Christians to copy them in this regard and to submit our memory, our intellect, and our will to God and to search only for God's grace in this life while desiring nothing more and leaving the rest in God's dispensation?

My only defense for my arduous search is that questions will arise and some answer must be given and for that reason my wager with Professor Moriarty may serve some final end if only to formulate questions that may later be set aside as this manuscript must also be set aside perhaps to gather dust and to be forgotten even as empires rise and flourish only to fall and to decay.

To grasp the age of the world as its true antiquity is revealed to the questing geologists and paleontologists has made us all feel lonely. Where formerly mankind only reached backwards to a garden and to Noah and his sons, now we are confronted by endless vistas of space and time and where are we on a stage so large? What place has a shouting evangelist at a tent meeting when his voice little reaches the woods beyond the firelight let alone outwards to the stars? Even the grandeur of Catholicism is as nothing against such an array of hosts once thought of as angels floating about above the dome of many waters in a heaven unattainable but by faith. However homely and even naïve was that vision it was something that might still contain us and serve as a goal for our aspirations; whereas now, dwarfed beyond all measure my physics and by chemistry, questions of good and evil seem mere locations of matter that can be plotted on a graph in which any ethical element seems a post-hoc judgment rendered on events that have already occurred and are negligible when set against so vast a universe.

All the weeping of widows and mothers over their dead extracted at so much pain from their loins is inadequate to erase even what has already occurred through war and famine and pestilence let alone what will happen tomorrow and tomorrow and tomorrow. How can I place all this before Professor Moriarty to some good effect unless I do so in such a way that I awaken within him a degree of compassion so that the vision of God dying on a cross will seem less vain and even insignificant and appear instead as the only great and abiding mystery that says we are not alone and that God is with us, of us, and in us ... and we in Him.

April 25, 1893
Copenhagen

I have arranged transport home to England. I will take a ship that will carry me to Whitby on the coast of Yorkshire. It is just sufficiently remote that my arrival will go unnoticed with the added advantage that I am familiar with the town and it is only a short journey from there to Sigerside where I plan on meeting with my elder brother Sherringford. It is an odd thing to feel a sense of dread when returning home. There is something about travel that gives one a sense of invulnerability. Even danger is at times a pleasurable stimulus, perhaps because it keeps the nerves on edge, so that each day holds a prospect of adventure. A part of ourselves dies when we have been long absent from home, so perhaps what I am describing is really a fear of encountering a ghost of my former self walled up in routine and certainty, whereas my now well-traveled self has become a new creation, vital and alive. To visit the site of one's early youth is even more fearful. Which of us does not recall with greater poignancy the fears and pains of childhood that leave imprints so deep upon the soul that they can mold one's dispositions or even one's character for life? I am no exception to this general rule. England at least has the advantage of not having had a revolution since the defeat of Cromwell in the 17th century and the restoration of King Charles II on May 14, 1660. These national convulsions can leave scars on a generation and Denmark is no exception.

At the time of the Napoleonic Wars Norway and Denmark shared a common identity as one nation. In two eventful years, 1813 and 1814, the tides of war sundered Denmark-Norway (the citizens of which had preferred to remain neutral) stripping the Norwegians away from Denmark and joining Norway with Sweden, but with Norway under a separate constitution from Sweden. Any effort to remain at peace when the world is at war can make a nation anathema to both sides of the conflict. Norway had managed to sign its own constitution on May 17, 1814, but after a short war with Sweden waged from July 26 to August 14 of that same year of 1814 it was partially united to Sweden under a common sovereign after being awarded to that country by the Treaty of Kiel on January 14, 1814.

Aspirations of nationhood have supplanted much of the feudal relations of minor kingdoms and principalities in recent centuries. Many of these divisions are based upon ethnic or religious loyalties. However many nations embrace even different languages yet still manage to maintain a unified national consciousness. The tides of influence and of trade are complex so that economics as well as politics have a role to play in the division of nations. Only America, that strange conglomeration of peoples, has managed even at the cost of a great and bloody civil war to maintain a sort of unity that may soon make it the most powerful nation on earth. I must visit there someday. I have read Alexis de Tocqueville of course and even dipped into *The Federalist Papers* in my search for some clue as to the attractive force that draws all people to this fabled land of plenty and new frontiers.

The Americans have the privilege of escaping from (to a degree at least) from the fatal embrace of history. The desire to make all things new was the promise drawn from the prophetic Book of Isaiah and repeated in the Book of Revelation. This has been the hope of whatever refugees have managed to gain passage to the pristine shores of North America. Thereafter they have pressed ever westward in search of an arcadia where they might prosper but first to forget. Lethe is the ultimate desire of mankind and perhaps of women also; to allow the dead to bury their dead as Jesus once advised a young man to do.

What is tradition but the record of the past failed attempts to make the earth ready for the return of Jesus on the last day? The evidence of Christian history is that what began as ardent anticipation has succumbed with the years to a desire to secure our position here on earth as best we may while the centuries pass. The adjuration to remain always on guard "for you no neither the day nor the hour" has given way to lethargy and to sullen discontent. Instead Catholicism speaks of the Particular Judgment where each soul receives its due sentence while the General Judgment is indefinitely delayed. This bifurcation has the unfortunate effect of blunting the sense that neither heaven nor hell is a merely personal affair. We choose in the end the community that is most akin to our desire for a permanent domicile in eternity. Each day and night as we age becomes revelatory of the choice we will make in that final dread hour when the moral universe shall break apart like a great fissure in the land or the sea and all things will find themselves to be, where in some strange sense they have always been, in that composite coming home or that composite exile, either into light or into darkness for eternity.

April 28, 1893
Whitby

I am home at last! How can I describe the joy which came to me as the mists lifted as we approached and I beheld again the grey cliffs that rise above the harbor and the dense green of the surrounding moors? I seem to have been absent for decades and not for a mere two years! In reviewing my journal I see that my return to England is but a few days short of the two year anniversary of my departure from Dover to Oostende. My arrival was a quiet one. A gentle fog hugged the coastline so that my first glimpse of England was a drab olive shadow that soon resolved itself into the cliffs above the harbor and I could see the black outline of the old abbey that rises out of the old graveyard upon the hill above the town. Whitby has a somber charm and I have always loved it. I remember well certain beaches where I bathed as a lad on family holidays. As the mists on the channel parted I heard the familiar sound of the gulls and smelled again that sweet scent that every Englishman knows so well, the smell of sea and land mingled together in a common freshness that speaks of home.

The local county bank where I keep a small account had not closed and I presented a draft for funds at once and soon I had shillings and sovereigns in hand rather than Danish Kroner. My passage through customs had presented no difficulties. The stolid Yorkshire men took little note of "another of them Norway chaps on holiday." I found an excellent room above a pub near the water and I was soon standing along the quay with a cup of cold cockles and whelks in hand. I ate these homely items while I stood looking out into the fog as the evening mists gathered again and settled down upon the village. Mine was just such a homecoming as that which I had pictured in the bleak deserts of western Persia. The fall of the mist this evening was therefore most precious to me.

I am again in my cozy room as I write this after my afternoon of sightseeing. I have developed a certain love of eastern tobaccos while in the Arab lands and the scent of Turkish tobaccos and Latakia, mixed with an excellent Danish Cavendish, fills the air about me as I lean over the guardrail on my balcony and listen to the sea sloshing on the breakwater at no great distance from me. From now on I need not use the name of Sigerson, as so recently in Denmark, because no one will demand to see my passport. I am a native of Yorkshire after all and my mastery of Yorkshire dialect still remains from my youth in my linguistic repertoire. I know that I will soon be accepted after I have bought some proper English clothes tomorrow.

How strange it is for me to see the streets that I remember here from holidays in my boyhood. They seem to have grown smaller both physically and in the unique significance that they once had for me. Boyhood is the realm of adventure and fancy and mine once filled these streets with characters drawn from my

reading. Spies and black knights abounded and I would not have
been startled to have encountered ghosts or cyclopean monsters
around each corner or to see a sea serpent rise out of the depths
beyond the coastal traders and fishing boats of the harbor.

Who can say when we exchange the realm of fantasy for the
grim prosaic world of our maturity? Only in love does there seem
to endure that former world of silver delights. Only the lover
retains the capacity to find the infinite in his beloved, finding in
her all that once characterized all that the world that surrounds us
once contained of imagined romance. But let me not tarry on these
vagrant thoughts. I have decided to remain in Whitby through
May Day and to enjoy the festivities that always accompany that
traditional holiday here. The country-folk still have their rural
ways about them. Christianity often floats above a residue of
superstition and of pagan ceremonials that are not so much heresy
as they are folklore. They fulfill a certain function in the collective
identity of the people and to censure them would take many simple
joys away,

April 30, 1893
Walpurgis Night

To those who have survived the rigors of winter, spring
brings the promise of renewed life. The cultures of
northern Europe still retain the pagan Festivals such as
Beltane or the First of May when life springs forth in the budding
of the trees. Trees themselves were once seen as sacred to the gods
or goddesses of fertility, agriculture, and the hunt. Goddesses such
as Diana, Minerva, and Bridget, from whom we have the word
"bride," would be honored by kindling purifying bonfires on
hilltops. Boughs were cut from the trees to bedeck every house
and cottage. Even today young people go about the town singing
and small children dance about the Maypole. The Christian
church, recognizing in itself the source of new life, celebrates the
feast by honoring the Blessed Virgin Mary on this day who is
crowned Queen of the May. The aspirations of the people were not

changed then, but redirected to their proper end.

It seems to me that to use violence to rid a culture of what it has formerly held sacred only creates resentment so that any conversion obtained by such means must perforce be superficial. To drive a former religion into hiding only has the result of strengthening the resistance of the people. The better practice is to honor what has already been honored, but to extend reverence to embrace the new faith. For this reason it takes at least a generation for a missionary to create a new religious community. To proceed too quickly or with an attitude of arrogance is to extinguish the fire of faith before it may be well-kindled.

In just this way the efforts of the early Jesuit missionaries in China were once brought to nothing by a misguided fear at home of Chinese practices and usages by a new provincial who was fresh from Europe and thus contemptuous of the Chinese culture. China was lost to Christianity for centuries as a result of this prejudice. The enemy of Christian belief is often Christian practice. Today China is ravaged by opium introduced into China by England to restore the balance of trade so that the English habit of tea-drinking would not enrich China to the detriment of England. I saw some of this practice and its lamentable results in Tibet when I was there and again in Afghanistan where poppies grow abundantly. The desire to subject foreign peoples of the east to our own economies is an evil and a guilt that must be soon addressed if peace is to prevail.

In my own travels I have never forgotten that England was once a colonial land of Rome. Even today the signs of Roman rule are everywhere to be seen in Britain. Yorkshire is not far from Hadrian's Wall in Northumberland. In addition we have the mysterious ruins of the Druids or their predecessors in relics like Stonehenge. Finally, we have the ruins of the abbeys and monasteries that represent a type of economic arrangement that once defied the modern state. I have often thought that the major economic result of the confiscation of lands and buildings belonging to the Catholic Church and the looting of the monasteries and abbeys by King Henry VIII in the 16th century was the destruction of indigenous Catholic culture. It was also at this time that the common grazing lands of the peasant farmers began to be absorbed by the landed gentry and later to be purchased by the rising middle class. The way of life of the average English farmer and herdsman, which had been attached to the land and that we still see celebrated on May Day was thereby changed forever. Crops needed to be sold now to pay rents to landlords. A mercantile economy developed; the land was overworked and the balance of nature was destroyed.

Human life demands its seasons of celebration, the foremost being planting and harvesting. For this reason Jesus uses homely metaphors such as sowing and reaping for the gathering of souls into heaven. To extinguish what the people need for joy is to reduce natural human actions to slavery and to make of the gifts of the earth mere commodities. The magic vanishes from life. The religious instinct is killed. Work assumes an aspect of the treadmill that simply sustains the source of production while leaving behind no surplus that is not profit. Nothing remains unclaimed to serve as a source of largess and gleaning. There is no surplus for sacrifice to the gods in thanksgiving as in pagan times. There is no remnant left in the fields for the poor of afflicted to harvest so that they may have something for themselves not dependent upon charity. Worst of all there is no sense that all that we see is a common gift of God to be held in common out of mutual identity as human beings.

The rich man is destroyed by his superabundance just as the poor man is destroyed by his want and misery. Injustice creates mistrust and enmity between men and these must be controlled by arms and the threat of reprisal. For this reason every modern state is based upon the threat of force. Even the laws, no longer derived from God or from the common needs of the community, are imposed from above to sustain the very order of injustice that they should be used to prevent. This is the grasp of evil upon the world. Its results are to deny the sense of the sacred which is innate in the people and is shown most clearly in their love of life and their joy in their labor, which only becomes work when it is imposed to serve a master and not the people themselves.

Superfluity in some creates want in the many. The existence of riches in some creates poverty in others. Perhaps only on these barren moors and in the southwest of England can one still imagine the life that was once universal in England, a life of local custom where each parish saw to the needs of the people, a life where even the poor man could repair to the commons to supplement what he might earn as a laborer. Since we are all equal in the prospect of death and must ourselves suffer the fate to be reaped like ripened grain, should there not be equality in life, at least insofar as to procure adequate means for subsistence to exist among us? All human beings should be free from the prospect of an early death brought on by penury.

If we are to obtain these goods, there must be a renewal of the sacred within us. We must turn to the young who still feel the fire of hope within them if we are to create a better world. The existence of the young is the joy of the old, for it is to their charity that the old must look for succor in their coming age and disease. The old pagan ways celebrate this abundance. It is the young girls cut boughs and gather early flowers to present at each house as they pass. Song and dance invite the coming year's fullness. There is hope in harvest before the seeds are even sown. Thus man and woman have confidence in life and in themselves. There is none of that suspicion and mistrust that strangles human intercourse.

All of these innate virtues show that even pagans feel the first advent of grace even before its source is ever announced to them. Pagans are the children of the earth. For this reason I have made a study of the old ways and I intend to do more of this now that I am home. Already I have visited many old booksellers in town and have acquired a thick tome on the origins of tree worship, which will occupy much of my leisure reading in the coming year.

How grand it will be to assemble a library around me again! My odyssey and the need to travel without encumbrance precluded carrying about a wide selection of books with me. The absence of books was no small measure of the sacrifice that my journey has entailed for me. I was thrown back upon my memories, those very memories that now crowd thick about me, of my own youth here in Yorkshire.

Among those memories is the celebration of the First of May. Tonight bale fires will be lit upon the hills to drive away the witches who, the old customs believe, have this day to exercise their waning power before life again embraces the land. In central Europe this last day of April is called Walpurgis Nacht, the night when witches are abroad and the rule of evil has full sway. Today this belief is looked upon as merely an instance of harmless folklore, but there were times when these legends of the various forms of the preternatural were considered quite seriously. Many cultures set aside days for socially tolerated forms of excess such as the seasons of carnival when the chaotic and disordered impulses of human life can be brought out into the open and effectively purged through humor and masquerade.

Evil is allowed its night so that it may be purged. The purging is done by the rekindling of the light and by invocation. Burning brands are held high to frighten the witches away, for witchcraft is held by one and all to be among those forces that sour milk, that blights crops, and that kills the cattle and the swine. Evil is what destroys the life of the people in other words. If that should be so, then the tools of modern economic life would appear to be witchcraft indeed! Would that a mere bonfire might thwart the baneful influence of the commercial spirit gone awry!

It might be argued that the old feudal ways and the absolutist government that prevailed in the past could not have sustained our present levels of population. Only enhanced trade has allowed Europe to create and sustain the technological marvels of the day. It would appear that advances in science, technology, and the rise of middle-class prosperity always proceed apace. It is easy to forget though how new are the forms of thought and the institutions created by economic liberalism, which owes its existence to the French Revolution and the conquests of Napoleon. In a very short span of years the remains of serfdom were ended, the prerogatives and tax concessions to the nobility abrogated; monarchs were deposed and replaced by republics; and the even power of the Catholic Church confined. Christianity no longer dictated societal forms or controlled state policy.

With the decline of feudalism the power of the guilds was constrained so that the trades and then the military caste and bureaucratic positions were open to men of every class. The Jews were freed from the many prohibitions that had contained them within ghettos. There has even been an effort to extend the rights of freedom to contract and own separate property to married women under English law in recent decades.

For a few bright years it appeared that a liberated society might be recreated along the lines suggested by the philosophes of France. These hopes were not to be fully realized. After the defeat of Napoleon, The Congress of Vienna in 1815 imposed the will of the Holy Alliance as it was called. This peace conference restored many of the time-honored institutions of feudalism on the continent. Russia of course remained sunk in its peculiar and eternal night. Napoleon was defeated by Russia's endless expanse and by the winter that will always be Russia's rampart against any invader. England existed in a state of comparative immunity from these developments on the continent after the triumph of Wellington at the Battle of Waterloo.

The 19th century thereafter has belonged to England and to mercantilism. England's aristocracy was never dislodged by revolution, so that there was no need to adopt draconian measures to restore order by extirpating anything that might stifle commerce and trade. The result has been that England leads the world in industrial production and in trade with the east yet still retains its peasant culture. Many of the old ways are intact and a measure of trust between the social classes prevails in spite of the temporary unrest caused by the Chartist Movement.

Yet the England to which I have returned is already different from the England of my youth. The old agrarian ways are slowly passing. People are streaming off of the land to seek employment in the dark mills of Lancashire and the factories of

Manchester and Leeds. For this reason, it has brought joy to my heart to see that the old ways are still alive in a few remote places in England like Whitby.

Whitby seems to be not very different from my memories of it as a lad. The fishing trawlers still ply the channel and seek refuge from the sudden storms that can make of that short sea a maelstrom. The net weavers still ply their trade. The markets are filled with produce from the surrounding farms. I have dined on Yorkshire lamb and mint sauce and listened to the curlews and gulls as they circle the vessels in hopes of being fed by the fisherman. Already my travels seem to me like a dream. Was it I who traversed the mountain passes of Tibet? Did I dare to enter Mecca? Could I have crossed the mountains of Afghanistan and Persia? Surely some other man wandered the Abyssinian wastes and crossed the great plains of the Sudan. Yet it was I who did all those things.

To read certain entries in my journal now one might have supposed that I had remained always in the comfort of England, for I did not dwell excessively in its pages upon the discomforts of the journey. I shall never forget them of course, nor the many fears that dogged our steps through those often hostile regions. I sought in my journal to record my theological conclusions and to assemble an armory of arguments that I might apply against Moriarty upon my return. Now I feel both hope and dread of that encounter that must soon come. In what condition of mind will I find the Professor? Surely these past years may have caused some alteration in him. I must gage his disposition before proceeding to lay all of my cards upon the table. I fear that he will gaze at what are proofs for me of divine intent, raise his eyebrows, and say, "Surely this is a poor showing. You disappoint me, Holmes. Your exertions were all in vain. I think that I shall have to proceed with my plans after all, if you have nothing better to show for all your travels." In order to distract my mind from these fearful and burdensome thoughts, I have entered into a quiet realm of my own mind and memories. I have imagined that I might begin everything again, that I could stand here as I did once on a remembered holiday in my youth.

At that time so long ago I stood upon the sea cliffs above the town and walked the old graveyard that surrounds the ruined abbey. The gravestones made of sandstone that now lichen-encrusted and beset by salt, by sea mist, and by storm are etched by epitaphs that are now so blurred that the writing that should have memorialized the lost and vanished lives is now largely illegible. The meaning of their lives and the mere fact that they ever existed is witnessed by only the stubborn refusal of the tilting stones to fall to earth. The shadow that follows me as I wend my way among these graves is the shadow of a man in his middle years. My sun is overhead but I can conceive that it may already have passed its zenith. How long can it be before I, like these lichen-tarnished stones, begin to bend earthward with inevitable age?

Each generation imagines that it is immortal, that time will always gather laurels and blossoms to deck the laps of the present inhabitants of earth. It is as though life had never coursed through other veins with the same force. The dead appear to the young to be like natural features of the landscape. The gravestones that remain as the last testimony to their passing stand like those rocks and hills bedecked with heather and gorse bushes. The dead were also young at one time and as impervious to any thoughts of mortality. They too were once filled with hopes and aspirations. These dreams must yield fruit within the few years allotted by maturity or be lost forever. How soon does that inner sense of limitation begin, an intuition of mortality that only grows greater with each year to remind them of the fleeting course of time that soon mocks the few years that remain by moving with greater rapidity as old age approaches?

Suddenly, the graves that had seemed so picturesque on a spring morning in youth assume the dire aspect of destiny as they do now to me and as portals to the netherworld. It seems to me now that had providence allowed this world to be more beautiful than it is, we would weep so to leave it that even heaven would provide us an inadequate solace for our loss. But Christian belief assures us that there will be a resurrection of the body also, so that we may imagine that we will scent the grasses of spring once more and that we will see the sun rising from the ocean and see the mists rising to a new day when our bodies will rise again. This is the comfort that allows us to revere this fallen earth as still redolent of Eden and to imagine joys that exceed the heart's aspirations when God's promises are to be at last revealed.

If my youth seems with each year more distant and more alien to my present self, I pause then and reflect that in a similar manner how distant then will appear all of our present sufferings. All the troubles and premature conclusions that lead many to despair will be placed in their proper order and perspective. No doubt a pattern will emerge that is completely indiscernible from our present vantage point. The joyful reunion of both soul and body on the last day, although seeming to be a futile dualism, will in fact be a marriage where the soul will so radiate through the body that every ill will vanish and every accidental distinction find a new harmony in God.

May 1, 1893
May Day

I stood last night in the moonlight by the old abbey and watched as the fires were kindled upon the hills surrounding the town in areas cleared for that purpose. The sounds of revelry and music came to me with the wind in snatches while the town slumbered peacefully below. I could see the shadows of the young lads leaping over the flames of one nearby fire. Doing so is said to shake off the evil of winter and to bring good luck for the coming year. That this feat requires no small daring also impresses any young maids in the area who are in attendance at these revels.

Mead is served in brimming beakers to all present and toasts are drunk to the Green Man and his consort, The Bride, and many young lasses look forward to the splendor of their own weddings when they may assume her lovely and immortal aspect and be surrounded by a court of their dear friends. It is simply life continuing in spite of all the problems that have beset history. It was a joy for me to witness such youthful revels although I could not share them at my age. Besides I wished to be up in time for early Mass and to witness the children dancing at noon about the Maypole in the village and distributing flowers from house to house as local custom prescribes.

The cyclic nature of human life is the most mysterious aspect of our human existence. For a time in our youth we appear to be fortune's favorites. Each year of maturation adds to our beauty. Life waxes within us until we reach the height of our life's summer powers. So great is that force of life within us that it issues forth into new life from our loins. One generation begins to grow before the prior generation feels even the first frosts of autumn. Then nature, satisfied that the spark of life will not be extinguished, begins to withdraw its favors one by one. The blush fades from the cheek. The eyes are not as bright. Disappointment and regret leave their marks upon the visage and wisdom crowns the barren brow of age. Wisdom is not always joyous though for with it comes the knowledge of evil as well as good. Life brings us knowledge; if only knowledge could bring us life!

But our knowledge is always tempered by limitation as well so that all knowledge leads outward to the vast and beckoning horizon of what still remains unknown. Only faith can extend our reach beyond the horizon of our days to imagine a land and a condition where what we have lost will be restored to us, so that we will wake to the dawn with that same grace that we knew only for the short season of our youth. Hours they seem to me now and not days, months, or years. Time hastens as it advances. Were we ever so fresh? Did the sun ever touch us with its glory? Who is now old who was not once young?

Perhaps our fear of witches is that they are the image of our own latent desire to restore power by converting the laws of nature to our use so as to restore by craft what has been lost by time. If witches blight the crops it is only because by doing so they may protest the loss that age has wrought upon them by denying to those still living the power and the beauty that they once enjoyed. Witches are always portrayed as ancient and ugly because the young fear the enmity of age and are perhaps conscious that the treasures that they now possess are not permanent possessions but will eventually be taken from them in turn. True restoration though will not come from witchcraft or by resisting that ebbing tide of life which carries all of us into oblivion. It comes only from our consent to the inevitable.

But age and death should not for all of that be embraced as if it was a good in itself. Life deserves its autumnal hours. When even December winds shake off the last clinging leaves and the poor pale limbs that remain are exposed, even then it is good to be alive and to use whatever hours remain to build a Phoenix pyre of our virtues and our hopes as an offering to God. Happy is the man or woman who has lived each season of life to the full so as to have the minimum of regrets. Still, it is the harmony of the whole that matters, a harmony dictated by the fullness of grace.

This very fullness of grace springs forth at the hour when what once sustained it is no more, the flame passes on even when the candle gutters and burns no more. Then out of death life rises anew, but not the life that was known on earth, but a new life in heaven. One that does not dishonor what was, but rather crowns it with glory in the eyes of God. This is what was meant when Jesus spoke of the entry of the Blessed Ones, those who ministered to the needy in life, into heaven.

The preconditions for that promised entry must always stand before the Christian so that his days and nights are spent going about doing the Father's business with acts of charity and ministration to the needs of others who share our fate, while recognizing their needs as identical with our own. The poor are not another species. Distributive justice need not be compelled when it is voluntarily embraced.

The commands of the law are redundant to Christians or at least they should be. Scarcity is always the result of superfluity elsewhere. Since all will in time be taken from us by life itself, surely charity, which alone brings enduring joy, would not seem to be the great burden to us that we assume it is, but rather a natural outgrowth of our humanity. Yet distributive justice is resisted to the last degree by many people who fear that they will suffer want through the pursuit of equity. Our ultimate fear is to be forced to share the fate of outsiders and aliens.

Where would we be if we gave all that we possess away? To join those who die daily through want of necessaries would be to require the charity of others in order to survive; it would be to swell the ranks of the poor while leaving the remaining wealthy even more powerful because they would constitute a smaller minority. If one might imagine though that charity would grow over time by the gradual defections of the rich into the company of the poor, then one might imagine a point of equilibrium where the majority would have enough to at least survive. Famine and excessive want as we know them would then be no more; to attain an adequately provided for human life for most people should be the goal of every government in the world. Then the wealthy, not honored as they are now, but rather held in disgrace, would be evaluated now as they will be before the court of Divine Justice. If even those at the very pinnacle of wealth gave only a fraction of what they possess, they might still remain rich and yet still reach the poorest of the poor, who having almost nothing, might see their wealth doubled by only skimming the froth on the crème of the very richest of mankind. Surely that could be the beginning of a new order among us.

As a world society, the political leaders could begin the task of this redistribution by a tax that began at the top and worked progressively downwards. The result would not be, as it is now, an abyss of poverty for the teaming masses of earth, but rather a plateau of sufficiency in a world that still had hills and mountains above the plain. Those hills and mountains could themselves be leveled gradually over time until all possessed all and sharing all would form one vast commonwealth of humankind

If this idea appears fanciful and absurd let us imagine the contrary where the few who are not gods yet aspire to live as gods while the mass of humanity lives in progressive degradation. The question then is in which direction should goods and services flow? Just as valleys are rich, because the soil flows down from the mountainsides, so should wealth descend over time to fill the vast valley of humanity.

It is the task of governments then, not to defend injustice, but to work towards that very end of redistribution in order to create a better life for all men and women of the world. Of course this would require mutual trust, the very thing that we do not accord even to God. This lack of trust in God and in one another is most likely the actual defining characteristic of Original Sin. The way of life as taught to us by Jesus Christ is therefore a narrow one and few there are that find it.

May 2. 1893
Whitby

Theology and the dogmas of the Catholic Church are the fruit of long experience and prayerful reflection. For this reason any summary, no matter how accurate, displays the weakness of human language to convey the full wonder and deepest meanings of the formulation. Nevertheless I include here a summary of my own faith during these precious days after Easter.

After Mass yesterday I stayed behind to spend an hour with the Mother of our humanity, she who is today crowned as Queen of the May. Mary is the mother bestowed by God upon all of humanity. When Jesus, speaking from His cross entrusted her care to the care of St. John the beloved disciple his care of her was to be our care for her as well. To honor Mary is to honor Christ who distributes all graces through her to humanity. She is the Immaculate Conception, as she called herself at Lourdes when she appeared to the humble French girl Bernadette Soubirous.

The Blessed Virgin Mary is the last, best hope of humanity in her very person. For this reason, the Catholic Church honors her above all others as the narrow gate of the temple leading to God. All prayers are offered through her ministration, she who advises us as she once did the wine stewards at Cana, to do whatever Jesus tells us. Mary is fully human, but alone of all who are human she was preserved without sin from the moment of her conception. She is what man and woman were originally created to be. She has arrived at that state of perfection that we possess only by virtue of redemption, whereas she possesses it by a sovereign gift of divine exemption exercised on her behalf by God. Thus the Blessed Virgin Mary is a new creation. What for us is promise is for her present fulfillment. This fullness is the Kingdom of God where body and soul are united.

Her fullness of grace is not for herself alone but for us, her children. Her only desire is that we as members of the Catholic Church shall join her in the Kingdom of Heaven. To that end she exerts all her efforts as Mother of the Church and as Mother of God. Mary shows forth the original intention of God towards all of humanity. When no resistance is met and grace is allowed to operate unimpeded the result is that simplicity and single mindedness that allows Mary to cooperate fully in the order of salvation. Her glory is not in herself but in her uncompromising desire to do the will of God and to trust God completely.

The opposite of this primal virtue is the insecurity, the doubt, and the anxiety that we associate with the human condition. For a finite being to know evil is to be victimized by it. Man and woman are quite simply unable to look at evil without being paralyzed like a bird before a snake. Although we are advised to imitate the virtues of Christ, the assumption that mere human effort is adequate to satisfy that injunction is the heresy of Pelagianism. We can at best cooperate with grace, grace that not only crowns our efforts but assists those efforts, so that God is both the beginning and the end of every action and disposition of our hearts, not because we are conscious of this divine aid, for we often seem quite alone and confused in our acts and dispositions, but because God lives in us through Baptism into Christ through the medium of His Church

Thus Divine Grace operates in us in a manner of which we are not always conscious. It shores up walls that we imagine are solid. It sustains us even in our sin so as to limit the damage done to us by that sin. Grace is most present when our own efforts are most absent. To presume upon grace is to wish to control it, but the Holy Spirit blows where it wills. To presume to map within ourselves its ministrations would be to understand ourselves completely, which is something only God can do. In this sense our salvation is always beyond us, a gift rather than a reward.

To be certain of one's own sanctity is more often the fruit of pride than it is of virtue. But to commit the contrary error and to assume that no effort is necessary on our part is the heresy of Quietism. God does not operate in a vacuum. Some measure of movement of the will must still exist. I will not go so far as to say that it is better to sin than to do nothing, but it remains true that sins may be forgiven, whereas to despair of human actions as irretrievably flawed by our human condition and by doing so to freeze into moral immobility would be to despair.

God does not quench the flickering wick. God works with what He finds within us to extract and nurture, to build up, to sustain, to heal, and to quicken. God heals us from the inside out, although we operate from the outside in. We attempt virtues that are alien to us and we find them ill-fitting at first. Only the passage of time reveals the changes that have occurred within us. To be confident in the merits of Christ to supplant all of our deficiencies sustains our hope.

Never to look down upon the way we have come prevents that moral vertigo of the spirit that may cause us to fall. For the Christian soul the peak alone is what matters; that peak which is union with God. Each step, however slight and hesitating it may be, brings us closer to Him. To stagger and fall then is not to turn back in discouragement. The one who helps us back to our feet and walks always at our side is the source of our confidence.

To ask why all of this moral processing is necessary for us and why God seems to be so far away is the legacy of the primal sin of the human race that wished to become in an instant equal to God by the mere eating of a pleasant fruit. The assumption that man and woman may simply snap themselves into holiness by an effort of will is the will's primal illusion. For this reason we are slowed to a snail's pace in our moral development. We tunnel through this world like moles through heavy soil. All is effort. We look into our hands for the fruits of all our efforts and witness there, from the barren fields of our lives, a few sodden grains of wheat, the hard kernels yield but little substance even for our own use with little surplus left as an offering for God.

The message of the gospel however was if five barley loaves and two fish were a feast for the five thousand, how much of history has offered to our contemplation anything other than smoking fields and blasted lands? It is as though the winter of our heart had so ruined this earth that no life could ever find soil for renewal; yet God has given us the May flowers that blossom, the trees that bud forth, the waters that flow again with winter's melted snows. We learn in spring to hope again and before long there is youth and new life again and against the witness of all of human experience the human race continues even as it always will until the Second Coming of Christ that will end history as we know it.

That history should have an end must seem arbitrary, as though God simply sent a top whirling and then suddenly and at a whim grasped it up again, as a child does only to run away. Providence sets its own schedule though; that schedule is guided by a secret reserved to God the Father alone. We are told that the end will arrive like a thief in the night.

Perhaps some vain historians will say, "Wait a bit, my synthesis is almost complete. One last sentence and it will be done." The historians will scribble their way into eternity and God will transpose them desks and all into heaven, so that when they look up finally from their task and place their pens aside they will mutter, "Oh that is hardly what I had expected. I must have made an error somewhere in my calculations. Let me see..." Or will the end of all things come as a thunderclap so that all creation will be frozen into immobility and awe. Will stars fall from the sky and the heavens be shaken, as Jesus said, or was this language chosen simply to magnify for our minds a change that we cannot conceive?

We have long blamed God for His seeming absence and indifference to our fate, but to invite a coming that may find us unprepared is only to hasten our premature end. Perhaps our prayer should be instead, "Stay awhile Lord since we still have many great cities to build. We are in the middle of a production run. We had planned a holiday at the sea and were just closing the business." But what if God is with us in all of these, even in our most vain pursuits?

For this reason Jesus added a note of urgency wherever the Kingdom of God was concerned. We are even advised to leave the dead to bury their dead. It is said that the apostles left everything after their call without a backward glance. Was the father of Peter and Andrew left with a boat-load of stinking fish? At the age of twelve, Jesus said that He was already about his Father's business.

May 3, 1893
Departure for the Holmes Estate at Sigerside

I left Whitby in the morning after one last stroll about the town. The old locomotive that was to convey me to Sigerside Halt winds through the high bleak moors on its way to Northumberland. From the higher hills there are occasional last glimpses of the English Channel, but then the moors themselves have an aspect of the sea in wave after wave of heather and bracken. There are deep dales and valleys crossed with stony rills. The sheep on the higher tors might be the foam that crests a wave. It is a fanciful landscape that breeds imagination and local patterns of speech through the isolation here of its inhabitants. They are a stoic race, not far removed from those ancient Britons who were their ancestors.

The stops that we made were frequent, since our train was carrying goods from Whitby to the inland villages. I soon resigned myself to the jolting of the train over the ancient tracks. It may seem strange to an outsider, but I recognized amidst the chaos of the land, familiar patterns that only a local inhabitant would ever notice. Each place was familiar to me with that particular memory and set of associations that remain here from my youth and boyhood. As the train came closer to Sigerside, those memories only grew sharper. Here and there I had walked these very fields, a thousand times along the common waysides and sheep-tracks that often pass as roads in these rural districts. I knew where to look for the small village church spire that suddenly emerged from around a bend, surrounded by a cluster of shops and the single old pub that was the only place for convivial meetings for many miles. The train station, as we pulled in to Sigerside Halt, had a platform filled with geese in crates for market and other local produce and wares.

I was the only person to disembark here. The goods were soon loaded and the train groaned and hissed as it was set again in motion. I stood alone on the platform with my two valises looking about me for some manner of transport to the manor. At last an old porter noticed that someone had remained after the train's departure. He hobbled over and picked up my luggage automatically before looking up at me for instructions.

"Where be 'ee goin, then Sir?" he asked looking up into my face. All at once he paused and dropped my baggage and broke out in a fit of coughing. I slapped him on the back until he could regain his composure.

"Why, bless me sir, can it be you Mr. Sherlock? Him as I knew as a boy? But no it can't be for we heerd you was dead off in Sweetzerland! All the papers were full of it at the time, even those as we get out here from Whitby."

I assured the poor old fellow, whose name was Old Josh Withers that I was very much alive, that it had all been a mistake, the reports of my death. I recalled him well from my boyhood days. I had ridden on his shoulders when I was a mere boy and he a strapping lad. Then he was a tall, smart, country yeoman and not bent as he was now with age. He had never left Yorkshire. He took care of all matters pertaining to the station. Since the train stopped but once every few days as he told me, his duties there were few. Since the train had departed, he would now be at liberty to close up the station building. He had a small dog-cart, which was his official mode of conveyance since he was also the village cabby.

When he had quite recovered from the shock of seeing me, he insisted on carrying my baggage himself. He was still strong despite his years. We walked then to the rear of the station to where the high street of the hamlet began. I asked him if he would join me for a glass of ale before we left for Sigerside. I wished to know something of the welcome or lack thereof that I might meet there from my brother Sherringford and to hear how matters were up at the estate.

He looked about him before answering, "Well if it be not above my station to be doing so, then thank you kindly, Mr. Sherlock."

It was mid-afternoon and the farmers had yet to come in from the fields, so the pub was nearly empty when we entered it. A smoky peat fire burned upon the hearth and the smell of homely cooking still lingered there from lunch. The bar-maid was a young woman and did not know me. She was no doubt the daughter of the proprietor and was little more than a girl at the time of my last visit home.

I ordered a shepherd's pie and a pint of bitter and ordered the same and pint of ale for Josh. We were soon engaged in quiet conversation at the secluded table that I had chosen. My back was to the door and I faced the fire. While I doubted that I would be recognized by many people after so many years of absence, I did not want to court public notice during my short visit. I merely wished to pay my respects to my brother as duty and propriety demanded. I must also confess that I wished to see Sherringford to see if the years since our last meeting had changed his views or modulated the disposition of gruff formality towards me that had always been characteristic of the man.

I have long held to a theory, one that the Chinese would not find strange, that the primary unit of society is the family and not the individual. Even kings and queens owe their status and position to their membership in the royal dynasty of their family. Individual achievements are soon assimilated to the group to nourish its stature and relative position with other families. Individual misfortunes or defects are soon plastered over by the passage of time, by being absorbed and their losses dissipated by the larger social unit to which they belong.

Which family does not contain both geniuses and fools? History simply moves too quickly to take account of any but the most extraordinary individuals who may deflect the stream of events through their own efforts. For the many anonymous members of any society there is only the small accretion to that smaller society, the family, of whose intimate circle they were once a part.

The history of the world is therefore that of competing dynasties. What we call statecraft flows from the inner virtues and foibles that appear in the individual rulers, but what is the source of that personality but the result of those values and influences imbibed from a single source, the family. The spring of family character waters all growths from that single source. The great trees, the flowers, and even those weedy aberrations that may finally choke the ground and prevent further growth, all take their nourishment and origin from the blended origin that begat them.

Even families perish however and others assume positions of prominence in time. No dynasty is permanent. Even in China, history is reckoned by those long successions that have brought an end to various dynasties, to the Han and to the Tang. Only the Popes may claim to change history by right of election with a dynasty of one, their own Papacy. The ring of each successive Pontiff is destroyed at his death. The only continuity of the Church is the Holy Spirit who even effaces the corruption of the Borgia Popes with time.

When family aspirations presume to advance their own ends at the expense of the good of the commonality of the Church, they do so in vain. In worldly matters though, the family is supreme and prior to the state, which it often claims as its servant. Thus is sovereignty finally exercised in a personal way by actual living people whose claim to rule is translated from divine right to its temporal exercise. Most history has been created by various dynasties both in the Eastern and the Western Worlds.

I asked Josh for news of the estate and prepared to absorb whatever I was about to hear.

"Ah, Mr. Sherlock, these be hard times and that's the truth on it," he began. "Wool don't fetch what it did, what with all them cotton goods out of them 'Indu lands. Farmin be alright and our horse raising does well. Coal comes out of the ground still up in Northumberland, but there be wild talk of starting unions there, syndicalism and all them foreign notions. All in all the estate holds together, but ain't what you might call prosperous, not like it were when your father Sigerson was alive, God bless him. As to your brother,'ee ain't a man what likes to speak of his private thoughts, as ye know well yourself, sir. Our cold winters have left a mark on him, that I do say. He sits a horse well enough still, but he shows the cares what come with his position as Lord of the Manor. It ain't easy bein' Lord of the manor and that's the truth."

I took the opportunity to inquire after his own health and wellbeing. He drank from his ale with a gentle smile before replying, "God has seen fit to keep me in a humble station all my life and it suits me fine. I still live in the gatehouse up at the estate when I ain't here in the village at my duties. I only comes down 'ere the three days a week when the train goes through. All in all I does well enough. I've a bit put aside so as to take a holiday once a year down to Scarborough. I'm an usher in the Church and I says my prayers at night. I'm glad to see you alive and home again sir and that's the truth on it! Though if you pardon my saying it you look a bit like one of them chaps out o the Arabian Nights, which I guess is natural seein as you say that you just come from them far-off regions of the world. Furthest I been is France and it were enough for me. The things them folks eats over there!"

He shook his head. I offered him another glass of ale.

"Another ale, sir? Well, since this is by way of a celebration of your homecoming and all, I will and thank you kindly."

We enjoyed out meal together. It was served in large portions to feed country appetites. The gravy set off the hearty meat and the crust was excellent if homely. It was served with oat scones and a particular sweet biscuit that is common to the region. Our meal served us well for a late lunch or an early tea. My brother always favored late suppers and I desired to see something of the estate before darkness fell, so I paid our bill and we left.

Few people entered while we were there and I am happy to report that no one paid us any mind or overheard our discussion. I was not surprised that the estate like many in England was not what it had been in more prosperous times. The rising middle-class and the succession of Prime Ministers were having a decided effect upon the landed gentry. Taxes were up and the great land-holdings were beginning to break up like ice on a pond. Some went up for auction, others managed to survive through thrift and the loyalty of the tenants. Sherringford had always been a kind if stringent master and Mycroft and I had little to say regarding how the estate was run. It had the benefit of diversity in products and was not confined to agriculture alone. What the estate lacked in scope it made up for in ingenuity. Sherringford had some of the same mental characteristics as his brothers after all. We were soon on our way with Josh's dog-cart jolting us along the country lanes on the way to Sigerside.

May 4, 1893
Sigerside

I begin this entry with a further account of the events of yesterday. The Estate of Sigerside occupies the high region of the local moors stretching northwards beginning about two miles distant from the village and extending into Northumberland. The Holmes coal mines have their own small hamlet on the very northwest corner of the estate. The railroad circles round the western edge of the Holmes Estate and after picking up coal from the mines proceeds onward to Newcastle, where it joins the county rail system that extends into Scotland.

The eastern part of Sigerside consists of small farm holdings and grazing lands for sheep, while the central part of the estate, which occupies a wooded dell, contains the horse stables where Clydesdale horses are bred and sold. There are also family investments in various businesses in Norway and Denmark from which various annual remittances supplement the small rents from the tenant farmers and shepherds on the estate.

These rents are low for the region. This comparative generosity towards the tenants is made possible because of the spare and frugal life led by Sherringford as lord of the manor. He refuses to apply the usual attitude of rapine towards his tenants. The estate is therefore dotted with comfortable crofter cottages rather than the usual dwellings manifesting poverty and squalor, which reflect the attitude maintained towards their tenants by most other Yorkshire landlords.

The manor house is substantial but not inordinately ornate. It was built of dark grey stone and dates from the latter 17th century. It is sheltered by stands of poplars and elms and surrounded by rhododendrons. Ivy climbs the walls and shelters the inset windows. There is no wall about the manor but a small gate house stands amidst oaks and chestnut trees that shield the house from view from the highroad that extends onwards to other hamlets in the vicinity.

We turned in at the gate-house and proceeded through the parkland where stags still roam. The woods had been planted in the 18th century by a Holmes ancestor to restore timber to our denuded county. The estate was always well-stocked with game. Hares abounded and our grouse and pheasants kept the Holmes' sideboard and larder well-supplied to meet all domestic needs. My father had kept a wine cellar of some local repute in the county. Sherringford has kept up this tradition. He must have his Madeira after his meals.

After leaving the woodlands behind we suddenly rounded a bend in the road and there was the great house before us in the slanting rays of the late-afternoon sun. The manor lay in its own hollow and a stream from the heather-clad hills trickled though the garden in the rear of the dwelling, where my mother had planted roses so many years ago. The park timber lands were behind us now and we were soon at the door. I looked up at the high walls of the house. All was silent and only a few whiffs of smoke from the great chimneys showed that the manor was even inhabited. The house wears an antique aspect and is still lit by candles, as it was a century ago.

These would soon be lit with the evening coming on. I knew the schedule of the occupants well, as though I were a permanent resident and not the occasional visitor that I had been in recent years. There was no need to seek a prior invitation for the Holmes estate by my father's will was equally open to all his sons. He desired that they might share the manor equally, although the estate lands were owned and managed by Sherringford as the eldest son. Mycroft and I shared a portion of the rents of the tenants while the coal interests remained with Sherringford to pay the expenses of the estate as the rule of primogeniture dictated so as not to split up the estate.

No doubt the sound of the dog-cart had alerted the staff for the door opened and our old butler, Robert, opened the door to greet us. His imperturbability made him the perfect butler for my brother whose own excitable nature was tempered by entrusting the running of the household to a man who was able to take all things in his stride and to proceed without excess direction. The brief look of surprise, which made his face comical for a moment, was instantly replaced by his usual air of strict calm and propriety.

"Welcome home Mr. Sherlock, you must pardon my brief hesitation, but your arrival was unexpected."

I had not been sure whether Sherringford had explained to the household, or at least to Robert, that I was still alive after the affair at the Falls of Reichenbach. I had requested that Mycroft inform Sherringford of the true state of matters, so that no efforts would be made to settle my part of the estate in my absence. Watson must have wondered why there was no talk of a will. Watson would of course have been my natural beneficiary. He no doubt concluded that with my usual habit of untidiness I had failed to prepare a will, which meant that my share of the estate would pass by intestate succession automatically to my brothers in equal shares upon my demise. No doubt his own delicacy would prevent

Watson from ever referring to the matter directly, but a momentary pang struck my heart that I had failed to take some measure to have foreseen this further insult to our long friendship. I intend to make it up to him as soon as I can.

Josh carried my baggage into the house. He set everything down in the chill foyer and touching his hat brim he bid me farewell. The door soon closed behind him without further formality and I was left to Robert's care. "Shall I inform your brother that you have arrived, sir?"

He had only had a few moments to conclude that I was not in Pluto's netherworld and he was already treating me as though I had been only absent for an extended weekend. "Yes you may do so, Robert," I answered. "I trust that my old room has not changed?"

"It will only require a fresh change of linens sir," Robert answered. "If you will give me a few moments, I will see that all is arranged to your satisfaction. Perhaps, you would care for a brandy. The fire is burning in the library. Your brother is I believe in the estate office speaking to the manager of the coal mines who reports to him once a week, as you perhaps recall. I will see that some biscuits and jam are brought in. You are perhaps hungry after your journey. Dinner will be served at the usual hour and I will see that the maid prepares your room and sees to your baggage."

We had been walking through the old ancestral hall on our way to the library as he spoke these words. It was still cold and draughty there, but not as forbidding or as dark as the similar room at Baskerville Hall. The purpose of the entry-hall here was to receive the tenants on formal occasions and for grand entertainments of the local gentry. As such it remained empty for most of the year.

Day-to-day activities were confined to the library and to the formal drawing room. The library had always been my own particular favorite. I had spent many hours in my youth there perusing my father's many volumes. I was allowed to remove them as needed to the school-room where Mycroft and I were privately tutored until he finally left for public school before going up to university. I joined him briefly there after my mother's death. Mycroft attended Oxford while I attended Cambridge for a few years until our father's death. After that I transferred to the University of London and forsook Greek and Latin to pursue my interest in chemistry.

It was originally thought that I would study engineering and succeed to the task of overseeing the family coal mines, but engineering was not to my taste. After our father's death I chose my own particular line of studies, which my brother, Sherringford, always referred to as "my little exercises in romantic fantasy." Practical science savored too much of the tradesman for him. He was not pleased by my choice to become as I termed it a consulting detective. The rift between us began with my choice of a career, or so I believe. Family models and expectations, even when they remain silent and unexpressed, are not to be ignored.

Sherringford of course attended the University of Edinburgh where he studied accounting and economics, after the usual grounding in the classics, in order to prepare himself to run the estate. He had little sympathy for any inquiry conducted for its own sake. He was also suspicious of any English city south of the Midlands. His sympathies were always with Scotland. He had acquired a certain Presbyterian bent while at school in Edinburgh, though he remained in the Church of England for form's sake.

He could never be a dissenter or an evangelical. Sherringford ran the affairs of his soul with the same efficiency as his estate. It was always difficult for me to restrain a certain air of levity and inconsequence in my statements to him on religion and on other matters simply to irritate him and to confirm him in his view of me as one who was always frivolous and governed by whimsy. Once one knows how one will inevitably be judged in spite of one's best efforts, it is always tempting to carry to extremes the very traits because of which one is judged to be inadequate.

obert had left me alone with a courteous bow after pouring me a snifter of brandy. I went to the window and looked out upon the green fields filled with waving alfalfa and at the distant poplars that had just unfurled their leaves. After a time, I turned to the fire and had just stretched out my feet to the blaze and felt the first warming touch of the brandy stealing in upon me when I heard footsteps out in the hall. The door was opened suddenly and I rose to greet my formidable brother. Sherringford stopped for a moment and gazed at me in surprise and then after a quick appraisal walked over and shook my hand.

"Well," said he, "So Marco Polo has returned ... and all in one piece I see. I had imagined your head on a pike somewhere in Africa. You seemed to be determined to become a legend Sherlock, like Chinese Gordon of Khartoum. If that is true then let me advise you, there is little profit in notoriety. But pray do sit down. Will you have some brandy? Ah, I see you have been served. Very well, I will join you. This has been a most unpleasant afternoon."

He proceeded to pour each of us a generous amount and sat down wearily in the chair next to mine. He drank silently for a minute, looking into the flames before speaking further.

"I trust that you are not returning for money. If so, let me say at once that many rents are in arrears at the present time. The price of coal is down and labor troubles are everywhere. No doubt in the regions you have recently frequented there is little talk of a modern economy. The advantage of subsistence living is that prices never change. Without money one exchanges item for item on a fixed schedule developed over time. But add capital and speculation to the mix and prices slosh about like laundry in a wash-tub from industry to industry. Speculation produces higher prices, overproduction occurs, then prices drop and there you are in another financial contraction. In this country we have been mired in it for the past year. I have even been forced to sell at a loss some stocks in American railroads in order to raise cash. I have not been alone in this. The mania of building railroads in America, fed by typical American enthusiasm, was bound to create something like the South Seas Bubble or that business with the

Dutch tulips. Excess Sherlock! Excess always sooner or later breeds penury and collapse."

Sherringford subsided then into a grim silence, which soon became uncomfortable, so I spoke up. "As it happens, my travels were not such as to leave me in debt. My writings have brought in some funds and I was even able to do a bit of trading in Persian goods along the way that my travels took me. So you may rest easy on that score," I explained.

"Well, that's alright then," Sherringford went on gruffly, after a brief pause during which an expression of relief crossed his face. "Mycroft sent me some of your dispatches. It appears that you have become something of a romantic figure. I have even heard that young ladies in London see this *nom-de-plume* of yours, this Sigerson fellow, (chosen in poor taste if you do not mind me saying so) as a sort of modern Lord Byron. No doubt they sleep with copies of your dispatches under their pillows. They picture you with piercing eyes doing battle with Arabian sheiks or defending yourself against natives throwing spears. It is bad enough, the figure you cut in those romances of your friend, Dr. Watson; but now you have exceeded all limits. What would our father say of all this? Next I shall no doubt hear that you are off to America, fighting red Indians like an American cowboy."

"As it happens I simply intend to resume my practice in London as soon as I may do so. First though I have a certain private task that lies before me. The prospect may involve some danger. But I wanted to see you in any case. I took the boat last week from the continent to Whitby, and after I leave here I will go down to London to see Mycroft."

Sherringford seemed to grow somewhat more genial under the influence of his brandy. "I'm sorry; you are welcome here of course. You must understand that I am not in good humor these days. I am getting older and this blasted climate...well you are lucky to have been for a time in warmer regions. Mycroft informs me that you spent the last year in France and in Italy. I may ask your opinion some day of a good place to go for a retreat for my health, gout you know. I have also heard that you have had a bout of lung trouble. That's not good you know. Perhaps you should have stayed longer in the Italian Tyrol or in Switzerland. It won't do to go back to that beastly London, not with bad lungs anyway."

"I will only be passing through," I said. "I intend to spend the remainder of the year in the west of England, in Devonshire."

My brother nodded in approval, "Good choice that: sea air and all that, warmer there too, at least in summer. Well, we shall eat well tonight in any case. I've ordered some roast leg of lamb. Killed the fatted calf for the prodigal!   The truth is I need it too. May as well eat and drink our substance as wait for it to be snatched up by creditors. I have had to sell off some the estate, not much, but some. Land prices are down and are likely to go lower still. The main thing is to preserve a central core and wait for the times to improve. If you wait too long to sell you take a thrashing."

I was surprised to find Sherringford in a mood of gruff but genuine hospitality. His troubles seemed to have made him forget our past differences. He was even showing elements of fraternal concern which showed themselves further at our late supper together.

We ate in the old dining room which was paneled in walnut. The generous table boasted a leg of lamb and a pheasant cooked in Madeira and stuffed with rosemary stuffing. I had brought along several bottles of Amontiado from Whitby as a gift. Sherringford seemed well-pleased. As the dinner progressed he even managed to shake off some of his melancholy, not enough to grow festive, which would have been foreign to his character, but at least sufficient to show some signs of geniality.

"Well then, tell me something of Moriarty," he said as he filled his glass.   "Mycroft confided to me that you spared the bounder when he was well within your grasp."

"Well the truth is that I was more in his grasp. He was accompanied in Switzerland by Colonel Sebastian Moran who is a most dangerous fellow. Let us say that we reached an agreement there between us to take a mutual sabbatical from our usual occupations. We were in a position to do so because each of us had come to owe much of our employment to the other. We each suffer from a dreadful *ennui* as regards life itself and its purpose. We decided then to divide our researches. He was to pursue a solution to the human dilemma without God and I was to pursue God and His will for mankind as the solution to the human problem."

"Bah, you are romantics, both of you," sniffed Sherringford. "Both of you assume that there is a human dilemma because you insist on exalting man above the beast that he is. Do you catch the animals going about speculating about their own dignity or worrying each other about their own death? No, they accept their lot and get about living. No hare despises the hound for dispatching it. No hound engages in bouts of guilt or attempts to wash the blood off its fangs. Atheism of course is bad form, but religion makes untoward assumptions regarding the nature of its God. The arbitrariness denied to man is reserved to the deity. We give to God the prerogatives that would be ours if we were able to assert our own wills to an extreme. Which of us would not create the world over again in our own image and to serve our convenience? Every man is a potential tyrant and each woman would be a goddess waiting for blood to be spilled on her altar. And what have we to contain such vile aspirations? Only the human condition, which by its very limits drags us into the dirt until in sheer disgust at ourselves we invent Gods to forgive our sins and restore us to the good opinion we would like to have of ourselves: virtuous even in our corruption."

He warmed then to his subject and began to show his Presbyterian sympathies. "John Calvin realized this of course, though his Christianity was only his own attempt to hide from himself his contempt for the human race. Any love of God for man in Calvin's view is without any merit on our part. He magnifies God by insulting man. But he is right to do so, quite right."

It was unusual for me to observe my brother to be so voluble on any issue. He usually had been reticent in the extreme to air his views, so that his comments took me by surprise. I could only attribute his excess of bitterness to the reverses in the family fortunes that he had lately encountered. "Have you left the Church of England for the Calvinists then?" I inquired.

"Of course not!" said he, "Though my own religious belief wavers with the state of my health, I do not say that religion serves no purpose at all. Religion keeps the masses in awe of something and justifies a hierarchical society that alone can govern the many who are dull-witted and who would otherwise unleash a reign of slaughter upon their betters as they did at the time of the French Revolution. The aspirations of the mob are always the same: drink, debauchery, and bloodshed in that order. Napoleon tried to give them their rights as a permanent possession by attempting to set up a French empire. Bah, they could not comprehend them. The law to the masses can only mean the threat of force. Once one gives them rights you ruin them. If the Czar of Russia should ever free the serfs they will be upon him like hounds in an instant. Why do you think that Britain rules the world, Sherlock? Is it because we let the House of Commons bleed off their gall in debate? Well perhaps, but they are Englishmen after all. But no, it is much more than that! It is because the House of Lords manages to restrain the enthusiasm of the House of Commons and because Victoria is secure upon her throne."

He paused to re-fill his glass before continuing, "Take America as an example. The whole bloody country began in revolution and this talk of rights, Thomas Paine and all that. What is the result after one hundred years? A new American aristocracy has arisen to govern the nation as it always must if the country is to hold together. But Americans still go on worshiping that rebellious blighter, Thomas Jefferson, and talking about their blasted Constitution! Did they ever understand for a moment what it said? Like all charlatans Jefferson promised rights to the common citizens, while knowing as he must have known if he was not a fool, that most men do not know what to do with any liberties that they are granted. Democracy can never work! In any case, the first thing that the great landowners of America did after 1783 was to try and recreate an aristocracy and to assemble a new labor pool of serfs from the off-scoured masses of Europe to work the land and the factories. When the labor-pool got too large they were sent west to conquer more land from the savages. If the fool citizens had known better they would have made common cause with the Indians who were the only real democrats on the whole continent! The Indians knew what freedom really was, which is to live as an honest savage, free of religion and free of civilization. Chateaubriand knew that much, romantic though he was!"

He paused and refilled his glass again before continuing, "What do you see in America today as a result of one hundred years of effort? I will tell you, a vile republic dedicated only to greed, in which the few prosper and the many remain, even after generations of effort, where they were when they first arrived on those fabled Democratic shores where "all men were created equal." The Africans are still slaves in the South with only this difference: whereas before they were valuable property whose lives and well-being mattered to their masters, now they are seen as merely expendable workers and hated and persecuted as a threat by white immigrant laborers in the Northern factories. In the northern states the workers are all slaves, only of different colors. Meanwhile, the supposed free land of the west is becoming America's version of Siberia. Once the open plains are well-subdued, the wealth of the west will be claimed by the few great landowners and railroad interests in the East. In the end America's talk of the rule of law and of principle is only a way of blinding the many to what is occurring before their very faces and to hide their own despoilment by the great and the wealthy. It has been like this ever since the American Civil War."

"But surely," I answered, "That is what our family here is, are we not also rulers of the land, aristocrats in our small way."

"Yes, but with this difference," stated Sherringford, "We know our place and have become accustomed to its moral burdens. Why do you think that I don't sell the estate for what it can fetch and move to Italy or to some other more salubrious climate to restore my health? It is because I know my duty to the land and to its tenants. They are, for better or for worse, Holmes tenants on Holmes land. I will not betray my forebears or my own dignity by absconding like a hound with whatever I may salvage of the spoils by a sale to the rising class of tradesmen."

"So you also are a romantic in your fashion, my dear brother, a modern version of those who still recognize the burdens of nobility," I remarked smiling, "But only where your own honor is concerned."

He looked up startled before breaking out in an unaccustomed and rusty laugh.

"You are an impish fellow, Sherlock; you always were, perhaps you are right though."

After a brief silence, he continued. "It is not an easy matter to be in a position where one's own dispositions can make the difference between life and death to others. Power is a burden if one has any conscience at all and I have been inoculated by that fatal virus from my youth. Our father, you will recall, enjoyed reading the great writers of his day. His was the generation that after the failed rule of Napoleon tried to re-establish the rule of republican ideals again in 1848. Our father believed in social advancement through education and class mobility. I mean no disrespect to his memory, but these are dangerous notions I believe. The existence of the British social classes forms the strata of a stable society. Once one introduces social ambition in the lower classes, discontent and fermentation always result. This breeds distrust and discontent within the lower classes in the limited circumstances of life. Soon there arises envy and emulation that finally results in a growing sense of entitlement within them. When this fails to obtain equality so they can find a place in another's station in life on a higher plain, through work or fortunate circumstance, even crime is believed to be justified to get what then appears to be essential to their self-esteem."

"When all men must be equal, the dregs begin to float off the bottom of the crock and the entire mixture of society in the keg of life is spoiled, all becomes a great cloudy fermentation with yeast obscuring the clarity of the ale above. Let me make my point clear with another metaphor. You have perhaps observed the rock strata along the seacoast where the land has buckled under volcanic forces from below. When this occurs, the land itself has no weight-bearing capacity. No structure can be erected there, because the land beneath it flows about in various directions. The foundation is soon therefore ripped asunder and any structure built upon it collapses."

"In a society where a sense of egalitarianism prevails, only force and ambition rule. This is what you see happening now in America. What appears to be the vitality of that nation is merely the violent fermentation as each man strives to outdo his fellows. Even the American cities are impermanent. You have only to visit any one of them in a hundred years and I doubt if you will find a single original building still standing. The city will already have gone through a score of mutations and the last built will be no more permanent than the first. Life flows through America like flood waters, leaving alluvial deposits here and there; nothing is built to last. America is a land corroded by the adventurers who took it from its original inhabitants. Even the American women partake in this ephemeral quality! Where is their grace, where the leisure of the sex to which mankind entrusts the delicate sentiments that should know nothing of strife and sordidness! Where will this pushing and shoving ever end?"

"Women have begun to demand enfranchisement, even here in England! Nonsense! What will they do when they have it, but vote for some charlatan who appeals to their feminine sensibilities to be a hero? Women, who were formerly the one sure guarantee of civilization, are willing to barter away their dignity for a mere paltry vote for whoever promises to better distribute the material goods of the democracy."

Sherringford paused and I pointed out that men make poor political choices as well as women; but my brother was still quite carried away by his own rhetoric. He continued as before.

"I have seen the British harpies with their suffrage signs on my few trips to London. What do they wish for but equality, to join the great unwashed polis that elects whatever liar will pander to their desire for power and what is that power but as in America the ability to oppress another and to force one's views upon them. In a stable society, one where each one of us has a definite role to play, freedom of thought is the norm though actions are constrained. In England the very man who shines my boots and tips his hat to me may think I am an absurd old walrus and laugh at me behind my back, but he will not assault me in the street. In America that same man will wish me to the devil, knock my hat off my head, and if I am in a dark alley leave me bleeding and minus my pocketbook and if you ask him why he has done this, to an inoffensive old walrus like me, he will say it was because I was a rich old scavenger and deserved as good as I got from him!"

To see my brother so voluble was no less surprising than it was welcome to me. For the first time I began to understand his own position, which in the past had led me to believe that he was one who valued his position as a lord instead of suffering under it. I could see now that his promotion at my father's death to the responsibilities of the estate was a burden to him, yet one that he accepted out of duty and a sense of destiny. I decided to test him further to see if all that he had said was mere bluster or was sincerely believed by him.

"Why don't you chuck it all in then, Guvner?" I said with an assumed cockney accent and a winning smile.

Sherringford started and then smiled again. "Still the imp I see! You may enjoy pulling my leg, but I am quite serious. I believe that democracy always leads to a series of new Napoleons. Each will promise the people everything and end by taking everything they possess. They lead the people to into wars for democratic ideals. One democracy will fight another for the same equality of nations that they first sought to give to each citizen. Only the rule of a few nations will ensure a stable world-order and even they must be in balance."

"The rule of sovereignty means that each nation by its very nature opposes all other nations. Only fear bred of past experience holds them in check. Only the fear of war among a few select nations can sustain a general peace. For this reason a balanced system of alliances is like a wall against warfare. Only when one nation perceives a marginal advantage in the power equation will it risk provoking a war. The international task then is to cement those inevitable gaps between nations by an ardent and honest diplomacy that makes the threat of war real but not immediate. A good diplomat knows when to show his fangs. The aura of respectability that surrounds the ambassadors of state relations is undergirded by the law of the jungle."

"Mark you Sherlock, Mycroft knows about all this. He is the puppet-master, the director of the entire diplomatic corps. He knows the personalities of men like Bismarck. He has studied the writings of Talleyrand. He exists in Whitehall as a force, bland and inscrutable, but like Poseidon armed with the trident of the triple alliance, he keeps the Germans and Austrians in check. The result is a general peace, which has held ever since the Congress of Vienna in 1815 with the sole exception of the Franco-Prussian War in 1871 that was waged over Alsace and Lorraine, which was really only a minor border dispute after all. There are also occasional flare-ups over colonial possessions I admit, but these are adjustments to the power equation and are not to be taken seriously."

He paused again to assess my reaction to all that he had said. "Ah you look at me with a censorious expression! Please recall, Sherlock, that the African native tribes were engaged in enslaving each other prior to the arrival of any Europeans on that continent. The plantations of America were merely an outlet for natives who might have died in internecine tribal conflicts had they remained in Africa. The death in the slave ships was appalling of course, but we must not forget that life in those African regions at the time was always short and brutish. The tropics are a cesspool of disease with Malaria, sleeping sickness, river blindness, and various parasites; they were well out of it. To assume the ideal in history is always to court disappointment. Each age witnesses to the arbitrary death of millions while the few survive. Why do they survive, because of superior virtues? No! Often the best people die, the morally superior ones die, those who are more compassionate to those who suffer about them die with them. What remains then of the individual and his virtues? What remains are only the forms of the society, the class differentiations that will reassert themselves ineluctably as soon as the fermentation of revolution ceases!"

Sherringford paused once again to catch his breath before concluding his reflections on the political process. "These are the very organs that must rebuild a civilization from the chaos of change, whether induced by wars or by revolutions. That is why I play my role here at Sigerside, though another might do as well or better in my place, but here I am and here I shall remain at the tiller of the ship of this estate of our father, Sigerson."

It was then that I suggested that we repair from the dining room to the library where we might finish the evening off with a treacle pudding before the fire. I don't believe I had ever heard the doctrine of *noblesse oblige* stated better. That my brother believed all that he had said sincerely, there could be no doubt. But I felt obliged to raise an objection after we were well-seated in adjoining armchairs and our dessert was brought in for us on a tray.

"You state your case very well, Sherringford, and your reservations regarding democratic governments make a great deal of sense. Perhaps this is why there have been so few of them, but let us say that the people in a democracy choose to run the risks attendant upon their independence. Are they not entitled to do so? May it even be true that the ruling class disguises the profits that it obtains in return for offering protection to the masses? Surely we are all finally visible before God, what man may claim superiority after death or exercise domination over another through unjust rule that denies others equal freedom and dignity? Eternity well set all matters right."

"Yes, but we are dealing with this world where struggle and strife prevail. No empty idealism may apply. Besides, Sherlock, it is you who assume the role of a feudal lord when you assume that people desire freedom and dignity above all other goods. The dignity that you would bestow upon them, or allow them to assume, is nothing but a source of care and anxiety; most people are like children, give then pinwheels and candy and they will be satisfied. The masses only grow cross when their amusements are denied them. Even to critically reflect upon their subservient situation is too much for them. Politics for the masses will always be guided by their perceived short-term advantage. They always imagine that they may obtain something for nothing, because the majority of the human race has no awareness of costs. For this reason someone must consent to take them in hand. Social experiments are always dangerous. Take this chap, Moriarty, our former stable boy, as an example. Our father, no doubt with the best of intentions, gave the lad an education equal to that of his sons. What has become of that noble gesture? Moriarty of all men is a threat to you, Sherlock. He bites the hand that fed him and why; because it is his wretched nature to do so. His father was a brute as you must remember and given sufficient time so has the son become a brute as well."

I objected, "You forget that he is also a brilliant mathematician and astronomer. His work on the binomial theorem and his astounding contributions to cosmology through the study of the movements of asteroids is renowned throughout the universities of Europe. The University of Heidelberg once offered him a full professorship and his own department of astrophysics, but he turned the appointment down."

"You only make my point, Sherlock. The fellow only shows thereby his true colors and his ungrateful nature. He shows that he prefers to be a lord of cutthroats and robbers. He has learned a few tricks of course, like a trained tiger, but he is a tiger still and will turn on his keeper the moment the keeper's back is turned. Mycroft tells me that you anticipate some sort of civilized debate with the fellow with the existence of God or morality as the stake between you. If you should win he will supposedly give up his life of crime for good. But what if you lose, Sherlock? What will then become of your own faith?"

Sherringford then explained his own position in regard to religion. "I find no grounds for believing in either the love of God or His wrath. I have continued to believe formally in Christianity only because I have no idea whether faith can ever be justified, but I am not ready to accept the vacancy of the alternative. It would matter little to me if I could prove that God exists and it would not dismay me unduly to find out that He does not. Religion for me is an essential to good government and that is sufficient justification for me to applaud its practice among men of good will. As for an afterlife, this life has been quite exhausting enough. I have no desire to join celestial choirs, nor can I imagine a more beneficent fate then a good glass of port after a foxhunt over the moors with my hounds and then an uninterrupted sleep. I gave up long ago wishing for a better world and decided to adjust to the only world that I know."

"Religion persists in seeking for an explanation, a purpose, or a recompense for what we endure or inflict. By doing so it breeds dissatisfaction and waste of the only life that we know exists, the one we are living now, here on this desolate and foolish sphere of earth. So my advice to you is to give it all up, Sherlock! To exhaust the mind with definitions of what the mind cannot conceive is nonsense. It is like the pointless pursuit of justice and equality among men. Equity will never arrive at a point where it will represent the general condition of humanity. The best that can be hoped for is the occasional exception of charity, which is virtuous precisely because it is so rare."

"If equality was ever the norm for mankind, it would not require laws or taxation backed up by force to achieve it. As it is, we institute governments to compel what the majority will never embrace, which is 'the common good.' Each man would be a master of others if he were able to become one. Only crucified Jesus ever taught that we should prefer to be servants of each other. What Christian society though has ever truly embraced that doctrine? Does not each Christian imagine that his own belief entitles him to preferment over the infidels whom he blithely consigns to the Christian hell?"

"I have met many a sweet little woman in my own congregation in the village of Sigerside who would turn pale if she had to observe a terrier worrying a rat, but she will not turn a hair when the vicar speaks of the babies in Siam who will receive eternal punishment because their parents taught them to be Buddhists!"

"Apparently it is better to be a hypocritical Christian than a devout Buddhist, Moslem, Jew, or Hindu to her way of thinking. Such people love to speak of 'the remnant' and of God's mysterious preferment for the elect, but it is only because they imagine themselves to be among the preferred ones beloved by God. I know that I hardly sound like the Calvinist that you accuse me of being, but you mistake a political preference for the rights of the Scots for sympathy with their religious doctrines."

"Regarding the self-satisfied Christians, I wish to ask them how they would feel if they knew that this short and sorry life was to be only a prelude to the unimaginable disaster of eternal torment inflicted for a sin that the Buddhist commits by simply being born, if they had themselves been born a Buddhist? Would they love God then and wish to praise Him forever? Yet this is the God that they prefer to worship. How does one explain such bloodthirsty attitudes among the pious?"

"If even religion becomes another example of the exertion of power over others, another occasion of pride and self-congratulation, then where are we? It is said that one of the joys of the blessed will be the contemplation of the damned. Can it be that one's favored place in heaven will then have so extinguished our natural compassion that the elect will form a sort of Greek chorus saying again and again of hell, 'It is just; it is just.' Where is the consolation in that?"

"As for me there is no animal, no matter how vicious or noxious it might be, that I would not wish to dispatch to oblivion rather than to sustain its life eternally, merely for the satisfaction of causing it pain. Instead I would purify the universe by extinguishing what I could not change. But if we imagine hell as a great stinking sewer preserved forever merely to make the smell of heaven sweeter, are we not more deserving of hell than those whom we have viewed as damned! Surely if heaven is sweet and God is good that should be an adequate reward for the truly righteous without the added frisson of the sadistic torture of those whose beliefs differ from our own."

"I do not need to drink henbane prior to savoring my mead. I need no study in contrasts to appreciate a good reputed to be absolute. God would be adequate without a grimacing devil to which to compare Him. I am only a Christian now because the world is a little better because some Christians are in it, the few, the very few who actually resemble Christ. As for the rest, I think that the hell that they anticipate with such relish for others might be better visited upon their own souls."

My eldest brother fell silent then. I was amused and impressed by the strength of his opinions. I have often entertained thoughts along similar lines, as the entries in this journal have shown, but perhaps never expressed my thoughts with such vigor and conviction as Sherringford displayed.

I felt that I must make some reply however. I was not ready to admit that my quest had been as vain and pointless as Sherringford implied. I had never for instance valued Christian formalism.   Indeed my entire approach to Christianity is predicated upon a less sectarian view, one that will embrace and explain the human condition in its most universal aspects.

After some time in reflection I addressed him, "Well, we must trust that the contradictions you have identified will be remedied when we see things no longer 'in a glass darkly.' As for Moriarty, I refuse to pre-judge him yet. I must say openly that I am giving him a hearing because I believe that beneath his malice there is a wound the nature of which I cannot know. Even he may be unable to explain the final source of his criminal motivations. As for my granting him a foolish liberty, let me assure you that the advantage has been all mine. Moriarty has stayed his hand now for three years. He has yet to break-out or make good his threat made to me in Switzerland at the Falls of Reichenbach. He has honored the terms of our wager thus far or I should have heard of it. His next crime will, he has claimed, shake the nation. I have bought time, yet sacrificed nothing but my own inconvenience in seeing a good part of the world, while guarded and protected in regions with which even my own daring and resources might not have sufficed to keep me from death. I was even of some use to Mycroft in the process."

"In any case, Scotland Yard did not have enough evidence to convict Professor Moriarty of his crimes. Neither Mycroft nor I could conspire to simply kill him by extrajudicial means, though some members of the government have advised precisely that course. He was after all raised among our family as a lad. What course remained then for us to pursue but the one I have taken?"

"I know that Professor Moriarty presumes a point of origin to exist in the universe, for the laws of mathematics show a pattern of regularity and precision tending towards the unity of forces. It seems to be then but a small step for me to assume that order does not spring out of nothingness and without some other supreme conscious agency, that we will agree to call God, that is behind all phenomena."

"If I can convince the Professor that the intelligible order of creation does not exist without a supreme mind that is its source and origin, I hope at last to awaken within him that universal desire for compassion that provides the best proof of our own humanity, which is still the residue of the image of God within us. I believe that universal trait to be latent, even in a man like Professor Moriarty! Beneath all experience there beats in Moriarty a human heart. Within him exists a path and a direct reason towards a humane world, and if humane then the world is also God-like, because God must inhabit in some way this world that embraces us for all its failings and disappointments."

I tried to sum up my feelings on the matter, "I believe that from our present perspective as human beings we may never know good and evil as God does, but even after the sin in Eden some spark of our former origin in God remains within us unimpaired. God does not so easily withdraw his gifts. We have sullied the image of God within us as a mirror may be clouded and distorted though unbroken. We did not leave Eden as shards of shattered glass, but as a mirror facing the wrong way in which we contemplated only ourselves and not the glory of God within us.

We did not know that we were naked until we became the center of our own attention."

"If we repent and turn to God, we forget ourselves and we can see God again within us; our dignity is restored when we cease to try and exist outside of God and His regard for us. We exist in the love of God or we cease to exist as human beings. What that would be is what is meant by hell, which is always spoken of as the Second Death, a condition that we can approach only by metaphor, rather than by the graphic descriptions that attribute hell to God rather than to ourselves in trying to be God."

"Man and woman now exist on the razor-edge of eternity. Our state here is but a transient one. What we shall be in heaven we cannot say, anymore than we can define the fate and experience of anyone who would be eternally deprived of God. All of life is only the great either/or of the choice once offered us in Eden in the person of our primeval parents, the dawn of moral consciousness, a mere taste of the fruit of that proverbial Tree of the Knowledge between Good and Evil that brought us the misfortunes of our present state."

"Death shall make available to us at last the fruit of that other tree in the garden, the one that has been guarded by an angel to this very hour, the one that would grant to us Eternal Life. In our present state to eat of that tree would have condemned us to eternity in our undecided condition, caught eternally between good and evil. Eternal Life is only safe and bearable for a being that is ready to grasp the eternal with love and in God, a being in other words that would resemble Jesus Christ who shows us the way. The same gift of Eternal Life under any other conditions would turn to ashes in the mouth of any being that would be its own God. Only God may bestow His own nature upon us through grace by living within us. If that grace is absent, then eternity would be like being locked in the echoing chamber of our own minds and prey to the most fearful dreams of our own imaginings. Only God may ever really give us peace." I fell silent then. This affirmation of my understanding of faith was the summation of my beliefs and our final word that evening. I took it as some measure of the efficacy of my speech that Sherringford made no comment after hearing it, but only bowed his head for our shared recitation of the Lord's Prayer before parting.

We both rose and proceeded into the darkness of the hall. The great rafters overhead supported the heavy stone roof of the manor-house like a protective shell; the Holmes estate of Sigerside had protected us both from some of the naked ravages of life and granted us the leisure to embody our thoughts into words. This alone was a great privilege granted to us by our father. Many people are forced to live similar lives to the dumb suffering of animals. These are God's true innocents. Perhaps having known purgatory here they are made more ready for heaven than we who have been allowed a space and time to question the nature of the life that we share with them.

To even take a position toward God is deferred for many souls until after their deaths. That twilight region of abated breath must reveal what now is but the ground of faith and speculation. Even the Catholic Church, its mission of proclamation complete, may only seal the cold foreheads of the dead with Holy Oil and dispatch the soul on its final journey made with the prayers and intercession of the Communion of Saints. I left Sherringford with a brief fraternal embrace that he returned and I went up to my former room where I have written this account before the sleep that must soon come.

May 5, 1893
Sigerside

It has taken me some little time to adequately complete and polish the last entry in my journal. I have somewhat condensed our conversation so as to make each of our perspectives into a coherent narrative. My reunion with Sherringford has shown me that he is not immune to those speculations about the nature and purpose of human life that so obsess me.

It seems as though the collective mind of our family has

been separated into three parts. Sherringford has been faced with the problem of creating a stable society based upon the traditional British class system. Mycroft has been given the task of creating a stable international order.   Meanwhile I have been burdened with the question of the fate of the individual when confronted by both a seemingly indifferent international social order and an equally indifferent physical universe. If everything can be traced back to God as the final cause, then it seems that a universal solution can be offered to all three problems.

God's primary concern is for the fate of the individual, since all social action and the actions of states and other polities is revealed in the last analysis to be the sum total of the decisions of and for individual human beings. Grace operates upon the collective freedom of man as well as it does upon the individual soul. To deny freedom though and to place the nature of the life that we lead in God's hands alone is to deny our own humanity and its collective responsibility for the nature of the life that we lead on earth. God does not supplant our freedom but guides it and strengthens it to embrace the decisions of the one God whose providence guides the larger segments from family to community to state to the universal assemblage of nations.

Providence coordinates all of human action so that the good is advanced, but always under the sign of the Cross of Christ. All of human destiny is summed up in that one unique historical event, the Crucifixion of Jesus Christ. The Passion of Christ is the absolute rejection of God by mankind in its collective sin and simultaneously the absolute acceptance of man by God in enduring that rejection without exacting vengeance, but rather using that same event as the pledge of eternal mercy. The Divine Son of God from His Cross said, "Forgive them Father for they know not what they do."

So integral and complete is this event that the Legion of Evil is robbed of its triumph in the very act of the completion of the task, which it had undertaken in Eden and completed in the Crucifixion of Jesus Christ: to sever man and woman from God and even from each other by their own free choice. The initial choice of rejection of intimacy with God in Eden was repeated and reached its fruition and climax by the rejection of the Messiah by the act of ordering the crucifixion of Jesus by the will and approval of the leaders of the very people who had been prepared to expect and to receive the Messiah when He came. But that very rejection failed in its purpose, because God will never abandon us, though we may abandon Him. Even death is conquered by this event in the assumption of our death, the penalty of sin, by taking it upon Himself in the person of Jesus, the anointed One of God.

This historical event is of cosmic significance. Hell itself received a corona at least of light that for an instant penetrated even those stygian depths of death when Christ entered the realm of the dead. In His death Jesus Christ descended into that realm of waiting where the virtuous dead had long awaited His coming. The dark realm of death could not then hold their weight of freighted souls for redemption was at hand. Jesus entered into death and left the netherworld depopulated by those souls that were liberated at that moment from the bondage that had held them in that state of being a living soul, but yet doomed to exile, until God Himself should restore that lost communion that had once allowed Adam and his mate to walk with God and see Him face to face.

If then the Cross of Christ is the center of history, if its shadow is cast over all events, so does that shadow point to the Second Coming of Christ that will bring an end to history and institute an order that we may only describe as a renewal of all things. The winter of our present age will pass, but not in an ordinary spring that begins with rain and mellow days and only gradually comes to its fruition, but rather in the twinkling of an eye; time itself will cease.

The border that has so long contained the universe, the membrane of time and space that has enclosed all events will open and give birth to a new heaven and a new earth. The grave-clothes that have long shrouded history will fall away. The General Resurrection will see all things made new. What is made new in turn will find its place in God so that God will be at last all in all.

Such an event of universal significance cannot be described in temporal or spatial terms since time and space will themselves be changed by it. Eternity must then have its own vocabulary, though we know even now that love will be its syntax. The love of God will be revealed as the constitutive element of all being. Evil then will be seen as what it has always been, a lie. Evil, robbed of its specious grandeur will be shown to be that presumption, that parasitic growth that it was from the beginning. It can only destroy, never create. God has no part in evil and evil has no part in God.

Once revealed as utter negation, evil will lose that pretense to being that it always claims to possess. Crowned with vanity it crumbles into dust and even the dust is blown away to those desert regions and ash pits where the demons are said to howl their blasphemy and despair. The event for which the Church prays daily is that very arrival of the fruition of the Cross of Christ when the seed long planted shall at last burst forth, that the order of grace will be revealed in the Saints and that final judgment be commenced that will cause evil to collapse forever.

Before that we are taught that there will be a final spread of evil. Just as the Redemption of Easter was preceded by the Cross, so will the Second Coming arrive at the darkest hour of history when evil will appear to have triumphed. Jesus on the way to His crucifixion told the women of Jerusalem not to weep for Him but rather to lament that hour that was to come when even the Cross of Christ would be spurned. That bleak season of death will be that of the dry wood when God will seem most absent. Perhaps even the Cross and the Church that proclaims it will be splintered into fragments.

We are asked though not to despair, for those signs will be the indication that the final hour has at last come. Each generation has imagined that it lived in that last season of the world, but history always surprises us with fresh iniquities. Each age for honest men and women proclaims itself the worst because it cannot yet imagine how much worse the world can be. Perhaps the worst will come when all of mankind is busy congratulating itself that its material needs have all finally been met but without God.

It will then be the perfect season for blasphemy when we may collectively turn to God and say, "See, it is as we always knew it could be; we did not need you after all. Our own resources were quite adequate and sufficient. You may take your cross and go stumbling off for men and women can still become as God, knowing good and evil. The devil was telling us the truth after all when he tempted us in Eden!"

It is then not when we are most miserable that we need to be afraid. It is when we imagine ourselves to be happy, if that happiness is in ourselves and not in God. The demands of the cross are not to be feared if Christ shares them with us. It is better to remain attached to the cross with Jesus, knowing that it leads to heaven, than to be among the most fortunate of men and to lose God at last as the price of a self-procured salvation according to our own estimation of where our ultimate happiness is to be found.

Dr. Watson's Narrative Continues

I closed the manuscript at this point. There was as ever much hope to be found in the composite tale of salvation as traced through the connected stories contained in the Bible. Generation after generation has faced the troubles of life finding in these stories the strength to go on after person losses. It brought to my mind those bleak days after the death of my wife when all existence seemed to cease for me. It was as though I found myself upon an empty plain in which any movement was impossible, for there was neither sign nor direction to guide me. When all actions become of equal import, no action may be taken.

For years I had first weighed any plans or aspirations by asking myself first what Mary would think or what would please her. Now there was nothing. I realized that beyond my medical practice I had no ties, no obligations, and thus no purpose. At that time I believed Sherlock Holmes to be dead and now my wife had followed him into that great silence. Never was my faith more tested than it was at that very moment when it should have simply told me that death is not the exception in human life, but rather the direction of our every action lived within the limited time that is allotted to us. The mere habit of living makes us entertain plans and set goals that may be interrupted, nay terminated, in the next hour or minute. Yet, if we were to focus always upon that undeniable fact, we would stand trembling rather than making death meaningful by seeking to live a full and joyous life within whatever lifespan is granted to us.

It is for this reason that there is something to be said for those who dance before the aspect of death. I have read that the Mexican people celebrate a Day of the Dead with masques and bright colors and even joy. To honor death too much is to please the devil, while to mock it is to recall that man and woman are made for eternal life and that to share in the joy of God is our appointed destiny. The stygian depths, the purple robes of Pluto, the mournful keening of the Scots and Irish, are not the only means to deal with death.

In my despondency at that time of her death I felt the need to live among a people of the south, to find a rich alluvial soil in which to plant again some new hope for my life. To be condemned to life after the death of a loved one seems a greater cruelty than it would be to perish with them in a shared disaster. It takes a wrenching effort to turn away from the grave, knowing that the mere clay and ashes of their remains are not the beloved-one, but only that barren chrysalis left behind by a winged soul.

I buried Mary in Dundee where we had gone on holiday and took the train south to London. For a few weeks I went through the motions of my practice as a doctor. I would leave Kensington to visit Baker Street after my days spent in my dispensary. I would stand on the street there and look up at the windows of 221B, the site of our old rooms when I lived with Holmes. Mycroft had maintained those rooms as Holmes had left them, both as a charity to Mrs. Hudson and as a tribute to the memory of his brother. I had been assured that I was welcome to use my old bedroom at any time as Holmes would have wished. Mrs. Hudson still lit the gaslight in the evenings as she had always done. As I looked upward from the street below I could imagine again that lean figure passing before the drawn blinds. I could see the past ghost of myself passing on the cold pavement where I walked so many times before climbing up those seventeen steps, turning left and opening the door to our old sitting room.

I would enter and hang my hat and cloak upon a coat-rack and take the well remembered cane-chair by the fire. Holmes would be gazing down into the street. At last he would turn to me and say, "You have come at an opportune time, my dear fellow. I have just received a most intriguing cable. It is lying there upon the table." I would take it up and read a message with contents such as this, "I must see you, Mr. Holmes, on a matter of the very greatest moment. I am at my wits end. I must meet him at the lighthouse, but before God, I fear to do so. I know that he will have the papers and that he will laugh in mockery when he sees me. He will be quite alone but for that dreadful trained cormorant with its dark outspread wings. I pray you do not think that I am mad, although madness may be at the door of my very soul. Help me Mr. Holmes! I will come to you at nine for it is only then that I may slip away. Please do not fail me or I am lost!"

"Well, what do you make of it, Watson?" Holmes would ask. "It is certainly an odd communication is it not?"

"I can make nothing of it," I would reply.

"Nonsense, you need only apply my methods, my dear fellow," Holmes would say. "Surely it is obvious. The letter was written by a young woman, who has been trained in stenography. She no doubt works for a politician and she has sustained a recent injury. Notice the tremor evident in her writing. The papers she refers to may be her own or depend upon the person who requests their delivery. But why meet at a lighthouse? Has it any personal significance? The reference to a cormorant may be a bit obscure, but I have no doubt that she will make it clear at the interview that follows. Hello, can this be her step upon the stairs even as we speak?" But that was all some years ago and the records of the matter have been sealed, perhaps forever. How many cases such as the one to which I have just referred still lay in various stages of incompletion in my files or in the memoranda made at the time of their solution. During the grim years of his absence I had believed that Holmes himself was sealed, dead in the fierce mountain torrent below the Reichenbach Falls. I supposed that he lay beneath that dreadful cataract held down by tons of plunging water. Mary was dead as well. Her poor thin body, free at last from pain, lay buried in an oaken box in the quiet cemetery of the Methodist Church in Kensington, a place I could no longer consider home.

From the Journal of Sherlock Holmes

May 13, 1893
Enroute to London

I am off by train once again, enroute to London. My last days spent with Sherringford at Sigerside were peaceful.   He showed me about the estate and I was able to see once again the scenes of my boyhood and youth. Even Sherringford seemed to enjoy the green countryside. Everywhere there is the yellow of the Scotch Broom. The oaks and elms and chestnuts are now in leaf. An early summer seems to be at hand.

Our final conversations were enlivened by those happy memories that make of our childhood a season of revelations. We recalled hearing our father read to us from the Waverly Novels. We remembered our dear mother when we looked at some of the landscapes that she had painted. They have been preserved in a small gallery in the music room and in the parlor where she once received her guests, the village women and even an occasional gentlewoman who would come to call in order to receive her advice or ministration to their needs. Her charity matched her beauty that I still recalled. She was well loved by all in the neighborhood of Sigerside where she is buried in the village churchyard. I stopped by her grave for a visitation on that last day before boarding the train today for London.

I might have stayed longer to prolong my rest after my travels but it is imperative that I see Mycroft as soon as I can. His repeated cables to me urged me to make all haste so that although I might have wished to remain longer at home, I am forced to bid Sherringford farewell. He looked downcast at my announced departure. I believe that my visit has lightened his present cares regarding the estate. I realize now how much he has been forced to bear alone without help from his brothers after the loss of his dear wife. His sons are away at university and can only aid him during the long vacation when they return home on holiday.

I do not know them well. I realize now how easy it is to defer some of the most important tasks of life under the impression that there will be more time next year to undertake or to catch up on neglected private matters. As my practice as a consulting detective grew through the years the demands placed upon me took a toll on not only familial relationships but even upon my health as I have mentioned previously in this journal. I must also confess to periods of wasted time due to a constitutional neuropathy that occasional manifests as depressive episodes.

All in all, my eldest brother has held together quite well. I tend to forget Sherringford's actual age, for he still loves his horses and engages in his habit of riding each day. This practice has allowed him to display an uncommon vigor in both physique and manner. But time presses upon us all and the Yorkshire winters here are harsh. I trust that I shall find him well when we meet again. In any case I need feel no longer the distant feelings that once existed between us. We are loving brothers once again. In our last days together before parting I even began to feel some comprehension and sympathy for his conservative views.

He is for instance steeped in English Jurisprudence. The English have contributed to the world the three great branches of English Law: Property, Contract, and Tort. The essential idea behind Property is the right to use or to exclude from using; as such it is more about relationships than it is about physical things. This view may seem obvious at first, but it must be remembered that there are societies in which all things are held in common possession. Even in our own society there are things to which no right of property may ever attach. If no one may own the air or the sea it seems strange to many cultures that anyone may own land and carve it up into bits and pieces; to say to another man that here he may not step without committing a trespass. Land after all is the creation of God. How then can any man expect to levy an exclusive claim upon it? How for that matter may it be claimed that it is control of territory that confers sovereignty in nations rather than having that power vested in some other basis independent of a geographical requirement for jurisdiction? Yet such was the nature of feudal concepts that the land determined a man's social standing.

There are other sources of power. The right of the Pope to govern the Catholic Church for instance is not dependent upon possession of the former Papal States, since the jurisdiction of the Pope is based upon a claim of right bestowed by Jesus upon St. Peter and his successors to guide the conscience of Catholic believers. No land is required for this, although the Papal States did once act as a source of personal security for the Pope in his person to protect him from the pressures exerted upon his freedom by overbearing monarchs.

Perhaps a time may come when all right to rule will be based upon human rights and all earthly goods will be distributed and used to procure the common good of all. The divine charity of the gospels would seem to mandate just such distributive justice. The world as we know it however is one that presumes a war of all against all as does much of English Law. That law then allows for the possibility of enforced inequality by recognizing property. It further allows for contracts, so that property, or its equivalent, in a recognized medium of exchange, may be exchanged for other property. Contracts require that each person surrender something of value where a promise takes the place of the property in question. Tort Law in turn grows out of contract principles in what was once termed a trespass on the case. Tort Law allows for certain instances where property may be forfeited in damages through conduct that inflicts harm upon another. Thus English Law attempts to create social order without an appeal to charity and assuming a state of affairs in which each man will follow his own way within the borders of certain social parameters rather than the mandate of God that may well exceed the demands of the law.

A state of mistrust prevails among nations. The creation of the nation-state assumes that no higher sovereignty exists under law within each sovereign state. Each is left to govern its own internal affairs as it sees fit. Thus, each nation is allowed to set up its own legal order, to protect its borders, and to provide for the common defense of its citizens. The international order is thereby often less civilized than that of individuals within a nation-state.

International law is the exception to the rule of the untrammeled exercise of power that each nation would exert against the others limited only by another nation's ability to retaliate. This fact makes each state seek power at the expense of its neighbors motivated by fear of identical conduct from them. The result is a general condition of mistrust and warfare that is only constrained by self-interest. A nation may make war as well from fear of attack as from the desire for acquisition. Thus the state of all people is insecure. War finally seems to be a plague as impersonal as that of flood, fire, and famine. Man becomes his own victim. The security of states may guarantee domestic harmony, but that domestic security entails an increase of power in the governing entity that may finally be turned from ensuring domestic tranquility to the effort to create an artificially imposed loyalty at home. It may lead to unjust policies and to subject alien people to the rule of the state by invasion of their land.

My two brothers have each in their own way devoted their lives to the belief that England should be the base of their loyalty and actions. They have accepted the world as presently constituted as the best that is currently obtainable. Sherringford has done his best to keep the family estate intact as the guarantee that the Holmes family still belongs to the class of landed gentry that will prevent our fall into the seething pit of social aspirations that one sees in America where the bourgeoisie rule. While Mycroft, turning his gaze abroad, as devoted his life to ensure that England and English Law will have the broadest possible international scope and that English trade will secure the prerogatives of English rule by making England the foremost temporal power in the world.

I differ from my brothers in this way: I have devoted my life to seeking that commonwealth of man and woman that will make for the realization on earth of the will of God. I have taken my own mandate from the words of the Lord's Prayer, "Thy Kingdom come, Thy will be done, <u>on earth as it is in heaven</u>."

If all sovereignty comes from God, then all right to rule may proceed only as far as God allows. This means of course that all just government must be an act of prayer and discernment. Any law that violates the will of God is no law at all and it is therefore permissible to break it. If at times this view has allowed me to display a certain degree of latitude in my actions (such as committing burglary if the greater good appears to mandate it) then so be it. In fact I have also been guilty of trespass on occasion.

Watson has often been shocked at my often cavalier attitude to English law, but my conduct has always been based upon the principle of conscience and I have been always willing to bear the consequences of my acts. This has created within me a self-reliant attitude that may have even approached anarchy but for the inner constraint of my conscience. I am not at all sure that among men of practical virtue anarchy might not be preferable to the actions of many nations and kingdoms when they are governed by evil men. It may seem a strange observation at this point in my journal, but I believe that the attitude to law displayed by Professor Moriarty is in many ways similar to my own. We are, each of us in his way, a law unto ourselves. For this reason, I believe that the key to Moriarty is to discover the source of that inner law that governs him. He is too much of a man of principle to act arbitrarily. One does not trace the dynamics of an asteroid and leave unfathomed the source of his own motions. If the great physicists, such as Sir Isaac Newton, sought to explain all motion from the first impulse, then I believe that Moriarty will not be able to resist a need for a first cause in both physics and in morals as well. He will need to ask himself why there is something rather than nothing.

The ability of the human mind to negate being does not imply that there is a way to conceive of nothingness. We are presented with being as a *fait accompli* by God. We may at least imagine however that the totality that we see might have hovered for an instant in abeyance in the divine mind before being summoned into existence. If God was not compelled to the act of creation, then God might have simply mediated creating and then changed His mind. If the Holy Trinity is self-subsistent being sufficient unto itself, then all creation is an act of supererogation on God's part, as is redemption after the Original Sin in Eden.

If humankind once desired to be the source of its own definition by becoming like God through our own choice, then God might have allowed us to suffer the full consequences of that choice. The result would be human history as we know it. Left to our own devices we make a sorry mess of everything. I believe that our present condition, constrained by matter and subject to death while encased in animal corruption, is actually God's mercy to us, to reflect back to us in a most visceral way our own inadequacy. These limitations prevent us from terminal fixation in the pride that condemned the fallen angels and makes their redemption impossible, at least within the bounds hinted at in the Biblical accounts.

The angels represent untrammeled will as exercised outside of time and space. The reason that the devil cannot repent is that his will has considered every alternative, weighed all data as it were, and reached an irrevocable decision, but contra God. There is nothing that can dissuade him from that decision, nor will eternity suffice to change his mind. Heaven of course lies open to him, for the love of God is never closed. The torture of the devil is that he will not consent nor use the key to heaven burning in his very hand. His only recourse is to devise means for his own torment; thus is hell self-created.

This brings up the question of necessity versus contingency. Contingency has two aspects: chance and freedom. We can never be absolutely clear that things that are apparently ruled by chance are in fact random events. It is possible that an underlying pattern of causality exists in things that appear to be random occurrences. Necessity similarly can hide under an aspect of apparent freedom. For this reason theology can never close the book on the relations between God and created being, let alone how God relates to Himself. For instance, is God free or is God a victim of His own nature and thus bound by necessity?

This reflection in turn raises the question of non-being. Ontologically speaking non-being does not imply that a transition into being is precluded. If God is free, then God can always presumably continue to create and by doing so instill being into what has not yet come into existence. Nothingness is another matter entirely. From nothing, nothing can come. Our entire notion of causality depends upon the inertia built into what does not even exist. Technically, nothing that does exist can ever become nothingness. In other words not even God is able to un-create something that has ever existed. Nothingness in other words requires causality to destabilize it in its non-being.

May 14, 1893
London

𝕴 am installed in the old Northumberland Hotel here in London as I cast about the old city to get my bearings again. I hesitate to plunge into Baker Street without first speaking to Mycroft. I shall therefore take up my disquisition on metaphysics from yesterday, a sort of preliminary exercise to get me prepared for my initial meeting with Professor Moriarty when I set off for Devonshire...

This question of nothingness is a corollary of the question posed by freedom as opposed to necessity. If God determines all things in advance by some underlying rule of necessity, then creation as contingent being would be either illusory or pointless. Why should God set out a row of dominoes only to knock them over? God would have foreseen the falling of the last domino no matter how remote it might be. By assuming that God stands outside of time and space and that God knows all things, we also presume that from God's point of view everything that we experience as contingent has already taken place. It seems trivial to assume that God has created a playhouse and written a drama in which He is the only audience and where He already knows the course of the play.

It is also pointless (from our point of view) to pose the first question of metaphysics, "Why is there something rather than nothing?" Could God create something and a moment later return it to nothingness as though it had never been in the first place? Can God erase all memory of His own actions by eliminating all traces? Or does the option of nothingness disappear the moment that God creates anything? God's complete freedom appears to cease from the moment that the quiescent state of non-being is disturbed. Even to think of creating contingent being would in a sense already have disturbed the former equilibrium maintained between being and not-being. In this sense our metaphysical concept of nothingness represents a great "maybe." Perfect freedom for God in a sense makes virtually anything possible. Nothingness lies forever balanced on the edge of coming into being if God should ever will it so. Once God creates anything that is not Himself the moment of perfect freedom ceases and necessity is born.

But then for God to further qualify necessity by implanting in creation a new capacity to generate chance, change, or spontaneous variation would appear to indicate that God can abandon His own freedom by delegating it to subsidiary causes. Why would God allow such potential to exist in secondary causes rather than retaining complete control under an interior rule of necessity? If then there is something rather than nothing only love may account for it. God must in this sense be the victim of a tragic flaw: His belief that Evil cannot be spontaneously generated the moment that anything exists that is not God.

These daring speculations take us from philosophy to the first question of Christian theology as a revealed religion, the nature of the Divine Trinity of three Persons in One God. When Jesus told his apostles that He and the Father are One how were they and how are we to understand that statement? The early Christian Church was divided by that question during the period of the Arian heresy. The question was resolved by simultaneously affirming two contraries at the Council of Nicaea: Jesus Christ as a person, one of three in the Trinity, is both fully God and fully Man united in a hypostatic union.

It is not as though Jesus alternates between two states of being, one divine and the other human; both principles are simultaneously active, even if conceptually they are distinct. This means that for Jesus to do the will of the Father is only theoretically a concession and a choice, because the divine unity would make any divergence of wills between the Father and the Son impossible. The Third Person of the Divine Trinity would also appear to be implicated by necessity in this union of will/wills. In other words Christian theology assumes and teaches that for God the offer of salvation after encountering sin was a choice that although free and not necessary was never in any way debatable. This was no committee decision reached by consensus. God's nature would accept no less when confronted with evil.

But the Holy Trinity is not diffusive of good as the philosopher Plotinus believed. God's creation of good things does not behave as though it were a squeezed sponge filled with water, for if God was the sponge then what higher God would have mandated its diffusive nature and caused good things to emerge? The Holy Trinity is not constrained by anything but its own essence and if that essence is to possess untrammeled freedom while remaining simultaneously good in all that it does then only God as the source of all things could have chosen evil rather than good without being judged for making that choice.

Evil is defined with God as its reference point. The first metaphysical problem then is not to prove God's existence, but to inquire why the God that exists is good. We must imagine that God might have hovered for a divine instant before creating at all with the full knowledge that to create beings capable of intellection and freedom might choose evil and by doing so oppose the will of the all-good God. Since God has a monopoly on creating being out of nothingness there is nothing for evil to do once it exists but to strike out on its own in imitation of God, but in an act of contrary willing to the will of God. Thus does evil come to be.

Since God's will is always by definition the ultimate good of the creature, then evil must will its own destruction as the only ground left for it to occupy. The next question is this: since God has created us (and even if we were to be somehow reduced again to non-being) we would still exist in the memory of God as having been, so what shall be done to remedy evil choices by created beings once evil manifests itself? Even God it would appear cannot simply cancel evil.

This is the problem set, not before us, but before God. What can be done to constrain or redeem evil once it exists?

The first option would appear to be not to create anything at all. But the nature of God as love is such that though the Holy Trinity might have done otherwise, creation did in fact occur and in full knowledge of the consequences attendant on that choice, if not in actuality then at least in potency, for freedom to choose God implies as a logical corollary the freedom to reject God as well.

This of course raises an intriguing question. Could the mind of God even conceive of any evil not properly attributable to God prior to its exercise in the angels and in human beings? Was evil then something of a surprise to God? Might we not think of God as morally innocent in that way, analogous to the purity of a child who is suddenly scratched by a purring kitten? Perhaps perfect goodness cannot even imagine evil let alone commit it!

If evil metaphysically manifests itself as the vain wish to be primordial, then it will turn to God in accusation (as perhaps the devil does) and say, "Why did you make me so beautiful if you did not know that I would make an idol of my own beauty and wish to be you, that I would envy my own source of being?" This style of twisted thought is a hallmark of evil, that it turns goodness into a condemnation of the giver. The devil condemns God for being God!

So what other options are left open to God post-creation when confronted by the utter alienation of evil? To will evil into non-being is to take back a gift that was good in itself. Evil may act as an *agent provocateur* to tempt God to destroy it. But Creation would appear to be an irrevocable decision on the part of God. Since what God does is good, it admits of no cancellation.

The next logical option would be to allow evil's challenge to stand and to admit it as a viable alternative vision of reality, which would mean admitting the devil as a sort of alternate deity (a position by the way that is strongly asserted by the devil himself in the last temptation of Jesus in the desert at the beginning of His ministry where the devil promises Jesus all the kingdoms of the world and all their splendor if Jesus will only bow down and worship him). This alternative is so absurd that it shows the inherent self-contradiction of evil, unaware that its being is entirely derivative. It is the last desperate effort of evil to create a separate realm in which all direction reverses itself and God worships what He alone has created.

There is a third way though! Faith teaches us that God in actual fact chose the third alternative, one so surprising that it scandalizes evil and brings the devil to distraction: God would Himself will be evil's victim! The Incarnation of Jesus Christ is inconceivable without the Passion and death on a cross. Jesus Christ's failed mission is its victory for had He been accepted, had evil allowed for the immediate realization of the Kingdom of God by the acceptance of Jesus, on Jesus' own terms, evil's own defeat would have been at hand.

Jesus Christ had to be rejected to keep the game alive for the devil. The death of Jesus was the fulfillment of the Incarnation, which assumes even that fact most characteristic of human existence, our suffering and death. These would all be visited upon Jesus in the course of His life and in a manner most unjust and terrible. The Resurrection of Jesus then was not a mere return to life as though death was a sort of spring-board to Jesus. It was final and transformative so that a resurrected body is in truth a new creation.

The suffering and death of Jesus is not merely symbolic; it actually happened. Death is death! The Resurrection then of Christ re-creates all things new in which there is no evil. Only God acting as God could have accomplished this. The degree of the metaphysical triumph cannot be overstated. The Resurrection of Jesus Christ is so complete in its scope and effects that even in purgatory God's praises are sung by those still burdened by the legacy of evil and only now awakening from the dark dream that once encased them and all created things with them. A beam of light was cast into even the dark caverns of hell on Holy Saturday and the devil was reminded that, however the devil had changed, God had not changed towards him. We may imagine heaven's door open, which to the devil is only a mockery of the self-chosen condition that is now his only destiny.

The answer then to the metaphysical question, "Why there is something rather than nothing?" only requires us to look inwards at our own nature, beset as we are by the choice of good and evil. To believe in ourselves is already to believe in God. If there were no God, then the question of our own being becomes insoluble. We alone in the universe would be an equation to which there is no answer, because we have the misfortune to know both good and evil within ourselves!

Not only is our own state of being doomed to death, but we know that the universe does not depend upon us and will go on after our death. Thus are we both in contemplation of the infinite and simultaneously aware of our limitations as men and women. This is a metaphysical contradiction in our very being, a vast disproportion in a creature with a hunger for eternity while encased in time.

Nor can it be maintained that we are mere cells in a larger

organism, for human consciousness always assumes individual form. Each of us is a world unto himself. We stand against all of creation in possessing this awareness. If we may at times suffer a merger of consciousness into groups or in a transcendent awareness that the whole relates to us as well as we do to the wholeness of creation, that experience does not belie its source in our own individuality. The consciousness of merger and union demands a simultaneous awareness of our differentiation in union. God's promise of redemption then is an individual as well as a corporate invitation and each of us has a seat reserved at the Wedding Feast of Heaven. Each soul is separate and eternal. Even creation's unconscious variety is conserved in the mind of God. When all things are made whole they will be at least what they have been, but purged of evil and transformed. A new heaven and a new earth will see all things partaking in some measure in the Resurrection of Christ, yet each body, though resurrected in Christ, will retain its individual and unique goodness and identity. The ordinary borders that make human communication so subject to misunderstandings will dissolve, but not in such a fashion that our integrity and personality will vanish. Of course even this image is an analogy to what the Kingdom of God will actually experientially entail.

May 17, 1893
My Meeting with Mycroft

How strange it is to descend from such metaphysical heights of speculation to prosaic London! The outskirts of the great city and its reflections in the Thames, this world of hansom cabs, fog, and the stench of coal smoke; I am plunged from heaven into what often has the appearance of hell. Can I have ever have called this place home? Where now are the high snows of the Himalayas? Where are the brown and scorched crags of the desert hills of Persia? Where is the blue Mediterranean Sea below Colonel Moran's house in Monte Carlo? Where is Rome with its marble and majesty and the gracious presence of Irene

Adler? If London is the seat of world-empire, then how poor every earthly empire must be!

I spent today with Mycroft at the Diogenes Club. He wished me to make an immediate and full report on the situation in the Sudan and he wished to acquaint me with the activities of Professor Moriarty as far as they are known to Scotland Yard and to the British Cabinet Ministers. He arranged to meet me at the Diogenes Club. I suggested that I should don a beard for the occasion to disguise my identity, but Mycroft wired me as follows:

Salutations, Sherlock, on your return; no disguise will be necessary. Members at Diogenes are islands unto themselves and will take no notice of you.
Regards,
Mycroft

One of the club's stringent rules is to take no notice of guests it appears. I acted according to his instructions. Upon leaving my hotel I was met at the entrance by a driver who preceded me to where a brougham awaited me by the curb. The driver soon whipped the horses up and we were off. A short time later I was deposited, again without a word, at the marble steps leading to that venerable club of misanthropes which is Mycroft's closest approach to human companionship and society. He makes it a habit to decline all other social invitations. No greater horror could be imagined for him than to be forced to attend embassy teas and to be forced to converse there against his will. His great brain functions best in the rarified atmosphere of his club. There, surrounded by books and a more than adequate dining-room and bar, where alone some discrete conversation is allowed to take place, but only between a member and his guests, Mycroft conducts his life when he is not in his simple but elegant townhouse in Pall Mall or meeting with the leaders of the British Empire at Whitehall or at Downing Street.

The Diogenes Club serves a unique function for its members. It allows its them to avoid a reputation as cranks (for the habit of maintaining such extreme isolation as that which prevails at the Diogenes Club would normally require the services of an alienist) while adding an aura of ease and respectability to lives spent at home in their spare bachelor quarters. All actual interaction is confined between the members and the elderly servants of the establishment who quietly see to it that newspapers are brought up, whiskey or gin mixed according to taste, and meals served properly.

These interactions are kept strictly impersonal and with the minimum of information exchanged. The members otherwise take no notice of each other. Even a nod of recognition, while not a strict violation of the rules, is held to be an extraordinary liberty, one to be avoided except under very unusual circumstances. The bylaws at the Diogenes Club are short and to the point: a first violation brings a fine and an admonitory letter, while a second offence brings expulsion. There is only a record of a single exception ever made to this practice, which was granted to a member who had just discovered upon reading his copy of The London Times that he had just won the Irish Sweepstakes. He read of his winning ticket in the Times and shouted, "By Jove! Congratulate me lads, I just took the sweepstakes!"

The silence of the club reading room had never before been broken. It was considered at the time to be a very grave offence indeed, but the executive committee at the time included two former judges who ruled that *mens rea* was lacking and the surprise of winning had been such as to impose an atmosphere of duress or momentary suspension of the higher mental faculties of the member in question that had temporarily overridden his reason and the ability to control what was a spontaneous outburst rather than a deliberate flouting of the rules. Therefore no sanctions were imposed and the member was allowed to enjoy his winnings without forfeiting his position as a member or other penalty.

I was met at the door of the club and my hat and coat were silently taken from me to the club's cloak room. The musty smell of the Diogenes filled the somber rooms. The high walls reached upward to the dark-stained ceiling with its elaborate carvings of walnut and teak. Grim portraits of past members, now deceased, frowned down upon me from the walls. The carpets were thick and well-woven so that even footsteps were muffled there. I was taken to a private drawing room where Mycroft rose to greet me from a great chair set before the fire. He has not aged too visibly during my absence, but his ponderous frame has if anything increased. He shook my hand briefly before motioning me to a chair. He subsided again into his own accommodation and lighting his pipe looked me over from head to foot.

"You are too thin, Sherlock, altogether too thin. No doubt you have spent time whirling about with those Sufi dervishes in Mecca or perhaps it was your time in Tibet while fasting with the Buddhist Monks that makes you look so febrile. There is a feverish look to your eyes that I don't like. Any excess of religion will do that you know. It breeds its own type of mania. Not seeing visions I hope? Good! Well it is high time to get back in harness with some common problems in the detective line. There is a backlog awaiting you here, I assure you. The past years have contained many unsolved cases due to your absence. Many a perplexed governess has had to decide for herself if she should take a position in Bedfordshire in a mysterious old house and Lestrade has had to use his own best judgment in arresting malefactors."

"I trust however that your journey has not been in vain. No doubt you have picked up some useful information in the Far East and in Persia. I trust that you took some notes as to the political situation there ... names and dates? No? Tsk tsk. That is too bad. Still you have always possessed an excellent memory and it is your impressions that will be of the most use to me. We in Whitehall are particularly anxious about the state of the Sudan. It is the key to Africa you know, that and the Congo."

"There are rumors of gold and of diamonds filtering out to the coast. The Belgians are pressing for every advantage in the rubber trade and the Boers are a concern to us in South Africa. Then there is always the threat posed by the Germans. We understand that the slave-trade still prospers in the Sudan. It still goes on there, you know. Poor blighters! Anyway, Her Majesty's government needs to secure the Sudan to anchor our position in Africa, perhaps not this year, but soon. We need to know the strength of the Khalifa, his arms, men, all that sort of thing. Is he supported by the local tribal chiefs? Does he fear any rivals? It is always best to stir up a bit of discontent prior to deploying any British expeditionary force. We prefer to appear as liberators and not as invaders."

It was difficult to answer so many questions so hastily put to me, but I gave Mycroft my composite opinion, which was that the Khalifa had succeeded admirably to the role formerly occupied by the Mahdi and that he had no rivals for that austere position. I did not believe that his desire to unite Islam was likely to succeed, but in the region of the Sudan he ruled supreme. I believed that his men would be willing to sacrifice everything for him. The bulwarks about the river at Khartoum would make a British attack on that city difficult and costly unless some prior degradation of the Khalifa's power there should occur. But to foment rebellion there was pointless. Mycroft nodded his head before replying.

"Ah well, perhaps we must wait then for him to attack us in Egypt. He will you know. He needs a stronghold on the Mediterranean if he intends to unite Islam. At present he is a big name in a backwater. He is far from Mecca. But whoever rules Egypt will control the Suez Canal and will be in a position to rule Islam rather than the Sultan in Constantinople."

"What about a desert force led by some Sheik upon Mecca and Medina?" I enquired.

Mycroft answered, "Tosh. Mecca is merely the locus of the axis of belief but not of commerce. Arabia is a wasteland. It would take a miracle to make it anything else. Religions thrive on emptiness, because there a mere idea may seem to have substance. But worldly power demands trade in real goods not in ideas or promises. Persia has some claim on Islamic unity of course, but it is Shiite not Sunni and hence it represents only a minority religious position in Islam. The Ummah will never be ruled by a sect. Of course the entire region is an unstable powder-keg of rival ambitions. There are no real borders, only tribal allegiances. We are lucky that the Ottomans keep the whole affair in check. The Turks are at least partially civilized. They also keep the Cossacks from spilling down out of the Caucasus and the Arabs from advancing northwards."

He paused to let me absorb these observations before continuing, "We need to maintain a military presence there, Sherlock. Egypt is ours already and the Sudan will soon be ours as well. Then it will be only a matter of controlling Abyssinia so as to protect trade in the Red Sea. The whole bloody place is the gateway to India you understand.   Otherwise we would let the poor wogs alone. India is the jewel of the British Empire!"

He paused again before turning to me with the first show of real concern, "I trust you were well treated at the embassy there and in Tehran? Good! I did try and smooth your journey. Frankly, I had my doubts that you would ever return home to England in one piece. Never did like that picture of General Gordon in your rooms at Baker Street. We don't need another martyr of Khartoum! Although in your case it would have been an anonymous martyrdom, at least as Sherlock Holmes. This fanciful concoction of yours, this Sigerson fellow, has become quite the rage among shop-girls and governesses you know. You cut quite a romantic figure in your dispatches. There have even been rumors of some musical play in the West-End called, oh some flowery and entirely inappropriate thing ... oh yes, 'The Viking of Tibet!'"

He laughed quietly, "It is all nonsense of course. By the way, how is Colonel Sebastian Moran? Is he still in Monte Carlo? Hmmff, just as well; we don't need that chap about London. Quite lucky he didn't 'do you in,' as my cook expresses it. No, all in all I would say that you have been quite lucky to be back here alive."

He smoked quietly for a bit looking into the fire. "Still determined to have it out with Moriarty, I suppose?"

After I assented with a nod, he shook his head. "Can't depend on that chap to play fair you know."

"He has taken steps then in my absence?" I inquired.

"No steps that we have been able to detect at least. He

seems quite caught up with his horses and his lectures in Exeter at the university there. Still, he did take that one trip to Amsterdam, but only to see a banker there named ... Maupertuis I believe, yes Maupertuis was the name. He appears to have substantial financial investments on the Continent. Just as well, since we do not need to have his ill-gotten gains invested here."

Mycroft smoked for a bit and then burst out with, "Our father was a fool to educate that bounder in the first place. An unnatural growth, that's what he is. How do you expect to influence a character that is formed; not only formed, but positively steeped in evil? Do you think that life is a mere syllogism to him or that logic has anything to do with the way that events in this world actually transpire? The world, my dear brother, is ruled by force and the men who have the cunning to exercise force. Religion is for the comfort of widows and children. The priests who earn their living by empty ceremony are little more than poor players who strut and fret their hour upon the stage, to quote Shakespeare. The ultimate source and end of morality is the use of power to achieve practical ends."

"But what is ultimately good cannot be defined without religion," I interposed.

"Do you really think that is the case, Sherlock? On the contrary, religion exists to gratify the vanity of man. Only take away the trinket of heavenly destiny and what is left, just dry precepts held together by improbabilities. At best what remains is the practical wisdom in the commandments brought down by Moses from Sinai and dishonored ever since."

"Everything comes down to practicalities. Are you aware that the stock market crashed in New York? Railroad shares collapsed. British speculators have been selling all spring. What will save the economy, religion? No, it will be gold and the stability of the British Pound that will stabilize matters. The Americans hope to inflate their currency by shifting to a bi-metallic standard. The whole country is drowning in silver from Nevada and does not know what to do with it all, while England remains on the gold standard. Inflation of the currency and money-supply causes waves of speculation that finally result in a general collapse of values."

"The present panic has caused a renewal of questioning, but whereas they should be asking if they have expanded too swiftly with this frenzy of the building of railroads, the Americans are looking inward and examining their consciences while praying for relief. The churches in America are filled. That absurd country will conclude that it is a judgment of God that their investments have collapsed, whereas it was merely bad policy and greed that have caused the present crisis. There is an economic depression ahead. Farms will be lost and factories will be closed, not because of sin, but because men do foolish things. They do them because they are men."

"The one who seeks moral perfection must live upon a mountaintop or in a monk's cell beset with feverish dreams. The man of affairs must take the world as he finds it and seek to minimize harm. Christianity fails because it manifests loyalty to a single idea. Islam will never work as a principle to organize nations, because it is beset by divisive tribalism. It is all a question of loyalty you see; but loyalty to fragments only brings on further fragmentation. So finally what remains to organize nations but political power and the will to exercise it; this is the ruling principle of national survival and prosperity."

I considered his words. To say that I found them harsh and shocking is only a testimony to the fact that I was able to live a private life. What private citizen would ever willingly and openly collude with the many atrocities that are committed each day by his government? We imagine that honor is the rule at the highest levels of our abstract governmental structures. It comforts us to do so. The reality though would not bring us comfort as we lie down to sleep. Nowhere does one find more compromise of principle, the rule of the venal, and the hunger for prosperity and advancement than one finds in governmental circles. I am not at all sure that those who advance to positions of power and influence are not the worst among us. I can still recall the bitter lessons that I learned in Russia when I went there to investigate the Trepoff

Murder. Russia exists on two major bases: the practice of intrigue and the drinking of Vodka. All nations however share much the same characteristics.

I tried to think of an adequate response to his indictment of religion and to his skepticism regarding the efficacy of prayer. "Yes Mycroft, I see your points; but what are nations finally but the creation of charters, agreements, and constitutions? People place their faith in the power of papers that memorialize agreements and constrain arbitrary conduct, what Rousseau called the social contract."

"But are these documents, even when they are formalized rather than remaining implicit in the general consciousness effective or even real?" Mycroft asked. "It all comes down to power; the nation can only exist by a veiled threat of force toward its own citizens. The people collectively create the Leviathan by agreement to forgo force towards one another, but in doing so they only become mere cells within that larger organism. We create nations because we prefer one tyrant to many. We seek enemies abroad so as to diffuse the hatreds that exist at home between the social classes. The task of government is the same as that of a magician. The magician focuses attention away from the hand that performs the illusion. The task of the politician similarly is to focus the natural aggression of the nation's people toward enemies outside."

"Let me be specific, Sherlock, my specific task is to serve the British Empire so that it remains unified and so that Britons do not return to living in stone huts and erecting monoliths to help them keep track of the seasons as did the ancient Druids. England has many real enemies abroad. Those who counsel peace have short memories. Or perhaps we should go back to living in terror of invasion by neglect of our defenses?"

I responded, "I only know that those who take up the sword sooner or later perish by the sword. These endless preparations are bound and certain to finally bring about the very war that they are designed to prevent. Readiness and preparation set up precisely the situation where a minor spark can start a conflagration."

"Well that is a vexed question is it not?" Mycroft asked rhetorically before continuing. "As I see it one either resists or one is trodden underfoot. Shall we take the Jewish nation as an example? The Jews as a people have been exiles for nearly two-thousand years from land supposedly given them by God, the all powerful God, to possess forever. They bequeath to the majority of mankind not only a collection of some of the oldest written documents of human history, but also bequeath certain profound ethical ideas that still enlighten most nations. Yet, how have they been treated? They have been confined to ghettos, killed and humiliated on the streets, not one is a member of this very club where we are sitting; so where is the honor that we should by right bestow upon the Jews as a people? Instead, a brief riot in a Roman courtyard in Jerusalem is held against them forever. Is this fair? Yet religion or religion's effects persecute them and hound them from our midst. The adherents of the Christian religion have allowed it, which would not even exist were it not for its preparation by the Jewish experience in ancient Canaan. Christians are asked to be peacemakers, yet they have not made peace with those to whom they owe the greatest debt of gratitude. I do not know if there is a God or not and I have no time to wait for Him to make an appearance. However, I do resolve that Britons will not be placed in the position of jumping off of the cliffs at Dover as the Jewish patriots did at Masada, at least if I can prevent it. I try to keep a grasp on what is happening and the probable course that events may take. I do not know that this pleases God; I must consult my own conscience and do the best that I can. And when I come to die..."

Mycroft was silent for a time. "I hope that those who knew me will say that I was a good Englishman. I will be buried in an Anglican High-Church ceremony, sprinkled with holy water by the Archbishop of Canterbury, and carted off to some bone-yard in Yorkshire only to have sheep grazing over my head. If there is anything else after death, I hope that I may meet it squarely and without prevarication. I don't dislike God mind you, but He has given us a bloody difficult world with which to deal hasn't he? If you don't think so, come and see me after you talk to Moriarty. If he is a philosophical agnostic, then I am a practical agnostic, based upon my experience of men and affairs."

I thought this response was both brave and honorable, so I said. "I believe Moriarty will make a similar set of arguments to those that you have made to me today."

Mycroft smiled and then said in self-deprecation, "They are not my arguments alone then. I would prefer you realize to be wrong. My melancholy is derivative rather than innate. I have perhaps seen too much for my own good."

"Or perhaps not enough," I replied. "In any case, we will talk again about these things. I am not without a fairly vast acquaintance with human nature as well."

After a significant pause I lightened matters by asking, "Do you intend to feed me?"

Mycroft smiled broadly for the first time. "Ah well, life has its comforts also does it not. Come along then, Sherlock. Our chef has prepared an excellent Beef Wellington and his Crème Brule is outstanding."

Mycroft held the door open for me. We left the private room where we had been speaking and made our way through the silent halls past other rooms whose open doors revealed men of substance reading or sleeping in their chairs before the hearth immune from the world outside with all its hopes and fears. That immunity did not extend to my brother. Indeed, he looked more harried than I was accustomed to seeing him. There is no greater way to witness the advances of age than to be absent for a time and then to gaze upon a familiar face. What I had taken to be simply a gain in weight was perhaps an unhealthy retention of fluid, a sign of bad circulation that only increases the strain upon the heart.

Mycroft labored under immense responsibilities. He was in a sense the clearinghouse for all British Intelligence. The amount of raw data retained in his memory would have required an army of file clerks and secretaries to duplicate. In addition, his extraordinary memory allowed him to retain data for a considerable time. He alone might recall a prior treaty or secret agreement that might be compromised by some new initiative of the government. The result could not be anything but a constitutional overload. I once told him that his great girth was simply an indication that his body as a whole had become an anteroom for the data that could no longer be contained within the precincts of his skull. He was not amused. Like many large men he still retained an inner image of himself as the athletic youth that he had once been. Over the course of our dinner he proceeded with the conversation that we had begun earlier.

Mycroft resumed our discussion by remarking, "You are no doubt shocked and may even be appalled as well by my frank disclosure of the reasoning processes of nations. You must understand that statesmen are actors. It is their business to appear noble for the sake of the people. It is left to functionaries such as me to deal with the sordid realities that make life possible for the citizens. There is a certain child-like confidence that people appear to retain regarding the governing structures and their personifications in leaders. Advancement in government circles is often proportionate to the ability of skilled actors to play up to what is expected of them in that regard. We imagine nobility and preternatural insight to be present in men whose primary skill is to read convincingly words that wiser men have written for them."

"Perhaps if I simply explain matters as a scientist would do this phenomenon will seem less amoral. Think of the nation as a whole as an organism. Its wants and needs are supplied by its collective energy resources. Cut off that source of energy and the organism will finally decay and perish after a primary period of desiccation. Look for instance at the great city of London. It functions as the heart of that organism, but it requires great energy expenditure in order to do so. I am sure that it would be possible to arrive at an estimate of the energy that is required simply to sustain the organism, but you must remember that every organism must grow merely to survive."

"This in turn requires a growing economy. Capital is lent

out at interest. The result is that any economy that cannot cover its interest costs has no choice but to borrow on the future to pay the interest of the expenditures of the past. The only choice then for an economy is to make a profit above the cost of simply servicing its loans in the hopes that the principle will someday be able to be totally repaid, which of course never happens. No nation can live long within its means and sustain a balanced budget, because the mandate of history will not allow it to do so. The rapid increase in a national population requires growth to proceed faster than would happen in the case of a sensibly balanced budget. Even to speak of a balanced budget of course would assume that all essential raw materials and energy sources might be obtained from the domestic resources, which is of course patently untrue. Most nations require extensive imports of raw materials in order to feed their expanding industries. This fact creates a sort of trade imperative among nations. This in turn is governed by the power differential that exists among them."

"All nations must trade in order to survive. All of that sounds quite peaceful of course does it not? Think for a moment though and the central problem becomes manifest. If every nation must grow and if that growth in a capitalist framework requires profits, then some nations will have to be sacrificed so that others may prosper and survive. There is simply not sufficient raw material and energy to sustain every nation under any system of government that has yet been devised. Capital cannot be created from nothing, at least in the long-term because sooner or later there will be a demand made by the creditor for payment or continued loans will cease. This is preceded of course by a period of rising interest rates in order to accommodate the theoretical risk of a default on the loan. Of course at the higher levels of government it is always understood that it is national military power that reminds too insistent creditors that demands for re-payment will be resented and then resisted if loans are not as forthcoming as usual."

"This means that in the race between nations to take their place in the power hierarchy some nations will inevitably lag behind others. I will not say more because the conclusion is so obvious. It is imperative for poorer nations to lag behind, for if they joined the same exclusive strata where the more successful nations reside then they would be able to charge a higher price for the raw materials that they export to the richer nations. The poorer nations must be kept then at a primitive level of consumption in order that social advancement may be obtained elsewhere. When you walk down Pall Mall, Sherlock, and gaze upwards at the elegant buildings that line it you can be assured that some village in Africa or South America or Asia is ultimately subsidizing that wealth and sophistication."

"Or let me pose another example. Imagine for a moment the state of affairs that would prevail if some obscure desert people such as those wandering tribes that presently roam about the Arabian Peninsula ever became separate nations in possession of some essential raw material rather than sand and an occasional oasis for grazing sheep. If that were to be the case, then a great deformation of the world economy would undoubtedly result, because a balance of payments in world-trade might begin to shift between producing-nations, like England, Germany, and America, and the resource-rich nations that would over time demand higher prices for their exports."

"The industrial nations then, unless they might obtain that raw material cheaper elsewhere, would have to pay the price charged or invade those upstart nations who dare to demand higher prices and simply take those resources without payment. The ultimate effect of refusing to invade would be similar to levying a tax upon the purchasing nations with every added shilling used to purchase that now essential raw material. When added to the ordinary interest payments on preexisting loans to the government at home this new foreign tax would cause prices to rise for domestic consumers. If wages could not keep up with the rise in consumer-prices the result would be increased levels of penury at home and a fall in the standard of living until the dominant nation such as our own England would become subservient to the nation possessing those rare resources!"

"There is nothing more humiliating than being forced to borrow money from one's servants in order to disguise a fall in one's fortunes. I may tell you that England will not consent to be so reduced in stature as to become a debtor nation. We do not have abundant resources here except coal, therefore we import them and we do so cheaply by possessing colonies. We are the engine and they are the source of the fuel that feeds our national prosperity. In return for the materials that we import, we export items that their genius has failed to invent and we provide stable governments to our colonies to curtail native warfare and religious factionalism. Over time we also export Christianity to replace whatever crude religious opinions have sustained them heretofore. The result is not only our own survival and prosperity, but the general spread of civilization. In any case, we have no choice. The entire international system is sustained by a precarious balance of power. Change any part of that equation and the entire system could collapse into general penury and warfare."

"To prove my point, let me be more specific. This very year of 1893 is involved in an economic contraction that may last for years and spread throughout the dominant nations of the world. Production will fall until prices grow stable once again. Under the pressure of human need alone demand will finally begin to pick up, the sinews will begin to heal, the volume of trade will increase, and before long the entire machine will be humming along once again. But in the meantime there will be suffering and dislocation in many places. When people suffer they sometimes go to war out of sheer desperation. The only thing that prevents this is that wars are so costly that they only extend the period of recovery after they are concluded."

"The result paradoxically is that most wars are fought when nations are doing well but fear that a crisis or a passing opportunity requires warfare as a means to sustain the level of prosperity to which the nation has become accustomed. No man is more desperate than a man who is used to living well who fears that he may not be able to continue to do so. He has forgotten what it means to suffer want and does not desire to reacquire that capacity. So also the nations that have known wealth and power do anything that they can to sustain their relative position among the nations of the world."

"You may take that statement as a general rule in world affairs. If England were to lose its position of dominance, it might take a century for a new international balance to emerge. During that time chaos would break out and millions would die. So my dear brother, if you are at this moment doubting the virtue and integrity of your brother Mycroft, based upon what I said in our earlier discussion, I beg you to remember that I am one who is engaged in sustaining the current international order upon which millions of lives depend. I often feel like Atlas with the world upon my shoulders. My only refuge is this club, where for a few short hours I may imagine a world where isolation and a private life are possible. You have no idea what a pleasure it is to have the luxury to cease all exchange of words or ideas for a time. The Diogenes Club contains some of the most independent men in London. It is the principle of the club that we are telling the world and also each other to go to the devil while we are here. "

"There is no need here for a balance to be reached between hypocrisy and candor, for we presume a level of mistrust and contradiction to exist even among the membership. We admit the needs of the outer society to the very minimum and the result is that we are able to enjoy a brief peace. There has never been a scene at the club and no member has ever said an unkind word to another. Bring human beings together too closely and you have the equivalent of rats in a cage. The whole mixture is unstable. Even husbands and wives kill each other. Why? Because whenever human needs increase or overly sanguine expectations promise to be disappointed, so does fear and anger increase. These in turn are the fruits of mistrust and betrayal. The Diogenes Club has no officers, but only a Rules Committee to see that the club rules are followed. The office of enforcement rotates and is seen as a great burden to those who occupy it. Fortunately infractions are rare. No one covets power here because we realize, as the world has not heretofore done, that the hunger for more power, although that hunger is the rule between nations, turns one into a beast if one seeks it individually."

"Switching to a different social institution may reinforce my point. You may think that I have no religious beliefs simply because I am weary of the struggle for power between religions. I have thought a great deal about religion and particularly about the death of Christ and the aftermath that created Christianity. I have come to the conclusion that it was nothing more than the struggle for power that resulted in the death of Jesus of Nazareth. I have often wished that I had been able to have a discussion with Jesus prior to his entrance into Jerusalem."

Mycroft paused because a steward had just entered to inquire after our needs. Mycroft's narrative was thus interrupted.

"Will you have some more wine, Sherlock? Here steward. Ah our glasses are now filled and we may continue.

'Oh for a beaker full of the warm south, full of the true, the blushful Hippocrene, winking at the brim and purple-stained mouth; that I might drink, and leave the world unseen, and with thee fade into the forest dim.'

"You recognize the lines of course; they are from John Keats, his *Ode to a Nightingale*. They make for a lovely toast don't you think? Cheers! Yes, well then as I said I have often thought that a bit of reflection might have put Jesus on the right course and avoided the whole sorry affair of His crucifixion. But then that might have worked the very devil with our hope of salvation. I would have pointed out to Him that the times were simply not yet ripe for His sort of message. The Jews were expecting revolution and the Romans were garrisoned in Jerusalem to prevent it. Now here comes this rather obscure folk-healer with talk of universal love in an atmosphere charged with hate, resentment, and the fear of the loss of religious power and the few freedoms conceded to them by the occupying Romans. Even the Jews of the time were divided in Pharisees and Sadducees. Herod acted as a nominal king, a Tetrarch (whatever that entailed) by keeping the people down, while the Sanhedrin kept the dream alive of a national resurgence. The Romans ignored the existence of the Temple.

What was it to them if the Jews ran a slaughterhouse for animals as part of supposed sin offerings? The Romans knew that there was only one sin for them as Romans, to disappoint Caesar and hence to lose their promotions to the rank of centurion or tribune or, in the case of Pilate, to retain his position as the governor of Judea.”

"The Romans needed to preserve power and control over the most contentious people known to history. The Jews were fighting even among themselves over the question of the existence of an afterlife, but all agreed that the Romans must be forced sooner or later to go. Everyone was waiting for the Messiah to come and remove the Romans. Now then, what does Jesus do? He rides into Jerusalem on a donkey, kicks up a frightful row in the Temple, and tells everyone that they should love one another, even their enemies!"

"Why if Jesus did the same things in Westminster Cathedral or over at the Bank of England today he would be in custody before nightfall and The London Times would publish an article about some poor madman who had kicked up a great disturbance. Jesus could not have chosen a worse time or place to give his universal message to mankind. It was virtually certain to fall upon deaf ears. Even his own friends and avid followers were jockeying for position for what they imagined the Kingdom of God would finally turn out to be. His parables seemed to them to be simply some mysterious utterances and not the center of his mission at all! Then suddenly the crucifixion and death; the death of the very man that they had trusted and believed in without reservations, now crucified and their hopes all come to nothing!"

"This strange but virtuous man dies and all of Jerusalem and even the Romans are revealed for the sorry part that they played in His destruction in order to preserve their own power. The Sanhedrin feared a challenge to their religious authority and Pilate to his peaceful rule over the people. Jesus dies and His blood runs down the Cross and over the whole world ever since. There you have the history of Christianity in a nutshell and I would have acted just as Peter did and tried to talk Jesus out of whole thing. With all of time to choose from why did God Jerusalem and why at that inopportune time? But then a quick review of world history reveals that as regards such a message there would never have been a proper time and place."

"But to return to Jerusalem in the first century: the known world of that time began almost immediately to doubt and to grasp, first in men like Nicodemus and men like Joseph of Arimathea, that something dreadful and irreparable had just occurred. Who was this man Jesus after all? What if Jesus was who he said he was, the Son of God? What if all of human history had been focusing upon this event since before the time of the founding of Rome or Jerusalem? And now it was all past and Jesus lay in a borrowed tomb with a rock rolled over the entrance..."

Mycroft paused dramatically and I waited for what he might say next. After taking another long drink from his glass of wine he continued.

"That should have been the end, just another of history's many disappointments. There should have been a period of dislocation and a few people, women mostly, would have cried for a week and then gone on with their lives. His apostles would have wandered away, gone back to fishing or whatever. There were no gospels yet written, no monasteries formed, not even an obscure temple like that of the cults of Mithras or Apollo. Nothing! It was all over. Pilate had washed his hands of the whole affair..."

"And then, in that great silence, a burst of hope: Jesus has been seen! He is risen! This man torn almost to shreds and bled as dry as a bone, pierced by a spear, has been seen! More surprising still, people believe it. More people see him. Finally, the appearances cease and he is said to have ascended to God the Father. Even then, the whole matter does not die out and suddenly even Paul who had once killed these poor delusionaries becomes one of them. Christianity survives without any written records for a generation based on mere popular conviction alone. Then the first gospels are written and the epistles of Paul are sent, but even then the Canon of Holy Scripture, sifted by the early church for what is most acceptable, is not finalized for over a century into what we now know as the Bible. It appears that people simply live according to this thing called The Way: slaves, illiterates, and even some wealthy Romans. They find in this tragic event and the teaching that preceded it the entire purpose for their lives. They are even killed for entertaining this strange belief. Yet still it does not die out. Finally, even the Emperor Constantine accepts it. Rome itself dies and what remains? The Pope! The Pope on the Chair of Peter keeps alive a faith that preserves what it dare not destroy. Soon even the savage Germanic and Slavic tribes are Christian!"

Mycroft paused and took another drink of wine before continuing, "Now among some thinking men like St. Augustine and the early church Fathers like St. John Chrysostom, or later men like St. Athanasius or St. Thomas Aquinas and it becomes conceivable that Christianity is not a mere historical anomaly, but is predicated upon what Jesus said He was. Jesus is the actual Son of God who had it within His power to bestow grace through the gift of the Holy Spirit to the Church. Jesus is the principle of all life and the final answer to the scandal of death and of evil. He will come again to be all that the Jews had ever wished their Messiah to be and more, for then He will restore all of creation in God and for God so that God will finally be all in all, the Alpha and the Omega, the beginning and the end of the world!"

Mycroft was silent again and then he said quietly at last, almost in a whisper, *The whole thing is so fantastic; it must be true.*

I believe that I saw a tear in his eye then. Perhaps the first that I had seen since our father died. He shook his great head from side to side as if to clear his vision and poured himself another glass of wine which the steward had left and filled my glass also. We were silent then until the clock began to chime upon the mantle above the fireplace in the quiet room where we had dined alone.

"Ah, it is late, this dinner has been somewhat prolonged," he said bestirring himself at last. "I will have to leave an uncommonly large tip for our steward. When will you be leaving for Devonshire did you say? Two days? Good. We shall meet again of course and talk of other matters."

He heaved his great bulk up and stood swaying there before the fire. I wanted to say something to him, but could find no words to exceed his own in elegance or perception and insight. We drove back in silence to his rooms in Pall Mall where my baggage had been transferred and I have remained awake in a comfortable but not overly ornate room to record the events of this extraordinary day.

May 18, 1893
Second Day with Mycroft

I awoke quite late to find that Mycroft was already up before me and off to Whitehall. His elegant townhouse above Pall Mall is provided to him free of charge by the government. It may be strange to say, but Mycroft owns no house of his own. I am sure that his monetary resources are substantial though. Should he ever leave his current position, he might establish himself anywhere in the wide world. As it is the Diogenes Club fulfills the functions that are usually associated with possessing a home. He has a drawing room available to meet friends or the heads of government departments. The dining room and cuisine are unexcelled.

The townhouse for this reason is merely a place to sleep and to enjoy a frugal breakfast before beginning his day. He keeps only a single servant to serve as butler and valet, a man named Hugh, a dusty old man but still possessed of the quiet dignity and excellent taste of his class of servant. It was he who prepared eggs and bangers for my breakfast and afterwards lit the fire in the parlor so that I could complete my journal notes this morning. I am to meet Mycroft for afternoon tea at the Diogenes Club. Until then I may do as I please, so I shall spend this time writing some reflections that I have had after my talk with Mycroft.

The past few weeks have been a revelation to me. I must

say that I am closer to both of my brothers in sympathy than I suspected these many years. Perhaps it is only by tracing my own credo in these pages that I have come to understand the beliefs and principles derived from a common family background and ethos that activate them. It was a relief to me to know that my brother Mycroft had not really lost his faith. He remains Anglican of course rather than Roman Catholic. Strange to say but his great reasoning powers have yet to bring him over to the Roman Catholic Church. Perhaps it is the visceral nature of Catholicism that puts him off. The Italians after all are so much more expressive than the English. Still, the ceremonial observances are similar so that perhaps it is some latent xenophobia that keeps Mycroft aloof.

The Roman Catholic Church is above all else rooted in the sacramental order. Jesus promised that he would not leave his followers orphans. For this reason the Catholic Church believes and teaches that the Sacred Species of Holy Communion is in all truth, the actual and substantial Body and Blood of Jesus Christ. Jesus was quite clear upon the matter. "For my body is real food and by blood real drink," he said.

The doctrine of the Resurrection of the Body is also nothing else if not visceral. The image of the seed that dies to create the Church that will thereafter bear much fruit shows the function of Our Lord Jesus Christ both in His life and in His death. Jesus Christ did not come to earth merely to spread the teachings of God *in personem.* The Incarnation is far more than that; it is God becoming man so that man may enter into the very life of God. God is thus granting, but in His own way, the wish of Eve and of Adam to become as God, but not in opposition and a prematurely grasped equality, but in an obedience and subordination made out of love for God and nourished by God through Divine Grace as mediated by the sacraments.

As Catholics we are asked to surrender all in order to become all. We die with Christ in order to rise with him. Jesus Christ embraces our death so that we may receive His life in return. For this reason Baptism is the reverse of original sin. In it we accept death as the price of sin by being humbly submerged in the primal waters from which all life springs. We become nothing in order to become everything.

A new creation begins within us at Baptism; thereafter to be nurtured by the reception of Holy Communion, reinstated and healed by the Sacrament of Penance, and strengthened by the Holy Spirit through the Sacrament of Confirmation. We are anointed again when our soul begins its last journey by the Sacrament of Extreme Unction. Finally, our choice of a state of life with a mate is sealed in Christ in Marriage and for the few there is also the Sacrament of Holy Orders that sustains the Church by passing on Christ's ministry to His anointed Priests and his teaching and governing role to His Bishops.

The Sacraments are God living with us and within us. They are effectual because they are fundamental, rooted in our constant need for God and in God's ready response to those needs. To imagine Christ coming among us simply to teach is to deny the radical choice of God to become one of us, wholly and completely. Jesus was not a phantom but real flesh and blood, without in any manner surrendering His Divine Nature. The Hypostatic Union of the two natures of Jesus Christ is the embrace of man by God, an embrace that is the fulfillment of every promise, for God will not relinquish us to our own feeble resources. Humans once redeemed may never again be unredeemed. The cancelation of the debt of Eden is absolute and need only be personally embraced to become effectual.

Final perseverance in grace is none other than our own complete and lifelong embracing of the source of that redemption. We are strengthened and sustained in that resolve by the Sacramental Order and by the Sacramentals of the Church as well, such as the veneration of the Holy Relics, blessings with Holy Water, and by the veneration of Holy Icons. These bless all of life's moments and allow us to consecrate everything in every day to God. To sever teaching and word from the Living Body of Christ present in his Church is by its very nature Pelagian, for it leaves to man and to woman the impossible task of an unaided embrace of God.

However we may wish out of despair or out of presumption to go it alone, this task is beyond our powers, to live a Christian life alone and unaided by grace; but by accepting and using the sacraments we simultaneously accept conversion of heart and the salvation that conversion bestows upon us..

Protestant doctrines in contrast often suggest that it is only when man and woman perceive their complete depravity that they may accept grace, which they then do once and for all in a unitary moment of conversion. The error in this position is twofold:

1. Man and woman are wounded by sin, but not depraved. The image of God is not eclipsed within us by the sin of Eden, but only shadowed. We still wear the stamp and signature of God on our very souls. We are made for God. In our very sin is already the promise of the redeemer. God did not send Jesus as an afterthought. "Where sin abounds, there grace super-abounds," says Saint Paul. The great poet Francis Thompson says that "fear was not to evade as love was to pursue;"

2. Divine Love awaits our response. Conversion is then the beginning and not the end of the Christian life. Just as conversion requires the grace of initiation, so does perseverance require the daily graces bestowed through the Church and through the intercession of the entire Body of Christ.

It is Pelagian to believe that any soul may do this alone. Jesus walks every step with us back to the Father. Salvation is not an individual contract made with God, but a continual merger into the Body of Christ. It is the Body of Christ that is saved and we as members of that body through union with Christ are saved by virtue of that intimate relationship that incorporates us into the Church and sustains that new life within us so that no man or woman is alone.

It is important to emphasize here that even those who might be spoken of in theory as being outside the Catholic Church are redeemed by reason of God's wish that all might be saved. The sacraments are not given to us as privileges, but as gifts and they are meant to be shared, not held closely as a private possession to which only the virtuous have access. To erect artificial barriers between various sects of Christianity is to confine God's choice to an 'elect' and to deny the universal desire of God that all men and women should come to believe and to acknowledge that Jesus came from God and is God. To even perceive God is already to love Him.

The Church leaves the manner of that introduction to God's providence, to God who knows best how and in what manner He will present Himself to the individual soul in life and in death. The Catholic Church knows that God will make up for our own deficiencies in promoting the message entrusted to our care. God can only be embraced to the extent that He is seen for what He is. Even the Apostles lived with Jesus but seemed unable to see Him as God until after the Resurrection. Even the Transfiguration awoke in Peter only the desire to set up a few tents. Their response all along was inadequate and misguided even though they were Apostles.

Is it surprising then that Christians often fail both individually and collectively to act as God would have us act. We often seek to exclude others as unworthy of God, as if that decision was ours to make. How much more must we who live beneath the comforting mantle of faith learn to truly know and acknowledge God whenever we see Him in others, no matter what provisional faith they profess. We are like the disciples on the road to Emmaus. We walk with Him but we do not recognize Him, except in the breaking of the bread that reminds us of our unity and of God's hospitality to sinners.

Even the Catholic Church can do little more than celebrate Jesus in the Breaking of the Bread and walk the lonely road to Calvary in His footsteps. Doubt and weariness lie in every step that we take. We may often be persuaded that we are abandoned, even as in that last hour of Jesus on the Cross. For this reason God meets the soul in our final hour, as though nothing had gone before, so that as we cross over into death, God is there beyond the portals of our senses. He will appear to us then clothed in that aspect of divinity that will most confirm whatever dim knowledge we have of Him. Those who have not formally entered the Church may do so then, for God will then make all things clear to us.

Our sole prayer then must be that we shall not be put to the test, that having fully known God in that meeting, we might prefer rather to persist in a life without God for eternity. What greater tragedy may be imagined than if God's last word to us as we turn away should be farewell? How tragic if we force God to endorse our own decision, as He then must, because our freedom once come to fruition and maturity leaves it possible for us to reject God, even though God will never reject us!

It is the mission of the Church to prepare us for that encounter and we join the Catholic Church so as to have at our disposal every available grace, which it is the function of the Church to bestow upon us as Jesus commanded that it should do. It is a legacy of the Donatist heresy to confuse the malfeasance of any member of the Church including the Pope for the Church itself. The Church shines through the sins of its members, for it is the lens through which the light of Christ shines. If its image is ever dimmed by personal sins, this is only a temporary condition. It will be wiped clean again by God in due season. For this reason no one need doubt the permanent presence of Christ in His Church until the end of time.

The essence of the Church is not in need of reformation. It speaks only the words of Jesus, given to her for all time. Reformation for this reason must never entail schism because to separate from the Church is to leave the unity of the faithful. Only the accidentals may be changed, for the very reason that they are just that, accidentals. They do not pertain to the integral mission of the Church but only its faulty articulation at various periods of history.

This is the real intent behind the infallibility of the Universal Magisterium that states what has been taught and believed at all times and everywhere as attested to by the Holy Spirit who will not deceive the Church as a whole. This does not mean that all teaching is provisional until confirmed by centuries or by taking a poll of believers, but that what has been so long attested to by time as a universal belief may be safely relied upon as a prudential measure for attaining the soul's salvation. This reliable teaching touches matters that human reason alone cannot discover, but how we formulate and understand that revelation is beset by the limitations of human expression and cultural habits of mind that may require a second look as new problems are presented. Therefore I pray that Mycroft will someday soon become a Catholic, but if in all good conscience he finds that he cannot do so, I will not fear for his salvation, but rather entrust him, even as I do myself, to the mercy of God.

This same rule applies to all men of good will who persist in any faith, even one that is not Christian. The imperatives of culture often make the Christian message too attenuated and diluted by the mode of our own cultural presentation to be grasped by alien cultures, particularly when their own notions of the sacred seem to be callously violated by our missionary efforts. To despair of their salvation is to cast aspersion upon the universal efficacy of the sacrifice of Christ on the Cross for all of humankind. On that note it is time for me to depart. It is time to leave for the Diogenes Club. The body needs sustenance as well as the soul. I will join Mycroft in that strange society of misanthropes, who like all children of a sour disposition, seem bound to resist the joy to be found in human intercourse and company.

Later—

This time I was shown directly into the dining room where Mycroft rose to greet me.

"Ah Sherlock, here you are at last. You are ten minutes late. My stomach is an infallible indication of the hour. I trust that you spent a comfortable morning and that Hugh saw to all of your needs? Excellent! I recommend the flounder ala crème. Shall it be Riesling or Liebfraumilch tonight? Our wine cellar is well supplied as you can see."

We ordered and Mycroft proceeded to inquire why I had failed thus far in our conversations to mention Dr. Watson. I answered at once that the subject was a painful one to me since I felt guilty for being so long away.

"I thought you might feel so," said Mycroft. "For that reason I have avoided telling you that Dr. Watson lost his wife to typhoid last year."

I received this news with both shock and bitterness.

"You should have informed me at once, I would have made every effort to return sooner, let the costs be what they may."

"I realized that, Sherlock," Mycroft answered, looking down at his plate for a moment before looking up again and gazing earnestly into my eyes. "You must understand. This was while you were in Abyssinia. I could not have gotten word to you. By the time you were able to communicate with me again from Cairo it was pointless to tell you. Dr Watson had by then left England for America. He had placed his practice in the care of his assistant and vanished. For a time we feared the worst. I put Inspector Gregson on to it of course. After diligent inquiry, we were able to trace Dr. Watson, first to New York and then to Louisiana. He is there now. He is involved in trying to set up an asylum for victims of leprosy in America. I did not tell you of this earlier because it took months to trace him. By then you were deeply engaged in your own chemical research and to abandon it would have been pointless. Even his assistant did not know of Dr. Watson's ultimate destination. He knew only that Dr. Watson had left England where he could not remain after his wife's death. The tragedy had shaken him to his depths. Typhoid is a beastly illness. She lingered for weeks before she died."

There was nothing that I could say to this news. I know how devoted Watson was to his wife, the former Mary Katherine Morestan, whom we both met in the adventure that began at Pondicherry Lodge. I had often chaffed him for abandoning me for a wife. I have often noticed that a married man is a different species from a bachelor. Domesticity kills the sense for adventure and many a sportsman and ally settles down and becomes like a lap-dog carrying parcels about for his wife while she plunges ahead into the entrances of various commercial establishments.

I had become selfishly accustomed to having Watson always at my side and ready to lend his incomparable aid should any danger threaten and to provide the perfect foil for me as I would lay out the facts of a case. His very incomprehension would often guide me to a solution. By knowing that I must finally explain it all to Watson, I was forced to connect every facet of the case and to make no untoward assumptions. I am afraid that the good Doctor became over time an extension of my mind so that it could barely function without him. He forced upon me those habits of systemic thought that temper mere insight. His plodding nature restrained that excitement that often overcomes me, so that I seem to race from thought to thought. His patience would also sustain me in those dark times when existence itself seemed pointless and when I would resort to even artificial means to kindle again the spark of life within me. For all of these ministrations he had asked nothing in return, but only to be my friend, to share my dangers, and to celebrate my solution of cases by making my name known throughout England and beyond. Now in his greatest need I had been absent! I blamed myself severely.

Mycroft broke in upon my thoughts. "Sherlock, there are ills to which no man may minister, even you. Even as a youth I could see that you wished to take the world upon your shoulders. Your ambitions often even exceeded my own. This quest of yours, to solve the mystery of good and evil by tracing the thoughts of the great religions is an example. What is this vast synthesis you seek? Who are you to seek it? Do you really think that you can place all of the elements of human life into a retort and to distill them drop by drop so as to obtain the final glowing essence of it all?"

"Do you realize that millions of men and women have died in various faiths and that each has held that faith to be the truth? Their lives are no less important than your own. Is your genius such that it can encompass in a single life all that has preceded you? Can you live every experience? What if you had been here? What could you have said to comfort Watson? There are losses that must simply be suffered through alone, where only God can give us aid. Is there anything more Pelagian than the belief that you can do all things? I often think that the holiest of men and women are those whom nature confines by dimming their intellect or afflicting their bodies. They endure their condition and accept their limitations. Is it not these who know best the afflictions of Christ? If Jesus took on human nature, then he also took upon himself all of human nature. Jesus is not present only in the hero but in the sodden and the degraded members of the human race as well. Grace is that weak pulse of conscience in even the most depraved."

"You seem to think that you can vindicate God, forgetting that God is vindicated every day by His quiet labors inside of each human soul where He pleases to dwell. Like many missionaries before you, you believe that God cannot manage without you while the truth is that it is you who cannot manage without God. I have learned by spending my life among the great how feeble and foolish are the men and women of power. They also believe that their lives have been set apart so that history must take dictation from them. Their illusions and pride are the tragedy of the world. Thousands die so that they may maintain their image of themselves. Some of the worst evils in the world are brought about by men of good intentions who are simply wrong, wrong not only in their conclusions, but in even assuming upon themselves a power that belongs to God alone."

"God alone is the universal solvent of hearts. Only God walks into the chambers of thought and event and bends all things to those universal ends and trailing means that alone we seek to grasp. Heaven is beyond our comprehension! Even to call it a Kingdom is God's condescension to our inability to comprehend His design for all things. I had hoped that the rigors of your journey would have bred in you a sense for what is possible. I warn you that if you approach Professor Moriarty with a frame of mind that demands victory for your own sake, then you will fail."

"Evil is not defeated by storming its ramparts with arguments, no matter how cunningly constructed they may be. Evil has left reason well behind. Evil exists in its own inverted realm where wound feeds wound, where canker breeds canker, where rot breeds more rot, where darkness seeks only greater darkness. Shall I tell you what the devil hates most? He hates to be laughed at, for evil in the last analysis is absurd. Evil has no sense of itself! The result is that evil is always derivative and must assault the good. It destroys because it cannot create. It wounds because it cannot heal. It freezes what it cannot warm. The Devil is himself because he is not God and cannot bear that he is not!"

"But how then can I defeat Professor Moriarty?" I cried.

"You can't," murmured Mycroft in reply, "But God quite possibly can."

After a considerable time spent in silence, during which my meal grew quite cold, I looked up at Mycroft again. "But how do you know all these things Mycroft?" I asked in perplexity and with some chagrin at the depth of his vision, he whom I had deemed a callous agnostic.

"Ah well, I do a bit of thinking from time to time. We are not completely idle at the Diogenes Club and Westminster Cathedral is after all not that far away from Pall Mall. I have even been known to kneel. It is a statesman's only comfort. I have had the misfortune to know the costs of power and to have the residue of guilt that must always accompany its exercise. I am more in need of mercy than most men, so I ask for it with greater urgency. I am not sure that I do not risk my soul in doing what I do daily, but I fear what might happen if I were to leave my position, for then one even weaker and more foolish than I might assume my place. So I go on because I do not know how to stop. If that sounds absurd it is because it is. I have not been a stranger to evil. But I refuse to find comfort in it."

Again we were silent, as only brothers may be when they glimpse each other's souls. At last Mycroft spoke. "I think we should have our lunch warmed up. It is always a shame to waste good food." He rang then for the steward. While we were waiting he spoke up again. "I think Sherlock that you are ready now to go and see that man Professor Moriarty."

Dr. Watson's Narrative Continues

It was on one of those dark nights, standing before our old rooms in Baker Street, which I could not bear to enter again that I knew that I must leave England. I must go to a land I had never seen before, a new land, at least for a time. I went home and consulted my atlas. I had always wanted to see the American southern states. I despised the institution of slavery, but I admired the fierce independence of the southern resistance to the domination of the northern union states that saw the south and the western territories as ripe for exploitation.

I needed to visit the land that had stimulated so many divided feelings within me. I had heard in a London hospital of an effort to establish an asylum for lepers at Carville, a small town near Baton Rouge. I knew something of the disease of leprosy from my time spent in India and I had kept up with the medical literature dealing with that fearful malady. I thought that perhaps I might learn to face my own grievous losses through ministering to poor people who had lost far more than I had lost. I was fortunate in having a most able assistant who could take over my Kensington practice in my absence. He would remit to me a rental on my home and dispensary. I had a bit of savings besides, so I would manage well enough. It was a comfort to me that I might make out of the ashes of my life some small contribution that I could dedicate to Mary's memory. So a month after I had made this decision I took a boat for Savannah, Georgia. I would then go by rail to New Orleans and from there catch a steamboat upriver for Carville.

I have retained a journal of that momentous trip. I seldom look at it, for those days are painful to me to re-live even now. As I read Holmes' journal it was a comfort to me to know that he had heard of my affliction with much sorrow and regret. It was not until 1894, after I had returned from Carville that we were to meet again. It was then that I was to discover that Holmes was still alive. By then I had recovered from the despair brought on by my wife's death and found there among the lepers the first vestiges of that affection for the Catholic faith that were to lead to my embracing Catholicism later in Rome as I have recorded here.

I return now to my narrative of the summer that Holmes and I spent in that memorable year of 1898 in Newport in the lovely state of Rhode Island. The events of the war crowded in upon us during those months as the summer progressed. On June 10, 1898 the American forces lay siege to Guantanamo Bay, trapping the Spanish defenders whose gallant attempt to reach the open sea resulted in the destruction of the Spanish fleet. On June 20,, 1898 the island of Guam in the Pacific was occupied by the Americans. Then on July 1, 1898 there began the battle for San Juan Hill that ended after much bloodshed and terrible illness and yellow fever among the American troops leading to an American victory.

It was also in July that Holmes and I met that stern and admirable man, Thomas Brackett Reed, the Speaker of the House of Representatives, whose views were similar to those of Sherlock Holmes in regard to the war. He had sought refuge during a Congressional recess at his cabin in Maine from what he regarded as the course of folly on which his nation had embarked. As the Speaker of the U.S. House of Representatives, he was the third in line of succession for the Presidency. He had used the full power of his office to try and make America adhere to that course of independence from the race for colonial possessions that had so engulfed the European powers. In this endeavor he had failed; but he was not a man to accept defeat easily. It was in his bitterness that he sought out Newport where he had heard that Sherlock Holmes was staying for the summer as part of his convalescence from an attack of consumption the preceding year. He therefore sought us out at Lands End to which we had just returned from our stay at the Breakers and where we resided for the remainder of that memorable summer season

I recall well our first meeting with that gentleman. He was a huge man, almost as large as Mycroft Holmes but more athletic. His presence seemed to fill the library at Lands End where we met him. Holmes and I had been out that day for one of those slow and leisurely walks that had contributed so much to his recovery. Since there is no specific remedy yet for tuberculosis, only the body itself and its own defenses must be employed to halt or delay the spread of the disease.

The progress of the malady is slow and insidious in most cases. The tubercular bacillus itself that was first isolated by Dr. Robert Koch on March 24, 1882 is almost invisible. It may only be observed when it is properly stained. Once it was possible to observe it, scientists discovered that it divides slowly and soon adapts to the particular constitution of its victim. The lungs which are its usual place of residence develop a spongy tissue in an effort to wall-off the organism. This aerobic bacterium requires an oxygen supply in order to survive. Anything that aids the body in building up those ramparts of scar tissue that will serve to wall-off the germ is therefore advantageous to the patient. An integrated recovery program of good diet, long periods of rest, moderate exercise, and fresh clean air are the usual specifics.

All of these were available in Newport that summer and Holmes had readily and faithfully availed himself of them. I tried in addition to spare Holmes all unnecessary excitement. I was glad that the contentious individuals that we had met at The Breakers on our first day there were replaced by the usual lazy summer crowd bent only on the simple lawn-sports like badminton, croquet, and other mild enjoyments of the season. The war with Spain seemed gradually to recede as a favored topic of conversation. Like all wars it seemed to assume an illusory quality to those not directly involved in combat.

The ladies displayed their summer finery at a series of fetes. We grew better acquainted with the small community by attending many of these gatherings along with Miss Irene Adler whose beauty and wit added so much to the pleasure of those occasions. Her dance-card was always full and she often gave dramatic readings by popular request. Even Holmes was prevailed upon to recount tales from his travels in Asia and Africa. Throughout all of this I maintained a vigilant watch upon my friend. I saw to it that he retired early. I looked for the first signs of any weariness or untoward excitement stemming from his ardently held convictions. I began to realize that social intercourse is largely a function of the containment of differences. The expertise of the women of Newport in providing a refuge from the troubles of the world for their husbands and male guests was impressed upon me. I knew that Holmes would prefer to be in Washington and engaged there at the center of the dawning American policies, or at least to be present in New York where news came first from the various fronts of the war; but I would have none of it.

"Very well Doctor," Holmes would say, "I will do as you say, for now. By September or at the latest October though we must resume our mission, for events are moving swiftly and we must not lose our initiative when the hour for action arrives."

The threat of excitement I had tried to ward off came again however with the visit of Thomas Brackett Reed. He had also sought refuge along the Atlantic seaboard that summer by traveling northwards to Maine to escape the sweltering heat of Washington and no doubt to lick his wounds, for his own position had been defeated.

On July 7, 1898 the 55th Congress had voted by the means of a joint resolution to adopt the Newlands Resolution and in order to annex the Republic of Hawaii to the United States. It was a day of mourning in Hawaii among the natives who had dreamed of shaking off the dominance of the traders and the sugar-cane planters who came just behind the missionaries to subjugate the native people. The entire story was one of perfidy and betrayal of a gentle people and the destruction of their way of life.

When Congress had gone into recess, Mr. Reed could not be too quick in shaking the dust of the Capitol from his feet and going up to his refuge in Maine. If he had stopped in Newport, it could only be because he assumed that the Spanish defeat was close at hand and that peace terms would soon be issued. In that case he would need to return swiftly to Washington. No doubt he had also come to consult Holmes after hearing of the great detective's presence in Newport and to gain his opinion as to what might still be salvaged of what he felt was the character and honor of the nation that was now being recklessly abandoned to enter uncharted waters as a new imperial power.

I recall that he rose to his feet like a great grizzly bear as Holmes and I entered. The room seemed dim after leaving the bright sunlight outside. It was as though we had entered a cave and a great beast had reared up to defend its domicile. He shook both our hands before asking us if we would be just as comfortable on the terrace where we would have privacy in our discussion. He had been quite alone in the room since the ladies had retired to their bedrooms after lunch for a nap and Mr. Reed had requested them to please do so as he had some papers to review and asked if the library might be at his disposal for the afternoon. That request had been granted. We therefore did not need to fear any interruption. At Holmes' request we adjourned to the terrace. A servant asked if we required anything and at Mr. Reed's request the servant left a bottle of a whisky distilled in Kentucky from what is called a sour mash, three glasses, and a carafe of cold spring water before leaving us alone.

The terrace was in the shade but we could still see the blue line of the sea beyond the hedges and the rose beds. A slight breeze was blowing inland and the bees hummed in the geraniums. A more placid day could not be imagined. War seemed inconceivable in such a place and I asked myself as I often had why history should ever bear the sound of alarum and the clash of arms, why the hand of man should be raised against man, and why life should ever cease but through the natural course of age and time. War seemed more than ever to be a creation of man and not in the nature of things. Surely the earth was one vast commonwealth entrusted to all people and therefore to be enjoyed by all. How came it then that divisions and animosities flared up among men if those very divisions and animosities were not infused from some source beyond what God had created? The festering iniquity of the heart of man must be its source or perhaps the dark angels who laugh at our woes.

After introducing ourselves and settling down on the terrace, each of us with a whisky in hand and a plate of ham and cucumber sandwiches before us, Mr. Reed opened the conversation.

"I have come up here to Newport to consult with you, Mr. Holmes. Your reputation has preceded you and I have read several accounts written by your friend here that explain your unique method of detection. Above all you seem able to see light where others see only darkness. Well, I am in that precise state at this very hour and it is not one with which I am able to easily reconcile myself. I have the reputation of being a man who usually gets his way. You may have heard that I am something of a juggernaut carrying all before me. I have even revised the rules of the House of Representatives to force a vote when necessary. It used to be the custom for representatives to avoid standing up like men and voting for measures that they did not like by simply withdrawing into the hallways of the Capitol. I took it upon myself to demand attendance in the chamber and when one member in particular sought to avoid an up or down vote by simply maintaining silence I asked that gentleman if he would care to stand up and deny that he was present."

Holmes and I smiled at this example of the man's conduct, which showed the character of the man before us. He was a man of courage and of wit who once said of a foe that the gentleman never opened his mouth without subtracting from the sum total of human knowledge.

The famous statesman continued, "I am not a man to be put off sir, nor do I entertain most of the illusions of my contemporaries regarding the innate goodness of mankind. I do not maintain a jaundiced view either however. I allow each man to show what is in him and proceed from there in dealing with him. But let us come to the matter at hand without undue delay. You have heard I trust, Mr. Holmes, of our recent annexation of the Hawaiian Islands?" He asked.

Holmes nodded in assent.

"Good. Then I must tell you that I was and am irrevocably opposed to the action that Congress has taken in that matter, though it was my own party, the Republicans, whose votes largely made this usurpation possible. I was ill at the time and absent, but I had made my wishes known and three of my fellow Republicans voted against the measure as I would certainly have done had I been present. I now come to you to seek your aid in procuring a reversal of this mad policy. The vote on the measure has unfortunately already been taken, so formally at least the matter is finished. The Hawaiian Islands are now ours. I fear that the Supreme Court may do nothing to oppose it, because the action was taken by the two political branches of government, the legislative and the executive branches. Besides, there is the procedural issue of who has standing to sue. Even if the action of the Congress was *ultra vires*, and hence illegitimate who has the legal right to point that out and reverse the legislation? The people's representatives have spoken. Shall the former Republic of Hawaii, which has now been annexed, bring an action at law? Where is the international court with jurisdiction to hear it? I think not since the Republic of Hawaii through various private machinations petitioned to become a territory of the United States. The sugar planters virtually controlled the now former republic. If the former government of Queen Lili'uokalani protested the annexation and by doing so hoped to have the former monarchy that preceded the republic restored to the people of Hawaii the answer is again no, for she was stripped of her sovereignty by the very minority of wealthy white landowners who hold the majority of the denizens of these islands in a form of labor bondage that is little different from slavery."

He sighed heavily, "It is too late for a point of order to stop the Congressional vote and as I said the courts will not touch it. Very well then, it will stand. But it is unconstitutional, by the heavens it is! America may attach lands seized in war, if we are attacked by a foreign power. America may even annex lands by the consent of the people of those lands, but only by adopting the means of a treaty. What may not be done constitutionally is what has in fact been done in this instance: to use a simple joint resolution rather than to adopt the usual procedure in a matter of such great importance as the one involved here."

"It is appalling to accomplish the annexation by using such a transparent device and only because a sufficient number of votes required in order make a treaty could not be obtained by the proponents of this outrageous annexation. The whole matter of the Newlands Resolution has the form of law; but it is no law. It was a cynical effort to steer this country from its traditional role among the nations of the world, a role that allowed the people of each nation to choose that form of government that they wish, the people sir, not some small oligarchy who happen to constitute a pretended government even while holding the people as virtual hostages."

Mr. House Speaker Thomas Brackett Reed then explained to Holmes and to me in detail how all of this change had come about. We did not interrupt him but sat fascinated by the strange tale that unfolded before us.

"There are at the present moment 3086 Americans in Hawaii. But there are 31,019 native Hawaiians, 24,407 people of Japanese origin or descent, and 21,616 of the Chinese by the last census. Hawaii is a land of refugees and of a few great landowners who trade in sugar and pineapples. The American settlers are the minority, yet they control these lovely and unspoiled islands. Is this popular government sir, is this democracy? Tell me has the vast majority consented to white rule by the Americans? Did they approve this annexation? Did they have any say at all? What form of government will now be imposed upon them? I fear to say! But more still I fear that what we have just accomplished in the case of the Hawaiian Islands will become our model for all future land acquisitions and that wars will become our normal manner of conducting statesmanship.”

He paused for breath and took a sip from his glass as he gazed out to where the sunlight illuminated the cliff walk and the waters beyond, “I do have an idea though. The text of the annexation resolution allows for despotic control of the inhabitants of these islands as the President so directs. Is the President now also to be a King and in foreign lands? Tell me sir if this nation may survive so blatant an abandonment of its own principles. Where will be an end to it? Our victory after the Battle of Manila has bestowed upon us the present control over the islands of the Philippines. Will we now subdue those people also? Having promised them freedom, will we now deny it to them? If so they should resist. It is their right to do so. There is also the outstanding question of the fate of Cuba and other Spanish territory in the Caribbean region.”

Mr. Reed shook his head sadly and poured some more whiskey into his glass before continuing his discourse, “What has become of the party to which I have devoted the energies of a significant part of my life? The party of Lincoln that once fought to free the black slaves has become the means to press the Hawaiians into virtual slavery. I can play no further part of in such doings. This shall be my last year in Congress sir. I am defeated, but more than my own defeat, it is the ideas that founded this great nation that have been defeated by actions such as these!”

I could see that it was painful for Holmes to see such a great man, a man who clearly had his nation’s honor close to his heart, be faced with such disillusionment and despair. Though not an American or a lawyer I could see that the points that he had raised appeared conclusive. The America of the new century had joined the imperial powers and would no doubt share the challenges of the coming struggle between the contending empires.

American affairs would thereafter be world affairs and world affairs would appear to be American affairs. Great power abroad requires the existence of great power at home. American citizens were already adjusting to the power of the great trusts and corporations upon whose beneficence their very lives depended. The small farmer could not get his grain to market when the railroads could grant or withhold concessions as they wished. The smaller railroads could not survive. As they were annexed one by one the larger railroads could charge any fares that they wished, without fear of competition.

The small farmers could not compete with the great landowners, the new American land barons. The independent oil producers were finally forced to sell out to the Standard Oil Company of Rockefeller. Everywhere a process of untrammeled mergers and acquisitions was taking place. The virtuous effects of competition were being thwarted by monopoly capitalism, advanced by the very men who liked to boast of the advantages of privately held capital and the dangers of what they called big government. In point of fact the laws favored the wealthy and held the small entrepreneur in contempt. As to the working man, he was seen most unrealistically as in an equal bargaining condition with the great corporations and, should he attempt to join a union and to bargain collectively, he was treated as a member of a criminal conspiracy operating in restraint of trade.

Women were in an even worse position if forced into labor in mills and factories or onto the streets in America's teeming slums. Famous names like Jay, Frick, Gould, Rockefeller, Carnegie, Astor, Morgan, and Stanford were the names on everyone's lips as centralized corporations and trusts took over in field after field that crushed the nascent unions and fired or killed union organizers as troublemakers. These new oligarchs were no longer mere names but institutions with more power than many European kings had ever held. This was the America of the new post-war administrations of both major political parties under Grant, Harrison, Cleveland, and McKinley.

Mr. Reed scoffed, "Newlands, is that not an appropriate

name for a land thief! That fellow after whom the resolution takes its name comes from Nevada. He is a protégé of that rascal William Sharon who was the former "Lord of the Comstock" as a banker and as a stamping mill owner. He was always a thorough scoundrel. The fellow did manage to get elected as a Senator, which bespeaks nothing as to his honor. The apple does not fall far from the tree. It is bad enough that those Nevada people have gorged this country with silver drawn from the bowels of that barren desert country. Of what use is silver but to make candlesticks? The world trades in gold! I accept the need for trade as long as we have a proper tariff to protect American interests. I am no isolationist. But I will have a nation first of all and one that knows its proper boundaries, those that are fixed by law and not by the force of arms!"

House Speaker Reed looked across at both of us to assess the effect of his impassioned utterance. "I ask you gentlemen, where does it stop? It is a complete transformation of the republic. Do you realize that an obscure case in California in 1877 defines corporations as 'persons' for all practical purposes? Imagine that! A corporation now has flesh and blood, shall it soon cry out as well, like Shylock in *The Merchant of Venice* and say in all foolishness, 'Does a corporation not bleed?'"

Holmes had been silent during this discourse but I could see that he had carefully followed this great man's exposition of the implications of the recent change in American ideals and practice. Still, our own mission demanded that we defeat Baron Maupertuis by encouraging the Americans in their dreams of expansion, so I was curious how Holmes would answer Mr. Reed.

We had listened intensely and with great interest to the problem that had been placed before us. Now Holmes spoke, quietly but firmly, in answer to the speaker's tale and its many observations.

"Mr. Reed, whatever you may have heard of my powers as a detective I am not an oracle. I am sorry of course to hear that you will be stepping down from your post next year and I deplore the circumstances that may have caused you to decide to follow such a course. It is a fearful thing to stand in the door of history and to attempt to block the often mindless rush of events. I have heard of your powers as Speaker of the House of Representatives in the American Congress. Perhaps you will find some comfort in knowing that where you have failed no man could have succeeded. If your nation is bound to follow the path of imperial ambitions it will soon meet with opposition from England, France, Germany, and the other powers of Europe."

"I might add that even tiny Belgium has a colony in the Congo region of Central Africa out of which rumors of the most diabolical kind are emerging daily. Empires always require the subjugation of native peoples or even their extinction. Empires exist by the systematic application of terror and force to exert their will. The only exception to this may have been the great dynasties of China. Their empire exacted tribute and emulation rather than overt conquest. The Chinese culture spread by consent and emulation rather than by the imposition of force. Wise administration benefits all with whom they come into contact."

"America now appears to believe that its democracy can be imposed from without rather than to develop naturally in the hearts of other people. If the theory of the rights of man is indeed accurate, then it will not require American aid to grow to fruition in other lands. They will adopt democracy when it is within their capacity to sustain it as a native growth and not as a gift from a foreign power. The graft will not take if the tree is not ready to accept it. Perhaps a later generation of Americans will turn from the supposedly easy path of conquest and restore a spirit of true democracy to your great nation. Until then you have acted the part of a noble servant to the trust that you have received in virtue of your high office in the Congress."

"Beyond these short comments I can have no impact I fear on the present question of the annexation of Hawaii or upon the war with Spain that has been brought I believe virtually to a conclusion with victory assured to the American forces in Cuba. I may suggest though that what has proven to be a care to Spain may become a burden to America as well when it assumes Spain's place and attempts to govern a fractious foreign populace.”

Holmes turned his gaze out to sea as if he could see there some hint of things to come. “In Hawaii America may have similar difficulties. The Japanese will not welcome the enhanced American presence in their near vicinity and region of the world. The sea power of Japan has grown since the Americans landed there some sixty years ago and pried open its doors to trade with the outside world. Who may say what course the future may take and what conflicts may break out as the Japanese apply their traditional martial spirit to a wider world with the added tools of our technology to the spirit of the samurai?”

“You show a remarkable grasp of world affairs, Mr. Holmes. You do not play a role in parliament, do you? Or perhaps it is your brother...”

Holmes started. “I had not thought that Mycroft’s connection with the British government was generally known.”

“It is not as you say, ‘generally known.’ But I have spoken to Mr. John Sherman who you know is our Secretary of State and he has informed me that your brother advises the Queen’s Cabinet Ministers on certain delicate questions. There is also some debate in Washington regarding your own presence on these shores. It is your first trip to America I believe. Are we then to assume that you come as a mere tourist and at such a time by accident when our nation is at war? I am not a man to mince matters, so I shall make so bold as to ask you directly sir, why you are here.”

Holmes smiled before answering, “Since you ask me directly, I will be as direct in my answer, for I see that you are an honorable man. I have come to America to urge your country to build a canal across Central America.”

Speaker Reed was somewhat taken aback by this direct statement. “Why should you desire that we do so? Is your interest personal or do you speak for England?”

Holmes then sought to clarify his position. “I speak for the interests of the world sir. There is a man, a Baron Maupertuis, who controls the Greater Dutch Canal Company. Perhaps you have heard of it though it is only of recent origin. It is his intent to take over where the French have failed and to build a canal in that region. He must not be allowed to do so. If he succeeds in his venture, there will be no stopping him. He is a man of immense wealth and power. He trades extensively in the Dutch East Indies. He is involved in the export of rubber from the Congo region. He is a man with the blood of thousands upon his hands. Without going into details, I may also inform you that he once entertained a plan, which very nearly succeeded, to wreak terror and destruction throughout England. To defeat his ambitions is the goal toward which I have bent all of my energies during this last year. Lamentably, the achievement of that primary and essential goal justifies me in asking that your own country pursue the very expansionism that you so justly deplore."

I could see that Holmes hoped to enlist Mr. Reed's aid by his added remarks, which I could tell were spoken with regret. "I appreciate your sentiments about imperial ambitions. My first intention in coming here was to meet with President McKinley and to dissuade him from war with the Spanish interests. I too believe that your nation has now embarked upon a dangerous course. It has however annexed Hawaii and may attempt to deny the Philippine people their freedom if only to protect them from the Japanese who have already annexed Okinawa and Formosa in recent years. America no doubt desires to dominate the Pacific region. That is clear since the extent of your country now reaches across the great American basin to California. It cannot sustain such a large country, even with railroads, without a canal to unite the two coastlines of America. The passage around Cape Horn is arduous and uncertain and impossible during certain months. A canal will also enhance trade with San Francisco and the Oregon region and with the purchased territory of Alaska. If your nation is to continue upon its course of expansion of its international power, it must build the canal."

After a considerable pause to consider this proposal, Mr. Reed asked, "Did you speak to Mr. Roosevelt about all this during his recent visit to Newport?"

Holmes chuckled, "No, as a matter of fact Mr. Roosevelt

and I had a slight altercation while he was here in Newport."

Mr. Reed joined Holmes' laughter, "I confess that I heard as much from the man himself. Teddy referred to you as "a damned pacifist" when he returned to Washington after his visit. In any case, he is the man you should have attempted to win over to your cause. President McKinley is too cautious to undertake such an extensive project at this time. Have you considered the expense or the lives that would be lost in building such a canal? Why the cases of yellow fever alone would require a constant supply of new men to take the place of those who fall victims to it and to other diseases and accidents. Even that ratty little railroad in Costa Rica cost thousands of lives to build."

He refilled his glass with whisky before continuing, "I seem to recall some intelligence reports regarding that Maupertuis fellow now that you mention him. He had a blasted tract published in this country that implicated some very important men in what practically amounted to the use of slave labor in the building of the railroad that traversed Costa Rica and connected its two major port cities on opposite coasts. It caused a hell of a row in some quarters, with Italian immigrant societies demanding the hides of those American businessmen who had helped to fund the project. The Hearst papers ran lurid tales of corruption. There was a tide of revulsion towards our policies in general toward Central America. Until the sinking of the Maine it looked like America was moving away from all talk of expansion, let alone any idea of building a canal. And now ... well who can say? You may succeed."

After another significant pause Mr. Reed continued, "In any case I won't be around to lend any opposition to it. You can talk to Bill McKinley if you wish. I will even provide an introduction. Bill and I are still friends, although I think he's gone quite mad. He was against the war a few months ago. Now he has become convinced that America can only prosper by placating the trusts and corporations. Well, I doubt that anything can stop them now. They are well on the way to turning Americans into a lot of vassals."

His eyes softened then for the first time. "I live in Maine you know. Damned beautiful state! We know what independence means up there. We are the state furthest from the south yet we fought as hard if not harder than any to preserve the union. We thought we would see a new birth for democracy when the war ended and instead what do we have but what my friend Mark Twain calls, 'a gilded age.' Look at these blasted imitation French Chateaux in Newport. Not a blessed thing about them is American. It won't be long until we get royal titles here in America. I'm glad I won't live to see it. Public service will itself be paid servitude to the highest bidder!"

He stopped and poured himself another whisky. He tasted it with approval. "We all want the better things of life but if the few must be wage-slaves to help the few to their aristocratic pretentions, then that's damn un-American that's all there is to it. This was a damn perfect land when we came here. The Indians had been here forever and not a mark on it. Now look at it. I tell you gentlemen there are times that I wish that Tecumseh had won in Ohio and we were still thirteen colonies. He was a wonderful man you know, that Tecumseh. He bid fair to unite the eastern tribes against us. If you British had stayed behind him I don't doubt that he would have won. He was that kind of gallant man. I know a patriot when I see one and can respect an opponent who is nobler than I."

He looked down at his lap in chagrin. "I should have seen this whole annexation thing coming. What was our policy to the Indian Nations but to provoke them to war by endless duplicity and then to annex their lands? I don't know if a nation that is based on systemic duplicity and rapacity will survive. God can hardly be asked to bless dishonesty and theft. Maybe that ghost dance fellow was right, that Wovoka the Paiute Indian who claimed to see the end of the rule of the white men. Maybe the land will have had enough of us finally and will roll up and over us like a blanket and take us all with it. If I was an Indian I would pray for that every day, but I am an American statesman and I have done my best for this country."

"President Lincoln feared above all else as the great war ended and the states that had joined the Confederacy were restored as part of the Union that the war had created a new threat more pervasive and insidious than slavery, the great corporations and the wealth and power that form of business bestows on the wealthy individuals that control them. Lincoln did not live to witness the triumph of those moneyed interests that are now imposing a new slavery upon American citizens, white and black alike."

"After the assassination of the President the following administrations allowed and even commanded the victorious Union Army that had fought to free the black men to turn their weapons and their wrath upon the last totally free men in America, the Red Indians. These brutal incursions reduced their numbers and condition to a remnant fewer than that of Israel when sent into exile into Babylon. The parallel is exact. Their children have been sent into captivity in mission schools. Indian families have been broken up. Their very language has been forbidden and stripped from them. Yet are not these people Americans if anyone is? If they were sovereign nations, then they should be restored as the southern states were restored after the war. Where is the state of the Cherokee? Where is the state of the Cheyenne? Where is the state of the great tribes of the Lakota Sioux? Or if on the contrary they are not to be regarded as independent nations, then at least they should be regarded as citizens just as the rebellious Confederate soldiers were after their defeat and allowed to settle on the land with the same equality as the European immigrants who are being settled on the lands forcibly taken from the tribes and not be pushed off onto reservations."

"Until this nation does justice to the Indians, it will not do justice to its citizens. A nation with guilt and blood upon its hands must live to expiate it. It will add crime to crime until God himself will demand that justice is done. I believe that the annexation of Hawaii and our lordship over the Philippines will habituate our country to precisely this habit of conquest. The hope of our forebears was that the idea of America might spread through emulation to other lands, but not by martial imposition and engulfment. I am appalled that in the hope of mere material gain my fellow citizens cry for the very means of their own destruction. Do they assume that a nation of abstractions and not of men will serve their interests? Do they imagine that corporations that do not die will be more merciful than men who do?"

"I believe a time will come when property that is so organized will impose its own logic upon America. That logic will be that of great worms or mighty slugs crawling over the face of this republic and engulfing all until the free citizens of this land are forced to beg from these abstract entities the very bread that their own hands once supplied in abundance on their own farms. There will always be work to do in America, but there will not always be employment. Employment is a function of the boom and bust cycle of capital investment. A free man who creates out of his own labor the means of life on his own land needs no job from another man, for he has his own work to do. Trade for him is a free action with other free men for those few items that his household cannot itself provide. When trade can only exist among nations and tariffs are no more than the unit of compromises and betrayals, costs will be so high that no single man can produce a sufficient quantity of goods for his own sustenance. When that condition arises and prevails and becomes well nigh universal, trade will be confined to just such vast entities, the corporations and trusts that even now determine the courses that our nation will pursue."

"The Hawaiian issue is paradigmatic. Hawaii is now not a state nor even a territory. It is a plantation held by five great entities. What you see in Hawaii today is what you will soon see throughout America, the many going with pleading hands to the few. I can no longer be a part of this process, so it is time for me to go."

I could see the eyes of Sherlock Holmes shining as these words were spoken. He stood up and walking over to him shook the hand of Mr. Reed warmly before saying, "You give me hope sir. I had not thought to find a man with these sentiments upon these shores. I can only lament that your voice will not be heard in the halls of Congress in future years. Perhaps I may dissuade you from retirement. The great men die in harness in the attempt to create a better world, while the evil men live long and easy in the world as it is. Evil cannot endure a determined adversary. Evil prefers always to corrupt and then to accuse. When the tide turns and evil itself must stand before the bar, then it assumes an air of virtue and of innocence to deny that it is evil at all. I am sure that this annexation and this war of conquest will be seen as liberation or portrayed in that light to the cheering of Americans. Only time will reveal the effects that will flow from these events. Perhaps in the clarity of that time a reassessment may take place. If not, then America may take its position among those powerful nations that must settle among themselves the question of a final supremacy by waging war; perhaps such a war as mankind has never yet seen."

"The wars of nations take no account of the individual. He is but a cellular structure in a larger whole, a greater conflagration. If war comes, a general war (and how can it not come in the face of such international ambitions) then those who survive will do so by joining smaller states in protective unions, which may safeguard their people by renouncing the very power and status that the greater nations always covet. Peace is always the product of humility just as war is the result of ambition. I fear that America will have no deficit of just causes to take up arms against as the years unfold." Holmes then resumed his seat. Our time on the terrace had passed swiftly and the late afternoon sun fell low over the sea.

It was as I have said a lovely summer day in late July when the events recounted here occurred. The wind was coming in with that late afternoon Atlantic breeze that dispelled the stifling heat of noon. To speak of these dire matters seemed to me a profanation of a day that breathed such peace and contentment. Surely, in such a lovely world as that which was presently displayed before us there could be no cause for pain or discontent. The earth itself seemed to wish only for slumber. Had I been alone I would have slept in the hammock that was placed beneath two large maple trees casting their combined shade nearby. I would have listened to the leaves rustling overhead as though they were answering the wind in their own quiet language. On such a day I could not imagine that autumn would return here or that fierce winter gales would shake the ruined boughs of the winter-gnawed trees.

What were wars or rumors of wars there in Newport with its great mansions? There war was only a news headline. Stout gentlemen read of easy victories that summer, which now in 1917 as I write these words seems so long ago. They sat reading the Hearst papers while fresh butter melted into the raspberry-red scones before them and fat sausages and omelets dotted with fresh parsley filled their morning plates.

I recall that I thought on that bright day back to my time in Afghanistan when I had served in Her Majesty's medical corps. I had known war in my youth. But I had escaped death, wounded even as are all men who go to war. I had lived through my time in Afghanistan, eventually married, and tried to heal. I had brought new life into the world as a doctor. I had known love and what it is to lose that love in death. My only desire now was peace.

I could well sympathize with a man like Thomas Brackett Reed, who having done his best to ensure that a wise course for his nation would be followed had finally come to acknowledge defeat and leave the scene with his dignity intact, proclaiming by his silence those enduring truths to which he had pledged his life. Truth will find its own voice in the hearts of men and women, even under tyranny and oppression. I doubted if America would ever forget the voices of its founders, even in its coming dark age which began in 1898. But if it did forget, then events themselves would eventually make manifest the source of those errors.

The passing years finally bring forth and reveal all things. History is not confined to a single lifetime. Its patterns are the slow accretion of decades, and often of centuries, so that suddenly the man of wisdom looks up and in the face of God assesses his state and that of those associations that have claimed his loyalty to see if they do not require the forgiveness of God. Penance becomes increasingly bitter for its long deferral in those who have believed too much good of their leaders. The penances of nations are often wars and from those wars the survivors must assemble the fragments that are left and begin to build the nation once again.

While I mused on these matters I realized that my companions had ceased to speak. Their silence seemed to me to comprise and to manifest a resignation in the face of the implacable nature of events. At times of decision alternative courses are abandoned never to be revisited. Historians may always speculate as to how it might have been had events taken a different course, but such speculations can have no effect upon the new constellation of causes and effects that follow a major change in policy.

Only if historical events followed a predictable parabola, then we might speak of progress. Instead there is only the chaos of particular events, strange accidents, reactions that may error in degree or in significance, the impact of personal bias, fear, or ignorance; any of these variables may vitiate even wise policies and may deflect from its course the most determined and virtuous of actions. But how much destruction may flow from actions that even in their insipient stages were based upon false assumptions or carried forward by frankly stupid men!

In order to continue then to engage with life and to risk taking action, it is essential to act with imperfect knowledge, hopefully guided by principle and performed in good conscience, but in all cases to accept that reflection at best yields only probable outcomes and that complete certainty lies only with God. Even to risk the production of great good is to court unleashing forces that may be deflected towards evil ends. Still it is not possible to enter heaven without risk. That premature state of absolute peace, that I so yearned to embrace on that summer's day, seems to me now to have been less a sign of virtue than an abdication. However natural it may be to feel disillusionment with all of human endeavors, particularly as one grows older, one must seek to summon forth the strength for a final assault upon the citadels of chance. But any enthusiasm one may feel in old age is tempered by the remembrance of former good intentions and sanguine plans that have come to nothing and of achievements that wilted in the very hour of their blossoming forth.

All of human life seems a sorry show after all. I am not a physicist, but I often believe more in the conservation of lethargy than in the conservation of energy. The friction of the universe seems to exact a terrible cost in entropy for every step forward in human effort. Still, there are those few individuals who give us hope. I knew that I was in the presence of two of them that day on the terrace as the wind blew in from the sea.

Part of the charm of what was originally planned as a reconnoitering mission among the American political leaders, industrialists, and financiers in Newport was our exposure to culture there. Evening entertainment after a lavish dinner often included music from small ensembles with chairs set out for the guests on spacious lawns overlooking the sea. As one who enjoys chamber music and motets these productions when set in such pleasant surroundings was an uncommon joy and one that I have never forgotten.

Then there were the more sedate and impromptu discussions on all manner of subjects but often including as topics literature and the visual arts as well. Although my own choice in reading matter is usually confined to adventure tales, I am aware that much experimentation is being done in literature at the present moment. Sherlock Holmes in contrast had always had a penchant for French literature since his mother was French. An interesting note is that the great American gothic writer Edgar Allen Poe was translated and popularized in France between 1852 and 1865 by the French poet Charles Baudelaire when Poe was sadly neglected in his own country of America. The French literature of the latter half of the 19th century, whether represented by Guy de Maupassant, Jules Barbey d'Aurevilly, Joris Karl Huysmans, or Stephane Mallarme dealt with similar obscure states of human consciousness. Holmes often chided me for lack of imagination and I must admit that my practical nature is suspicious and perhaps a bit fearful of the more *outré* elements in the decadent movements that Holmes found fascinating. Perhaps he reasoned that to understand the criminal mind it was necessary to have some insight into those strange and elemental cross-currents of madness and compulsion that appear like a ghostly penumbra around the ordinary sphere of human consciousness.

Our conversation with Thomas Brackett Reed and the stillness that had followed it was interrupted just before formal tea-time by the entry of Miss Irene Adler and by Mrs. Edith Wharton who joined us on the terrace in the late afternoon. The sun had declined from its zenith and the day had grown somewhat cooler. It was no longer essential to seek refuge in the cool and darkened rooms of the house behind us to find comfort. We men stood up to greet them as the ladies entered, who were looking as cool and white as the sunlit day. An excellent tea was soon served with sandwiches, scones, and iced tea flavored with fresh mint leaves. The conversation shifted from politics to literature and to the remarkable novels of the expatriate author, Mr. Henry James, who was a friend of Mrs. Wharton. It was a relief to be able to discuss art, which operates from the perspective of the eternal. As we drank our tea and helped ourselves to raspberry scones, Mrs. Wharton expressed the opinion that the best artists are those for whom plot is secondary to character and atmosphere.

"Great literature," she opined, "Should resemble the graphic arts and architecture. The task is to assemble sentences so that when the book is set aside one has a feeling of the integrity of the work as a whole. There should be no awkward edges, no unfinished cornices, no disproportion, but only a sense that each word, each paragraph, has added to a sense of beauty in the whole. It is not important that the characters be familiar or that they remind us of people that we have actually encountered; it is only important that the responses of the characters should evolve and illuminate the situation in which they find themselves placed by fate or by intention. Mr. Henry James manifests this virtue in his unique style. He customarily slows action to a crawl. He shows that in any complex situation character manifests itself slowly and by minute accretions. To rush the narrative headlong as we actually experience time would be to miss the tiny degrees by which the will is brought to assent to a course of action and to deny how many threads or filaments of motivation attach themselves to the character as the story progresses. A point is reached where the balance begins to tip and a revelation occurs. The balance of character and personality shifts from the position formerly occupied. If this seems absurdly artificial, as lamentably it does to some of his critics, it is only because Mr. James errs by being more of an artist than most novelists are. Many modern novelists seem caught up in what is termed vulgar realism and are only journalists in disguise. If the public is growing weary of Mr. James' mannerisms it is because the habit of reflection that he imposes on the reader belies our desire to reach what is often a rash assessment or conclusion. Many readers cannot tolerate ambiguity or conflicted motives in fiction. The average mind has a habit of generality that is deplorable. To apply a rein to our habits of premature conclusion by explaining that even marginal human actions may imply a world of unseen consequences seems to me to be a good thing in fiction writing. Do you agree, Irene?"

Miss Adler looked up and smiled prettily before responding, "I may only answer as an actress. My art form is of course always derivative. My responses are dictated by the playwright. The task of the actor or actress is to assemble face, voice, and manner so that the character that one plays is believable as an individual. Even a madwoman is not arbitrary. She will manifest the consistency of her particular form of madness. The actress is not responsible for the success of the play as a whole, but only for her particular part. She plays but one instrument in the orchestral work of the play. She must know when to draw attention to herself and when to seem to disappear. An actress who must always be the diva destroys the integrity of the total performance. In that sense I agree with you Edith; in art the impression made by the whole is everything."

Miss Adler paused then for a moment before smiling wickedly and saying, "Still, I must say that I have a certain penchant lately for the plays of Ibsen."

Mrs. Wharton looked displeased. The works of Ibsen were still considered to be somewhat shocking at the time.

"He is too ... well, too topical for my taste. You have always been sympathetic to those who claim to be social reformers." Mrs. Wharton chided her friend before continuing. "The best authors have no message. It is sufficient that they map out a tiny area of human life and portray it accurately and completely. A moral artist would be better employed giving sermons than writing plays or novels. Art is a method and not a subject matter. Mr. Zola for instance is a sociologist disguised as a novelist as was Mr. Dickens before him. We all know that life is sordid; we need no reminders of that. The task of art is to ennoble the whole of life by showing exceptional behavior in exceptional circumstances. If one must embrace a sordid theme, then let it have the dignity of a Greek tragedy so that one feels a sense of awe and terror and not mere disgust at the conclusion. What do you think, Mr. Holmes?"

Holmes spoke demurely, "In matters of literature I always defer to my Boswell, Dr. Watson. I will say this though. I enjoy Wagner, not because of his majestic themes, but for the sheer energy of his music. But then I am a detective, one who craves the excitement of the chase, and as such I am hardly qualified to discuss questions of aesthetics. Perhaps Mr. Reed has an opinion."

Mr. Reed looked up from the brown study in which he had been engaged. "What's that? You must pardon me, Mrs. Wharton, my mind was engaged elsewhere. I will venture this though insofar as I follow your line of thinking: aesthetics it would seem to me is always subordinate to ethics. If a work of art is not morally justified and ordered so as to improve human actions, it had best not exist at all. Most books are a waste of time for a man of affairs. It is enough to read Cicero, Seneca, and Marcus Aurelius. The task of the statesman is to know when one is being told lies and how to marshal consent by the construction of compromises. In addition one must know procedure well. The man who makes the rules can best apply the correct one to achieve a noble end. Still the real work is always done behind the scenes. When the moment of the final vote is taken, it is comparable to when the actor comes on the stage after the final curtain to receive the applause of the audience."

"Oh come now, Mr. Reed," chided Miss Adler, "Surely the business of Congress is more serious than a mere play."

"Democracy is largely a show put on for the people. We are a republic thank God, not a democracy. The people never know what they want. It is the task of the legislator to avoid the more obvious popular follies and to convince the people afterwards that the course of action decided in Congress will serve the wishes of most of the people. Congress is the team of horses pulling and the citizens are the load in the wagon. I do not intend by this statement to denigrate democracy; I merely wish to point out that the nation functions best when the people are not overly involved in government. When political passions run high, demagogues arise to fan the flames of social bonfires."

"Let us take this recent war as an example of how things would be if it were otherwise. President McKinley is said to have consented to the war because the people demanded it after the sinking of The Maine. But when the war-fever passes and the bodies begin to pile up, what will he do then? The President must concentrate his energy upon foreign affairs now. He must of necessity then neglect domestic matters, which in the last election seemed to be paramount. The whole election at that time turned on the issue of a gold-backed currency versus the bi-metallic standard that included silver. Who speaks now of a cross of gold upon which the nation is being crucified? This was all pure demagoguery. If public policy is to be governed by mere whims of the working class or for that matter by the interests of capital there can never be any question of a nation, but only a marketplace and statesmen become like auctioneers."

The ladies had not heard our previous discussion, so Mr. Reed offered a summary of it to them at this time. "Our nation is an extensive one. Surely we have enough to govern ourselves without colonial attachments and their attendant expense! The price of involvement abroad will be less freedom at home. The costs of empire are prohibitive!" He then showed them how the question of the annexation of the Republic of Hawaii was merely symptomatic of a national change of heart. He concluded his discourse by saying, "I am much concerned at present by what I regard as a fatal change in our national policy. Pardon me if I say, Mrs. Wharton, that for me art is the reward of leisure and when I have any leisure at all; I go fishing."

Holmes broke into laughter at this homely observation, while Mrs. Wharton lifted her nose into the air, indignant at what she must have viewed as a trivialization of the aesthetic occupations that she so valued. Meanwhile, Irene Adler I could see was endeavoring to suppress signs of her own amusement. I was happy to have escaped the need to render any opinions. I am after all only Holmes' biographer, not an artist or a novelist. I am also a man of rather strict habits, a legacy of my early life in the military. As the discussion on the terrace turned to less weighty matters I excused myself and set off on my own to consider the import of the discussion among people whose approach to life exceeded my own poor capacities.

The long afternoon had left me in need of a brief walk before dinner. It often took me a certain time to assimilate what I was hearing from minds whose insights exceeded my own. I therefore made my excuses to the company and left them still engaged in a lively discussion. The cliff walk was thronged with strollers. Young gallants escorted some of the young ladies who were spending the weekend attending one of the summer fetes. The lawns that surrounded each of the mansions that I passed sported gaily attired young people playing croquet while their elders enjoyed tea on the enclosed porches or terraces. There were occasional benches where lone artists sketched the scene before them, with the sailboats and motor-driven pleasure craft, some from as far away as Boston or Nantucket.

Nowhere did I see signs or detect a sense of urgency that would indicate that matters of life and death were being decided across the sea in Cuba or in the Pacific. Here only good fortune reigned supreme. The only question was whether one had done well to spend the summer in Newport rather than in Europe or at one of the many lakes of New England. All were happy to have at least escaped Baltimore, New York, or Washington, D.C. with their many responsibilities and stifling offices. But I tried to keep my mind concentrated on the beauty of the scene before me and to quell any resentment or envy I might feel as only a visitor to this illustrious resort. The times of life when fortune casts the possibility of happiness before us are few enough, it seemed to me then, and were not to be wasted dealing with the inevitable tragedy and struggle of which most life consists. I was happy to have seen Holmes in such good humor that day.

The summer had greatly aided his recovery. The state of our mission to America was still undecided, since it was now apparent that only the state of the people's excitement and enthusiasm would be able to provide the support necessary to build a canal. Whether President McKinley would be the man to take on such a project was an open question at the moment. In any case I was in no hurry to go to Washington with the Murillo Papers and while there to present them to the President. My only desire was that Holmes would be allowed to continue the process of his recovery as long as the good weather in Newport lasted.

This was a most congenial period in our lives together and a unique experience to live so far beyond our own usual means and customs. The food and company had been excellent, the conversation stimulating and the sea-air was delightful. Holmes slept for an hour or two most afternoons. I doubted if even Switzerland could have more aided his recovery from his most recent attack of tubercular infection.

As I have already mentioned here, this was my own second trip to America. I knew that this brief season of our lives would probably not be repeated. Holmes would resume his life in Baker Street where I hoped to join him as in our former years together. It appeared that my own desire to retire in Cornwall had been premature after all. I knew that summer that I would never leave Holmes' side while he required my assistance as in the days of our long partnership.

Mr. Reed stayed with us only one more day before departing again for Washington where he had been summoned. His last word to Holmes was that we should attempt to see Mr. Roosevelt once again when we finally came to Washington if he had returned.

"Teddy is a Tartar! There is no mistaking that Mr. Holmes," said he. "But he has all the energy of a young bull moose. Once you get that energy behind an American canal you can be sure that it will be sooner or later be built. He'll see that the damn thing gets done come hell or high water. He's quite mad of course, but don't let that deter you. He has a definite future in politics and he exercises great influence over William McKinley. I advise you to put your case in his hands. Goodbye now, and if you are still over here in the autumn or spring, come on up to Maine. We'll go fishing for some Muskie!" He left us on the following day.

On August 9th terms of peace were proposed by the United States to end the war with Spain. The series of defeats were to lead to an early capitulation. The long summer that we had enjoyed in Newport ended too soon for me. The last balls and parties of the season began to wind the summer's festivities to a close, but in the long still afternoons I was often able to return to the journal kept during those lost years of 1891 to 1894 by my friend and to read at last in that account of unfolding events of the long anticipated moral duel between Sherlock Holmes and Professor Moriarty, which had been postponed since their encounter at the Falls of Reichenbach. That duel was now about to be commenced in earnest in my reading of the journal and with many rather surprising developments (as will be seen), on the haunted moors of Devonshire.

From the Journal of Sherlock Holmes

May 20, 1893
Exeter

I bade a hopefully temporary goodbye to Mycroft and took the early morning train from Waterloo Station on the London and Southwestern Railway for Exeter, where I am to meet the Professor at the University of Exeter. He teaches there or rather lectures since ordinary teaching is beneath his dignity and stature. He is just finishing the Spring Term there where he is presenting a seminar on advanced astronomy.

I sent him a telegram from London announcing my arrival that was answered promptly but briefly as follows:

> *Very well then, come ahead.*
> *Rooms reserved for you at the University.*
> *Professor Moriarty*

My train traveled to the south-west at first through Surrey and Sussex to Portsmouth and then on to Hampshire. I passed on the way through Aldershot to Dorchester and Weymouth and from thence onwards to Exeter. As the train gathered speed between stops I sat gazing from the window at the bright fields and the dappled sky. What a relief to emerge from the London smoke again and to be among the fields and farms of the English countryside. I spent some time reviewing in my mind my remembrances of the character of the man I was soon to meet and imagining what his opening gambit might be.

At the time of our wager we had not come to any agreement as to the exact rules of combat to be pursued when we met once again. There was simply no time. I was then as anxious to begin my travels as Moriarty was to end his trip to Europe and to return to the comforts of England. Now we are to meet and we do not know the size of the chessboard or what our separate pieces will be. Perhaps I have fooled myself in thinking that our encounter will be a quiet one of move and counter-move. Perhaps the Professor will seek an immediate checkmate through more violent means, but I doubt it. I believe that he is as curious about my data and conclusions as I am about his. It is part of the paradoxical relations that exist between us that I have come to look upon Moriarty as more of a collaborator than an adversary. This is because Moriarty insists upon principle in his evil. Only for that reason can we enter into a dialogue at all.

There are varieties of evil just as there are varieties of goodness. I will go so far as to say that principled evil (if evil can ever be termed principled) seeks to advance some good through evil means. It usually involves taking a quick course to an end that could have been achieved by slower but more virtuous means. It is a paradox that tolerance for a degree of physical evil seems to be a prerequisite for achieving moral goodness. In contrast, principled evil always seems to rebel in some way against the human condition rather than learning to endure it with grace.

The most extreme form of evil is what might be termed metaphysical evil. Metaphysical evil cannot be addressed or comprehended directly because it is like quicksilver. It yields at the slightest pressure and fragments into many parts. For this reason the satanic realm, when forced to identify itself by Jesus answers, "We are legion, for we are many."

These words of confession carry the usual satanic pride, the desire to appear to be omnipotent and thereby to instill terror and dismay; but these words are also a rare outburst of satanic honesty. I will explain what I mean by this strange statement.

Metaphysical goodness is by its nature one, for love is from God and God is love. Love acts so as to draw all good things to God through the affective metaphysical desire or tendency within every nature to perfect itself by finding its proper place in the Divine Order.

In contrast, evil acts in by using force, distortion, and trickery in order to mimic God and assume His attributes but without love. The devil wishes to draw all things to itself by fraud and by bribery. It subverts goodness by claiming that it is the lord of all proximate goods as "the prince of this world." The devil acts like a politician who buys votes by dispensing gifts.

God does not act in this way. God desires to be loved for and in Himself and not for any mere proximate goods that He may bestow upon us as gifts. Instead God bestows His gifts without precondition and requests our love without demanding it. Even the First Commandment telling us that we should love the Lord our God with all our mind, soul, and strength and not to prefer or worship strange gods is not meant to enhance God's vanity but to preserve us from being misled by imitations. To use God as a means to an end rather than the ultimate reason motivating all of our actions is a fundamental metaphysical confusion. Since God alone is the source of all goodness, no gift that He may give can exceed that of the gift of God Himself through being granted a share in the very life of God through the gift of Divine Grace by means of the indwelling presence of the Holy Spirit.

The devil on the contrary, being a mere creature and a fallen one at that, can rely only upon bribes to purchase whatever qualified and contingent love it may obtain from its slaves. Thus hell is a realm characterized by radical self-interest and utterly devoid of community. The reward of the legions of hell is similar to the share of the spoils of conquest distributed among the scattered legions of Rome by the later Roman Emperors. These soldier emperors were peripatetic generals who at last could not even retain the City of Rome, because they had so exhausted themselves waging war on the frontiers of Gaul and against the inhabitants of the regions of the Germanic and Slavic tribes.

It is one of the greatest paradoxes of divinity that God is one and therefore simple whereas evil is multiple and superficially complex. The mind of man is impressed by vain show and grandeur, so it often yields to the lure of the chaotic, whereas real complexity always manifests an underlying principle of order. Evil mocks what it cannot successfully imitate. The legend placed upon the cross of Jesus that said, "This is Jesus, the King of the Jews," was the ultimate in Roman mockery at the pretentions of the subject people of Israel, but it was also the mockery of the devil, for the means that God used to definitively defeat evil.

God always uses the little to shame the great. God uses the rejected, the outcast, the foolish ones, the woefully inadequate, the sick, the lame, the ugly, the aged, the infants, the lepers, the beggars, the prostitutes, the starving, and even the weakness of sinners (to whom He shows immeasurable mercy) to snatch from evil the spoils that evil would claim. I will go so far as to say that perhaps one of the reasons that no one in hell would dream of leaving it for heaven despite its tortures is that to do so would be such a perceived downwardly mobile social step for the august and exalted denizens of hell that they perceive themselves to be. I expect that hell has rather strict zoning regulations to keep out of each particular corner of hell those deemed unworthy to reside there. The deepest pits are the most envied.

In contrast, in the Kingdom of Heaven the Doctrine of the Communion of Saints proclaims that the virtues of the merits of the Saints are credited to sinners to reduce the temporal punishment due to sin. In heaven the desire is to share goodness, so that no one is abandoned or left empty and alone. In heaven "the last shall be first and the first shall be the last." Heaven up-ends the expectations of human nature so that love simply makes no sense from the perspective of hell! The entire point of the Crucifixion of Jesus Christ is that it seems so unnecessary! Surely God could have found another way to accomplish our salvation! Even the human nature of Jesus prayed to His Father (who would refuse Jesus nothing) that this chalice might pass him by. But Jesus acquiesced at last in assent to the strange necessity of the

Father's will, and of Jesus' own divine nature as well, accepting His suffering and death on the cross.

Jesus had no desire for power, kingship, or worship, but only to draw souls to the Father. So complete was this emptying, this *kenosis,* that Jesus claimed nothing of the divine prerogatives, not legions of angels, not the aids promised with a mocking grin by the devil to impress the mind of man and by this means to win converts, not a life of comfort, not freedom from pain and death, but chose instead to endure rejection and death.

Jesus took upon Himself the burden of all evils and of the condition attendant upon evil itself, which is alienation from the Father. The final glory of Jesus as the Christ is His radical obedience to an absurd requirement, simply because God appeared to ask it of Him by His silence in the Garden of Gethsemane. The Father's silence issued no command. No ringing voice warned, "Do not eat of the fruit of this tree for on the day that you eat from it you will die." The Father appeared to demand nothing of the Son at that moment. Why then did Jesus die? Why not pack up his sleeping friends and leave that troubled city of Jerusalem for a quiet Passover in one of the quiet hill towns? Let Judas look in vain for someone to kiss! Yet Jesus stays; he does not abandon his people or his mission. He leaves to God the Father all hope of any later vindication.

And in that last hour when Jesus cries out, "My God, my God why have you forsaken me?" many people have assumed that His cry was that of despair at God's utter absence at that moment Did Jesus think, "What if there is nothing there after all? What if I have been deluded all along regarding my status and my mission?"

What if there is no God, no God, *no God at all;* but only the spectacle of three obscure men dying on crosses outside the city gates, just as they do every day? Was this the perception of Jesus or was it instead the awareness of the Triune God of what it actually means to be a creature at odds with its creator? Jesus as God for just that instant completed the last element of the Incarnation, to know what it is to die.

But these words of Jesus are not in fact the memorial of His despair but the affirmation of the Psalmist who first wrote those prophetic words. They are not words of despair but of that same unconditional trust in God that Jesus had always manifested from the beginning, so that for the Father to leave the Son to die upon the cross was the final proof to humanity of the love of God the Father for all men and women, that love, which is unable to deny itself, even to those who would destroy all love by crucifying Christ!

Evil simply cannot cope with Love of this kind and measure, nor can death claim dominion here. The glory of the Passion of the Christ is not that God's justice demanded it, but that the Trinity would allow itself to be made subject to even such an absurd requirement at the request of evil: that after having given all in this manner, no more remained to be given!

God surrenders to evil to defeat evil from within its own emptiness. The lie is made manifest in the face of Truth. Hatred reveals its malice when confronted by such radical love. Evil ends its vain revolt by creating for itself its own dwelling, not in a palace, but in the empty arena of its aspirations, which is hell. The legions of hell are therefore all of the multifarious and absurd evils that we witness each day, the thousand cruel words and insults, the murders and mindless destruction, the betrayals, the waste, the vanity that vitiates so much of life. In seeming defeat God's victory is consummated. There is compared to this, no Napoleon of Crime.

Dr. Watson's Narrative Continues

In that waning August of 1898 I seemed more than ever before to notice the young couples who would pass me with their children on my daily walks along the cliffs of Newport. I would stop now and then to talk with the groups of young artists who were sketching the scene before them and remark at their choice of form and color. Out on the bay the pleasure-craft would be dipping their sails to a passing breeze as they traced their intricate patterns that always just managed to avoid collisions.

Matrons and nursemaids could be seen in the sheltered beaches building sandcastles and fortresses against the onslaught of the waves as the tide rose during the course of the long afternoons. The sun would then be further behind me and the water would take on that darker hue of evening and I would suddenly remember teatime and the stimulating conversations of the evening ahead among the good company provided by the Newport intelligentsia who would often gather at Mrs. Wharton's mansion in the evenings. I knew even then that I would always recall this summer with unique pleasure. To have known even one such perfect period in life would cancel the sorrows of other years when I had been a captive of the great city of London with the burdens of an active medical practice to face each day.

I had adapted well that summer to the carefree life of Newport. Over the summer I had for instance taken up that peculiar American custom of the drinking of coffee and cream served up with chocolate and crushed ice. It was with that particular treat in mind that I left behind the pleasures of the seashore one day. The chill wind of the advancing evening was rising and I had forgotten to bring a summer coat along with me after lunch. I knew that my chair on the terrace would be waiting for me with the tall chestnut tree overhead for shade and that Holmes would look up at my arrival with merry eyes at my discomfort as I made my usual apologies for having tarried so long in my solitary perambulations by the sea. Later that same evening Holmes and I had a most interesting discussion as I recall. I told him that I had just reached that point in his journal where he was about to confront Professor Moriarty after a long period of travel abroad in preparation for that dramatic encounter. I recall asking him if he had any advice for me as I approached that great battle of wits between the two adversaries in my reading of the journal. He thought about my question for awhile, gazing outwards to where the great ocean shone in the moonlight before answering.

"Well you must bear in mind that at this point of your reading your own exposure to its contents is fresher than what my unaided memory can provide. Like many battles of a physical nature I recall that we exchanged blow for blow with now the advantage going to Moriarty and now to me. Our discussions were wide-ranging and discursive in nature I recall; but if I might provide a few preliminary remarks I would ask that you bear in mind that my own approach to faith is somewhat paradoxical in nature. It is so because I find that God's dealings with the human race are also paradoxical in nature.

God seems always to take the long way round when seen from our point of view. Why for instance should God choose an obscure Semitic people to be the custodians of his revelations? Would the message not have proceeded far more swiftly and efficaciously if the Greek philosophers or the Roman poets had been the chosen oracles to convey divine wisdom?

Or again consider the poor timing of the advent of Jesus during a time of particularly zealous patriotic fervor among the Jewish people. Was not a message of universal love for all mankind doomed almost from the start when addressed to a people who expected a glorious and militant Messiah who would restore past glory to Israel? It would certainly appear from one point of view that God likes to court disaster. Why for instance does Jesus constantly ask his disciples to keep it to themselves whenever he acts in a particularly wondrous or 'God-like' capacity or fashion such as at the Transfiguration? Why was not the miracle of the loaves and the fishes performed daily and in Jerusalem? Why did Jesus flee worldly Kingship and adopt such a lowly and humble guise among men?"

"Why indeed?" I replied, for I was anxious to hear what he would have to say on the matter.

"Well let me begin by assuring you that I mean no impiety by asking such questions. I mention them only to show the state of mind that I encountered in Professor Moriarty when I returned from my travels – one of scorn and ridicule. Moriarty was of the opinion that the more that he showed me that Christianity was absurd, the greater was his chance to prevail in the course of our discussions."

"He could not have been more wrong in that supposition, for in me he was not dealing with a dried up old rationalist as he supposed, but rather with one who was willing to observe and to learn and to question even my most firmly held convictions, while not forgetting that as Pascal once said, "the heart knows things that reason knows not of." How often I have repeated to you that it is a capital mistake to theorize without data. If this dictum is true in everyday life then how much more this adage should be kept in mind when dealing with God. For instance, can we notice any common themes in salvation history? What facts do we observe?"

"I cannot say, unless it is that God appears to proceed by surprise and indirection and to approach us from oblique angles," I replied.

"You have chosen a very apt metaphor Watson! You are quite right, God appears to ask of mankind precisely what mankind may not provide. For example, why should God have posed a test in Eden to two young innocents with no prior experience of evil and hence with no built-in defenses against temptation? Later God asks the chosen people to navigate among rival tribes virtually all of which practiced some form of idolatry, without succumbing to the same natural human impulse to visualize the power upon whom they were asked to rely for their security by embodying it in the form of an idol. Was this not in a practical sense asking too much of them?"

"Then there follows the prophetic period of Jewish history when God's prophets systematically point out the virtually constant failures of the Jewish people to abide by the terms of the covenant. Can we be surprised that the prophets were not popular in their lifetimes? Yet the writings of the prophets were preserved rather than destroyed or watered down into a more acceptable form.   Other cultures celebrate their triumphs while only the Hebrew culture celebrates its failures. Of what comfort or use are these constant messages of accusation of betrayal and demands for conversion of heart? Were any other races or nations acting with greater morality at the time?"

"Finally of course we have the example of Jesus who is born to deliver the consummate message of God to His people and from them to the world; His mission appears to end in the ignominy of the cross. Christianity grows slowly from a mustard seed planted in Jerusalem and even that great city is destroyed in 69 A.D."

"And yet Christianity exists among us to this day for all of its failures and indirections. What do you see in all of this my friend?   Is God unreasonable or is He merely consistent but paradoxical? What do all of these examples have in common, but the revelation that God asks that we rely, not upon ourselves or outer circumstances for reassurance, but upon God alone. The whole point of the temptation in Eden, the giving of the covenant and the law, the witness of the prophets, and finally the testimony of the life and death of Jesus is that God frustrates our every natural conception as to what the divine nature should be like. God does not seek power, but abjures it and appears to court failure the better to reveal His true nature. God must then be sought less by reason than by direct apprehension and appropriation in faith. We grasp God, if at all, in a synthetic awareness of contrasting elements that if not actually absurd are at least not self-evident."

"By this means God teaches us trust, surrender, and love. God tolerates evil so that evil may be mutated into something else by actually utilizing the power that God has refuses to use - but by doing so evil defeats itself and shows its own essential emptiness. It is God's refusal to pursue the obvious course that indicates that it is God that we are dealing with and not a mere natural phenomenon. God appears for instance in a burning bush that is not consumed – a Torah that finally cannot save because its strictures exceed human capacities – a Savior who is rejected and killed saves us by rising from the dead!"

"So Watson, in approaching my adversary, Professor Moriarty, I did not try so much to contradict him as to enlarge his preliminary criteria for verification to include the paradoxical - not that reason is inadequate to lead us to God, but because there are minds that are best approached by an oblique attack and I judged Professor Moriarty to be one of these."

It took me some time to grasp the full implications of this unique approach to converting an adversary - by simply admitting from the start that science, the study of objects, can never approach God who represents the ultimate in subjectivity. Even our subjectivity is not impermeable by grace. Each of us mediates grace to others by merely existing. We encounter God; we do not prove Him!

I wondered how Holmes would approach another problem that had bothered me in my private reflections on Christianity, the problem of pursuing private happiness. One of my own primary temptations has been to wash my hands of this sorry world and to retreat to a realm of my own devising in order to simply live a quiet day and seek repose at night. Was this too much to ask in a world where greater evils occur every day?

So after mulling over all that he had said I asked him a further question. "Then, if you are correct Holmes, God creates human nature and then asks the impossible or at least the improbable from it, the exercise of perfect charity? Is that fair?

Does that not manifest more than what we might have expected of God that He should play fairly with us and not take advantage of our lowly position in a manner that would appear to torment the human spirit and not to honor it or to love it? Why ask more of us? Did we ask to be created in the image and likeness of God? Why should we not pursue knowledge and happiness on this earth by any means at our disposal, even while seeking to minimize harm to ourselves or others? In other words what is the place of what might be called the natural virtues, those that refuse to look beyond our own limited nature for any eternal purpose? Or would you advise that we dispense at once of any conception of the self and the private happiness that our insurgent desires seek to obtain?"

"You have asked me to answer several questions in one, old fellow," Holmes answered smiling. "Your argument, for an argument is hidden in your question, is that we know what will make us happy and what is fair. The mind of man covets the short route to pleasure and thus what most men or women mean by happiness is a combination of the maximum of pleasure with the least risk and effort and the greatest security against the interruption of our blissful state."

"It is the morality of the hedonist and the coward that has the greatest immediate appeal for us. Which of us covets effort, sacrifice, labor, and delay, let alone our own final extinction at death? Yet these are the parameters allotted to human existence. It is not that we are asked to completely abjure private happiness, but to place God's will first and when our own happiness leads us to make gods of ourselves and idols of our pleasures, to take the contrary course out of our love for God and to honor Him."

Holmes continued, "I will say this though, as a purely practical matter, that many people create for themselves a narrative of private happiness that is impossible of any realistic prospect of fulfillment – then when they encounter the failure of the world to live up to their entirely presumptuous vision of what is their due, they blame God first and not themselves. In that sense we are well advised to abandon what you have termed, 'a private happiness.' In any case we do appear to be made in the image and likeness of something and it is up to us whether that likeness should be of God or of something else."

It was shortly after this that our hostess beckoned us within and we rejoined the assembled company by the evening fire in the drawing room for liqueurs. I could not but reflect that life did have its comforts as well as its tribulations and it was in a tranquil spirit that I retired that night to sleep.

From the Journal of Sherlock Holmes

May 21, 1893
Exeter

I have arrived in Exeter. I will meet the Professor tomorrow, as per a brief and formal invitation, sent in answer to an evening telegram from me that I have arrived as arranged. I ate alone in my hotel near the railway station where I am at present staying. I have been invited to attend tomorrow's lecture and then to join the Professor for lunch in the faculty dining room. I assume that we may then adjourn to his chambers to begin those discussions that lie before us.

In my writings as set down in this journal earlier this afternoon I tried to explain to myself the difference between metaphysical evil and the evil that is displayed by a man like Professor Moriarty. In the former instance no dialogue is possible for the two levels simply do not meet. Evil for the mere sake of evil has as its very purpose the subversion of the good and the avoidance of any effort to justify its position. This means that no common principle of verifiability may be arrived at to support a dialogue with evil as such. To call into question the very rule of God as is done by metaphysical evil is to deny the very jurisdiction that might provide a measure of the fruits of victory let alone the rules of engagement.

This means that metaphysical evil is aware, at some level, that its pursuit is mere vanity and finally pointless, but the mystery of metaphysical evil is that from that knowledge, any insight is not forthcoming. Metaphysical evil cannot turn from its course once that course is chosen. It can only add to the number of its offences. It is a tear in the fabric of the rationality that governs all things that are not subservient to evil.

This is the great gap that exists between heaven and hell that is spoken of in the gospel. To identify then with metaphysical evil is to need to shift one's ground constantly, to adopt new standards always in the hope that some unidentified technique might still yield a way around God, to circumvent His purposes, to escape His love, and to obtain the fruits of love without the cost, which is simply to allow God the room in which to act in the tiny crucible of the soul.

All of my words as stated here are simply my way of saying that I do not believe that Professor Moriarty is irretrievably evil, for if he were he would be the devil and not what he is, a mere human being. Human beings are made in the image and likeness of God, which fact alone draws upon them the wrath of the devil. We are so negligible in ourselves that we might have escaped the notice of hell's minions if we were less beloved of God.

It is God's care for us and the fact of the Incarnation of Jesus, the Second Person of the Divine Trinity, that makes us of interest to a being whose own exalted nature would spurn to give us a moment of thought or effort were it not for the fact that it sees within us the love of God and the image that it does not reflect. This discrepancy is the source of the jealousy and hatred that is encountered in metaphysical evil, the realm of the fallen angels and the preternatural modes of action at their disposal. Although our sin may mar our ability to receive God's love, it still does not impair God's desire to give all the love that we will consent to accept from Him.

If this is the character of metaphysical evil, then how shall I describe the evil of a man like Professor Moriarty? Evil for human beings is chosen under the aspect of a misplaced good. This means that human evil is a departure from the will of God, which would set all things in their proper order and relationship. Human evil then is an act of insubordination that growing impatient with God would substitute its own judgment for the time and manner in which God always works to perfect the good of His created order. The restless quality of human nature is a direct consequence of our primal sin in Eden and the disorder that it instituted into created things.

To know good and evil and to attain eternal life are fearful gifts. It may have been that God preferred for men and women an extended period of innocence. Certainly it would seem folly to covet the problems of decision, the fear of bodily death, and the endless contingencies of human life from which we now suffer. If God might have given us a gentle and easily graded road to Him it would have been better for us to have taken it. This impatience and rebellion are similar to that of the devil and its minions, for it would seem that any servitude of so beneficent a master as God would be preferable to staking out a claim to whatever is not God. That is the only estate that may be claimed by the Lord of Darkness referred to as Satan.

It may be that our entire comprehension of the mystery of good and evil is biased by Adam's and Eve's erroneous decision. We have lost the ability to comprehend the terms of the choice that was once offered to the unity of Adam/Eve, a duality of persons that may have mirrored in its fashion the Trinity of God. This primal rupture of God's previous plans for the human race forces even God to communicate to us now by means of metaphor, for we have long since lost the ability to perceive God as He is. Our former familiarity may now only be viewed as though looking through a long tunnel of human evils from the abyss where we now reside and from there to catch what is now only a dimly glowing spark of the great fire of our origins where the heart of God once beat close to our own.

Perhaps Plato intuited this truth when he described all of human knowledge as an act of remembering what was once known totally and in completeness. Even the pagans were aware that human life, as it is now lived, is deficient in some way, marred by some primal wound or catastrophe. We are born in chains, unable to move. Our restoration to our former state of being was and is beyond our own ability.   It would appear that only by The Incarnation of Jesus in a human body followed by actually living the life of a human being that Jesus substantively implants again the former spark of the divine in man and woman through the gift of unmerited grace. A corollary of this is that absent the Incarnation of Jesus we would otherwise by the terms of our fallen nature have sought to create a spurious and ersatz eternity of our own and imbue that eternity with a God of our own creation, Man-and-Woman-without-God. Our human nature as it now is hungers for progress without pain, achievement without sacrifice, forgiveness without contrition, glory without effort, to attain the eternity of the angels though we live as beasts, to be loved though we are hateful, to be honored though we embrace disgrace, and to find heaven although we create hells for one another on earth.

If Professor Moriarty is evil, it is because he manifests human nature without the benefits attendant upon grace. This means that he would prefer that God would admire the genius of Professor Moriarty! It must have been very humbling for the Professor to discover the dynamics of asteroids and not to be able to prescribe and determine those very dynamics. Perhaps he desired to prove that these relational dynamics were chaotic; this might have left him free to instill a dynamic into creation not already to be found within it. Instead he found order in an unexpected place. Could it be this discovery in mathematics that first awoke the germ of doubt within him that perhaps there is a God after all? From what source comes such an elegant balance in a world without an observer to appreciate it? If so was the existence of a man like Moriarty not a mere accident of evolution, but a directly willed interlocutor who might address his God in prayer?

Moriarty evidently wishes to be like God, a Creator. It must gall him to be a mere creature. His very being screams those words of Milton's Satan, "Better to rule in hell than to serve in heaven." Moriarty's pride is such that he would wish to usurp even the devil's throne at times. HeI am counting on this fatal flaw within him: that as a creator Professor Moriarty at present would no more wish to serve the devil than he would wish to serve God!

For this reason my first step must be to convince Professor Moriarty that the devil exists. However much human beings may doubt that God exists, any honest appraisal of the sorrows and ills of life must indicate the devil's presence among us. The devil at least shares with us a created nature. As such we exist on the same plain of being that is to say contingent being as opposed to Necessary Being, which is possessed by God alone. I will start then with the devil in speaking to Moriarty, for the devil and Moriarty have a long acquaintance and although they are not friends (because evil of course tolerates no friendships to exist) they may still be termed to be allies in opposing the will of God. I shall use this tiny morsel of an opening and see if my efforts may breach the complacency of Moriarty's citadel.

May 25, 1893
A Seminar with Moriarty

The past few days have been quite eventful. I will attempt to sketch in the series of events based on the few notes I was able to make at the time. I was able to observe Professor Moriarty at his lectern for an hour without being observed as I slipped into the back of the surgical theater where he was giving a lecture attended by a substantial number of the science faculty and students of astronomy, physics, and mathematics.

The position of Professor Moriarty at the University of Exeter appears to be that of an endowed Professorship. He is spared the burden of teaching mere undergraduates. His entire duties are confined to giving a series of university-wide lectures on an immense variety of topics. The lecture that I attended was entitled, "The Role of the Axiom as a Source of Further Primary Postulates: A Philosophical Inquiry."

The surgical theater was quite filled and only my height allowed me to peer over the heads and shoulders of those who had come there before me to hear the lecture. After some time the room grew quiet. Professor Moriarty's stooped and diminutive figure emerged from a door and he walked across the platform to the lectern, without a nod of greeting to any of those present. He spoke without using any notes. I must say that I paid more attention to his manner and to his physical presence than to the substance of his lecture, much of which exceeded my own knowledge of mathematics, but there were elements in his comments on his equations that caught my interest. I will attempt to reproduce them here with as much accuracy as my memory may provide.

The Lecture

entlemen, the study of mathematics is the study of relationships, of patterns that exist between numerical values. These patterns are constant and unchangeable and are therefore certain in a way that knowledge in other fields of inquiry can never be. A prime number for instance is one that fulfils the definition of a prime number with absolute exactness such that no doubt may remain of its proper inclusion in the set of prime numbers. If mathematics was confined to a series of definitions and simple operations this certitude might always be retained and since numbers have no upper limit mathematics might embrace a subject matter that is infinite in extent and perhaps in scope of application. There would remain though the question of why the patterns that we observe in nature exist to which we may assign numerical values.

As scientists we do not of course presuppose the existence of a universal mind that out of its discretion has chosen to arrange matters so that the various numerical relationships exist, yet we observe evidence of patterns in the unalterable order of numbers. There are two ways that we can account for this phenomenon: the first (which we have rejected absent greater proof than mere theology may ever provide) is that God has created the rules that govern this universe; the second is that these relationships are the only possible ones and that not even God could alter them by His supposed discretion. There is of course a third possibility and that is that the human mind finds these relations of numbers unalterable because of a structural inability of the human mind to think otherwise. This latter belief we dismiss as what might be called a philosophical "dead-end" because to entertain it is to assume that the human mind may not know truth, but only itself through its own idiosyncratic operations.

If mathematical certainty is merely an illusion of our own minds, then all talk about verification must come to an immediate end, because we cannot abstract from our own minds any statement that we may choose to make. How we symbolize these relationships is another matter of course. We are condemned as it were to the prison of our minds from which there is no escape. Even so-called objective observations still require that the human mind do the observing. For this reason the mind must begin all inquiry with the presumption of its own abilities in certain areas. At the same time we are aware that human error and contradiction exist as well. We must account for error with the same assiduity if not the same accuracy as we account for truth. How then will we know when we may be certain of a set of data and when we may not? How can we be certain that our statements do not represent mere functions of language rather than resting upon some deeper foundation for operations in mathematics? In other words is mathematics self-referential, a case of mere tautology. If so then mathematics can only be used to provide an explanation for a closed-universe.

A truly dynamic universe would be one that cannot be described by the use of fixed linear equations. It would remain like a hollow sphere in which everything reverberates back and forth like sand in a glass ball. Every possible configuration, granted infinite time for these configurations and combinations to occur, would take place and then repetitions would occur until every possible combination would be reached a second time and then a third and so onwards to infinity. A description of this infinite process need not await its accomplishment. Once the insight happens within the mind a short descriptive statement will suffice.

Professor Moriarty paused then for a moment in order to allow time for the significance of his thought thus far to resonate through the crowd before continuing.

The traditional approach to this problem of insight into fundamental relationships is to begin with certain axioms which must be presumed to be true without achieving empirical closure by running repeated tests. An axiom forms the first link in a chain of knowledge. By being fixed in nature it will allow for a chain of postulates to be bound to it by logical inferences of a deductive nature and by ever more refined definitions, which if sufficiently discriminating, may lead to what we call certitude.

Linguistic definitions of course are inherently vague because words are, in the last analysis, mere metaphors of reality, the pairing of symbol and sense. Only the science of mathematics, since its definitions are self-contained and hence strict, admits of no exceptions at least in the case of real numbers. Thus mathematical truths may claim the highest degree of certitude. The inductive knowledge of most of what we call scientific truth is uncertain in nature by the very fact that many observations must be made to ensure validation by an inductive rule. Inductive rules are merely probable because unless we grant an infinite series of trials an exception may always emerge. The accepted rule of most scientific truth statements is then a mere sticking-plaster that adheres to the facts but does not emerge from them with absolute certainty.

A so-called intuition of truths that precedes the formation of a hypothesis may seem to provide certainty, but that intuition when it is reduced to its minimum atomic components will be revealed to be a mere global sensation of unity and coherence within the mind and therefore non-demonstrable to anyone who does not share that intuition.

He paused again before turning to the realm of what he referred to scornfully as "poetic truths."

But shall we leave certainty and truth aside for a moment? Mathematics may describe the tonal sequence in a symphony, but it cannot in itself reproduce the experience of listening to a symphony, nor produce the sounds that issue forth from the various instruments. Again we are in a closed universe with only one set of possible variations. But once again we have truth of a sort, aesthetic truth. An example of these aesthetic truths is that absurd statement of the poet John Keats in his "Ode on a Grecian Urn."

"'Beauty is truth, truth beauty. That is all ye know on earth and all ye need to know." It may have been all that Mr. Keats needed to know as a mere love-sick youth, besotted with nightingales and Grecian Urns, but to universalize his experience to all of mankind would have condemned us to that wistful state of the dying consumptive poet and his ilk. To float about upon the clouds of subjectivity may excite the senses, but gentlemen, it is not knowledge. Any truths which cannot be shared and assented to universally are not true at all!

Instead, they are a unique pattern of the nerves of the individual. There is nothing so absurd that it has not been ardently maintained at one time or another by a small set of mankind. I will suggest that the degree of their ardor is set by the degree of the inherent improbability of the assertions that they make.

Was it an illusion or did the eyes of Professor Moriarty seem to pierce through the crowd to fix themselves on me as he looked up into the darkness of the lecture theater?

But now let us move from the realm of so-called aesthetic truths, which at least possess the virtue of placing an object before us to be dispassionately evaluated and enter that region of inquiry that may be called the search for transcendent truth. I submit to you that here, to use an analogy, we have moved beyond the visible spectrum and entered a region that is beyond our apprehension and cognition and for that very reason should also be beyond our affirmation and belief. I am speaking of course as a scientist and not as a theologian. But I further submit to you that the very word "theology" is a misnomer, because we can know nothing of God except by whatever evidence we can produce from the world around us, a world that appears to be remarkably ungodly in every area beyond the precincts of houses of worship. So let us dispense with theology and simply deal with religion as simply another social phenomenon, religion as a branch of anthropology.

The religions of the world are the best example of this phenomenon of unbridled subjectivity. This is because the explanations that they make are said to be universal that they fall infinitely short of obtaining their objective of compelling assent from a reasonable man. The very universality of their claims leads to their downfall as seen from a rational perspective. I, as a presumed member of the class of reasonable men, would be far more likely to find truth in a tiny god who ruled over a molehill in my garden than to believe in a bug god who rules over an entire universe. The god of a molehill could be studied. I could walk out into my garden on a summer day and watch his operations as he is worshiped by the moles, the centipedes, the beetles, and all the other fauna and flora. I might even gain an insight into that 'god's' own peculiarities, the reason why he chose that particular mole hill on which to exercise his influence or why he prefers to be worshiped rather than ignored; and if he chose to give any 'divine commands' I could judge whether they were for the good of his creatures or a mere sign of his divine vanity and desire to rule over all that he surveys.

Perhaps the various 'gods of religion' are unsure of themselves and demand worship to define for themselves the nature of their own 'godhead.' But let us look at this entire subject matter from the point of view of the prospective human knower. If even the operations of a mole-hill (and they are complex as any entomologist will explain to us) exceed our complete knowledge, then how much more inexplicable must be the universe as a whole. Thus any assertion of a universal dominion by any God whatsoever must be empty of verifiable content and any statement of religious 'truth' must be absurd in its presumption!

When we add to this the record of blind religious persecutions and the inevitable counter-persecutions, the self-interest of religious establishments that use their supposed spiritual powers to lord it over others while always ensuring a comfortable living for themselves, and the sheer hysteria and folly of most religious observances, it will be readily understood why I as a reasonable man assert that any "moral truths' that we possess must seek another source than religions for their sanction.

He looked about the crowd with a lofty expression to see if any opposition was emerging before he continued once again.

"But let us go further still. Of what use are 'moral truths?' If you observe the power-relations of human life you will observe that the powerful are usually precisely those least constrained by moral considerations. This is proven by the race to acquire armaments of most nations. Every nation assumes that it alone is honorable while the other nations are greedy and mendacious. Would it not be more probable that every nation is mistaken about itself and that it is also greedy and mendacious as well? How then can there be virtue or honor among nations?

But do not congratulate yourselves, gentlemen, for it is not nations alone that disappoint the man who would seek truth and virtue in human affairs. If nations are but cads and swindlers are not their citizens also? Would it not be best simply to summarize human affairs by saying, in a re-phrasing of Keats, that it is not the case that beauty is truth and truth beauty, but instead that power is human truth and human truth is the ability to exercise power and that is 'All ye know on earth and all ye need to know.'"

Again his eyes seemed to search out mine where I stood in the back of the surgical theater listening to this extraordinary diatribe. He continued, smiling at his auditors and with that peculiar side-to-side movement of his head that I had often noted as a characteristic of the man.

But of course such a definition of human truth would be only slightly less fallacious than that of Keats, for truth does not yield to power. Truth is inherent in the nature of things and may not be coerced. So let us leave behind those shadowy regions of induction and intuition: the induction of the sciences and the even more fallacious intuitions of the poets and the men of 'moralities.'

I do not, you observe, dignify so called 'religious truths' even as intuitions, which are at least 'true' to the poet who records them or the artist who paints them, because religions are merely extended metaphors, adopted under compulsion by fools and cowards. Religions are always collective phenomena and such truths as we may possess are always the fruit of individual reflection combined with a principle of verifiability such as that which I have suggested to you today, which only exists in the strict sense within mathematics."

Professor Moriarty looked about him with a probing mien.

Perhaps I have offended the pieties of some of you present here today. If so I have not done so from any desire to dominate or subdue any worthwhile criticism of my position. We may debate these matters further after class; but allow me to complete my synthetic global proposition first so that you can stand back and either admire or deplore the entire structure. We may even have some philosophers present with us here today. Philosophers claim to take the idea of truth very seriously. Let us not disappoint them.

Let us summon up the spirit of one of them, one Herr Leibniz, a monist who devised a system to tune all things to the will of God by positing certain "monads" each existing in splendid isolation, but programmed by God to act in some marvelous synchronicity to obtain the good in all things so that the problem of evil simply disappears.

He might agree with me when I say that from the point of view of truth it is irrelevant if the laws of the universe might have been different had God so willed it. It is only essential that we come to understand the laws of the universe that are accessible to us. To doubt our capacity to make truth statements at all would invalidate our own nature as seekers after truth.

Descartes once said, 'I think therefore I am.' By this statement he no doubt meant that I may not doubt the fact that I am thinking and if thinking, then I must at least exist in order to do so. But gentlemen, let us pause for a moment. What if it is only my thought that is I? What if what I call my own being is simply the process of conscious thought itself? If I ceased to think would I cease to be as well? Or perhaps something else is doing the thinking and I am only a particle is some larger framework? Descartes has been guilty of an exercise of sleight-of-hand in leaping to the conclusion that because thought is going on that it was he who was doing the thinking rather than being the thought itself.

Like all metaphysical idealists Descartes insists upon being able to sign his name to the universe as though he was the painter and not a corner of the canvas on which the painting is happening. If we wish to speak of statements or of truth, which is always one step away from any statement we might make, then we must first agree to confine ourselves to the happening occurring around and about us of which we presumably are not the cause.

In other words gentlemen, we must simply acknowledge phenomena as they are and cease all attribution either to God or to ourselves as causative agents that things are in fact occurring, even when they stand still in time. This persistence in being that we term existence is already a conclusion and not a primary datum. We know nothing of substances but only of the languages by which we seek to grasp them. We adhere to habits of thought because they are convenient and may even promise us tenure someday in this institution.

His audience laughed at this statement and I found it significant that Professor Moriarty seemed for a moment to brighten into congeniality. But he immediately became serious once again.

This habit of positing gods, monads, atoms, essences,

substances, etc. is precisely what we must abandon if we are to know anything at all. It is no excuse to throw names about as if the great men of history were any different than we. Are we to drown forever in a sea of dogmas and of articles of faith? Dare we allow whatever is doing the thinking that has brought us forth to proceed unburdened by what it has done before? Why must God be consistent? If everything simply disappeared, of God were to put His toys back into His toy box, who would we be to complain? We complain that we must die; we who cannot prove that we are even alive and not some stray drop of paint running down the canvas, a flaw in a painting of which we play no part at all. God may have already set the canvas aside and we with it, never to return.

What is death then but the cessation of the process to which in its continuous operation I owe my own conscious being? Can the thinker think himself back into thinking when his thought stops at death?

Poof! Immortality has just gone out of the window and my thinking becomes not participation, as Plato would have it, in the eternal realm of ideas, but merely an organic process contained within the humble cranium of a clever monkey, one perhaps burdened by an intelligence that exceeds what is useful for its mere survival. What entity shall mourn our passing if perhaps some symmetrical virus succeeds in its organizing capacity and its ability to replicate its unique pattern of existence and by doing so kills the greatest of human philosophers; will the universe mourn that it is now not comprehended? In the face of infinite time what does it matter if a little delay in expression occurs or for that matter fails to arise at all so that the universe fails to ever produce its own sublime and all-encompassing description of itself?

The room had grown deathly silent. Professor Moriarty looked about him from face to face as if asking someone to dispute him, as if even he was not willing to admit the position that he had just outlined. At last he spoke.

But our hour is almost up and each of you no doubt has

other commitments. We must proceed as if everything that I said is just so much bilge-water, but isn't that precisely my point: we must persist, we must continue, we must imagine that some entity called us really exists in a world that really exists and that everything was once nothing and that from that nothing God fashioned a universe and then threw us into it saying, "Swim, swim for your very lives!"

Professor Moriarty smiled sadly before demising the class.

It may be that you will leave here today and find that you disagree with me, but I challenge you to find wherein I have erred. So let me conclude today by saying that if I may not abstract from my own being sufficiently to metaphorically gaze back upon the ground on which I stand, then how shall I describe those very processes that I hope to judge as a philosopher when I practice epistemology?

My own knowing apparatus and the processes in which it is engaged must be qualified by the very fact that an 'I' turns from its own consciousness of itself as thinker to describe its thoughts through the distorting means by which it attempts to communicate to other minds, which it assumes can even receive its communications sent into the metaphorical 'ether' that separates all human minds from each other. You see of course the conclusion that is forced upon us then do you not? All knowledge becomes subjective because the human mind cannot abstract from itself. I am aware of myself thinking, while aware of myself thinking, while aware of myself thinking like the infinite regress of images between two mirrors!

Professor Moriarty looked about him as though for a moment he doubted if he was not quite alone and we had all disappeared, perhaps re-absorbed into his thought processes, as he had described them to us. But in a final addendum as the students began to gather their books and umbrellas he said.

Wait a bit; sit down, sit down gentlemen!

The entire room as one body came again to restful attention as though they were a single army of thought processes.

Shall we then despair, gentlemen? We might of course.

We might grasp a butterfly net and go skipping through the meadows as the madmen that perhaps we are. Or being young, as most of you are, you might fall at the feet of some Olympian Goddess and ply her virginity with importunities. The rest of us might purchase a general's hat and claim to be Napoleon.

Or gentlemen, we might get busy and know what we can know and presume that it is true. In other words we return to the first axiom of all thought, that knowledge is possible! The opposite course would be to entertain epistemological anarchy! Still, it must be admitted that the human mind rebels at the need for such axioms as those which allow thought to proceed. The most perfect knowledge would not require that we make them.

For this reason a perfect knower, which we may call God if you will, would not require such axioms. His knowledge would be complete and immediate. Perhaps then the reason that some of you believe in God is because you believe that just such a cosmic knower is possible. I do not believe as you do, but lest I be thought to be too dismissive of your views I will attempt to make your argument for you.

It would be too absurd for the universe to be greater than the abstract principle of such a universal cognition. Could mere materiality be greater than that which is able to comprehend it in its totality? Surely that would imply that to be is always greater than to think about being. But the world simply stands against us, mute and pointless, whereas we can take a position toward it by our will, our intentionality.

But let us not insert another axiom here where it is not required or justified. Let me state simply that if the universe cannot be comprehended by an ultimate knower, then it becomes God by default and by exceeding comprehension by any Supremely Conscious Being it would be acting out its own frivolous and arbitrary nature that would deny the possibility of complete truth; because any truth that is inexpressible is not truth. Being, in other words, demands an explanation beyond its mere presence.

Why should the parameters of truth be confined to the

small part that we human beings claim to know, with various degrees of certainty? Knowledge then, as such, demands its own completeness. This is the best argument that I know for a universal knower, for a God, to exist.

A corollary of this assertion is that if something can act with such carelessness as to abandon a universe that eludes complete cognition to mere monkeys such as us, then it must have the will to do so and if that is true then we are back to a God, but an arbitrary one and even an evil one."

He smiled at us all and his smile seemed to combine contempt for all who were present and also a great sadness, before he went on to finish his lecture for the day.

The net result of all of this is that we have two fundamental options according to this particular universal view of things, or so it seems to me. And I beg you to recall that I am making this particular theist argument for you out of my, let us say, goodness of heart. The three options are:

1. To believe that the universe is an act of pure willfulness by a God inventing the rules as it goes along and that cognition must follow behind in its traces, sniffing like a little dog behind a cruel or willful master, or;

2. That cognition comes first and that the universe is guided (at least in the only instance that we know, which is the case of the one universe before us) by God or what we would call God reacting to the tasks we pose for Him."

3. There might also be a third view (if we abstract from time and into 'eternity') which would approach the metaphoric language of the creation myth in The Book of Genesis. That God creates and reflects upon his creation simultaneously. God makes a thing and immediately recognizes that it is good. Creation and cognition then become one simultaneous act of the divine will.

"You may take your choice, gentlemen, of these options (they are only options because none of the three may be proven from the molehill where the human race now resides). But we can only use the springboard of philosophical idealism by assuming that if within us the thought and the thinker are one,

then so it is also with God. For God to think a thing is already to accomplish it.

I reject, ab initio, the unconscious pantheistic God of the Jewish philosopher, Baruch Spinoza, simply because his idea of God is that 'God' is co-extensive with what we observe. If that were true, then all things become a vast simultaneity and we are back to poetry once again in a truism, which states that: God is all things and all things are God; or stated differently, all things are the maker of all things.

Such a statement conveys nothing to a philosopher; it is a mere equation with both terms undefined. I have no quarrel with a metaphysical God you see, only with the smorgasbord of supposed deities presented to me by the world's religions. They may be gods of molehills of various sizes, but I cannot imagine one of them being sufficiently subtle and sophisticated to create the universe that I as a man of reason inhabit.

I think that will be all for today, gentlemen. It is May and you are young, most of you, and perhaps you long to go tripping through the fields with your butterfly nets in the company of a fair young creature and to address her as the poet Andrew Marvell once did when he said, "Had we but world enough and time, this coyness lady, were no crime ... but at my back I always hear time's winged chariot hurrying near; and yonder all before us lie, deserts of vast eternity. Good day, gentlemen."

There was a short burst of laughter, appreciation, and applause, which Professor Moriarty ignored, as he walked to the small door in the back and exited the theater. I had agreed to meet the Professor in the faculty dining hall so I joined the exiting scholars and asked directions to the hall from a Professor Bruce Gilbert Whitney who said that he would be happy to escort me there as it was his own destination as well.

"Professor Moriarty is a capital fellow," he opined in answer to my question about how Professor Moriarty's lecture series had been received by the students and the members of the faculty. "He enjoys tweaking the lads a bit with his sarcasm at times, but they enjoy his somewhat sour nature. Today was a bit of a lark you know. He usually simply scrawls equations on the blackboard and then glares over the lectern and asks for questions, assuming that they are following him. The man is quite a Socrates in his way. He teaches by example rather than using the traditional lecture method. It is always a sort of duel between them and him. He picks us all up again when necessary and is soon well ahead of us again along the trail."

We came at last to a splendid hall of three stories located on the hill and overlooking the green courtyards and lanes below, threaded by the scholars and professors.

We entered the spacious hall and walked past a line of busts of past professors and teaching fellows to the dining room. It was immense and similar to the cloisters of my own former college at Cambridge. Professor Moriarty had already obtained the elements of his own sparse meal and was eating at a small table in the corner from which he could observe the room. I was still surprised by the comments that he had made during his lecture regarding religion.

Could his seeming acceptance of at least one of the philosophical proofs for the existence of God be only a ruse to knock me off my guard? Was he attempting to draw me from cover by tethering a young goat to a tree as Colonel Moran would have done to draw a tiger out of the undergrowth in India? Or perhaps he had simply fired a shot across my bow to alert me to the fact that I did not possess a monopoly over the literature of the world. He was in a better position at a university where he could access resources directly, while I was primarily dependent upon my own experiences for the most part during my long absence from England.

I saw at once that he was not ignorant of philosophy and that I could presume no advantage over him from that quarter. I crossed over to him at once though and he surprised me by rising to shake my hand briefly while saying with a grim smile, "Ah Mr. Holmes, late of India, Tibet, Persia, and the Sudan I believe. Colonel Moran has kept me abreast of your travels. Pray take a seat and a steward will take your order. My own meals never vary. I keep to a bland diet as you can see for the sake of my constitution. My digestion is not what it once was, but Professor Whitney has recommended a regimen of various vegetables ground up into a mash and eaten four times daily in small quantities."

I sat down as he had requested and a steward was soon at my side with a menu. I ordered a steak and kidney pudding and a glass of claret and a moment later I found myself eye to eye with the man who had haunted my days and nights over thousands of miles in Asia. He was drinking a cup of lapsang souchong tea and gazing at me with his sunken and piercing eyes that have always reminded me of a beast of prey gazing out of its lair.

At last he spoke up. "You have grown if anything thinner than you were that day when we last met at the Reichenbach Falls. You are no doubt a bit stronger though with riding camels all day. I hear though that you have shown signs of your old lung ailment. Not good. You showed signs of early consumption as a boy I recall, so you were tutored at home. Perhaps it is time for you to consider taking up a less strenuous profession such as your fabled beekeeping. Crawling about rooms with a magnifying lens looking for clues can prove exhausting you know."

I had not thought that the Professor possessed such a satiric wit, but then our conversation in recent years had been confined to a brief meeting in my rooms in Baker Street when the Moriarty organization was coming down all around him. Still, I believed that I could follow the course of his thoughts. I could see that he was feeling me out just as I had done by attending his lecture that morning. He seemed to read by thoughts, because he brought the matter up immediately.

"How did you like my presentation this morning?" He said breaking into my thoughts.

"You knew that I was there then?" I inquired. "No," he replied. "But I believed you might be. It gave me an opportunity in advance to rehearse the discussions that lie before us and if you cared to be present by giving you at least some point of entry into my thoughts. After all you have been gone for some time and memories fade. In any case I prefer to make the first move of the game. Consider it the privilege of age. You may also recall that since I am the challenged party to our little duel, the choice of weapons, place, and time falls to me."

"And that choice is?" I enquired.

"Oh, nothing too strenuous," he replied airily. "My age precludes wrestling on the brink of waterfalls, as you pointed out to me at our last meeting in Switzerland. In addition, I am accustomed to being shown a certain degree of deference. I have become a sort of Professor-at-large in this budding Arcadian academy. I am something of a polyglot, as you may know, so I am able to address a wide variety of fields, though mathematics and physics are my forte. However, I do hope you will not engage me in extensive parsing of the scriptures in the original languages, for I have shamefully neglected my Hebrew and Greek in recent years and my knowledge of Latin is not quite up to the mark. So you see my choice of weapons is simply to engage in an amicable discussion of the points that lie between us."

I was not deceived by his deliberately bland manner. "If I recall correctly the stakes of these discussions that you suggest are quite high, since you proposed two years ago to devote your time and efforts towards the furtherance of a scheme that would determine the fate of the entire British Empire!"

"Ah, I do recall something of the sort. Well I may have spoken a bit rashly at the time. You will recall that I had hoped at that period to draw your brother Mycroft into our battle. It would be quite something to defeat both of the Holmes brothers in a single campaign."

"You forget Sherringford," I replied.

"Not at all," said he, "But Sherringford was always the dullest of the three of you. It is as well that he is the oldest and that as a farmer and herdsman he is quite consumed by his duties in Yorkshire. Have you seen him yet? Oh, you have? How unflattering; I thought you would rush to Devonshire the moment that your boat landed to confront me all breathless with insights and scriptural passages to confuse me. But Sherringford! I trust that he is still a Tory and follows the tenets of the High Church of England. I doubt that you will ever make him a plebian Catholic like you for he is the virtual epitome of a provincial English lord. He assumes that the British Empire is engaged in doing the work of God on earth. He will never yield to the Pope the spiritual supremacy that the so-called Roman Pontiffs have claimed to possess since the Roman Emperors absconded to the East, because they could no longer hold the western empire together. Thereafter, if it had not been for the temporal control of Rome under the Popes, the Church would never have been able to spread over the western regions of Europe. It would have had to seek sanctuary in Antioch or Alexandria. The possession of Rome was the key to a spiritual empire, as Constantinople could never hope to be, threatened as it still is by the Moslems."

"I have always thought that it might have been better if Carthage had succeeded Jerusalem as the center of Christendom. All of the really important ideas were coming out of Africa at that time. Christianity began, if you do not object to my saying so, as remarkably deficient in complexity. Jesus left everything up to the first Christians to work out. Was Jesus God or simply a good man who was later exalted by God? There lay the ground for much contention and it kept the Church Fathers busy for two centuries trying to decide what should be the true position of correct Church teaching. The first three hundred years of Christian history is simply a matter of the working out of definitions. It was nothing other than a great family squabble. But what choice was there for the early Church when it began with only the threadbare legend of an executed Jewish wonder-worker?"

Jesus was not above using what St. John's Gospel calls signs, but the rest of Christian history rests its believability on the sheer intricacy of the weaving together of the fragmented views of just who this Jesus was and what possible significance His death might have for us."

"This whole matter of vicarious atonement seems to be the key, though how it can achieve its supposed end has always seemed to me to be logically inconsistent. Why this emphasis upon sacrifice? The whole thing is so primitive. It took the genius of St. Paul to even enunciate it clearly. That poor guilt-ridden former Pharisee, St. Paul, had trouble though even keeping peace among the members of his nascent and dispersed Christian communities let alone to be the first theologian. Most members of those new congregations were no doubt drawn from the simple folk of the region who thought that Christianity promised more than whatever local faith had heretofore sustained them. They were unlikely to grasp the subtlety of the man who had come to them with this new faith, this 'good news,' that required no geographical nexus, but only conversion of heart and conduct."

"No wonder that St. Paul had trouble with them! As a man he is interesting though in his way. He is the perfect example of a man who is forced to create the improbable as the only path out of an intellectually untenable position. Here he had spent his life believing that the absurd rituals of the Torah were in some manner pleasing to God when their only obvious function was to be sufficiently inconvenient that no other Semitic tribe would ever care to adopt them. It gave the Jews an identity and a history."

"But to return to St. Paul; the poor man discovers that he is killing Jews right and left who have gone over to this new belief. Suddenly it dawns upon him that no decent God could mandate such conduct in order to preserve a mere code of conduct most of which governs areas that are morally indifferent to anyone with reason. Why should God prefer that one not wear garments woven of two different fabrics? What is it to God if some object is made to represent Him as long as that object is a mere symbol? So it was that Saul, the Jew who had always honored the laws of Israel, became the worst heretic that the Jews had ever known. He set the law aside and made of Jesus the foundation for a new and universal sacrifice for the entire human race! Religious genius? Yes, but hardly a man with a message that the more faithful Jews were likely to appreciate."

"As for St. Peter, bah, he had trouble, for a while at least, in even realizing that Christianity had no hope of converting the majority of the Jews, nor has it done so to this day. The central message of Christianity is too simple and that is the problem. The Jews revel in complexity. Give them a code of priestly admonitions and they are happy. Tell them to wash to the elbows before eating and they will spend years and miles of scrolls debating where the elbow begins."

"No, give me Carthage to Rome every time. Augustine was the Bishop there and he set the stage for the later phenomenon of Protestantism by his contempt for human beings. Things were going bad in Africa with heresy and barbarians everywhere. Augustine had finally given up his mistress. And by the way that is always a mistake for a sensual man; just ask Colonel Moran. This sacrifice left him bitter towards the human race. He trotted out that threadbare story of Eden from The Book of Genesis and made it the center-point of his whole theology. "

"I lean of course toward the views of the discredited Pelagius who had some hope for man's unaided efforts to build a better world. The great pessimists like Augustine always win of course. Just look at your brother, Sherringford, who is as sour as the old bog water standing in pools on his beloved moors. Augustine was a literary man though and he didn't mind confessing his sins to the whole world. Drama is the very essence of religion and Augustine was the first to really understand this. He also didn't mind taking chances. Imagine selling Christianity to the Romans of the time by pointing out that people whose religion prohibits stealing or lying make good citizens."

"But I believe we were talking about something else. Oh yes, Sherringford; I never thought that I needed to consider him in my scheme. I went for Mycroft who is probably the most innately intelligent of the three Holmes brothers..."

rofessor Moriarty paused and I could see that the contest between us had already begun in earnest. In one brief opening gambit Professor Moriarty had insulted my brother, my faith, and my convictions regarding the place of Original Sin in an assessment of human history. He hung fire now for a moment, waiting for the smoke to clear, to see if he had done any damage with his first salvo. His head assumed that sinister side-to-side motion that I recalled from past days, the sinister dance of the cobra that is about to strike.

I spoke in response to him in my most laconic manner. "You were never fond of Sherringford even as a youth I recall. He was after all my father's oldest and favorite child. If Mycroft and I often felt slighted by him, how much more so did you who as a mere ward could make no claim to our father's largess but that of simple acceptance of his favors."

I could see my dart had touched a nerve. After a moment the Professor returned with the comment, "Your father was a good man; anyone would have valued his esteem."

"As for history," I continued. "Providence does not admit of hypothetical propositions. It is pointless to ask what might have happened had not the supreme authority of St. Peter as the Head of the Apostles not devolved upon the later Bishops of Rome, the Popes. The fact remains that authority was passed and has remained ever since in a continuous line of succession."

"A mere formality;" interrupted the Professor. "The point that I am making is that church history displays a process of aggregation over time that appears little different from any other series of historical events. Shall we trace more of Church history? Very well, the Papacy was often valued for its material benefits, the spoils to be claimed by the most powerful families of Rome during most of its benighted history. The Papacy is and has always been only a great carbuncle growing on the nose of the Church. But since the Church itself has been only a burden to humanity's aspirations by casting doubt upon the value of life in this world, it is not surprising that one absurdity has begotten another."

"The primary source of all religion is envy of the powerful by the weak, of the few by the many, of the noble by the ignoble, even as Mr. Friedrich Nietzsche has written. The Church has never escaped the burden imposed by European History. Its spiritual empire was sanctioned by other Empires. Even today the decrepit corpse of Austria is sustained by the pretence that it is the Holy Roman Empire and not a hodgepodge of Germans and Slavs held together by tyranny and oppression."

"But let us now turn to Mycroft, since it is he who enables the fools in London to interpret correctly the events occurring on the continent. My little scheme as you may regard it does in fact exist. I admit it. It is not complete however, so I do not propose to tell you what it is at this time. I have been quite busy you see with my work at the university, with my writings and research, and with my horse stables. My quarrel with your brothers and with you is only an avocation and not a full-time occupation with me. You must forgive me for being so remiss in communication, but I have commitments of my own to consider and do not have the leisure even in my retirement to devote to trotting about Asia or sending you updates on my activities."

I pointed out that he had at least kept a close watch upon me.

"Well I owe your father something. I would not have you fall victim to some accidental death if I could prevent it. I have no such obligation to the British Empire and if Mycroft chooses to go down with the ship; well, that is his affair."

I felt a certain sting of alarm at his words. "You agreed to withhold any execution of your plans until I was again home and able to convince you that there is a moral order in the universe and that one may look to religious doctrine as a guide to moral action, that the individual will may not be the creator of its own moral code without consideration of the objective order willed by his creator."

The Professor laughed. "Yes, I do remember something of the sort. I recall that I was so startled at your naiveté that I have even honored my promise. You have certainly set yourself a major task, my dear Holmes. I stated that I was willing to abandon my project if you were able to simply give me any valid reason to abandon it. You see, I have never believed that you could achieve your goal. I have been granting you the indulgence of your own folly simply to see to what lengths you would go in order to preserve your delusions. It has been a pleasure to me to think of you grappling with those marauding Arab tribes who veil their lust for conquest under the guise of spreading the message of Mohammed. I pictured you in the snows of Tibet casting yarrow sticks so that you might know which path to follow according to the mysterious hexagrams of the I-Ching. I could see you on a mat in India, seeking a premature oblivion through meditation on the nothingness of everything. I pictured you in Palestine with some room full of rabbis consulting the Babylonian Talmud and looking for a proper path through the bizarre commands of the Torah. I even wondered if you would stay with one of the countless forms of Christianity by going to Jerusalem to stand before the question of an empty tomb at the Church of the Holy Sepulcher. And now here you are after having sifted the sands and cultures of Asia and I can barely restrain my eagerness to hear what your investigations have yielded!"

"I do hope that you were able to be persuaded by some deity other than the ones that have emerged out of the Middle Eastern region. That is a region of tribal vanities and an unfortunate ability to write them down. That region of the world has saddled mankind with conflicting but absolute mandates. Too much of history has already been saddled with the result in wars, crusades, and impertinent missionaries. But I have allowed you time in order to discover this for yourself."

"You ask if I will delay the execution of my scheme. I answer that I am more than willing to do so until you come to your senses and aid me. Yes, aid me Holmes to destroy this ghastly British Empire by creating chaos. That is your little hint. My scheme will shatter the delicate machinery on which oppression depends. Power is more vulnerable than it appears to be. That is why every tyranny must root out and destroy the very least opposition. It must finally control even the thoughts of free men. "

"Freedom and power are the only morality; to impress one's vision for good or for evil upon the world. There is no judgment to be made but that judgment that we make upon our own values and actions. The reason that every morality differs and that the religions of the world have never reached a consensus with regard to the truth and never shall is that even religions are only the will to power in both individuals and groups, which they would gladly impose upon all other men through converting them. The will is everything, my dear Holmes; the individual will is God."

"There is no other overseer of our fate, no concerned deity to impose rewards or punishments. If a higher being existed he would give the lie to his greatness by any partiality in our regard. Man has only the facts of the struggle for life at his disposal. Any theory that he makes to account for these facts is provisional and finally pointless. The best that we may do is to contemplate the tiny navel of our own experience. To abstract from that in order to judge the whole is to attempt to swing the world as if it were a piece of lead dangling from a string. It is simply beyond our powers; but we attempt it anyway."

"Revelation is simply a word to veil our presumption. God does not speak to man. Even the universe as a whole may be waste, some cast-off garment of God's idle hours. God may long since have forgotten all about us. What we call evil may simply be those inherent imperfections latent in what was after all a first attempt at creation. If God exists and has not caused our universe to collapse again into non-being, it may be because even to do so would require an effort that He is unwilling to make; God may have simply forgotten our universe and cast it off into some obscure corner of eternity there to rot away in due season. Our entire pulsing universe may sit in some divine museum of the gods to be goggled at by the children of the gods while they are licking celestial lollipops and waiting for their nannies to urge them along to the next exhibit. Why take the trouble to destroy what has been discarded? God may have littered heaven with discarded universes. We are alone, Mr. Sherlock Holmes. No one will come to our aid. All depends upon us alone."

"Mankind has wasted five thousand years upon the delusion of God's existence. If the predictions of Thomas Malthus are correct we will in one hundred or two hundred years, through simply breeding like maggots in a corpse, have strained the ability of this earth to sustain us. We will then turn upon one another like rats at bay and rend each other to bits, while all the while looking over our shoulders for a God to intervene and save us. But I have chosen to intervene. Any chaos that I can bring about if chosen now may avoid a greater chaos later. The strong and the willful accept the burden of their inconsequential lives and seek no forgiveness but their own for the actions that they do, whether they be judged to be good or evil by some system of thought that should rather be engaged in judging itself."

The Professor had spoken throughout this discourse in a hoarse whisper, which was audible to me alone at our remote table. I saw at once the depths of his despair. The position of Professor Moriarty was one that betokened a wound that had become infected until the poisons had gone through all of the tissues of his soul. I began to comprehend why the Professor had always been such a fearful opponent, the very Napoleon of Crime. Crime for the Professor was not crime at all, but the mad assertion of his will. Professor Moriarty was the end result of the thoughts of the arch-heretic Pelagius, who assumed that there was no Original Sin.

If there is no Original Sin, then all humans are doomed to assume that they may become as God knowing good and evil, which means in the last analysis determining good and evil by themselves. If this ultra-Pelagianism was true, then the Professor would be right and all of human virtue would be restricted simply to the will to power. But! And upon this "but" all our sanity and our morality depend: there is such a thing as Original Sin and the results of that sin are ongoing, for that sin has blinded us to God. The words spoken by God to Adam and Eve in Genesis were spoken to their backs. Adam and Eve were already on their way out of Eden and so we have remained as their children alienated to this very day. It is not God who has abandoned us; but it is we who have abandoned God!

This is not a discarded universe in which we are left to ourselves to define good and evil. Our very limitations are the tutors of our compliance to divine law. Charity is the proper response to suffering, not scorn. I knew in that moment that I must probe that ancient wound, which in Professor Moriarty is a double-wound: First, there was Original Sin which afflicts all of humankind and therefore the Professor as well. But there had been another wound, one from which the Professor still suffered, a personal wound. That wound had come close to destroying what I began to realize was potentially a noble soul. Besides his great mind, the Professor has within him a greatness of soul. Perhaps my father had intuited as much and so had paid for the lad's education. The old Latin phrase, which when translated states, "The best when corrupted becomes the worst," comes to mind. Professor Moriarty was dangerous because if not enrolled among the saints, he would gladly serve the devil. He would serve out of his disappointment and despair, those precursors of all evil. He would serve under their tutelage because no man may ever be his own reason for being. We must serve something beyond ourselves and if that something is not God, then what remains for us but to serve evil.

"You are very quiet, Holmes," gloated the Professor. "I thought it just as well to set out at our first meeting the task that lies ahead for you. But you need not feel any immediate pressure. I prefer that the British Empire shall perish at a time of my own choosing and in its most glorious hour. I will delay puncturing the great balloon until its girth expands for a few more years. During that time Mycroft's efforts will undoubtedly add to British prosperity and a few more inches to his own girth as well. You may inform him that you have obtained from me by this meeting a reprieve, but that the clock is still ticking. Mycroft will still admire the genius of his younger brother and you may resume your detective practice in Baker Street. I will keep you informed of events and give you ample warning before the axe finally falls. We may of course have other discussions upon these matters from time to time. At least you now know my position, though I have yet to hear yours. Today's discussion is simply an aperitif for the real meal that will come later. Its purpose is simply to walk the dueling ground together, to decide upon the number of paces, and to choose our weapons. Now, let the duel begin!"

He rose and with a stiff bow was about to leave the table when I asked. "When shall we meet again, Professor?"

He turned and said. "You may wish to remain in Devonshire for a time. I intend to spend the summer at Kings Pyland. I will receive you there at any time that you may choose to visit. I will leave the next topic of our discussion to your choice, since I have taken the majority of our time together today to outline my views. Of course you may always withdraw from the duel, since my scheme is addressed primarily to Mycroft and to the British nation as a whole. You are quite free to resume your rather harmless practice of locating lost jewels and helping governesses decide whether to accept a position. The storm that will break upon England will appear to be quite natural in origin and that is your second little hint."

"Meanwhile your reputation will be secure as will my own. No taint of any crime will appear, so your reputation, such as it is, will remain intact and your business will not suffer as a result of any actions that I will take until the final fruition of my plans, which will be so great that none will think that you might have successfully intervened to stop it."

He smiled most disagreeably before continuing. "In any case I have read your dispatches under the name of Sigerson. Perhaps you were meant to be a travel journalist after all. You may consider abandoning detection as a foible of your youth or better still retire and move on to your beekeeping. You may then become the lord of all those tiny harems of industrious females working away to supply you with honey. You will make the world a sweeter place if not as safer place in which to live. My advice is to leave the sour discipline of religion alone. Religion has never done anything but spoil the few hours of illusory happiness that mortal beings may know. Beekeeping, my dear sir, is a more estimable undertaking. Farewell."

Those were his last words to me. I watched the grim figure of Professor Moriarty cross the room, acknowledging with the briefest of nods the salutations of his colleagues, before disappearing from my view. I resumed my seat heavily. I could see that our battle of wits would not be met with any easy victory for me. I was comforted however by the fact that he had pressed the first assault with such vigor. The old Moriarty would have sat back and allowed me to strike first, so as to know the range of my guns. He clearly hoped to unsettle me and demoralize me from the beginning of our discussions. This makes me think that perhaps his stamina is not what it once was. There was something school-boyish in his mockery of the solemnities of religion that ill becomes a gentleman. Then there was his closing *ad hominum* attack upon me. Am I wrong to sense that he may be more desperate than he appears? In any case I am determined to settle down for a long summer and if necessary to fight a winter campaign.

Dr. Watson's Narrative Continues

So at last the combatants had entered the field of battle. In my case the outcome had long been decided, for I had already cast my lot in with Sherlock Holmes and with the *One, Holy, Catholic and Apostolic Church* that had managed through every trial and tribulation to survive for two millennia. The Church was one, because Jesus had prayed that His followers would be one in charity towards each other. It was holy, because God willed that it should become holy with the help of the grace that the Father would shower out upon those who followed Jesus and therefore received the gift of the Holy Spirit. It was Catholic, because it was universal and all-embracing. Finally the Church was apostolic, because it was commissioned to carry the faith as one sent out to the entire world with its message of salvation.

At this point I could see that Professor Moriarty had devised an entirely different conception of human life than that offered by the Catholic Church. He perceived mankind as alone in an insensate universe. Worse still, he believed that each of us is equally alone and must construct whatever meaning might allow us to prosper and to survive. Even language floated upon a sea of uncertainty so that each constructed narrative was an exercise of arbitrary power. Perception itself was largely a matter of focusing attention upon one of the tiny particles of human experience that we found inexplicably attractive or persuasive, but with no reasonable certainty that this preference was communicable or compelling to anyone who did not coincidentally share that point of view.

I could not but reflect that these questions are for the majority of humankind answered, not by reflection or debate, but by the life-force itself as it is asserted in each new life. As a doctor I have attended my share of childbirths and seen how the great confraternity of women face up to the ultimate price exacted by nature to bring new life into the world. I have seen how the child emerges unprepared from its former comfortable aqueous world into a world of light, of air, and of change. No longer does the infant dwell in that comfortable realm, which must resemble eternity in its silence and its stability. All the extraneous noise of this troubled world is filtered out by the body of its mother who sustains its life. All that remains is the regular beating of the mother's pulse that drives along the essentials of life through the placenta. Is our dream of heaven and of immortality really a recollection of those hours and days and months when all made for sense and safety to this dawning human life?

We do not recapture again that plentitude that nurtures and perfectly fulfils our growing capacities on this side of death. Instead, all that we know, all that we build, all that we create exists in advance of us and we struggle with all of our means to catch up with a reality flying on before us into endless distance. We are a late-stage growth upon this planet. Even at our birth the earth was aged beyond all our conceptions. Countless lives have come and vanished; all that remains of them is the skeletal remnants that resemble nothing so much as the grains of sand along the shore. If there is no grand conservator of all things that have ever been, then time becomes the ultimate agent of mockery to all thinking beings who must witness change not only in the world about them, but within their very being as well.

I would have asked Professor Moriarty if had I been present at that initial meeting, what use can it be to formulate truths that will merely join the eroded paragraphs of all past generalizations so that thought itself becomes the equivalent of the mindless passages of sand blowing like smoke before the winds of night while the sea beats its eternal dirge and the waves keep coming, coming, coming without end.

I imagined asteroids, the very ones that so occupied Professor Moriarty; were they anything more than planetary refuse dodging among the established planets, tracing an irregular and pointless path against the silent background of the stars? Even if their orbits and motions could be frozen and then set again in motion, would not some irregular or unforeseen force soon make tracing their motion and position uncertain and incalculable? And what of entropy, that inscrutable law that would have the entire universe finally terminating in a state of maximum disorder; where was God to be found in all of this?

Was religion after all a tale that children tell each other in the dark to banish their fears? Did religion not entail terrors that were all its own? What is the offer of salvation worth if so many people, according to its own dictates, will fail to achieve it and be punished as a result? Could God have made everything good, as Genesis claims, only to see evil claiming the great majority of humankind and leering at God in triumph as a result? It was against this background of my troubled thoughts that I vowed to continue reading the Journal of Sherlock Holmes and to see if my own intuitions would be supported by one or the other of the two titanic minds and spirits now locked in combat over the nature of both life and death and what may be the purpose of both to the troubled souls upon the earth.

Book Twelve

The End of a Season

Dr. Watson's Narrative Continues

It was September in Newport. Once again I turned from my reading of the journal to resume the adventure that lay close at hand. An armistice had been declared and negotiations for a peace treaty were well underway between the United States of America and Spain. I had always been sensitive to the approach of autumn. That year of 1898 seemed redolent with change and the transfer of power. The century itself was old. The poetry of the *fin de siècle* had about it that peculiar and poignant aura of regret for opportunities wasted and of sorrow for brutal actions committed. The optimism of the age of reason had yielded to the extravagant hopes of the Romantic Period only to see all thought for a new age of mankind drowned in the dull luxury of the reign in France of Louis Philippe from 1830 to 1848, the Europe-wide revolutions that took place in the fateful year of 1848, and the resurgence of reactionary movements that followed with the advent in Germany of Bismarck as Chancellor from 1871 to 1890. The Franco-Prussian War upset the balance of power on the continent while England, secure across the channel, emerged as the supreme power among the imperial empires.

The literary tide had turned and new visionaries emerged to attempt to fulfill the role assigned to them by the poet Percy Bysshe Shelley of being "the unacknowledged legislators of the world." The Victorian Poets in England sounded a new realism and mourned a vanished classicism. That autumn I often read from Matthew Arnold's poems and reflected on these lines from *Dover*

Beach that seemed to sum up so well the prospects for the new century as we left the 19th Century behind:

Ah love, let us be true to one another! for the world, which seems to stand before us like a land of dreams, so various, so beautiful, so new, hath really neither joy, nor love, nor light, nor certitude, nor peace, nor help for pain; and we are here as on a darkling plain swept with confused alarms of struggle and flight, where ignorant armies clash by night.

A mournful aspect had emerged in the verse of Tennyson, Browning, and Arnold as well as in the so-called poets of the decadence. These men sensed that the verities, upon which men and women had long since based their lives, were coming to an end and that nothing short of some great and unprecedented event could act as a final point of punctuation where one historical era ends and another takes its place.

As September proceeded great cloud-wracked thunderstorms advanced upon us from the south. Many days our walks were interrupted and we were confined to the dull rigors of drawing room conversations. My growing familiarity with the people of great wealth that inhabited this little summer colony had relieved my mind of any envy I had once entertained towards them. I saw clearly now that great wealth is more of a mockery of the human condition than a relief from its ills. To be able to afford virtually any material object is only to know with greater clarity that those objects will outlive one and that mere trinkets will survive us as do the seashells when the tiny polyps that had once inhabited them are no more. The condition of man and woman is then revealed as even more irrevocable when the alleviation of so many ills and inconveniences is so close at hand through the abundant use of money. The primal human condition remains still the same.

Pluto, the god of the underworld accepts no tribute and the ferry to the land of the dead asks no fare from us but the cessation of our breath. The rich begin to realize this as they age though they fight against their mortality still, assuming that their money may purchase immunity from the human condition. The women deck their bosoms with pearls that sit awkwardly on the pale and withered flesh. The men grow great bellies and sit about discussing trusts and dividends while their bleary eyes try and focus on an endless series of reports from bankers and lawyers. The young heirs and heiresses go off to Harvard, Yale, or Columbia and have a few summers on yachts, a few grand balls, a glimpse of the glories of Europe on the Grand Tour, and then they too begin the slow decline of age and must face the unsigned withdrawals exacted annually from the bank of time.

The rich are deprived of the simple joys of the poor, who take note of each instance of alleviation of pain and each instance of unexpected felicity with celebration, glad for any respite from their usual state of misery silently born. Truly a rich man will find it difficult to enter the kingdom of heaven, for he will not believe that heaven is a gift when all his life only constant vigilance as to his affairs had approximated a state where things were subservient to his will. To the degree that one imagines himself to be completely fulfilled on this earth, one may judge of his lack of preparation for what is to come. All that we relied upon is taken from us by time. Daily the surfeit of our ashes grows and the fuel that abides is but the charred remnants of our dreams.

Some attempt one last brave assault of the citadel, which has long resisted the trials of prior years in one last attempt to make their lives bear fruit or to carve into the resisting granite of time some minute tribute to a vanished strength. Others may begin one by one to light the long-neglected candles of repentance and to grace their final hours by unlatching the chest of prayer and daring to look into the empty box before them. The poets of the 1890's whose restless slumbers revealed a life misspent, record for us our own ill-composed but no less urgent sense that what youth finds foolishness, age finds undeniable – that time is merciless and that in the regular beating of the sea we hear our own unspoken words of doubt and of reproach.

The poet, Francis Thompson, writes well of this when he says:

I stand amid the dust of the mounded years – my mangled

youth lies dead beneath the heap. My days have crackled and gone up in smoke.

My freshness spent its wavering shower in the dust; and now my heart is as a broken fount, wherein tear-drippings stagnate, spilt down ever from the dank thoughts that shiver upon the sigh-full branches of my mind.

Ernest Dowson has perhaps expressed most beautifully that middle-period where one is still too young to have begun the final descent into death's spiral dance, but where youth has long since been left behind.

They are not long, the weeping and the laughter, love, desire, and hate: I think they have no portion in us after we pass the gate. They are not long the days of wine and roses: Out of a misty dream our path emerges for awhile then closes within a dream."

Sherlock Holmes did not share my autumn melancholy. During the summer he had rallied and there was no trace of the persistent cough that had so alarmed me during the preceding winter. The presence of Irene Adler had acted like a tonic to him and I could not doubt the very real sympathy and mutual understanding that still existed between them. Still, I had watched them carefully during our walks and at the social gatherings over the summer for some sign of a budding romance, but I was unable to perceive signs that would indicate that a love relationship existed between them. The relations between them instead appeared to be an example of one of those rarities in human life, a genuine friendship and equality existing between the sexes.

He listened carefully whenever she spoke and seemed to take delight in her witty observations upon the character and personality of the illustrious people who surrounded us. I could see that her friend, Edith Wharton, also enjoyed her ability to sum up character in a phrase. The summer had been one of those magical periods in life when a company of intelligent minds comes together. I wish now that I had taken better notes so as to be able to reproduce the many subtle and penetrating observations on life, art, and literature made by members of that distinguished company.

Added to the charms of social intercourse during that summer there was the beauty of the scene. I would often sit on a manicured lawn or terrace with a cup of tea or a glass filled with a French Cordial and gaze at the sea or at the ladies whose pastel summer gowns and graceful hats, designed by milliners to keep off the summer sun, would seem to float about the lawns as they joined or parted from various groups.

The dinners were always sumptuous and I am afraid that I added a good three inches to my waist by autumn. Fresh crab and oysters from the bay served on ice were always present and there was roast pheasant and venison from local field and forest to supplement the usual fare. The evenings often featured dancing or a recital from a string quartet. The music would play as the sun sank behind the western trees. The sea would grow dim then and the night would grow enchanted by the flickering lights of fireflies. At last I would smoke a final pipe in the library and when I was already nodding off to sleep would climb the silent stairs to my room.

The weeks had passed all too swiftly for me and now that it was September once again we would soon be on our way. We did not return to New York. Instead we were to take the train through rural New England. Holmes wished to see Concord where Ralph Waldo Emerson, Henry David Thoreau, and Nathaniel Hawthorne had once lived. We would then go to Pittsfield, where Herman Melville had once maintained a farm. Our itinerary would then take us to Lake Winnipesaukee in New Hampshire and then on to Vermont. We also planned to see the great Falls at Niagara in New York and to visit Lake Champlain. Only then would we proceed south to visit the coal regions of Pennsylvania and West Virginia before going on to Washington D.C. where we were to spend the winter.

Irene Adler would return to New York where she was expected for the rehearsal for a new play. It would be difficult for both Holmes and I to say goodbye to her. We took comfort though from the knowledge that her play would be performed over January in Washington when the company began a tour to other cities. We would see her again at that time.

Inspector Hopkins had been absent over the summer. He had been confined to Boston where he was taking a course in police forensics and comparing notes with his American peers regarding methods of investigation as practiced by Scotland Yard and by the American police. We were to meet him in Boston and he would accompany us on our rail journey through New England.

As I packed for our trip and took the last of my walks by the sea, I knew that I was saying goodbye to one more of those precious seasons of life spent in a special place and that even if I was to return at a later date, it would never be quite the same. The moving finger of time allows for no repetition. It is as though the stylus of time writes in granite. No time or hour may be recreated as it once was. We must move on and hope that what lies before us may be as fair as the past. How short are such periods of repose in a busy life! Having once found contentment anywhere it is only natural to loathe to leave it and to begin the great journey of pursuit and discovery once again.

Sherlock Holmes had arranged with Mycroft prior to our departure a system by which he could be kept informed of all events that might impact the success of our American mission. The news of the summer had been for the most part slight and inconsequential. We knew that Baron Maupertuis had purchased a substantial controlling interest in the Greater Dutch Canal Company and that he had accomplished this through several interlocking directorates, trusts, and corporate entities. As was customary with him his name appeared nowhere, but his presence could be inferred through lists of major stockholders obtained by sources on the continent working for the British government. The shares of the company were still listed with the London Stock exchange and the price had vacillated over the summer. At every fall in price, the Baron had increased his number of shares in the company by buying out the initial investors, which included many British Banks.

The company had already begun operations in Central America with the purchase of the railroad that had been built so many years ago in Costa Rica by American investors with the cooperation of the dictator Don Juan Murillo, the Tiger of San Pedro. That purchase was a wise move by the company. The American investors desired nothing more than to divest their ownership of a railroad that was linked with scandal since the publication in Europe of extracts from the Murillo papers, the forgeries in control of Baron Maupertuis. Even most Americans were now aware that the railroad had been built with slave labor gathered from many nations and that the railroad had been built under conditions of extreme squalor and brutality.

The Greater Dutch Canal Company was now in possession of one of the major railroad transit points for goods crossing the barrier of the Americas. Until a canal could be built, the railroad would be the shortest point of transit for goods traveling between the two oceans. Since the building of a canal still remained somewhat speculative, the company's ownership of an actual producing rail asset had caused the stock to rise precipitately, once the news of the acquisition became public knowledge in Europe. It was at this time that Sir Henry Baskerville sold the last of the shares that he had acquired when the company was first underwritten. His name and resources had added to the prestige of the venture in those early days and Mycroft had arranged that other well-placed British investors would provide an impressive list of incorporators.

After acquiring a controlling interest in the company, Baron Maupertuis had changed the initial board of directors. Its operations were gradually assuming a more sinister nature. The Baron was unconcerned with any public outrage that might affect his shares since his ultimate ownership remained secret in any case. He had learned from the tolerance shown to rubber operations in the Congo Free State that oppression in remote regions of the world often remains unnoticed. This region of Africa was a virtual personal colony of King Leopold of Belgium. The darkest rumors were beginning to circulate at the time about the Congo, including tales of severed limbs in order to instill fear in the native population and to increase production. It was no doubt clear therefore to Baron Maupertuis that any atrocities would be tolerated in precisely such out of the way regions where the profits to be obtained were great.

At the time of which I write the American conscience had yet to extend its early idealism that recognized certain universal rights of man to all races of the earth. Although the Costa Rican railroad had been sold there was still virtual slave labor on the fruit plantations in places such as Guatemala. If Americans were behind the Europeans in atrocities visited upon subject peoples, there was still time to close that initial lead. The initial plan was for us to wait until Baron Maupertuis was all in and for the initial British investors to gradually slip away. We would then spring the trap by revealing that the papers controlled by the Baron were forgeries. This would vindicate the American financiers that had made it possible for the coast-to-coast railroad in Costa Rica to be constructed during the Don Juan Murillo administration. A burst of nationalist enthusiasm would follow and the Americans would throw their support behind the building of a canal. The Greater Dutch Canal Company would be placed under severe competition and as a private company could probably not compete with the American government acting within its own hemisphere. This in turn would cause the company's stock value to collapse and Baron Maupertuis would be financially ruined in consequence.

Now the unforeseen war with Spain and the American victory would seem to make our own efforts less necessary if our revelations were calculated primarily to reinstate American pride and ambition to build a canal. The stimulus to build a canal was now far more likely to come from a desire to trade with Hawaii and to retain control of the Philippines. In any case the Baron's initial success did not trouble my friend. Holmes had read of events over the summer with interest and satisfaction.

he man is playing his major pierces, Watson," Holmes said to me one day. "This is what I have been anticipating. He could hardly keep the company together by simply doing engineering studies in Central America. He needed an actual acquisition of some sort. He will now be committed to Costa Rica. If there is a bid to build an American canal it will make his railroad useless. He will therefore do everything that he can to prevent the spread of American hegemony in Central America. That hegemony is already deeply entrenched however by the American victory in its war with Spain. American companies now control most of the assets and governments of Guatemala, Costa Rica, and Nicaragua, while the British are confined to Honduras. I can foresee a great struggle for domination emerging in that poor region of the world."

"The Baron, once having sunk his fangs into the kill, will not easily surrender his position, even though it is a minority one at present. If we can fan the flames of the American appetite to build a canal there soon, it will threaten the position of the Baron. By annexing the Hawaiian Islands and by gaining control of the Philippines the government of the United States has declared its intention to dominate the Pacific region. It simply must have a canal if it is to be successful in its bid for dominion there. Otherwise Japan and even Russia will threaten that dominion. Then there are the French who are in Indochina and the Marquesas while the Dutch control the Indonesian Archipelago."

"A pattern is emerging Watson. Spain has been eliminated as a contender and the sun of Portugal has long since set. The great struggles of the new century will be between Great Britain, France, Germany, the United States, Russia, and perhaps Japan. The Dutch cannot be counted out though, not as long as a man like Baron Maupertuis exists. He has bet his all on this venture. If he succeeds and is able to build the canal, he opens up trade with Indonesia from a western route without going around Cape Horn or the Cape of Good Hope. He dare not let such an opportunity to escape! The man is well within our trap; we must only spring it when the time comes, so that the door behind him closes.”

“He can always sell his shares if they begin to decline,” I objected.

“That he will never do,” answered Holmes. “The Baron is a man who cannot admit an error of judgment of such a magnitude. He has pledged everything on the success of this venture. His reputation would never recover from such a blow. He is at that time of life where one last coup is essential to his self-esteem. For him the building of this historically significant canal would be to join the immortals, the builders of the pyramids, the likes of Columbus and Magellan. No, he will not retreat. His character will not allow it. I have known from the first that I was dealing with a man for whom retreat is impossible. To know a man’s fundamental flaw is the secret of attaining power over him. Every man possesses at least one fundamental flaw; but it often takes the devil himself to find it.”

“My own role in this affair has been an unsavory one from the start. I have had to use the devil’s own tricks to defeat a devil in human form, Baron Maupertuis. He is a man before whose evil even that once shown by Professor Moriarty is as nothing. The Professor’s evil was of a sort of principled evil in which there is always a spark of goodness. The Baron’s evil is of another sort entirely. The Baron believes that he is a sort of god. He is still of the mind of Adam and Eve in the first blush of their illusion of triumph, when they thought that they could face God eye to eye as gods themselves. It was only then that they discovered the trick, that they were naked and that any glory that they imagined for themselves was only derivative of the love of God for them.”

“To awaken to the fact that it is the love of another that bestows upon us our own beauty and goodness, and that what is kept within us as a possession is only our nakedness; that is to know the difference between good and evil, which is finally the difference between necessary and contingent being. The derivative goodness of contingent being turns to God, just as a flower turns toward the sun and becomes radiant in its gaze. Evil in contrast turns in upon itself and franticly tries to illumine its own darkness only finding that it cannot do so out of its own derivative nature. No creature may ever be like God except insofar as God allows it as a gift and not a possession."

I saw at last why it was that Holmes who was a proud man himself and one who did not tolerate failure easily had become after all a great exponent of Augustinian thought. The problem with Pelagianism and the reason that it is a heresy is that it flatters the vanity of man. Only Augustine and perhaps Saint Paul fully realized the need of man and woman for a savior. Saint Paul knew that the law can never redeem mankind. No man may both keep the law and avoid pride in doing so. The beginning of the moral journey is the conviction of our own inability to conform in all respects to what is ultimately in our best interest.

Radical hope must therefore be preceded by an equally radical despair. Holmes had been broken time and again. He was a man who treasured vitality, yet he labored under the mortal threat of tuberculosis. He sought to find God by searching among the great religions of the world, yet it was always God who was searching for Sherlock Holmes who had once denied His very existence when I first made his acquaintance. St. Paul's conversion was similarly preceded by blindness and helplessness. He had to be led to Damascus.

Even the Apostles needed first to be sent, for no one may choose his own mission. We are placed by God's providence in tiny places, places that we may deem unworthy of the great dreams that we once entertained of our destiny. Each of us would with to be a hero of the short drama that is our lives, but we awaken with the coming of age to realize that all that we have achieved is still short of the glory of God. Even the great St. Thomas Aquinas called his great *Summa Theologica* mere straw compared to what God had shown him in prayer. To stand then, not simply before our sins, but also before our virtues and to attribute all things to grace and not to our own efforts; therein lies the humility that opens the gates of heaven.

These were my thoughts and reflections as that blessed summer of 1898 neared its end. I spent the last days of our sojourn among the fabulously wealthy denizens of Newport in long walks down the lane that connected the carriage drives to the various manor houses along the sea cliffs. I thought often of my own simple home in Cornwall by my own quiet bay. Surely my life there lacked nothing. My wine cellar, if not as filled with expensive vintages, was adequate to my tastes. I did not need to feel the burdens upon my conscience that must come with great responsibility. I had power over no other human being. Even my housekeeper would consider that it was she who controlled matters as she kept my house up to her own high standards of cleanliness and order. My years with Sherlock Holmes had accustomed me to the presence of clutter and disorder, which were anathema to the new regimen that she imposed upon me. I learned to eat vegetables in season and to strengthen my teeth upon the crunch of undercooked greens. That woman was of the opinion that too much cooking "boils the life right out of them," and perhaps she was right. My life in England then was such as a man might live who called his soul his own, the exercise of simplicity and the quiet virtues that one may know by one's own fireside and humble hearth in a Cornish village.

It may seem strange in a world of men bent on the acquisition of wealth, power, and fame to hear me extol a life of simplicity and obscurity. It may even seem disingenuous for me to proclaim these virtues to be present in Holmes as well when I had done all in my power to publicize his name and make him famous across three continents. These efforts of mine were motivated though by more than a desire to create a national hero or to acquire literary fame by riding along in the shadow of the great man.

My desire was always to celebrate the man as well as to celebration his methods. In my own way I desired to create a school of the art of detection. It was always my belief that Holmes reached his remarkable conclusions by a conjunction of acute observation and attention to facts that could then be set against various templates of human nature based upon his innate grasp of human motivations. For this reason I did not abjure romance because I felt that there is something romantic in all situations of human conflict and desperation.

Most of our clients were in situations that a doctor calls, being in extremity. They came to Holmes when every other avenue had failed, hoping that he might see the light where they saw only darkness. My stories then were accounts of gradual illumination and the reader by following me could see how from chaos a certain order emerged in events. Is it not this the very assurance that is provided by religious faith? Is it not this very order that is the primary benefit of living a simple life? It seems to me that to be beset by constant demands is to be deprived of all satisfaction. Desires that are too widely dispersed leave one feeling each day as though one's vital forces have been similarly scattered. From this diffusion of energy and commitment comes anxiety and unrest.

In contrast is that sense of identity and integrity that will allow a man to proceed to meet any challenge in life or if fate should so decree even surrender his life at a moment's notice. What fate can be more disastrous than to be summoned forth out of life by sudden death while possessing no idea who one even is, because the pace of life has allowed no time for reflection? It takes leisure and concentration and a habit of contemplation if one is to assemble a central core out of the many conflicting motivations and desires that assault us daily. So many lives fail in seems to me for want of an axis about which all else must revolve. That axis is what Holmes always sought and I did also in imitation of my friend.

When I returned to Holmes' journal I was to discover that his travels had brought him to a new determination: to take up life in a quiet cottage in an obscure corner of England and very close to Baskerville Hall!

From the Journal of Sherlock Holmes

May 28, 1893
Exeter Train Station

I do not intend to tarry long in Exeter after my first discussion with Professor Moriarty. I know that he will be finishing his lecture series and classes and giving exams before the beginning of the Great Vacation when he will return to Kings Pyland. He has already indicated that our discussions, if one may term them such, will take place over an extended period. I have no choice but to comply and to see as we go on how we progress. He cannot be arrested for a crime that he has yet to commit and even a conspiracy, if there is one, may be sufficiently indefinite and remote at this point as to foreclose proof that he has anything actually criminal in mind.   Whatever he intends will require a means beyond imagining in order to match his threat. The upshot of all of this is that I must devise a way to ensconce myself for a time upon Dartmoor where I can be close at hand. I did not imagine that I would ever pursue an investigation here again after that most perplexing, and in the end horrific adventure, of the Hound of the Baskervilles, a story which has yet to appear in print. Watson may someday share it with his reading public.

I will clearly need to acquire a small domicile near here. To that end I have consulted with a firm of land-agents in Exeter. A young chap by the name of Gour Abernathy has agreed to accompany me by train from Exeter to show me a cottage, one with its own grounds, that is not far from Grimpen-on-Moor.

It may just suit my needs. Its situation lies close to my friend, Sir Henry Baskerville, so that I need not want for company should I require it. The cottage itself is sturdy and could be altered to fit any particular requirements that I might have. The economy of England has been for some time in a depressed state that has affected prices in the rural counties more than in the cities. Here commerce has declined into a virtual desert condition. The result is that the price being asked for the property astounded me and the land-agent intimates that any reasonable offer I might care to make may elicit a favorable response. Ah here is the man himself just coming through the turnstile onto the platform. I shall continue this later.

May 29, 1893
Grimpen

The result of all of this was that I soon found myself aboard the small steam locomotive that links Exeter, Launceston, Fernworthy, and Grimpen and then goes on to Taunton, Barnstaple, Ilfracomb, and Clovelly and the other hamlets on Exmoor that borders the Bristol Channel. The land-agent is a voluble chap and he gave me all the information that I need in order to appreciate what he calls, "the glories of Devon."

"Some calls it bleak," said he. "It is nothing of the sort; it is England's Riviera. You may easily reach the sea from any point for a quick holiday. In addition there are the charms available for the student of history, for geologists, and for antiquarians. The moors themselves are like a stormy sea with its great hills and tors. We are warmer here than in most parts of England and the winters are mild, not like the bitter cold of the Yorkshire Moors. The big landowner down here is Sir Henry Baskerville who is married to a great beauty of some Spanish extraction. The two of them have a great reputation here for philanthropy. They have built a free school for the village children of Grimpen and brought in agricultural specialists to help the farmers of the district. If you like colorful stories there is one that he was once stalked, or even attacked some folks say, several years ago by a giant hound. Very mysterious it all was! The beast was killed and Sir Henry suffered no lasting ill effects from the incident, which is a great cause of joy to the many people who have been helped since by his ministrations. As for Grimpen, well there is not much to speak of there, just a village Church and a small Catholic Chapel, a pub, a general goods store, and a wee bit of a library started by Sir Henry. But as you say that you desire quiet and peace the village should be well to your liking. The only other establishment of note in these parts, besides Baskerville Hall, is the stables over the moors at Kings Pyland. Excellent racehorses come from there."

"Who owns the stables then?" I inquired, seeking to hear something of the Professor's reputation.

"They are owned by a strange fellow, bit of a Professor, you know. Keeps to himself he does, not the sort you might picture as a sportsman. Still, there's a tale about that no man knows horses any better. He has an uncanny knack with them, sort of what we call a horse-whisperer. He can calm a horse down in the paddocks by a mere word or look or gesture. He comes down to Exeter on occasion to give a course or lecture at the university. Bright chap, from all that I hear, knows all about stars and comets and such. Beyond that there is not much more that I can tell you. You will be left to yourself if that is what you wish or you may seek company among the few gentry of the parish. As for the cottage, it is built like a fortress so you won't feel any winter gales howling in as they do at times in winter. There are two guest rooms and a fine central hall on two levels. There is a kitchen and a pantry as well. The grounds contain a garden that could be brought back in a trice with a bit of labor and there is an attached orchard with apples, plums, figs, and cherries. It has been empty for a year so the price of the whole isn't half what it ought to fetch. Quite a bargain and that's for certain! Anyway we have a few places in town also and if you wish we can proceed on to Barnstaple or Ilfracomb if you want a place with an overview of the channel."

"No, I prefer the shelter of being inland and the community

you describe sounds like it will just meet my requirements," I reassured him.

"Well, that's alright then," said he with a little squirm of pleasure. "Sales haven't been what they once were and I hate to see such a lovely place going untenanted. And don't give any thought to tales of Druid spirits and fairies and such. This is a quaint region and its folk have their superstitions. There are Christian folk that won't go abroad on Beltane and Lughnassa, but these are celebrated in this region still. If there are any devils on the moors they are locked up tight at the prison at Princeton. The last escape was a man called Seldon but that was some years ago now. The country folk are poor but honest."

I put fears to rest by assuring him that I had no fear of will-o-the wisps or goblins. At this he subsided into a satisfied silence and I was able to transfer my attention to the lovely hamlets that we passed along the way and to the great sweep of the moors which were green and lush at this season of the year. I liked the part about the garden at my proposed cottage. I could hire some local help to restore it and put out a few bee-hives for honey.

I thought at first of proposing a leasing contract of the place, although I have always wanted to possess a bit of land of my own. I could also decide after all to purchase the place outright. It might be a good investment for some funds that I possess in the form of a trust from the Holmes estate that has been growing for some years through various conservative railroads and shipping investments. In any case when I retire I can always sell it and go off to France or buy a townhouse in Bloomsbury. I have spoken to Watson over the years of Sussex as a possible retirement site also in order to be close to Canterbury and the Oratory located there. I have even hinted at beekeeping as a possible avocation, but the notion has always been somewhat whimsical although the dear fellow may have taken me too seriously.

Devonshire will do quite well for now. I have no idea at this time how long my contest with Professor Moriarty may take or how many moves there will be in the game we are playing. I shall certainly seek him out at every possible opportunity as we thrash it all out between us. I did receive one clue from the land-agent's discourse. Apparently the Professor still retains his love of horses, a trait that I recall he possessed in his youth. The sympathy that he lacks for his own species seems to have been reserved for the animals. But since sympathy of any sort may be the beginnings of grace in operation, I shall attempt to build upon it since I am deprived of any more obvious point of entry. It is not much of a starting point perhaps, but I must follow the example of Our Lord and take each soul as I find it.

At last we stopped at the way-side halt at the village of Coombe Tracey. We needed to take a carriage from there to Grimpen, which is just off of the rail line. We disembarked and had a bit of lunch there before hiring a carriage. My baggage was soon aboard and we were off behind a fine pair of bays through the moorlands en route for Grimpen. The carriage seemed to me like a vessel with its bow cleaving the sea-like land before us. The great waves of the moors slipped away on either side as we pursued the narrow track that wound about the hillocks and the piles of rude boulders that surrounded us. I saw again the old stone huts in one of which I had resided for a time during that strange autumnal period several years ago when I was engaged in helping Sir Henry to lay to rest the familial curse of the spectral hound.

I seemed again to hear the strange baying of the beast at night that echoed over the Great Grimpen Mire, that region of bogs and sinkholes. I recalled that strange man, Stapleton, who had combined a fascination with nature with contempt for mankind. Even nature however was treated by him as a possession. He had a passion for classification, as though all knowledge consisted of transcribing a reproduction of events upon the blank slate of the human mind. Surely knowledge requires more than a mere tracing out of formulae and equations. To describe nature, even if that description is accurate, is still not the thing itself, the *ding an sich* as Kant refers to it in his philosophy. If all that we call knowledge is only a grasping at the slippery surface of things, then we cannot really know them. True knowledge is more akin to participation, to engagement, and even to play.

221

This means that what we call knowledge is only the coordination of accidental qualities possessed by some inner essence that we can never grasp. This entails that all of our images of things are metaphors at best. We know only qualities, as John Locke would say. Some of those qualities are not even inherent in the source of our perception, but only appear as they are translated through our sensory apparatus so that they can become meaningful and useful to us. There is a principle of selection based upon prior acquaintance even in elementary perception. Knowledge is to that extent never value-free, because there is a selective criterion applied by how we direct our attention toward things. What we call knowledge is less a direct apprehension than it is a turning away from what we do not wish to perceive and regard as irrelevant to our present inquiry.

For instance there is the entire question of useless knowledge, which is a neglected area of philosophy. Human beings desire what they call knowledge primarily so that human existence may be oriented to the world and to use its resources to procure the necessities of life. Our animal nature is never left far behind us. My summary expression for of all of this is that we know as any primate knows. Monkey see, monkey do!

We know little of the languages of the great cetaceans, of the whales and the dolphins; but I have imagined that these ancient and intelligent creatures, whose evolution precedes our own, may be vast reservoirs of adaptation and insight into the global environment of water that surrounds them. They do not need to manipulate nature as primates do, so knowledge of hand-to-eye relationships is unnecessary for them. Instead they live within an amniotic and acoustic world of their deep soundings.

They leap into the ambient air as if into a foreign element otherwise necessary to them only for breathing. They exhibit no nostalgia for access to the land, for them the sea is all in all. If the great whales comprehend anything at all, then that comprehension must be much closer to the thing in itself, a vast contemplation of existence as mediated through sound and the sense of touch. Perhaps what we call science is only monkey knowledge, adapted to our own capacities as primates and our primate interests and not the thing in itself at all. But these are fanciful conceptions since the various species have yet to bridge the gap of communication. It is quite enough for us to communicate with other human beings.

Perhaps the whales though have found a philosophy and a language to express some great epic narrative of the world in which they live. But perhaps they could never communicate those insights to us, because our brains are structured to receive different impressions and to interpret them differently. We are condemned to having "monkey minds," so we act and react like monkeys, chattering to one another of our finds, our discoveries, and meanwhile gathering up as many bananas as possible to keep in a secret hoard.

At least I have met the Professor at last. His summary lecture, even if not a final synthesis or statement of faith at least serves to focus our joint thinking by providing a point of departure. During recent days I have thought often of his search for a science or a philosophy that could exist without prior axioms as a foundation from which to build. Of course as a theist I am committed to the idea that only God can manage without axioms, because only God was present as the first cause of all things; everything else is contingent upon something prior to it in time. An axiom serves the function of setting a point of departure for further reasoning, usually because it is self-evident; yet it is more than an arbitrary assignment. The axiom serves as a primary definition, a place to begin while resisting any desire or compulsion to peer behind the curtain of appearances.

If I had thought that the time was apropos I would have posed a question to Professor Moriarty that might have functioned as my own opening gambit. I would have pointed out that no matter what position he decides to take regarding the world within which he exists it is impossible to escape from prior meanings or to step out of language and then to re-create it so as to arrive at different conclusions. It is the fact that the world is already given to us that restricts us to understanding it on its own terms – where good and evil already exist.

We can dispute the definitions of those terms, but the human mind continually returns to the intuition that something is fundamentally wrong with the world in which we live. The problem with good/evil is that like most binary terms they are subject to being hijacked and assigned to things, persons, or events at our convenience. This tendency to assign evil is perhaps the best definition of evil.

I was interrupted in my meditations by the sudden appearance of a village steeple in front of us as we rounded a bend. It was a sign that we were approaching the village. Grimpen, floating about like Melville's ship Rachel looking for its children. Few people lived here who were not born here as well. Has Grimpen found in me another orphan? Will I cling to this obscure outpost as my only source of civilization during the months or perhaps years ahead? At least Sir Henry and his dear wife are here. I also remember Mr. Franklin and of course the obsessive anthropologist, Dr. Mortimer. He once announced that he coveted my skull as a possession, after my natural demise of course.

Dr. Mortimer at least shares with me a passion for archeological investigations and a fascination with the Druids that once inhabited this region of England. Perhaps I can spare a bit of time to seek for those ruins and artifacts that would indicate the presence of ancient Chaldean traders along the shores of Cornwall and Devonshire. My evidence of this is that tin-mining has flourished here since ancient times. It is a pet theory of mine that the populace here was also seasoned with ancient near-eastern beliefs before the advent of Christianity, which therefore found here a natural root among the former pagan inhabitants.

I have no idea when or how often I will be called over to Kings Pyland for an intensive debate with the Professor. I am forced to assume then the uncomfortable position of simply waiting to be summoned. During recent years I have gone where and when I wished throughout vast regions of the earth. Now I am to be hemmed in by the moors and in the society of simple farming folk who are content to read only the Bible and The Book of Common Prayer, if they are able to read at all. For most of these people theological controversy is simply unnecessary. Is not the Queen the anointed head of the Church in England? For them the local Vicar knows what to say even if like last week his sermon was, in their collective opinion, "a long time in the hearing."

What would folk such as these care for the questions that divide Professor Moriarty and me? I recently asked our old gate-keeper at Sigerside during my visit home if he ever considered becoming a Catholic. His direct answer had amused me, "What? Me follow that Italian fellow with the pointy hat? No, Mr. Sherlock, I'm English pure through. The Queen has what one might call advisors and the Queen now; she ain't Catholic is she? I'm a poor man and I ain't got bishops to advise me, but I thinks to myself, why shouldn't I use the same what advises the queen? When they advise her to become a Catholic, why I'll just tag along at that time! Besides I'm that old that I don't want to be a-learnen a new set of hymns."

I decided to leave his conscience thereafter in peace. To extinguish a partial grasp of dogma only to replace it with something even more dimly understood might have left him with no faith at all. For this same reason I try not to unsettle the fundamentalists among us. I prefer not to debate how many species were lost forever because they did not survive the cramped quarters on Noah's ark. The inclusion of an elephant pair undoubtedly extinguished many lesser creatures trod into non-distinguishable organic mush in the bottom of the boat.

We had no sooner glimpsed Grimpen than we passed it by and moved off toward some marshy lands with great dark grey and black patches where the Great Grimpen Mire begins. After a bit I saw in the distance the towers of Baskerville Hall as they emerged now and again over the hilltops. We must have been about four miles away at that point, though it was further still by carriage, for the earthen carriage paths were such that one could not follow a direct route to the Hall.

"The cottage is just ahead," said the agent sitting at my side and sure enough we rounded a bend and there it lay, as pretty a little place as I have ever seen. There was a small court in front paved with cobblestones and a great elm tree lay along one side of the house. The roof was made of slate, scoured clean by the winter winds. A bit of ivy twined around the window of what I took to be the sitting room. The entire cottage lay elevated on a small knoll so that it must appear somewhat like a fortress to any intruder. The front door was inset into the granite walls and the windows, which were thick and made of leaded glass, were inset as well. The second story was topped by twin gables and a small central tower, about six feet in height above the roof, allowed for a view in all directions over the moor. The small room at the top of the tower was reached by a winding stair.

I was later given to understand that it had been built by a retired sea captain some sixty years ago. Its unusual architectural scheme showed traces of the tall sailing ships that had been for so many years the man's only home. The land-agent placed his key in the lock and soon the great oak door, set with carvings, brass, and ornamental figures, swung open to reveal the dark hallway beyond. The place was unfurnished, which was just as well, since I prefer my own choice of cabinets, chests, and book cases. The entire place was as solid, as if it anticipated sailing off the moment the anchor was raised.

The cottage had been well-maintained. The wainscoting was not worm-eaten or rotten, for it was made of solid teak. The stairs did not make a sound when I climbed them to the tower above. The entire place was silent and snug. No drafts would wend their sinuous way through it. It had been lived in most recently by the Sea Captain's son until two years ago when that worthy gentleman had decided to spend his own last years in America.

It had been untenanted ever since, but still kept clean by a charwoman from the village. She was willing to stay on it appeared if I would be pleased to retain her services. The below-stairs fireplace was large and there were also fireplaces in the two bedrooms upstairs. The ground floor consisted of a large sitting room, a great warm kitchen, a pantry and servant quarters, and a bedroom for the master of the house.

There was ample storage space throughout and a root cellar for refrigeration. The central tower room, which acted as a sort of observatory, could be used as an indoor reading room on winter days. It rose above the level of the fog shrouds coming from the Grimpen Mire that often blanket the surrounding region. From it I was just able to see Baskerville Hall in the near distance.

I do not know whether my profession is most responsible for my ability to reach quick conclusions when necessary or when action demands it. But in any case my mind worked swiftly in this instance. After being shown about for an hour of careful inspection, during which I'm afraid that I asked a great many questions to the consternation of my patient guide, I turned to the house-agent and simply said, "Very well, this will do nicely. I will take it."

June 1, 1893
Grimpen

I am writing this entry in my room above the humble local public house called the Grimpen Arms where I have retained a bed and sitting room until the furnishings that I have ordered arrives. The last few days have been extraordinarily busy ones. After viewing the cottage and hearing all manner of details from the well that supplies my water, to the lavatory and laundry facility located on the lower level of the property to facilitate draining. After exploring the borders of the grounds that go with the dwelling, I am even more satisfied with my decision to settle here.

After my inspection of the premises we took the carriage back to the larger village of Coombe Tracey where we were able to procure overnight rooms at the Golden Dragon Hotel. From there we sought out a solicitor to review all the necessary papers. He met with us on the following day and gave a favorable report on the title from the local land office. I signed the necessary papers at once, including a draft on my bank in London, and the matter was settled.

I now have, not a mere collection of rooms, but a home. I must say that I am startled at my own speed in making so momentous and uncustomary a decision. Perhaps the habit of needing to resolve matters swiftly in dangerous regions during my travels has strengthened my ability to weigh all the necessary factors and to determine an immediate course of action. In this particular instance the decision was made easier by the fact that I have always loved Devonshire. The strange and haunted scenery reminds me of my youth spent on the moors of Yorkshire. I appreciate the openness of the hearty people who manage to eke out a living from such an outwardly hostile environment. The sea is close and the weather is mild for England. Besides, my good friend, Sir Henry Baskerville, is within a short walk from my cottage.

But above all I am close to Moriarty, the man who has a priority claim upon my professional attention at this critical time. If I should fail the Professor will make good his threat and all of England is at risk. I have no doubt that even should his plan succeed, he at least will be apprehended and held based upon what I will be able to discover before his plot goes into actual operation, yet I have the feeling that Moriarty is indifferent to his own capture as long as his plan succeeds. He is pursuing his course with unaccustomed passion and personal commitment, while making every effort to complete his research and to pass on his knowledge to students before the hour arrives when he may need to surrender his liberty to Scotland Yard. He is like a man pursued by the specter of death who is rushing onwards to complete his life's work.

I understand this frame of mind, for I am engaged in something of the same quest, to formulate my own theological synthesis in this journal. Of course as a mere member of the non-ordained laity my speculations and conclusions must be seen as tentative and subject to correction by higher authority. In this sense my journal is merely a prolegomenon to theology rather than theology itself. Its ultimate function then is more to submit questions that only the Catholic hierarchy can answer rather than to assume that my synthesis, no matter how enthusiastically and persuasively presented is true.

To everyone but the simple and the sensual life must pose a problem, what the great philosopher, Arthur Schopenhauer, calls the need for metaphysics, which may be an even greater need than the need for religion! Religion is the remedy, whereas the need for metaphysics must remain even for those persons who reject the answers posed by various religious doctrines. Professor Moriarty is no exception to this rule. It is not enough for him to be a simple criminal or to lose himself as does Colonel Sebastian Moran in hunting, gaming, and women. For Professor Moriarty, as for me, the drive toward a general explanation of all things is the supreme challenge. He must explain existence to his own satisfaction or leave this life with bitterness and disappointment, not in the universe, but in his own inability to solve its riddles.

Why does this need to comprehend everything exist in some men more than others? Why spend a lifetime filling a skull with knowledge when after death the skull may contain only the equivalent of two cups of sand? What is knowledge finally but a transient excitation of the nerves and not even a guarantee of happiness? The pursuit of such global and universal knowledge is often a prelude to despair rather than the way to happiness if it does not yield finally to the hope of reunion with God. If the pursuit of faith is deemed to be a vain pursuit, then how much more is such knowledge vain when acquired by a materialist or an atheist? Why should a man work all of his life merely to prove that the brain within the skull is the equivalent of a soft snail within its shell? Is atheism such a comfort after all that a man must exert so much labor only to prove that he is nothing after all? If there is no God, then we are all on our own and we can hope for no greater purpose and futurity than the brief years and decades of our troubled and inadequate existence on this earth.

Each year I develop new interests and my bookshelves

grow exponentially to accommodate new volumes. Each year another language beckons for me to learn it. I would gladly acquire Gaelic and Chinese, but of what use would these be to me in my retirement years, which now loom ever closer. I would learn Chinese only in time to read the lamentations of the melancholy Chinese poet, Li Po. I would no sooner learn Gaelic when the Banshee would be keening at my door to foretell my death. This forces me to an unaccustomed selectivity in every book I now read. I know that each such choice precludes other volumes that will then be left unread. I even forebear to write a will, for to do so would be to admit that the reading tasks that I have laid up for myself will never be accomplished.

Instead I will leave to my heirs a library of unread volumes and partial manuscripts, which will be only hints of the grand synthesis that I dreamed of leaving behind me. Even should I record here all my conclusions I would be tempted to add innumerable later supplements and appendices to modify the very conclusions that I had reached with such effort in the main body of the work. But then I comfort myself with the thought that it is a poor artist who does not die with a new canvass stretched upon his easel. If Professor Moriarty is like me at all, he will not be satisfied with this plot of his alone, but will dream of destroying future empires. But first he must defeat me, a task that has occupied him for most of the years of his life.

Or has Moriarty made England and England alone the focus of his ire. But why should England be the target of his especial wrath? If chaos is his goal, as he told me it was during our first discussion, why has he concentrated what may be the last major effort of his life to produce such chaos first at home rather than in the even worse governing structures and jurisdictions that prevail in other places like Germany or Austria? I suddenly realize that I have just discovered my first clue in my effort to bring the beast in Professor Moriarty to bay.

June 2, 1893
Baskerville Hall

Today I paid my first visit in many years to Baskerville Hall. I gave my card to the servant, who has replaced Barrymore as the Butler, and a minute later Sir Henry rushed into the hall, crossing that immense space at a remarkable rate, he came up and embraced me in his enthusiasm at seeing me.

"Sherlock Holmes! Can it be? My heavens man, I trust you are not some phantom from the moors? No indeed, for I feel strong flesh beneath my grip upon your shoulder. But this cannot be! Dr. Watson wrote me the sad news of your death in Switzerland. He did not give me any details, but I understood it was due to some climbing accident in the mountains. He told me that he was engaged in writing an account of your last adventure together, but if he has done so, it has yet to be published since I never received the promised advance copy. I tell you that you have been mourned sir, not only in this household, but among our friends who still recall your assistance rendered in that affair that almost cost me my life."

He was still out of breath with excitement at seeing me, so to put him at his ease I took up the burden of discourse between us.

"I trust that you have not been troubled since by devil-hounds from hell, Sir Henry, and that I am the only specter whom you have encountered? Excellent! We have laid to rest at last then your family's curse. Yes, it is true, I am alive and I will explain matters fully if we may sit down in your estimable library for an hour. I trust that I am not interrupting important business for you elsewhere, but I did not wish you to hear of the new tenant at the small estate over the hill and think that I had delayed paying my respects to you and to your dear wife."

Sir Henry answered in some surprise at my announcement, "I know the place that you speak of well. But it has been empty for some time! So you have taken it! You might have put up indefinitely here at the hall you know. I assure you that you would have been and are most welcome, my very dear fellow."

Sir Henry said these words with the great openness and hospitality of one who had in his past shared only a tent or cabin in his former life in the wilds of Canada. There are ways in which Sir Henry still retains the common touch of the democracies of the new world. I am happy to see that he has yet to assume those airs of a British Lord that would have been foreign to his character that still retains the charm of the young frontiersman whom I first met several years ago in London.

"You must not think of it, Sir Henry," said I. "I assure you that I shall be quite comfortable in my new abode, though I do hope that I may see a great deal of you now that we are to be neighbors. Besides, I am a man of irregular habits and it is better that I maintain my own domicile. It will be my first actual home you know and I am looking forward to moving in with the furnishings that I was able to purchase by order from Plymouth to be sent to Coombe Tracey and then onwards to Grimpen."

Sir Henry still protested, "Good heavens man, we have scores of rooms here that remain unused, all of them furnished to the hilt. If you would not object to gold-brocade, you are most welcome to take your pick of anything that appeals to you. In any case I shall send over some of my servants and farm hands to assist you in moving in. Where are you staying for the present, The Grimpen Arms? Nonsense! I shall send Perkins over to pick up your things at once. You shall remain with us until your house is cleaned, well stocked with food and provisions, and your furnishings are installed. My wife would insist upon it. She is away for the day visiting the elderly among our tenants, but she will be as delighted as I am to see you once again. Here, let us retire to the library. Perkins, this is my good friend, Mr. Sherlock Holmes, of whom you have heard me speak. I think we will have some Madeira in the library and some sandwiches if you will inform cook. There's the good fellow."

Perkins bowed and we retired to Sir Henry's extensive and elaborate library where I took the proffered seat by the fire and Sir Henry sat down facing me. "Now Sir, you must tell me how it is that on this bright summer day I find sitting before me a man whom I never thought to see again in this world."

I began my story, "I will unburden myself to you in all respects, Sir Henry. I have been among foreign regions to pursue an inner quest of the soul, a luxury granted to few men. I may have found some of that for which I have searched only time can tell. But I desired to find in my travels as well that greatest of life's benefits, a dear friend, one who knows one so well that even a hint is sufficient to convey meaning and where sympathy and good fellowship may mute one's faults and errors. I must begin by answering a question that you have been too well mannered to ask. How is it that Watson is not at my side? I have had to keep my survival a secret, even from one whom I trust and esteem as I do you and who has always been my most loyal companion. I am engaged at present and have been over these last years in a most dangerous series of exploits. I have traveled to regions where death rode always at my side. My only guardian in those regions was a man who was formerly allied against me, a man who at a single command from my arch-foe, would have dispatched me willingly, yet it was to his very knowledge and resolution that I entrusted my life over thousands of miles of travel, through hostile regions in Tibet, in Afghanistan, in Persia, in Arabia and finally in the region of the Sudan. At any point in my travels I might have been killed."

"Watson, had he known that I was alive, would have rushed to my side despite all risks. It was better that having once thought me dead, that I remain so to him until this affair in which I am engaged is brought to its completion. Even now the outcome is uncertain. Perhaps my enemies have only toyed with me thus far. They may have allowed me to escape the perils of three continents only to dispatch me now when I imagine that I am safe again in England and in my own home."

"I have not chosen my domicile without considering this very possibility. The place I have chosen is, despite its comforts, a veritable fortress as well and looks out in all directions. I am quite well-armed and anticipate purchasing an Irish wolfhound from a London breeder as a guardian that will be delivered to me presently. It is a most excellent breed, quiet, well-mannered, but fiercely loyal and quite capable of running down any foe. It has a wide jaw and sharp teeth and the heart of a lion. They were bred by the noble former kings of Ireland. So I hope that with these precautions in place I will be quite safe after all."

"No safer than you would be here, Holmes," expostulated Sir Henry.

I answered him with a self-deprecating smile, "It is a poor guest who repays his host's kind hospitality by forcing upon the household an attitude of constant vigilance and a new pet as well. I am sure that Lady Beryl would soon grow weary of such a houseguest, one who has grown immune to polite society from sojourning for years in the rugged regions of the world."

Sir Henry expostulated with me, "But we are already on the alert. I am afraid that we have never completely recovered from the anxiety and terror of the days when you first met me. The cursed hound is gone and my villain of a cousin is dead, the man we knew as Stapleton, but there are still nights in winter when the wind is howling over the moors when I imagine that I hear again the haunting cry of that spectral nemesis from which my family has suffered throughout the generations. When the mist rises from the Great Grimpen Mire and the skeletal fingers of sleet blow against the windows on a winter night, I seem to hear it still. On such nights I fear to look at the windows for fear that some fiend with blazing eyes may return my glance. Time and again I have imagined a face at the window, only to realize that it was but by own distorted expression of fear, reflected back to me from the glass. I cannot feel that our troubles are really at an end. It would be a relief to close at last with an actual foe. If you will not stay here at the hall, you must at least know that I shall see any lantern waved as a signal from your upper turret or hear a shot fired from a window; or if not I, then one of the tenants and we shall hasten at once to your aid."

"That is most reassuring Sir Henry. It will allow me to concentrate my forces upon my more immediate goal, which is to convince my foe to abandon his current course and to join me as, if not a friend, at least as one that no longer poses a threat to England and to me."

"You speak quite broadly, Holmes. How could any one man menace all of England?" asked Sir Henry in surprise.

"Yet, I assure you that it is possible," I said solemnly. "The man to whom I am addressing all of my strength and energies to defeat has promised that should I fail, he will in fact destroy the British Empire."

"He is quite mad of course!" muttered Sir Henry.

"No, I think not, unless genius is a form of madness. The man is the most formidable theoretical scientist in Europe. I doubt that any man living may follow to its end his equations. His mind is like a great explosion of light that leaves behind each area that it traverses, as fast as even light may traverse it. While I have been riding upon camels and eating dried lizards, he has no doubt been reading and planning and plotting. I can never hope to catch up to him. My entire strategy has been from the first to return to origins, to fundamental principles. Since I could not keep pace running beside him or scale the intellectual heights that he has reached, I have chosen to address his roots, for no matter to what heights a tree may grow it must draw its strength from its roots. Each man has a point of origin. No man may quite escape his memories and his antecedents."

Sir Henry thought for a moment about my statement before answering, "I presume by your statement that you believe that no man starts out as evil. That within all of us there is still the child that we once were."

"Yes Sir Henry, but I mean a good deal more. I have come to believe that the decisions that we make in life are for the most part trivial. There do occur though moments when our entire lives seem to focus for a moment and at such times we may, as St. Ignatius of Loyola would term it, elect a course of life. These moments are the great branch turnings, the major crossroads where we decide more than what we do, we decide who we are, and more importantly who we will become. Sometimes it is a chance meeting with another person who may influence us for good or ill. It may be a sudden illness, loss, or catastrophe that sets us on a different course. The boom of our lives comes over, the sails shake for a bit, the vessel heels over, and then the wind catches the sails and we are off on a new tack. At other times we head into the wind for a time and with a sea-anchor off our bow we lie-a-hull and take the waves as we may, we let the storm pass, then raise our sails and start off again on the voyage of our lives."

"I believe that most men and women spend their lives trying to solve one or at most a few central problems. The problems with which they grapple may have spanned generations. The wounds that we seek to heal may be, not our own, but instead our father's or our mother's legacy to us of unfulfilled dreams or bitterness or the need for revenge."

"The Japanese are quite clear on this point. The religion of Shinto contains the obligation to repay family debts, even if that debt should span generations. It is a point of honor that may not be avoided. How different is that concept of intergenerational obligation from our statutes of limitation in English Jurisprudence, which set a limit to even criminal liability to a single life. Our civic laws do not deal with forgiveness as such because the legal concept of a wrong committed seeks to apportion losses and to restore a prior condition as far as possible rather than seeking to convert the heart of the malefactor and to save his soul. Even our criminal laws, though they deal with the inner state to some degree by the legal concept of *mens rea*, are for the most part concerned with the selective use of force to influence future conduct by a threat of punishment. Evil thoughts alone do not provide a reason to say that any crime has even been committed. A man may harbor a vicious heart, but until he acts upon his evil thoughts the law can do nothing."

Sir Henry interrupted the train of my discourse at this point by observing, "Evil thoughts lead though to evil deeds, do they not? At what point may society intervene if it is to effectively forestall criminal actions?"

"That is a delicate question Sir Henry. The laws of our modern world exist to preserve a general peace among citizens rather than to form the conscience of citizens along any specific lines. The nation or state relies upon other institutions to advance learning, culture, and conscience."

"But those institutions seem to lack the persuasive force in the general marketplace of ideas," objected Sir Henry. "Can it even be said that there is uniformity in the quest for meaning. Perhaps your Professor Moriarty considers that his greatest contribution to the times in which he lives is to embrace the very evil act that you fear he may commit."

"A very wise observation, Sir Henry; that is why in my foe's particular case I cannot rely upon the force of the English laws alone. He is a man who is willing to be a martyr to his own convictions, even if they are wrong. Such men are dangerous," I replied.

"Yet the progress of events is often due to the most dangerous men among us, is it not," Sir Henry remarked.

"Yes, Sir Henry, but it is my contention that beneath the conflicting goals of men a primal moral order exists that we neglect at our peril. Actions and even dispositions carry with them a weight of objective consequences in an objectively moral universe. Catholic dogma recognizes that even after the forgiveness granted by God to reinstate Divine Grace within the soul of the penitent some lingering element remains unsatisfied to put matters right. The act of forgiveness for sin removes any eternal spiritual punishment, but sin is still so disruptive of the moral order that some degree of temporal damage remains. In a material world, a world subject to the irrevocable nature of space and time, all sin leaves damage behind if only a state of unused opportunities for good acts. This temporal residue brings its own temporal punishment in Purgatory. For this reason the Church recommends penances, prayer, voluntary sacrifices, fasting, and almsgiving, all of which serve to ameliorate to some degree the residual damage that maims our world. Above all else the Catholic Church contains within its spiritual treasury the infinite merits of Christ, the love and gifts of the Holy Spirit, and the merits of the saints in union with Jesus. These gifts may be used, in a manner beyond our comprehension, to heal and to replace and to enliven the temporal order so that all that was lost may be found, all that was wounded be made whole, and all deserved punishment may be surmounted."

"Though this point is often misunderstood, when the Catholic Church grants indulgences, it draws upon that treasury of merit. The power of the Church granted by Christ to bind and to release is above all else a mandate to use this power with the largess that charity commands. But the Church may also bind, or rather, since the bondage of sin is never imposed, to leave sinners for a time to their own resources. To leave them is not to abandon them to the devil, but rather to allow the soul to feel its own emptiness, caught in the web of its own machinations and ill-intentions."

"The Catholic Church is you see Sir Henry well-schooled in the dark ways of the human heart. Most sins are rather prosaic as befits human limitations. The detective and the priest share a common knowledge, one that is gained over time that most evils are dull, unimaginative affairs, due more to our incompleteness than to our malice. The detective solves a crime, while the priest hears a confession willingly revealed."

"I as a detective can only lay bare the facts and show the result. My powers are confined to the thread of the temporal order that links events and uncovers mysteries. Mine is a comparatively humble profession. My task is to reveal, not to heal what has been revealed, until that is this unique case of Professor Moriarty, for it is he of which I speak. If I do not heal this man I will not be able to prevent the crime in prospect. For this reason I am stretched far beyond my usual limits as a detective. I am on ground that belongs to another profession than that of a mere sifter of clues. I have been forced to assemble an arsenal of knowledge drawn from most of the religions of the world and to be a philosopher as well, even to function as a retreat-master although I am not a priest. My task is to force Professor Moriarty to confront the actions and modes of thought of a lifetime and to apply a different standard than the one that he has heretofore employed in judging himself. I must make him the prosecutor of the case against him. I must show him that he is wrong. Professor Moriarty, the master intellect, the man who of all men might explain or attempt to share with God the great pattern that governs the entire universe; Professor Moriarty who manifests the true nature of original sin: to wish to be like God to the degree of determining for himself what is good and what is evil; this man is the one whom I must confront and perhaps even convert."

"I quail before such a task, for I alone know how much it exceeds my poor powers. The strange thing is that he knows this as well! So why have I been allowed by him to live? Is it because the Professor imagines that I can do him no real harm? He toys with me as a cat toys with a mouse or a bird. He will meet me yes, but only to demonstrate the inadequacy of my powers when compared to his own. That will be his revenge for my destruction of his criminal organization. In the end he will dismiss me and carry out his plan of destruction and then simply return to his usual studies. It is a peculiarity of his revenge that he will not even allow himself to relish his victory. He is above all of that, so great is his pride. In the last analysis his contempt is so great that he despises even himself. His dark soul says, 'What are my triumphs to me but another occasion for boredom.' True evil, Sir Henry, is finally bored even with itself. I sometimes think that the devil pursues his courses through sheer inertia. The devil knows that it is defeated; it is no dummy after all, though he may be a fool."

"Why then does the devil oppose God? It is simply that the devil has fallen out of love. The devil is left to its own resources.

These are essentially the inverse of real power, because they stem from nothingness. Evil can only twist and distort what already exists from God. The devil cannot love for this very reason, simply because it will not love, and knowing this has brought it to a despair that is (thanks be to God) beyond all human comprehension. I must seek to discover during the course of the coming months in my new abode if the Professor is willing to be a man or if in his pride he wishes to be a devil."

Though I had often spoken thus to the solitary witness of my journal, I had not spoken so extensively to another human being. Even as I write down this discourse I have eliminated many of the pauses during which I attempted to discover if Sir Henry was able to follow my thought and empathize with my fears. At times he perhaps concluded that I was suffering from brain fever, but I trust that in the end he realized the extraordinary strain that I have been under without my Boswell, Dr. Watson, at my side to hear my tirades and to allow me to use his own remarkable patience and calmness to restore me to order. My mind often tends to race faster than an interlocutor, no matter how able and willing he or she may be, is able assemble my initial presentation and conclusions into a coherent whole. In this instance I had been quite carried away. It did me good to finally explain to a friendly ear the thoughts that have haunted me over so many miles and to outline the method that I intend to pursue with Professor Moriarty, insofar as I am able to formulate it. I could see though, when I had finished, that Sir Henry was puzzled.

He spoke up finally with a great laugh. "I see now Mr. Sherlock Holmes what poor Doctor Watson has needed to endure while living with the greatest detective of the age. You amaze me Holmes! The man you speak of, is he by any chance that same Professor Moriarty who now owns the horseracing stable over at Kings Pyland? Good heavens! And to think that I have been living for three years next to a man that even you fear. I have seen him of course in the owner's booth at the annual Wessex Cup. I even put a fiver or two on his horses from time to time and always come out a winner. I must say he does not look to be a devil. I once saw him hit a jockey with his own riding crop for laying it on too fiercely on his horse in the stretch. I even recall his words on that occasion. I overheard them clear enough. He said, 'Take that you wretch! My horses run for the joy of running! All you must do is guide them, the motive to win lies in their great noble hearts. Touch even one of them again like you did today and I shall see you skinned!' I must admit that chills ran down my spine at the time; I could not doubt that he meant every word. But the fellow understands horses, that much is clear."

"Yes, Sir Henry," I replied in agreement. "Now if I can only enable him to know something of his own soul."

June 4, 1893
Baskerville Hall

It is now several days since my last entry and I am now comfortably installed as a guest at Baskerville Hall until my new home has been cleaned and the furnishings delivered. My only hope is that I will not be so accustomed to the comforts of my present situation that I will be unable to assume again the habits of a single man, dependent upon his own company and resources for amusement. It was a pleasure for me to meet Lady Beryl once again. She recalled with gratitude my efforts of some years ago that perhaps spared her husband a dreadful death through the agency of the great hound, that was kept by that unlamented man, Stapleton, who was her husband at the time. Now there was a man of a most peculiar type; I have yet to comprehend him. If I was forced to try to come to some conclusion about him it would be that there was a man born without any sense or moral aptitude at all. There are cases of such individuals who seem born without the full measure of human nature. They exist in a peculiar universe in which they imagine that all things are directed towards them for their own use and pleasure. The human emotions of compassion, empathy, and insight into the feelings of others are completely absent within them. Their every action therefore assumes the character of pretence and the calculated construction of a mask to hide those fundamental deficits. Their interior must be rather like a stone. For them life is merely a game of predation and acquisition for they are always preternaturally selfish. A life that has no sympathy must of its very nature be contracted to a hard core like a boil constituted by self-idolatry. People of this type seek to fill the universe with their own petty goals. All other individuals exist simply so that their own needs may be satisfied.

They often maintain certain pet projects. Stapleton's own peculiar passions were for collecting butterflies and the subject of taxonomy. I doubt that he even had affection for his wife. She was a mere butterfly to add to his collection. Perhaps he was puzzled by her character that was so unlike his own. Like a monkey with a looking glass, he would use her to confirm whatever illusion about his own nature he was entertaining at the moment.

He bought himself a school in the north of England and filled it with paying pupils only to watch in indifference while an epidemic swept through the school. It was only after several boys had died that he was forced to send the remaining students home to their families. His wife found a curious notebook in which Stapleton recorded the deaths and made calculations on the likely rate of spread of the disease to those not yet affected. The entire school was only a laboratory for his own curious experiment, as though it were a mere Petri dish in his laboratory.

Still, the noble Lady Beryl had loved him. He must have had a certain charm in his way. Each new idea was embraced with a totality and enthusiasm, which only went to show the feverish nature of his internal emptiness. She undoubtedly imagined that her continual devotion would finally awaken a spark of love within him. But alas, it never did. His one desire was that she be there as a witness to his triumphs. He seemed even to enjoy the aspect of her increasing horror as the true depravity of his nature became clear to her. I must say that I am still surprised that he would go to his death in the bogs of the Great Grimpen Mire without dragging her along to witness and to partake in his terrible final end in those sucking pools of stagnant water. It was an end appropriate to such a man as he, a man who had sucked so many poor souls as victims into his own dark depths.

I could see at once that the life now led by Sir Henry and his wife was just that life of benevolence and concord that she had always desired. Sir Henry in turn would do anything for her, as would her devoted servant, a Mrs. Castillo who is I believe from her own country of Costa Rica. I may as well express my conviction here that this devoted couple of Lord and Lady Baskerville would do anything for me as well, not from gratitude alone, but out of the boundless resources of their own shared nobility of heart.

I have been quite overwhelmed by their solicitude. When they heard of my recent attack of consumption, I was promptly bundled up in wool comforters and fed such hearty fare thereafter that if I remain here long I will be as plump as Watson, whose game leg prevents long walks and allows him to put on weight at times. I wonder how the dear old fellow is doing in Louisiana among his lepers. I must say that he has shown by that choice alone the bulldog tenacity in the defense and aid of others that made him the very first among companions that one would wish to have by one when encountering any source of danger. He is one of those who would charge across an open field into enemy fire to rescue a fellow soldier. It was in just such an action that he was wounded so many years ago in Afghanistan, although I had to pry from him the circumstances through which he had received his wound. He would never admit to heroism when it was for him a mere question of duty.

I have been curious about when he will return, since he still retains his practice in Kensington. Through some discrete inquiries made by Mycroft it appears that he is scheduled to return after a year's commitment to the study of that ancient malady at the Carville Leprosarium. Strange as it may seem we have cases of leprosy even here in London through it is quickly hushed-up to prevent panic. Actually it is difficult to contract the illness, but so great is the horror of it as reinforced even by Biblical passages that it is feared beyond all other illnesses, even those which are far more easily contracted and certain to lead to a quick death such as cholera.

As for me, I have a peculiar fear of Yellow Fever, a truly ghastly illness, and one that Lady Beryl often witnessed in her homeland of Costa Rica. Fortunately, if one manages to survive, lifelong immunity is granted. Lady Beryl had a bout with it as a child and survived. Most others are not as lucky. There may be ample reason to risk the rigors of Cape Horn rather than to attempt to cross the Central American nations or southern Mexico to reach the Pacific. In any case, there is a region of the world that for all of its lush beauty, I am unlikely to visit.

It occurs to me from time to time that I tend to underestimate the horror of my own illness. I have lived with it for so long that absent the occasional flare-ups of symptoms I often quite forget that my body is inhabited by that treacherous organism, the tuberculosis bacillus. It likes to live at peace with its host. It shows a sort of beastly cunning in not killing its victim swiftly. Yet, it is no less deadly for all of that. Perhaps more people have died from tuberculosis than from any diseases other than Bubonic Plague and Malaria. Consumption has even developed a certain cachet among poets and artists, as though to suffer from it is to be ready to compose music like Chopin. Many a poor man and woman die in London of the disease. Their only remedy is to drink a hot gin or rum punch. The disease is democratic in nature and is not confined to those of rarified sentiments.

Leprosy on the other hand is seen as a degrading illness, a sign of moral blight. One does not suffer from a mere disease, but from some obscure curse of God! It is even felt that to have the disease is to have been already judged by God. The people of ancient Israel did not discriminate causes. All that occurred was thought to come from God in some manner and if one was ill, why then he must have sinned!

No doubt there are other afflictions and mental or physical variations similarly misunderstood. The Old Testament concept of

God is not to be seen through a single lens, nor was all of The Old Testament written at the same time. The Old Testament is a redacted composite that shows the contribution of many hands. That any final version should now be considered the definitive "Word of God" belies the mode of its composition and the service it was meant to perform among various communities. Only the message of Jesus Christ is eternal and for all time because it comes directly from the Divine Son who was able to look back definitively upon the laws of the Pharisees and to see which elements led to life and which did not.

Even had The Bible been dictated directly by God, with no possible reference to place, time, and circumstances; surely God should be allowed the latitude to amend a later edition of his own book. It is true that Jesus inculcated respect for the old law for the reason that it had performed the function of uniting a people to witness to Him when He arrived. When the nation failed to do so, the writers of the New Testament left a written record to embody the community's understanding of the significance of Christ in the first age of Christianity.

The Bible did not completely resolve in detail many questions as to the Eternal Nature of Jesus, which led to the early heresies. It required the judgment of the Catholic Church in several councils under the guidance of the Holy Spirit to resolve those questions as they were presented. God lives now among men and women in the fullness of the universal Church and it is the Church that determines what is true and what is false, when to bind and when to loosen. But the Church is slow to define and tolerates diversity upon unsettled questions so that when it speaks at last it may be with the voice of tempered experience and the fruit of much prayer.

Any new insights and innovations in theology must then of their very nature be merely hypothetical. Only the Pope and the Bishops may finally pronounce upon the questions at hand, for that is their mission given to them by Jesus and carried on in the Sacrament of Holy Orders. Catholicism is not a science; it is an organism, feeling its way under the impulse of Grace towards God.

Because it is living and incomplete it is subject to hesitations, to partial formulations, but it is never devoid of the final promise that Jesus and His Holy Spirit will be with it until the consummation of the world.

This is the consolation that enables all Christians to encounter evil with hope and even to suffer defeat to the point of martyrdom without falling into despair. This consolation is not derived from relation to a book but to the Living God, Living in the Church. No mere message, however inspiring or true it might be, is adequate for salvation. Relation requires a meeting of mind and heart which cannot happen between mere structures or organizations. For this reason the Catholic Church cannot be conceived of as an organization, even as one with a mission. Instead, the Church is present wherever Christ is to be found and Christ is to be found wherever two or more are gathered in His name.

This presence of God in small groups does not detract from or contradict the totality of the Church because the function of the small group is analogous to individual prayer in that its function is not teaching or definition, but worship and service. Such groups are in Christ to the degree that they are in union with the Church as a whole body with many parts. Any facile reliance upon scripture alone merely opens the door to a quagmire of personal interpretations that soon become as various as the individuals who claim to exercise an individual charism in preference to the universal mandate to the entire corporate body of the faithful under the Bishops as Successors to the Apostles.

Holy Scripture is reflected in and interpreted by the ongoing experience of the entire Church acting in unity with Jesus who is present with His Church as sacrament and in the One Holy Spirit which is the very life of the Church and its principle of unity. For this reason the ancient creeds speak of the Church as One, Holy, Catholic, and Apostolic. This great unity of the Catholic Church exists for the unification and consolation of the entire exiled human race.

Our exile is shown by our fragmentation and alienation

from each other.   The will of God is that the Healer and the Consoler of man and woman may be allowed to complete the work of this present age, the healing of all of the wounds that we refer to as evil. All proximate evils are paths to healing because they allow for the exercise of charity and of compassion. When this work is done, we are consoled. Thus it may be truly said that evil is the refusal to be consoled, to remain in the human condition as we find it and even to exacerbate the ills from which we suffer by adding to them a new component, our cooperation with evil rather than our resistance to it. If evil is the great refusal to be consoled then we may imagine the triumph of evil as a desire to bask in self-created miseries and to lash out in all directions in order to increase harms wherever it may.   If this is true, then the motivation of the devils is finally made clear for us; the devils (and for all that we know the other denizens of hell) are the ones who refuse to be consoled. Jesus said that he did not come to condemn the world, but to save it so that we might have life and have it more abundantly. God does not appear as our adversary then but as our advocate and on that we may rely.

June 12, 1893
Baskerville Hall

Progress on my home is rapidly proceeding. I walk over each day from Baskerville Hall over the moors to observe the progress being made and to give instructions on the placement of the furnishings. I am surprised to find in myself, now that I have made the decision to purchase a domicile, all of the instincts and emotions of the homesteader. I take a delight in walking the borders of my land. Each tree has become precious to me. Every stone is an element of delight. I begin to realize that man is not essentially a wanderer. The desire for hearth and home is innate in us. It is a hunger for attachment to a particular climate and soil from which to draw strength and sustenance, from which one may also draw community.   It is natural to seek support in life's trials and to share one's joys.   This seems to me the better way and essential to one's growth into full humanity. A man who prefers always to seek a higher hill is like a whirlwind: formless, chaotic, and finally unproductive of any real good for himself or others.

The need for containment is the beginning of civilization and of culture. The first technology was likely confined to pottery making, the weaving of baskets, and the decoration of funeral urns. What cannot be contained cannot be passed on to future generations. The beginning of the concept of wealth may be traced to the good fortune of a surplus harvest stored in jars. The grain must be contained. This containment was also the beginning of trade, for what may be contained may also be carried from place to place. Trade implies by its nature the idea of mutual advantage. Good fortune may be shared and through exchange widen the avenues of benefit by stimulating the further invention of other crafts. Humans learned to make various artifacts to trade for commodities. Thus all of culture may be traced to a combination of luck and insight, which leads to invention and to the beginning of an economic order. This in turn leads to the formation of laws and of governments among men and women.

Unfortunately, theft and warfare also stem from the idea of containment, for what can be contained may also be stolen, extorted, and expropriated by force or duplicity. From this in turn comes that natural defensiveness that makes an individual or a group guard their home and to erect barriers to make invasion difficult. For China the barrier was once its Great Wall to bar entrance to the barbarians. For Europeans it is currently the barricade provided by our guns, cannons, and battleships.

For me, since I am only a simple landholder, it is the walls of my cottage and the alert wolfhound that trots along now at my side on my walks. I have been at great labors to train him to remain with me and not to go dashing off in pursuit of every rabbit that he starts from hiding. I have a whistle that can be heard from a great distance and I reward him lavishly for obedience to its summons. All in all I feel sure that I will be safe here. I doubt that the Professor intends me any real harm.

As to other threats, certainly Sir Henry and his household have suffered no harm in recent years. Still, I cannot seem to shake an eerie feeling that there is still an evil force present upon the moors. I dare not mention this to Dr. Mortimer who is quite convinced of the reality of fairy mounds and of dark revels held by them in the bowels of the earth. He does not blush to leave a bit of milk on his doorstep every night to placate "the fair folk" as they are called. He will not be found cutting down an elder tree or near an oak circle at the full of the moon and he prefers to get home before dark.

The Midsummer festival of June 21st is not too distant in time when throughout the southwestern counties fires will be kindled on the hills. The old Pagan deities may have been vanquished by the advance of Christianity, but the instincts and celebrations live on here still, to the distress of the local Vicar of the Church of England and superstitious revels; yet they know that their discouragement will have little effect on customs so persistent and enduring, retained from antiquity.

My own belief is that to keep human nature on too tight a leash is always a mistake. The instinct of inquisition comes from a desire, deeply suppressed, to join the ribald celebrations. Perhaps it is better to pay a small toll to the devil if one is to walk the turnpike in peace. Not that the devil keeps his word in pocketing the toll, but we are reminded of our own imperfect natures and thus less likely to condemn with too much haste the faults of others while forgetting our own.

There is a degree of uniformity even in the variety of Pagan practices. Most deal with fertility or to propitiate death and are thus concerned with the purchase of a spurious brand of immortality. The otherwise quite enlightened Romans had a place for gladiators where even the most civilized men of the day came to watch the spectacle of people being slaughtered in the arena. The Aztecs practiced human sacrifice and perhaps even the Druids. Perhaps even the practice of warfare is in the final analysis symbolic. I will go so far as to say that the greatest evils stem not from so-called savage practices, but from civilizations that have evolved to the height of sophistication in their modes of killing. It is always a mistake for men to forget how much of the beast still lies within us. I should prefer a shaman, dancing about clothed in a bearskin, who does no real harm, to a general in epaulettes who may blandly order a regiment to its doom or a monarch like Ivan of Russia whose cruel and sanguinary temperament is now legendary. What we term civilization is quite often simply a means to hide the practices of rapine and murder by enacting them on a grand scale while invoking the blessings of God to cover our crimes.

Nor do I spare the fair sex from possessing these same sanguinary characteristics. Countess Elizabeth Bathory of Hungary bathed in the blood of peasant girls in order to preserve her fabled beauty. It was the Huron women who bit the fingers off of St. Isaac Jogues who came to them as a Jesuit missionary in what was then New France. I always look for the hollow ring filled with the poison of Lucrezia Borgia that may lurk beneath the scented handkerchief, the blushing smile, or the tears that quiver on an eyelash. I have found that the most threatening of men will often come over to one's side if one treats the fellow to a pint of ale. But a woman who is thwarted in her designs may hold a grudge for years and lash out when her victim imagines that he is at last safe from the prospect of revenge as recorded in some of the cases set before the public by Dr. Watson.

I fear the hearts of living men and women more than I fear the ghosts of superstition. I never really feared the Hound of the Baskervilles when its howl once echoed over these moors, because it was then that I knew the course that it would take and I could take measures to repulse its attack. It is the evil that creeps like a leopard on silent paws that I fear, the evil that with delicate tread, hidden in a veil of leaves, springs suddenly forth with its fangs upon one's throat that awakens terror within me. Evil is never more likely to wreak havoc as when all seems placid, calm, and secure or when the company seems too polite and well-bred to suffer its presence among them.

After my daily forays to my cottage I return to share tea with the Baskervilles. The neighboring gentry have heard of my return, though I have requested that the matter not be made public. I prefer to remain a quiet presence among the inhabitants of the moor. Our circle is one of old familiarity and is usually confined to Doctor Mortimer or Mr. Franklin or others of the gentry. Few gregarious natures can tolerate the isolation of our situation here. Country living in a district like this forces one in upon one's own inner resources and most people are not well-stocked in that department. The need for entertainment and diversion seems a constant in human affairs.

I have no trouble with solitude. I enjoy a night of a Wagner concert or opera on occasion, but I would be exhausted by a week of the London social round in the winter season. I prefer to visit Bath or Brighton in the off-season and am more likely to prefer a stiff hike out to Hartland Point on holiday than to find joy in the contemplation of the esplanade at Newquay or St. Ives with their strolling couples. I only seem to grow more contemplative with age. Whenever I have pictured the prospect of my retirement it has been to seclude myself with hives of bees and to hear the chorus of their industry on a summer afternoon. To see the sun arching over the heavens and to look beyond the downs to the leaden line of the evening sea off the coast of Sussex would be magical. But then retirement is something of a dream for me, since I have a most restless nature at times.

My present location in Devon will be a chance to see how well I tolerate the quiet life. I trust that I shall soon hear from Professor Moriarty, but he has made no promises to me. I must learn not to be discomposed by his methods. I must proceed as though the matters between us have already been resolved. In any case I can think of no further preparations that would be of any use. He will seek out my weak points in any discussion; I am sure of that, but where those weak points lie, ah there I may not say in advance. I must await his assault to probe my bastions and redoubts and then recover and redeploy as best I may.

It is only natural to desire a complete victory against such a foe, as if victory against Moriarty would end the reign of evil forever. But the world is always celebrating what it imagines are new beginnings, having arrived at last at what might be termed a definitive position. Yet one need only return to the site of victory in a few years time to find that the new order has become as tyrannical as the old. Whatever its boasts may have been with the acquisition of its power, it will have created about itself its own oligarchy and assembled about itself a list of victims for its own renewal of oppression and of violence. Whatever growth toward virtue may occur in individual souls, there is no real progress in politics. The extirpation of evil must by its very nature address social ills and conflicts, therefore that effort always assumes a political dimension, which is bound to fail. For this reason I have concluded that it is not the business of Christianity to make a better world, but to encounter the world as it is while acting as Christ would have acted in similar circumstances. To act in a Christ-like fashion of course always brings about a response that is similar to the experience of Jesus. Whenever the world encounters a Christ-like man or woman it will not be long before the cries to crucify them will be heard. This means that it would be well for the individual Christian and for the Church to reconcile itself to the inevitable failure to achieve anything like a substantial victory over evil in this world. The so-called "Prince of this World" is likely to rule until God the Father in His own good time simply says, "Enough!"

Yet it is the mercy of God that delays that dreadful hour. The fundamental mystery of life is that good is made manifest through the presence of evil in the world. Goodness is always growing from the soil of evil. That growth of goodness is something over which evil has no power. The soil may despise its own function as a catalyst of the good, yet it is powerless to alter that assigned function. Each age grows out of the detritus of all prior ages. The blood-soaked soil, glutted with the bodies of the dead, still yields its grass in due season. To the philosopher then the proper question is not. "Why is there evil in the world?" The question is rather, "Why amidst so many manifest and manifold evils is there any good at all?"

The world does not abound in gold, yet the value of gold is recognized at once. Evil is cheap because like stone it is so common. We live by the exception then and not by the rule. If virtue was universal we would take it for granted. Much of human history from this point of view may be seen as superfluous. Rare are the hours and occasions when virtue seems to assume the robe of dominion over evil in this world, one that is ever jealous of its prerogative on mediocrity. It waits in suspense to snatch it up again. Virtue then is not known by its effects, but by its inner disposition to follow the will of God, without regard to consequences or in hope of attaining a lasting victory. Everything is a matter of prayer and discernment. To pursue the good without the humility born of meditation before God is to suddenly awaken to the fact that the very pursuit of the good has been subtly transformed and that soon one is serving evil again after all. For the above stated reasons I am unlikely to win over Professor Moriarty though reasoning alone. If he is to find goodness, it must come from within that region of the soul that God alone may enter. It must come through the advent of grace.

I may make that event more likely through my own efforts, but I am incapable to do more than this by a mere personal command made to him that he should see things my way. As I said in my last journal entry, there is an evil which delights in its own misery and seeks finally to make a habitation out of it, perhaps forever. Despair is spoken of as the sin unto death, because in despair we lose the orientation of the will towards the good. Even proximate goods still retain some hope of fulfillment even if partial and temporary and subject to loss and to decay. But in cases of despair, where evil has its final way with us, we give our assent in principle to misery and pain as our final goal and desire.

The gate to Dante's Inferno reads, "Abandon hope, all you that enter here." I have always thought this idea of Dante's to be a misunderstanding of cause and effect. The fact is that the abandonment of hope must always precede the entry into hell, because it denies the efficacy of God to save even the most hardened soul. There is a corollary to this statement of all-abiding faith and hope that is most consoling for one who has not abandoned hope: such a soul will not be allowed by the mercy of God to enter hell, except by its own final decision and because it demands it.

June 13, 1893
Baskerville Hall

I spend my days here at Baskerville Hall with a great deal of freedom. I desire nothing more. Sir Henry and Lady Beryl are the perfect hosts, courteous but unobtrusive. Their community duties, a product of their generosity, keep them much occupied and I am in consequence left to my own devices. My walks about the estate leave me time to speculate and to add to the arsenal of arguments and strategies that I am assembling for my eventual confrontation with Professor Moriarty.

Since I am adopting religion as my primary point of entry, it may be of no harm to use these quiet days to make explicit why I am relying on religion and specifically upon Roman Catholicism as my heavy artillery. First of all, I am no match for Professor Moriarty in his own chosen field of science and when it comes to mathematics my expertise is confined to practical chemistry. This leaves only history, philosophy, and theology as my primary sources for meaning since psychology and sociology are still in their infancy.

Literature is of some use, but as an art form it is primarily expressive rather than explicative. Literature must rely upon some formal structure to support its weight and that critical structure must come from outside itself. Certain critics like Matthew Arnold and Walter Pater are doing splendid work to define the realm of literary criticism as a separate field of study, but beyond Arnold's comprehensive genius the field is still largely amorphous and undefined. All argumentation requires language of some sort in order to proceed and natal sciences like linguistics and philology are focusing our attention on the linkages between thought and how we express thought and whether the two are coextensive.

Is it ever possible though to express an idea that has not been already formulated in some way within us? But how is any thought formulated unless it already exists in some mental image or intuition? Does this mean that epistemology is always and necessarily a refinement of a prior set of conclusions regarding the scope of linguistics; that thoughts beyond simple sensations are innately tied to expression? Thought and expression would appear to occur simultaneously. We may mull over a problem, but its solution once it springs forth is already clothed in language.

From this point of view religion by claiming to explain and almost to capture God in authoritative texts like The Bible would appear to be caught up in an essential contradiction. If God calls forth everything, both substantially and relationally from nothing, then God as that causative source might presumably have chosen differently, including not to have created anything at all! This would have meant that God would have had nothing to reflect His nature and glory but His own self-containment and inner perfection as the Divine Trinity. But if the universe is flawed by evil, then God must somehow have factored in evil as an ontological possibility by creating anything less perfect than God Himself.

Is it possible then that creation was therefore a great gamble that gratitude and a proper evaluation and admission of dependency alone would keep any conscious created being from ever straying into the pit of self-idolatry? Is God actually a great gambler or is He instead a Lover of such magnitude and generosity that even evil is worth the price of risking everything for love? How shall we ever answer questions such as these or is it blasphemous to even pose them? However, when assent to religious doctrines becomes automatic they lose their full depth of meaning. Religion must be startling or it will cease to be religion at all.

When confronted with the multitudinous versions of Christianity it is natural to call to mind the image of children playing about in a pond making mud-pies to throw at each other with little real sense of the source of that pond where they spend their days in quarrels and disputes. What are these distinctions to a God who makes even the possibility of drawing such distinctions available to us His creatures in the first place? If we must first become like little children before entering the Kingdom of Heaven, then perhaps a first step is to get out of the pond! Nevertheless, since Catholicism has excellent historical credentials and any reform of the Church should come from within the Church itself as a single discerning body of believers I have made Rome my intellectual point of departure. I cannot tailor Christianity simply to be appealing to professor Moriarty.

My presentation to him of necessity must begin by drawing distinctions among various religious claims while still retaining as a basic attitude the universal love of God for all things to save us from our own worst human impulses. I have taken Christianity as the normative presentation of God to all western minds. However, some manner of dialogue should be tolerated between all religions. But since with professor Moriarty I am starting with a man who has a bias and anger that simmers just below the surface in his atheism, it is with the man himself that I must begin.

There is no doubt that he is a strange soul, but religion itself may be thought of as the product of those strange but favored souls: the mystics, the prophets, and the saints whose writings are still our primary source for everything that we claim to know about God. In this sense God is not the author of religion, but rather God is the subject of religion. This distinction is essential to enable us to properly approach any written text claiming to be the Word of God. Theology has as much to say about us as it has to say about God. Faith informs us that man and woman were created in the image and likeness of God; but our daily experience reveals that we often create God in the image and likeness of ourselves.

Even Holy Scripture has in parts a spontaneous and circumstantial quality as though it was prepared to meet a sudden exigency that is inconsistent with a prepared and definitive treatise composed under less pressing and insistent circumstances. This style of composition leaves lacunae that point to many connective gaps to be filled in later by the authoritative discernment of the Catholic Church. In fact later Christians must encounter God and the events of the life of Christ not directly, but only as already filtered through the early estimation of the followers of Jesus who had already defined who Jesus was to them.

We meet Jesus Christ therefore only within the circumambient enclosure of the proclamation of Jesus as the Christ. Even the mission entrusted to the Catholic Church is defined in the same documents that record the granting of that authority in a historical pronouncement or commission. We cannot step outside of this source material in order to approach Christianity from a purely skeptical position of non-commitment. The act of faith and the proclamation of faith would appear to be simultaneous events; to hear is to believe.

June 14, 1893
Baskerville Hall

While speaking of strange souls, as in my prior entry, I should like to comment on the sheer variety of obsessions that one encounters over the course of a lifetime. It seems unlikely that God could allow such diverse individuals to exist if they did not in some way manifest the abundance and delight of God in His creation in all of its forms and varieties. For this reason I am impatient with the theological view that sees our life like walking a tightrope. I prefer to imagine that we dance our way into heaven and that God enjoys movement rather than a rigidly static position frozen into immobility for fear of Him.

Dr. Mortimer, a man whom many might call "an odd bird," came over today and we had a most stimulating discussion about the Chaldeans and the origins of the Cornish Language, topics that I may someday have the time to explore more fully. On the present occasion Dr. Mortimer has suggested that we combine our efforts to explore the vicinity for relics of the Druids and for evidence of the Picts, a people that may have been the source for the belief in fairies.

I am quite willing to humor him since his company in my walks across the moor may at least be diverting. The man is a genius in his way. His knowledge of phrenology and of variations in the shape of the skull is extraordinary. He possesses an immense collection of skulls from various regions of the world and could discourse by the hour upon the differences between the skulls of the Negroid, the Mongoloid, and even the skulls of the Australian aboriginal people. He has even gone so far as to claim that he can detect differences in a French skull dating from the time of Charlemagne and one from the same region today. I may say that he is a connoisseur of skulls. On this occasion I asked him for the reason for his unique interest in this arcane pursuit.

"You ask this of me Mr. Holmes, when as a detective you must certainly come upon the answer if you only reflect for a moment?" said he. "I should have thought the answer was obvious. The skull is the most ancient temple of man! Within the cranium lies not only the origin of man but of his destiny. What separates man from the apes but the cubic capacity of his skull? It is simply a matter of increasing that cubic capacity over time so that the cerebral cortex may increase proportionately if mankind is to evolve to occupy a higher plane of existence."

"What is the human brain at present after all but a great refuse heap of what we once were? The present human brain contains that of the fish and the reptile that preceded us. Indeed, these residual brains dominate the greater mass of the human brain. I tell you sir that it is this vestigial apparatus that may doom the human race before we have time to evolve to our full stature. Our entire civilization depends upon the control over our passions by the pre-frontal lobes. The majority of the species barely manages that control by the time that they are over fifty! Until then the primary drives differ little from salmon swimming upstream. The species only manages to produce one genius for every thousand men. What if that dismal ratio could be improved?"

"I always judge a man by his brow. Show me a man with a

receding forehead and I will show you a criminal! If we could only enlarge the room for the pre-frontal cortex by some means we might jump centuries ahead in evolution. A day may come when brains constituted as ours are at present will only qualify one to be included as an exhibit in a zoo. The mutterings of our most renowned poets will then be perceived as mere gibberish by the speakers of the exalted language that will then be the *lingua franca* of all people. I have great hope for the advancement of our species. This may perhaps be procured by glandular means. I have been in correspondence with a man named Professor Presbury who shares my views. He is currently working on a serum that may prolong life and thus extend the period of human cranial growth. He considers it a tragedy that the minds of our greatest scientists are extinguished by death at the very moment of their highest evolution attained through a lifetime of study."

"The brain shrinks as we age, did you know that, Mr. Holmes? Show me a centenarian and I will show you a man with a mere walnut for a brain! The convolutions become muted and blurred, the entire organ calcified and filled with various plaques and obstructions. Ugh, what a ghastly spectacle! Professor Presbury is experimenting with various hormone preparations that may extend youth, lubricate the brain in its cerebrospinal fluid, and thus preserve it from desiccation."

I attempted to hide a smile at Dr. Mortimer's vehement exposition of what I regarded as purely fanciful ideas. Having attended university lectures it is my considered opinion that only the fact that the faculty retire or die allows human knowledge to progress without being obstructed by set ideas. However, the good doctor continued his speech, not having noticed my amusement. I voiced a few mild comments to see what he would say. His answer was pointed and immediate as though he had already considered and rejected any objections that could be made to his pet theory.

"All that is very well of course but beside the point in my view; what do I care if my own little set of memories should die with me? What am I but a mere cell in the larger organ of humanity? It is always the species that matters! Let me pass on so that the man of the future may finally arrive! My only regret is that I must bequeath the characteristics of the ape that remains within me to any offspring that I may produce. What are my emotions for instance but a legacy from some forgotten monkey troupe chattering in the trees because a leopard was passing below? What is the sexual drive but a mere conduit of the nerves so that the females of that same monkey troupe will remain pregnant, so that the size of that same monkey troupe may grow larger in relation to competing troupes? What is the great city of London for that matter but millions of similar monkeys in a larger tree, all chattering away? The whole business of human life is pointless of course from any exterior point of view. The universe takes no note of our existence. Our mission is ours alone and there is no allowance to be made for mere decoration. Much is subtracted from utility by the mere aesthetics of contemplation. Our true humanity exists in that part of the brain that can retain knowledge, that area that discerns meaning, patterns, and is capable of reflection and self-directed will. All else is merely a mechanism governed by instinct and oriented only towards brute survival."

I did not comment further on his spirited discourse since I wished to learn as much as possible of his views on human evolution. After a few moments of thought and seeing that I made no comment, he continued as before.

"Life appears to wish to preserve itself, not only of the individual, but life itself. Everything is directed to that end. Most men and women live longer than they should and doing so they begin to reflect. They grow accustomed to living and begin to imagine that they should live forever. Thus religions grow up among us. Meanwhile the young, for whom the prospect of old age and death as applied to them is a pure chimera are satisfied to procreate and then to die in the fullness of their young powers if death should come upon them unawares. Meanwhile the old can only take note that unaccountably and seemingly overnight they have become another species and a stranger in their own eyes. Nature itself comes to the rescue. Aging serves the process of the species by clearing the ground of cellular debris. We become a burden to evolution by the mere fact of existing as individuals. We continue to consume resources long after we have exercised our one essential function of passing on the genetic heritage, the torch of life to others. One need only look at the way that nature deals with the female of our species to know the virtue of aging and death. One is always hard-pressed to gaze at the shrunken and wizened beldames that hobble about among us and by a mere subtraction of years to see again the goddess that she may once have been, when nature filled her with flesh and substance, when her fertility breathed from her every pore. What has she become but a carcass on the site of her former splendor? Or look at the elderly men in their London clubs whose rheumy eyes recall only faintly the vigor and purpose of their youth, when as young athletes their bows shot forth the arrows of desire and they entertained dreams of being conquerors of all that they surveyed? Too soon the former conqueror is lucky if he may carry a spoonful of soup to his toothless mouth! To see the end of life is to perceive the futility of living as far as the individual is concerned. This is why I study the races of mankind above all else. What to me are even nations? Even they shall pass into oblivion. Where are the Druids today? Where for that matter are the Romans? Where will we Britons someday be?"

"Yet you believe in the fairies," I said with a smile.

Dr. Mortimer started and then laughed softly. "Ah well, I am a man after all and what man does not like to believe that somewhere at least immortality may exist. If I imagine fairies it is because they are not of corporal being, but are merely the embodied substance of ideas. They are the tutelary spirits of the intellect. They are pure beauty and as such my aesthetic sense demands that they exist."

"So you are a Platonist after all, Doctor?" I remarked with a smile. "This is not surprising to me. The scientists are the direct heirs of the early Greek philosophers. While the Pre-Socratics such Parmenides were busy determining the primary substances of which all things consisted, a new group of philosophers gathered who asked even more preliminary questions those on which metaphysics is based."

"What are they?" Dr. Mortimer inquired, "And in what way are they more basic than primary substances?" I answered him, "I think the best way to answer your question is explain that metaphysics sets up the rules for all of existence. To begin then surely the first basis of all thought is bring up the possibility of negation. The negation of being is non-being. Until we ask why anything exists at all, it is futile to inquire into what, why, how and in what specific manner individual things exist. So the first metaphysical questions are two in number:

1. Why is there something rather than nothing?

2. What are the essential characteristics of all existing things?"

Dr. Mortimer objected, "Is it really necessary to go back to the beginning of all thought before affirming or denying the existence of the fairies?"

I replied, "Well Dr. Mortimer I could not help but notice the contrast between your belief in fairies and your minimizing assessment of the human race. Whenever I note such a contrast I ask myself whether some rooted prejudice or bias of mind is in play. When these invitations to fallacy rear their hydra-like heads I deem it wise to return to fundamentals and build from there."

I thought it was time to correct Doctor Mortimer's cynicism about human life and to point out the transcendent value of the individual, so I addressed him in this manner. "If I may proceed, the first question of metaphysics addresses the origin and purpose of all things and these are essentially religious questions. For instance the Book of Genesis provides no guide as to how it is to be read or interpreted or even approached as a text. The probable reader, the communal audience if any, and the purpose and occasion of its composition are not specified in advance. Instead the Book of Genesis plunges from an account of creation directly into a series of morality plays and from thence into the tribal history of Abraham and his heirs. Surely this is a mixing of genres. These are not scientific or historical accounts in the sense that we understand them today. As part of the Bible, which is actually an anthology rather than a single work, the average reader presumes that the reading and comprehension of today is identical to what it would have been to the initial audience that received the text. But these texts have been interpreted as self-evident and cohesive for so long that any new reading is well-nigh impossible."

"Yet we must turn to religion for ultimate answers, because philosophy cannot supply the details of the origin of all things or the purpose for their existence beyond their simply being in existence. In other words there is no knowledge imperative in the universe. The universe might still have existed without ever being known. Even as known by us we can never escape the fact that our perception adjusts itself to the questions that we pose and the language in which we pose them. This seems unnatural to us of course because our very existence implies the need to understand and to reflect."

"This inability to abstract from our own need to know brings on the second metaphysical question, the need to understand the particular characteristics of being. There is no escaping our sense of design in the universe and therefore of a designer. The alternate proposition that the universe in its laws and productions simply is as it is because it is as it is with no outside purpose or design whatsoever frustrates our expectation that perfect order in any system must have a first cause that is separate from itself. This sets up the bifurcation between God as the single necessary being and everything else which is contingent upon the act of creation by God."

"God is posited as the first cause of everything else that exists. But we enter upon this play of existence in the middle, somewhere between the beginning and the end. Our primary experience therefore is of change and duration. These two seem to be opposed but are in fact comparative in nature. Duration may be considered to be a slower rate of change. We can perceive time because we witness change; slower change is duration. The second law of thermodynamics gives us our next insight: change cannot be reversed. Time runs in only one direction. From this we arrive at the fundamental acceptance of cause and effect relationships, both of them mediated by time and running in only a single direction, towards increasing disorder and dissolution. From perfect order and potency the universe is moving towards diminishing order and potency. This law of entropy implies that the direction of the universe as a whole is towards increasing disorder. The idea therefore of an absolute beginning as narrated in Genesis would make no sense unless that maximum state of potency where no energy has been expended and no events have yet occurred sprang forth from nothingness at the will and command of a creator, who is God."

"Returning to the second question, the one that puts aside any talk of origin or purpose, we place the question of God aside and simply admit the existence of a knower and the existence of things that may be known. This world-view simply assumes that the universe as we know it simply but inexplicably is: that it was in a state of initial stability and perfection and that now it is running down like a clock along the arrow of time and the dispersal of space. From this point of view the God question simply disappears and we are left only with our present position midway between two opposing states of the universe, perfect order and perfect disorder."

"By ceasing to go beyond these two states of being in either direction (note the metaphoric use of space here) the first question of metaphysics essentially disappears as being a trick of analogical thinking that makes of God a great artist in the sky. However the second question brings God in through the back door by using the definition of God that appears in the philosophy of the Jewish philosopher Baruch Spinoza who maintained that God is not a person, but rather that God is the sum totality of everything that exists; everything is therefore part of God. This view implies that the primal act of worship actually lies in science and the desire for a deep and complete knowledge of whatever exists, because as far as any super-consciousness exists, it is only present in the distributed being of all things rather than as represented by the focal personality of the Hebrew concept of God as reflected in the

Old Testament.”

“To those persons who are preoccupied by the second metaphysical question, the first question may therefore appear to be an irrelevant cultural residue of Hebraic thinking in a modern world. For such persons we may only seek to understand what things are in themselves. They assume that we may ignore the question of origins or ends, since all that matters to the second question is what is here now and how it may alter over time. Any speculation regarding any ultimate purpose for existence becomes pointless and futile because to understand all things completely would be also to comprehend God.”

“Since western religion begins with God as the ultimate source of everything, those persons who prefer to start further downstream by concentrating all their efforts on the second metaphysical question of achieving a global understanding of particular being, and only then to paddle upstream to a source for everything never manage to arrive at their hoped for destination. Atheism may therefore be thought of as an infinite deferral of asking the first metaphysical question.”

“The true adherent of religion of course has the option of simply affirming what he cannot understand by refusing to ask either of the first two metaphysical questions. His concern is with what the religion demands in belief, conduct, and ritual. The believer affirms that God exists and in doing so to also know as well the purpose that God had in creating things. This of course implies that God is not a mere force but instead is analogous to us in possessing a personal existence. The book of Genesis of course reverses that supposition by stating clearly that God is the original while we as human beings are the deficient and subsidiary image of God.”

“But returning to those persons who are still shipwrecked upon the reef of question two: if God is defined as the totality of the potentially knowable and not as a being standing outside of time and space, then to know all things would be to know God also. But the religious instinct, properly speaking, is based on the intuition that the first question of metaphysics, again stated as,

'Why is there something rather than nothing?' implies that a self-aware existence standing outside of all that we may know in space and in time may have called forth everything from nothing."

"This intuition sees a level of discretion as standing above the totality of all that is, in other words it implies that God's will is greater than existence. The problem with this stance of course is that it may simply be an anthropomorphic view projected out upon the universe. It is certainly a bold step to imply that all that we see as true and real might, had God so wished, have been otherwise, even to the extent of simply not being at all! God could presumably simply have refused to create anything at all and we are back at nothingness as the primal stuff of reality! But what reality, since nothingness is all potency and no act?"

"It is a peculiarity of being that once it exists, its non-existence becomes inconceivable. This may also explain the human longing for immortality that you have just now decried as mere vanity and only the result of the persistence of the habit of living. Once attaining consciousness of ourselves, we imagine that we are in a sense the center of gravity for all the phenomena that surround us and that all being is deflected in an essential way by our being here to observe it. We may grow disgusted at times with our lives or appalled at our limitations as we age, but still we are aware that every act of perception makes the world transparent to us to a degree. Our knowledge is a wedge into being. Once we take the first steps of the use of our human intellect and will, we are committed to at least a latent desire to comprehend the whole. We are condemned to philosophy and not least of all to that first tantalizing question of metaphysics!"

"Thereafter we cannot cease to question, so that even death may not act as a terminus of our desire to know all things. This fact of our reflected experiences is one of the most persuasive reasons to believe in God. It would surely be too absurd for a being to exist that has the capacity to know, only to have that capacity be so limited, so unlikely of any real fulfillment in our short span of years so that we would be doomed to frustration. No, my dear Doctor Mortimer, it is not even a consolation to leave the trust of knowledge to the entire species of mankind, for the desire to know the infinite and to join with God at last through contemplation of God is always a personal one. The desire from the beginning is to comprehend the whole, not simply its parts. Plato desired to escape from the cave, to leave the shadows behind, and to ever succeed in doing so one must be immortal."

Doctor Mortimer had followed me closely. "But Mr. Holmes, you speak only of the exceptional man or woman. Since the majority of the human race takes only the first steps along the road of philosophy before accepting the relative and exalting the trivial or accepting the merely metaphorical solution mediated to them by some religion, should being actively engaged in philosophy be a prerequisite for the gift of immortality to be granted to us by God?"

"Human nature in many cases may quail before the full task imposed by our own potential. Still, the matter is one of potential ability and not of the actual use of all of our faculties. It is sufficient that one might ask the first question of metaphysics. Even if a baby should die in the womb, the destiny of all of mankind might be placed by God before the child at its death so that it may reach a decision regarding the final destination of its soul. Potency is sufficient to grant the entire estate and dignity of man and woman to any soul, however short his or her life may be and however full or absent the measure of human faculties may be, even if impaired by what are in the last analysis only the accidents and not the substance of life."

"As you see, I am also a Platonist, at least in my willingness to discuss essences. I do not share your contempt for the fate of the individual, Dr. Mortimer, because it is only in the individual that we may witness the summation of the progress of the species at any given moment."

It was then that Sir Henry joined us. "You are still at it you two as I can see. I was about to ask if you cared to join Beryl and me for tea. These things of the mind can be exhausting. The brain runs on sugar I have heard, so perhaps some scones with bramble jelly or marmalade may aid your thought processes, should you care to resume them later."

We both rose from where we had been sitting in some comfortable antediluvian seats of what may have been an ancient council chamber of the Druids. We joined him and proceeded to the hall where we soon adjourned to the dining room where Lady Beryl awaited us.

While we were being served with steaming scones by that good lady, Sir Henry continued, "I overheard the end of your discussion, Holmes. I am afraid that you must classify me among those for whom philosophy will always be a closed a book. I am afraid that I am like those water beetles who skim over the surfaces of life. It makes little practical difference to me what a thing may be in itself. What difference for instance does it make whether the scone that I am eating consists of atoms or of essences? To me it is a scone and I eat it as a scone. If through some miraculous transformation it was to alter and become a rock then its use to me as a scone would cease and I would not eat it. Do I sound very foolish?"

"Not at all, Sir Henry; the world as we know it is one that contains certain central relationships that make it meaningful to us on a variety of levels, the existence of the pragmatic does not foreclose further enquiry as to origins and that second mysterious metaphysical question of what a thing is in itself. Let us return to the humble scone that you just mentioned. You relate to it as something you may eat, but let us assume that there was no Sir Henry to eat it, but only a scientist to study its chemical composition, or a baker to duplicate its flavor in a new batch, or a kitchen maid to scrub off the residue from the sticky plates. Each deals with a different aspect of the whole. The question might still be asked by a philosopher, "What is the very essence of the thing, when viewed from every possible perspective including that of God whose knowledge we presume would be of an order to embrace the whole object of inquiry in all of its aspects, to see it from every angle, to see it as part of a chain of causality reaching to the very stars. Now your humble scone becomes a window to the eternal realm, does it not?"

"Of course the perception of God would reach beyond a mere summation of characteristics and be able to answer the first question of metaphysics as well, which is why the scone even exists? Some philosophers have suggested that there is no 'sconeness' but only individual scones. These philosophers suggest that what we call the eternal forms after Plato are really merely nominal in nature and have no metaphysical reality at all, but only exist in language.

"What is the relationship between a thing and whatever statements we make about it? Another key point to stress here is that if the mind can only know essences and eternal forms, then why do particular examples exist of any genus or species we might name? Why should the mind stoop to description in detail rather than remaining placidly ensconced at the mountain-top of highest generalities?"

"If everything that we claim to know has always existed in some form, then how do the new qualities attach themselves to form the essence of the thing in itself? Is this assembly of accidentals into essences traceable to some inner necessity or does this process of formation arise from some reservoir of potential qualities, selected and pasted together so that we can describe in detail what we have already grasped, the thing in its wholeness and integrity?"

"Is philosophy merely a name for how we think and how we express our thoughts rather than a mirror of a world that would exist without us precisely as it exists now? Or does the world that we see beg for an observer, and more than that, for an interpreter before it truly comes into full existence? One may choose either alternative, very well, but whence came that very necessity or that set of acquired qualities? One is always led back to a first cause and a final purpose for everything that we observe."

Dr. Mortimer spoke up. "Well in any case, I must be so bold as to ask leave to place a few scones out in your garden for the Fairy Folk. We dwell in these lands by their sufferance. You mark my words! If the government cared to allocate a proper sum to archeology right here rather than digging up tombs in Egypt I would find evidence of their existence that would surprise many scoffers. We may live in a remote corner of the world and Stonehenge may be no match for the Great Pyramid of Giza but both show a longer antiquity than the writings of the Jewish prophets and the literature of the Greeks."

He continued, "The world was already old when the first Hebraic writings were set down. There is a wisdom that must have presaged the earliest writings of mankind. Surely these latter civilizations that now dominate our world-view and our aspirations for eternal life did not erupt without some preparation and cultivation in the humus of a preceding culture. From whence came these startling insights into human nature if human nature was not already well developed.

Was Oedipus the first to undergo his tragic fate? Was Moses the first to see the natural morality in the ten primary commandments of the Torah; would Mosaic morality even be meaningful to us if we did not have a moral sense prior to the issuance of those very commandments? Literature and philosophy are always *post hoc* formulations of intuitions that stem from a prior source that lies innately within us. My desire as a scientist is to probe antiquity, to discover the roots of our present dispositions as left for us to find and to decipher in the traces of the artifacts left behind by our ancestors. Was Cain the first to murder his brother or is he only a type for a thousand murderers before and contemporaneous with him? What preceded the great awakening of the human race to language and to abstract thought? If we are substantially the same species as we were for thousands of years before human cultures as we know them recorded their experiences, what were we like then? Were we savages or did we perhaps study under a prior tutelary race which instructed us in the elements of our humanity?"

"What of those ape-like and beetle-browed ancestors that we call the Neanderthals? Are they no longer among us because they were gentle, dim-witted, and trusting folk and not savages at all? Perhaps the more brutal species has survived! The men and women living today may be only the most successful murderers.

The best of humanity may be dead, leaving only those stained by crime remaining to pass on the divine injunctions that they have never lived-by or followed! For this reason I choose to believe in the Fairy Folk who dwell beneath the ancient barrows of England and are satisfied to make the flowers grow with their blessings and who will even condescend to accept a mere scone or a jug of milk in offering for their many services to us."

On that affirmative note Dr. Mortimer ceased speaking. I dared not attempt to sway him from his strange but detailed pagan beliefs. Dr. Mortimer is a strange chap and perhaps quite mad, but he is an excellent companion and interlocutor and the moors gladly tolerate all manner of eccentrics, even me. I have certainly surrounded myself with interesting company here. Perhaps, I might have stayed home after all and not needed to wander over half the globe in pursuit of an answer to the primal questions that still elude me. Or perhaps it is time that I became a humble keeper of bees in the glade. These at least may produce honey for Sir Henry's beloved scones! To be of use in some fashion was the center of the thought of Thomas Carlyle who knew Emerson well, both of them individuals and both of them examples of those rare men who manage to create a creed without a church to support it.

June 16, 1893
The Black Dog Pub

If the desire for religion in one form or another lies at the base of every conceivable anthropology, then the belief, or at least the entertainment of a possibility, that the British Isles and Ireland are inhabited by fairies of various types that have withdrawn into hiding in caverns beneath the earth is less strange than it might otherwise appear to be in a man of science like Dr. Mortimer. Paganisms of various sorts either people the heavens with gods and angels or the underworld with various helper figures or demons whether they be benevolent or malign called Leprechauns, Brownies, Kobolds, Gnomes, Trolls, Banshees, or Kelpies.

Providence alone would appear to have ordained that certain earth-bound spirits serve the function to coordinate and supervise the operations of nature. Any supernatural way of looking at the world will result in some manner of religion, because to do so is natural to humankind. Where Christianity differs from this universal pagan characteristic of being human is in its concept of God as a Trinity of Divine Persons all of which are deeply concerned with human fate and the redemption of human nature in order to take it to a higher moral plane and to bestow as a gift the personal and corporate participation after death in what is called the Beatific Vision, to share in the nature of God, in love for eternity.

So exalted is this concept that any mere folk vision, no matter how quaint and amusing it may be, cannot be considered or compared with the supernatural faith of those religions derived from the experiences of the Jewish people and whatever they encountered in their unique history of wandering, warfare, and redemption after exile. While the eastern religions considered as a group tend collectively to adapt human nature to its inherent evils and limitations by prescribing an ordered and well-balanced life, the great western religions presume to offer the ultimate victory over fate, over suffering and death, by offering personal immortality. Nevertheless, for all of my reservations on the subject matter, I enjoy a discussion with good friends in an atmosphere of genial good-fellowship so I consented to a recent outing to take my mind off my anxiety and the many cares attendant upon establishing my first solo domicile.

Sir Henry and I met Dr. Mortimer this evening in a quiet corner of the Black Dog Pub in Grimpen. I thought that the choice of a name that recalled the famous devil-hound might be offensive to Sir Henry and recall most bitter memories, but thanks be to God he is not one of those squires who impose their own feelings or insecurities upon the common folk of the neighborhood by various implied strictures. Sir Henry had decided that the best way to lay old ghosts to rest in the public mind was to treat them with humorous contempt and by doing so to reassure the country-folk who still hesitated, even years later, to walk abroad in the locale of the Great Grimpen Mire on nights when the wind would sigh about the old stone huts on the moor and recall the darker legends of time gone by.

So it was that we were gathered by the fire that night, for it was a decidedly chilly evening. We sat with great bowls of mutton stew and pints of local ale before us. Dr. Mortimer had brought over a manuscript to read to us. It appeared that the good doctor has literary aspirations of the penny-dreadful sort. After dinner we gave him our respectful attention and he read the beginning of what promises to be an interesting tale of the usual sort to send spinster ladies to bed with a feeling of reluctance to extinguish their bedside paraffin lamps.

"My story has no title as yet but in any case here is what I have written thus far," said he. Dr. Mortimer then proceeded to read to us as follows:

The fire burned brightly in the great stone fireplace while outside an early winter storm battered the ancient window panes of the great Georgian mansion where our little group was gathered. The Professor had explained that whether or not we made contact with the beyond depended upon our willingness to suspend our reluctance to believe in wraiths, ghosts, specters, or other manifestations. I could see that the ladies of our group were nervous because a light ripple of laughter filled the room and seemed to dispel the darkness that lurked in the corners. The storm outside that howled over the empty moors only made it more natural that we would all seek solace within the shelter that the old manor house provided for us. Why was it then that I felt a sudden impulse to flee at once into the storm outside rather than to face whatever might dwell in the greater darkness of the silent upper chambers of the house where we were all situated? I began to regret leaving the jolly company of my London Club at this festive season where I might have been reassured by the dull litany provided by good company and the prosaic talk of the London stock exchange and the reports from the outer fringes of our British empire. Instead I found myself seated at a great round table lit only by a single candle burning bravely amidst the draughts of the vast drawing room and illumining the faces of those about me, the pale and lovely faces of the ladies and the grim faces of the men, as our host bid us all to rid our minds of any exterior thoughts and to focus as with a single will upon the invocation of the dead on that dreadful night that haunts my memory to this very day.

He finished reading and folded his manuscript looking up brightly to Sir Henry and to me to see what our reaction to his prose had been.

"Promising very promising indeed," said Sir Henry.

Dr. Mortimer then turned to me with expectant eyes.

I attempted to be honest, but not overly encouraging to his compulsion to pursue occult topics and studies that the Catholic Church considers to be very irreligious and ill-advised. "You must forgive me Doctor Mortimer, but it is my business to abjure romance the better to discern the all too usual course that events pursue without preternatural interference. Where would I be as a detective if I allowed emotional atmospherics to bias my judgment? No I fear that ghosts and goblins must seek elsewhere for a home, but as to the prose, you have certainly captured the prevailing tone of the Christmas tale of terror. I should think that you would be quite popular among the ladies if you continue to write in this manner. It is a peculiar trait of the female of the species that suspense and foreboding seem romantic and entertaining."

My rather qualified praise seems to me now in retrospect to have been a bit stuffy and lacking in the courtesy due to all writers. It is my considered opinion that writers who begin with little promise often grow gradually by the mere habit of continued writing to achieve some degree of dexterity in the style of their prose as well as in plot and characterization. So it was that I used this occasion to ask the budding writer why he did not rather compose a thesis upon the entire topic of specters and preternatural monsters.

"I confess that I have often considered doing so," said he,

"And I would do so now, but that I fear ostracism and rejection from the more hard-headed members of the medical profession if it should get out that I submitted monographs on these topics. Perhaps when I retire I may dedicate my efforts to a complete compendium of the occult. It would certainly provide a helpful corrective to the bland confidence of men like Thomas Huxley and others who scorn whatever science may not immediately prove and verify. I often think that there is nothing that has been more deleterious to mankind than the invention of new instruments for observation. We allow our instruments to constrain what may be conceived. What has become of imagination in science? I for one believe that the unaided intellect may intuit truths that far exceed the ability of any measuring device to capture. I find our British empiricism to lead to a shopkeeper version of reality."

"You prefer the German idealists then?" I inquired.

"I do sir, but not Bishop Berkeley or even Immanuel Kant, who as far as I can see has simply muddied the waters of the philosophical pond by speaking of the unknowable thing-in-itself so as to do justice to David Hume's skepticism. He doubts that we can know about substances while still positing various moral absolutes that float about in the ether as it were. What is his categorical imperative but his own inner Germanic conscience? A cannibal in the South Seas might feel an inner obligation to eat his enemy as a sign of triumph and to absorb his life-force; is that also a categorical imperative rather than a particular cultural belief; from whence comes this whole categorical imperative nonsense but from the latent Christianity from which Kant cannot be extricated? The Germans are among the most sentimental of the races yet they always insist upon relying on cold reason when they are not stuffing themselves with sausages. It will be the ruin of them, for from cold and distant reasoning there comes about fixed ideas based on inadequate data that will later be reinforced by the emotion that is only deferred by its radical denial to emerge later on. The German mind then promptly turns sentimental again and to impose its fixed idea upon the world turns to the force of arms. Meanwhile the British, who if I may say so have a precisely contrary affliction of thought, begin with a restricted vision based on empirical data and then quite unsentimentally take an attitude that some obscure sense of national duty demands national sacrifice - two different routes to one common end of joint destruction. Both nations are skeptics in their way: British empiricism ends in linguistic parsimony while the German idealists reduce everything to the mind and then proceed to exalt whatever power it has lost in cognition with a substitute, the force of the unaided will."

"And the corrective for all this mutual failure to arrive at a ground for all things is...?" I tentatively but suggestively inquired.

Doctor Mortimer answered me immediately, as if my question was one that he had often posed to himself. "Read the writings of William Blake or Samuel Taylor Coleridge if you wish to find an answer Mr. Holmes. The remedy for sterile philosophy is to allow the mind's fancy free play, give in to the imagination, because it is there that culture resides in embryo and it is from culture that civilization proceeds. Note that it is not the artists and poets who take us to war, unless they first prostitute their talents to patriotic zeal. The faculty of fancy that the poets possess above all other sorts of men and women grasps the world entire in image and symbol. The poet appeals to the feelings before he addresses the intellect and by doing so ensures that the intellect is fully human by awakening first a deeply human response within us."

"How does that differ from mere sentimentality, which you have condemned in the Germans?" asked Sir Henry.

Dr. Mortimer answered, "The distinction is that the Germans are rapturous about ideas that lead to power, whereas mere fancy creates images and from images the poet communicates beauty and the static emotion of wonder that beauty awakens within us. As John Keats once said, 'Beauty is truth, truth beauty; that is all you know on earth and all you need to know.' You will no doubt point out to me that images and symbols are vague and fuzzy things. You will point out that philosophy like science demands replication and authentication. Ah you see, I was right! But why is the world of thought so determined upon certainty as opposed to using premature suggestiveness to stimulate further thinking? Art feeds on precisely this need to communicate in new ways so as to make experience more rich and gratifying. Artists work on the periphery of thought in that shadow-land of dream and illusion. But even when we speak of truth in its most bare and brutal elements, what you might assert (after reading John Locke) as secondary qualities are not secondary at all, because we are closer to them than any other qualities that once abstracted out of human experience may just as well cease to exist, for we may know nothing of them. Even Pragmatism, for all of its protestations to be merely the exercise of common sense is opposed to our primary experience of value as mediated by art directly without passing through the selective prism of truth. Art is apprehended at once and prior to reflection as immediately meaningful. Art should be more of course than mere tautology. There must be some external reality to which the image must attach if only as its inspiration, but the image falsifies itself to the degree that it mirrors reality exactly. The truest image comes freighted with what fancy provides! We change things in the act of perceiving them and the creative artist changes them the most, not by obscuring the source of his image, but by elevating it into meaning by the activity of his art.”

“So you would agree with the romantic poet Percy Bysshe Shelley that poets are the unacknowledged legislators of the world,” I concluded.

“No, Mr. Holmes. The world does not need legislators pursuing various agendas and programs for human improvement. It is these programs to create a newer world that stifle the life within us! What we require is finer perceptions, not of what is, but of what we create – therein does what is Godlike within us reside.”

“And so you plan on writing more ghost tales,” chided Sir Henry. “Is that your choice for the use of the exalted faculty of fancy?”

“Fancy has no use; that is the very point,” answered Doctor Mortimer. “It simply is and that is sufficient.”

“It is closing time gentlemen!”

Suddenly our animated discussion was interrupted by those dreadful words of dismissal when all merry revelers are sent out into the unforgiving auspices of night. I was loath to terminate what had begun as a mere recitation from a romantic tale such as one from the pen of the German author, E.T.A. Hoffman, or that macabre American writer, Edgar Allen Poe. From this inauspicious beginning we had touched upon that ground where the aesthetic realm merges with the metaphysical - all of this to the vast amusement of several local farmers who had overheard much of our discussion.

"Didn't I tell ye; all the gentry are mad?" I heard one of them mutter to the other as we left, no doubt unaware that he had just impugned the sanity of Sir Henry, the squire and chief benefactor of the entire region round Grimpen. His companion explained this fact to the speaker while doffing his hat to our group. The speaker regretting his hasty words apologized at once. "Sorry Your Lordship, I surely beg your pardon; but as I'm but a poor man visiting from Staffordshire and didn't know ye, and as I've had a bit too much to drink, I'm sure I meant no offense."

"None taken my good man," said Sir Henry genially and in that good spirit we concluded a most enjoyable evening.

June 18, 1893
Baskerville Hall

My home is almost complete and ready for habitation. Sir Henry and I walked over today to inspect the progress that has been made thus far. I have had the grounds and gardens cleared of brambles and heather. The moss on the roof has been removed, the drive has been smoothed and new stone put down. Ruts and small ponds are no more. Vermin have been eliminated by a chap who keeps rat terriers. Inside all has been scrubbed, the woods polished to a high veneer, ceilings and wainscoting buffed, cobwebs removed and chinks caulked. My furniture has also arrived. Sir Henry and I spent the morning seeing it placed properly.

I have in my own way recreated my rooms at Baker Street here. My new chemical apparatus has its place in the corner. There is a settee. I have replaced the old cane-back chair of Watson with a more comfortable armchair with a matching twin. There is a fine oak dining table in the dining room with a substantial sideboard. The bedrooms have sea chests instead of closets and wardrobes so that there is room for a desk and bookcase in each room. The pantry and larder are well-stocked and I have opened accounts with the local butcher, the baker, and a fishmonger who supplies fresh fish from Plymouth.

Sir Henry has offered to supply me with fresh game from the estate, pheasants, grouse, and ducks. I have engaged a cook and housekeeper from Grimpen on Sir Henry's recommendation. Indeed, so much progress has been made this day that I need do little more now than simply to move in. I have arranged to have the house blessed by the pastor of the local parish church and to have a small housewarming party with my friends. For the rest I have laid in a brace of pistols and a Winchester rifle, all gifts from Sir Henry, to enable me to repulse any assaults from any quarter whatsoever. I am still not without enemies from of old. I have kept my presence here known to only my small circle of friends and perhaps the villagers who recall me from prior visits to Baskerville Hall. The latter care little for any name or fame that I may have. If I am referred to at all it is merely as, "that detective feller."

I am well supplied with tobacco and pipes thanks to Mycroft who knows my habits well. He sent me these as a gift addressed to Baskerville Hall. I was delighted with his choices since they correspond with my new affection for Turkish blends and my usual Latakia mixture. Watson has made much of my preference for vile and cheap shag tobacco, a reminiscence of my early years when I could afford little else. Watson always loves to paint me as an eccentric, no doubt to sell his little stories about me to the Strand Magazine. It is his little revenge for my occasional curt comments. I can be a bit nervy at times and Watson retaliates by giving evidence of a strain of pawky humor latent within him.

He also is not above altering details in his stories to enhance their dramatic appeal and even to make errors in dating through relying upon his faulty memory or perhaps out of a desire to avoid libel actions by altering circumstances to prevent any too close identification of the actual parties involved in a sensitive case.

Since I am speaking of the dear old fellow I should record here that Mycroft has received word from America that all is going well for him there. The good doctor is immersed in his labors with the small group of lepers and medical workers at Carville, Louisiana. The climate is quite stifling there no doubt, with the Mississippi River so close and at that latitude. He writes Mycroft that he has developed a taste for alligator and turtle stews served up with red peppers. I can only imagine how appalled Mrs. Hudson, that good Scotswoman, would be at this sort of menu. Her idea of the arcane is any article of French cooking. Her specialties are confined to roast beef, grilled onions and potatoes, and kippers and bangers for breakfast.

I have learned to supply any needs that I have for variety in cuisine by a visit to Simpsons or to a Russian tea house nearby in Chelsea. The proprietor's wife is French and will whisk up many provincial French dishes at my request. Alas, here in Devon I must make do with the traditional British grocery goods offered in Coombe Tracey and Grimpen unless I run out to Barnstaple where there are a few foreign restaurants. Still and all I believe that I will be quite happy here. My lungs are improving and I have cut back on tobacco use in spite of Mycroft's gifts that recall earlier times. My walks are brisk but not strenuous and undertaken largely to keep my wolfhound in good trim.

After seeing to matters at my cottage Sir Henry and I returned to the hall and I went up to my room to rest. I found myself still thinking about the strange character and opinions of Dr. Mortimer. I find his passion for Neolithic antiquity to be most intriguing. He appears to be quite the pagan, preferring our own native deities no matter how obscure they may be to any that he would deem of Near Eastern origin. No doubt he like so many others has been put off by the sanguinary history of Jewish origins and the conquest of the land of Canaan and the ritual of the blood sacrifice of animals. It is a vexed point how much of the Judaic vision of Yahweh is more a sign of the expectations and needs of the Jewish people, who were to be formed into the nation of Israel, rather than a transcendent revelation to them by God.

To assume that the Bible as we have it today is a univocal document and not a collection of separate texts is to deny the historicity of the communications to a tribal people with a mindset dictated by the needs and preconceptions of the age and place in which they lived. How much of these teachings may now be directed to humankind as a whole living in different times and conditions? To read Sacred Scripture without a proper hermeneutic and awareness of the time, place, and manner of its original reception is to imply a universal and univocal message to a differently situated audience and an equal capacity in every age to interpret and to apply the texts to present conditions.

Without a central and informed teaching authority of equal weight to scripture and a living body of believers inspired by the Holy Spirit as well, without this is to say the Catholic Church, that task of referral of the Biblical texts and their interpretation becomes impossible and various absurd splinter groups always tend to emerge with time. The historical result has been the fragmentation of Christendom and the encouragement of various sects and fanatics who would seek a specious unity through the charism of an assumed office to minister and to worship based only upon selective personal appeal. There can be only one true and complete synthesis of the Christian faith and that is the one provided by the solid structure of the Apostolic Succession which guides the living body of the one universal Church.

The Roman Catholic Church embodies within itself the Holy Spirit, present within it and guiding it to ever greater conformity with Christ, the head of His Body, which is the Church. Since Our Lord is the final and complete revelation in his own person of the will of the Father, He is not mythological but historical. All of Holy Scripture then must be seen as a gradual revelation that prepares the way for the coming of Jesus as the definitive Word of God made flesh and dwelling among us. All prior teachings and images of God must then be either validated in Christ or be seen as mythological. The roots in Judaism show by the gradual revelation over time of the interventions made by God for the welfare and advancement of the Jewish people, the way leading to Jesus Christ. The Bible must be read through a wide lens to be understood properly. To assume the validity of each line of scripture on an equal basis is to be placed in the awkward position of maintaining endless contradictions and opposing demands. Without the Catholic Church to serve as a guide Christianity becomes impossible, because without the Church any sect of Christianity that is being practiced is only a fragment and not the whole.

None of this of course would trouble my dear pagan friend, Dr. Mortimer. He is quite content with what he would call "the God of nature lord of nymphs and satyrs." For him all concepts of revelation are absurd because they appear to interfere with benevolent nature by putting it in second place. He is quite content to see mankind as merely an extension of the beasts. Even his "Fair Folk" are immanent in seeing to their various functions, such as making flowers grow, streams sparkle, and the rain to bead on leaves. He sees the world much as does a child and with a similar sense of wonder. There are no demons in his pantheon of spirits. If there is death and violence to be found in the world at times, it is because there are also bogies and kelpies among fairies. These are for the most part more mischievous than they are truly evil.

"Violence is part of life, part of nature," says he. "To strive to eliminate evil is to assume that this world exists for our convenience, pleasure, and comfort. The strange thing is that so piteous and futile a being as man or woman exists at all with all our pretentions. Surely that we exist at all should be enough without expecting heaven as well after we die. Besides, we need a bit of misery to stay sane. It is said that for a man to descend into fairyland is to return a madman, not because of the evil that he finds there, but because it is so beautiful there that no man who ever visits there can bear the exile of returning here."

Dr. Mortimer is impervious to all my efforts to imply a greater destiny for our aspirations. He can see no substantial difference between man and beast and stone. All are one. All enjoy living in that measure of being granted to them. He would prefer to assume that stones are conscious rather than to assume that man and woman are to be advanced so that they may dream of immortality in company with God. But when I try to speak of this Dr. Mortimer says, "Why the whole thing would be so boring! Imagine never ceasing to be. Can any worse horror be imaginable? Think of the sheer burden of successive memories! It is already intolerable to me to have decades of experience behind me so that I deem half of all that I have experienced as having happened to another man than the one that I am now. What then shall we make of centuries, of eons, of eternity without begging for the beneficent gift of extinction? What if this morning I were to watch a Brontosaurus feeding and by the eon's nightfall to see the species of tomorrow arising from the swamps of the present time as men? Yet this is the experience of God. Who would dare to ask for such a gift as immortality? Do you not see that it would be a curse for any human creature, as we are presently constructed, to live forever?"

I attempted to point out of course that heaven so exceeds time and memory that we will be adapted to eternity in heaven as we are now adapted to living in space and time.

"Ah yes," said he, "But then what becomes of your doctrine of a resurrected body? Was that doctrine after all merely a sop thrown in to aid those believers who could not imagine living a purely spiritual existence?"

This was a good question for one who does not believe, but still I think I answered him properly when I said, "The doctrine of the Resurrection of the Body represents the recognition by the Church that even in our present state our bodies are Holy and that the Holy Spirit of God dwells within us. The body once so dignified must share in some fashion in the resurrection. God does not despise matter. The Incarnation of Jesus Christ shows us that God does not wish to keep aloof from His creation, but that all created being is already by virtue of the Incarnation of Christ permeated with God. Creation is like a vast sponge desirous of being penetrated and filled with God. What we shall be after death, as St. John has said so well, has not been revealed. The Catholic Church teaches that Christ has put all things under his feet, that Christ is the beginning and the end, the alpha and the omega. What was veiled beneath the single human, in Jesus Christ of Nazareth, who was an actual person, is eventually to be shared by all of creation. This cosmic vision of the Resurrected Christ exceeds the historical drama of the thirty-three years of Jesus' earthly life, but is integral to seeing the divine efficacy of those events for all of humankind."

"If the whole thing seems disproportionate, it is only because we cannot imagine the infinite entering the limited. To say that God has become man is not the same as saying man has become God. The latter option was the one chosen by Adam and Eve and it brought about ruin for both man and woman. These two could not on their own initiative become like God. For this very reason God has become man, doing what only God can do, the one true God for whom all things are possible even to lay aside divinity as though it were a cloak or a crown and to assume the guise of the least and most suffering of men."

"In doing so God has left no corner of our desolation un-probed by the light of God's grace. There remains no dark corner of sin not comprehended and forgiven. Only the heart of man may close God out and only then with the fullness of its faculties and in a manner that includes both death and judgment as a simultaneous event, a test. We pray daily that we may be spared the full measure of that test. We pray that we may, during this life, so begin to live as children of God that when the time of testing comes we may find that we were already living in the life of grace, so that heaven when it appears at last will seem to be our natural abode after all. Then all that we have been, and yes even our bodies, will share that new life that at present exceeds any full measure of comprehension."

"Holy Scripture you see is merely indicative rather than definitive in this matter. It awakens the imagination to heaven, to picture what it cannot define. The Catholic Church as one body thus lives in aspiration, lives in faith, knowing grace now, but still not the full measure of what God has in store for those who love Him. The proper measure of Christian hope is to hunger for the unseen while not despising that which is seen now, but ministering to it in charity for as long as we shall live."

Dr. Mortimer shook his head. "Well, so you may say, but even if this is so, why may I not have the comfort of my own religion, which finds this world's consolations to be enough for me? I do no man harm. I find my shrines all about me and I share my views with the animists of every nation who have learned to live at peace with the earth. As I see it, most Christians spend so much time thinking of heaven that many of them feel no compunction about making a hell on earth for anyone who disagrees with them."

I smiled at this observation, "You may be closer to the Kingdom of God than many Christians, Dr. Mortimer. But dare I say that even you would not find a wonderful shard of pottery and not desire to know something of the artisan who made it. I suggest that if you keep turning over rocks and looking for fairy-circles in the fields of grain you will eventually search further still and find God waiting for you." Those were my last words to him. Dr. Mortimer made no reply at the time, but left soon after shaking his head to return to his own home no doubt and the comfort of his unrivaled local collection of skulls and rocks.

June 19, 1893
Baskerville Hall

One of those sudden storms blew in today from the sea and the air was quite as cold as it often is here in April. It put me in a ghostly frame of mind and I found myself thinking of the strange case of John Vincent Hardin the American tobacco millionaire and the strange persecution to which he was subject.

That persecution was of a decidedly preternatural nature and took the form of a haunting of the old family mansion located on the coastline of South Carolina. Though a kindly man himself he was descended from several ardent slaveholders and his older brothers were all killed in the cause of the American Confederacy. The estate that remained was largely preserved because it was in liquid funds deposited in English banks and it was to England that the young heir repaired after finding it impossible to remain in the family mansion with its current ghostly tenants.

The phenomena observed were typical of such reported haunting incidents. There were loud knocking sounds in the halls at night and unexplained lighting effects that might have been corpse-lights were seen hovering over the family graveyard. Mysterious writings appeared on the walls that appeared to be traced in blood and peculiar smells redolent of death and decay, which were traceable to no earthly source, made habitation unpleasant at odd hours. At last, the young man booked passage for England after first renting the estate to a local land magnate who saw that the acres of tobacco were worked at a fair wage by the newly liberated former slave population. The manor remained vacant though and was destroyed a year later by a fire of mysterious origin. It was said that as it burned cries were heard from the windows and flaming shapes were seen within though neither bones nor bodies were ever discovered afterwards when the ashes had cooled. I was able to share this story with Doctor Mortimer over dinner who nodded sagely and placing his finger alongside of his nose gave me to understand that such phenomena were familiar to him through his own researches into the occult.

"But what are they," I inquired.

"Who can say?" he replied. "They may be traces of past events preserved upon the ether or they may be communications from the dead, perhaps by providential design to enlighten the living in some way. Then there is the possibility that they have a demonic origin and are meant to frighten and confuse us. It may be that the dark forces exist beneath a sort of crust analogous to that which covers the earth and protects us from the molten rock below our feet. Certain events of a more than usual violence or evil may as it were cause this crust to thin so that the chaos beneath erupts in these very manifestations like a sort of psychic volcano. These cases tend to be the exception though and not the rule which breeds in us that skepticism in which a comfortable scientism takes its root. Still a primordial part of us knows that such things do exist and fear hovers about even the most unimaginative of us when we pass a graveyard at night.”

“As to this universal dread of the supernatural that you speak of I would have said with Aristotle that the instinct of terror to which you refer is more attributable to our sense of the innately theatrical,” I commented. “Pity and terror allow us to seem immune and above the ever-present threat of misfortune from such intractable or unforeseeable causes as nature always provides.”

Dr. Mortimer answered, “Why then not fear more ordinary catastrophes like a runaway carriage or sudden drowning, rather than ghosties and ghoulies and long-legged beasties and things that go bump in the night? No, Mr. Holmes, there are deeper origins for our terror than mere natural dangers; we walk in dread because we feel a fiend treading behind us who may whisk us away on the instant and into its dark realm.”

“But what have you to say about witches then Doctor?” I inquired. “Would you make common cause with those fanatical zealots who once put so many supposed witches to death for having entered upon a supposed pact with the devil in return for power over their neighbors, to obtain love or revenge?”

“The remedies of the times in question were no doubt excessive and ill-applied, but who is to say what entities if summoned by proper means may still pierce the veil of our mundane world and once having entered it remain to work their maleficent ends among us?” replied Doctor Mortimer solemnly.

“Gentlemen,” Sir Henry spoke up. “Let us leave these lugubrious topics. You forget that my own family was specter-haunted and such topics can only awaken in me unhappy memories.”

We both apologized to our host and the conversation drifted to a discussion of local horticulture and other matters of ordinary gossip in the country round about us. But as I settled in for the night I seemed in fancy to hear again the distant baying of that spectral hound that had once menaced our gracious host with death as it had done generation after generation ever since Sir Hugo Baskerville had summoned it forth by a rash promise to sell his soul to the devil in exchange for the virtue of an innocent girl for whom he had conceived an ill-starred passion. In just such matters it seems possible for evils to awaken or to gain entry through some spell or incantation and thereafter to spring forth unbidden so that once having done so the evil remains as a family curse.

Dr. Watson's Narrative Continues

The day of our departure from Newport had finally arrived. The month of September was well advanced. Already the leaves were showing the first signs of pallor that precede the deeper yellows and reds of fall. My readings in Holmes' journal had shown me how deep was the concern for me that he had entertained, even during our long period of separation. I recall well my time spent in Louisiana among the lepers. I primarily recall their patience in their affliction. How strange it seemed to suffer in modern America from an affliction that appeared to many people more of an ancient curse than a mere instance of disease; yet all diseases distance us from our peers. Disease is the great reminder of our mortality and what man or woman cares to contemplate his or her own demise. As we age we push the debt that we owe to time further and further ahead of us, imagining that we may rely upon the credit of the past to ensure that we will always remain in our present abode among those still living. Surely, we think that death busy as it is might make an exception in our case. Perhaps the decrepitude of age and our withered faces is a mercy to us. Who would let go of life suddenly, in the spring-flower of an eternal youth, without a sense of the stolen years that lie ahead; but when the years heap up like snowdrifts or blowing yellow leaves from burning pyres, we may at least acknowledge, accompanied by a measure of resentment, the fact that we must all finally die.

As I left behind the exquisite summer colony of Newport, I

was perhaps more aware of the permanence of things compared to the transience of those who pretend to own them. All of life is finally a long-term lease on all of our goods and chattels. We have a fee-simple absolute only over the six feet of ground that will be our graves. The only true free-hold is the tomb. I buried not a few of our leprosy patients that year of a prior trip spent in America. Many patients discovered in the leprosarium at Carville only a place to finally succumb to another affliction like pneumonia or malaria. Having lost my wife I did not care at that time what my own fate would bring. The result was that I nursed the dying with a charity and resignation that brought me undeserved admiration. I doubt if I would have run such risks during many happier periods of my life.

When my time came at last to return to England after my year of service, my departure in excellent health came as something of a surprise to me. I began to realize that I still possessed a medical practice in England and a proper home in Kensington. I would have again a clean dispensary at my disposal where I might meet my patients. I could appear again with a top hat and collar and not wearing a smock and an old planter's straw hat while doing my medical rounds each day. To return to civilization was as great a shock as it had been to leave it.

I caught a train from New Orleans to Knoxville and from there to the Port of Baltimore where I caught a ship a week later that was bound for England. I did not tarry in America. I preferred to return there at some later day when I might enjoy wandering about sightseeing without carrying about with me the recent memories of the leper hospital whose denizens would live the rest of their lives and die in Carville. My own freedom seemed to mock them; I had no heart for the pleasures denied to them for which I had no interest.

I arrived in England in time for the English autumn, a season in tune with the remnants of my despondency. I knew that I needed to begin to live again without my wife and without the companionship of Sherlock Holmes. I could not know at the time that Sherlock Holmes was back and alive and residing to the west of me in Devonshire, deeply immersed at the time in his struggle with Professor Moriarty. The struggle that I had assumed was concluded on the brink of the Falls of Reichenbach was still to be waged in a duel where only one party might hope to prevail.

I was engaged in recalling that painful autumn of 1893 when I was interrupted by the very man himself, Sherlock Holmes. "You were looking somewhat melancholy Watson. No doubt you will find it difficult leaving these fleshpots of Egypt to assume the role of a mere British tourist once again. We shall meet Inspector Hopkins at the station in Newport as arranged *en route* to Boston. I trust that he has learned all that he may from the New York constabulary. He is due for a bit of a holiday after so much study. We will spend the night in the village of Concord near Boston and tomorrow we shall walk the shores of Walden Pond. I have a series of maps at hand if you would care to peruse them. In any case, our hostess awaits us below and we must bid her *adieux*."

I proceeded after Holmes down the now well known staircase where Mrs. Wharton bid us goodbye graciously with two outstretched hands as she had already said her farewells two weeks ago to Irene Adler who was off to New York for the fall season. The carriage took us down Bellevue Avenue to the center of Newport. My morning walk to Rough Point along the sea had allowed me time to bid farewell to Marble House and to The Breakers. I could just glimpse their upper spires above the trees as our carriage passed.

A short time later we were aboard our train and heading through the green hills and deep woods of Rhode Island. The cheerful Inspector Hopkins was grateful to be reunited with us at last, and to carry on by our side as we explored New England's charms. Holmes attempted to cheer me up by getting the Inspector to inform us how his summer had been spent.

"It is all about gathering evidence," he said in answer to Holmes' query about what he had learned over the past months in New York. "They refer to it as scientific investigation. It involves building an airtight case for a prosecutor. The entire criminal system is oriented around the goal of conviction: fingerprints, miniscule traces of fabrics, plaster casts of footprints, physical clues of all kinds. The rest of American police science is to set up a police presence of sufficient size to deploy rapidly after a crime is reported and to use weapons effectively."

"What of my own methods of simple observation and deduction?" Holmes inquired.

"Ah, there sir I am afraid that I encountered the same skepticism with which you are acquainted from your dealings with Scotland Yard. As an individual you are respected and even admired in New York, but it is the general consensus that your methods are not adaptable to general use. Your peculiar genius is held to be an unusual quirk that will perish with you. I attempted to explain your methods and was given a polite hearing, but there the matter was allowed to rest."

Holmes pondered this with a shake of his head. "I imagined as much. I did not have great hopes of founding a school of thought here in criminology. I am finding as I grow older that the problem of criminal detection should take second place to the problem of crime prevention by understanding what leads people to commit crimes in the first place. Of what use is it to burden the land with prisons? What is a prison but a condemnation of the society that is forced to build them? It is true that evil will always be present in the human heart and that a criminal code must exist to define and condemn behaviors that may disrupt the social order, but what then? When that code is violated, does the mere passage of time in the brutal society of the prison properly reform the criminal? Can any sentence do anything more than lengthen the period of non-productivity of the criminal and add to the burden placed upon the rest of society that must in consequence support this enforced idleness of so many of its members? You speak of the emphasis upon physical evidence; excellent, all well and good in the effort to prove a chain of causality between actor and crime, what is called in terms of the law the *actus reus*; but is not the essence of the crime in the mental state and purpose of the criminal, again in the terms of the law the *mens rea* of the crime?

However the problem of criminality exceeds that of mere detection of crimes and the means by which society levies a sentence of guilt; the real problem surely is one of social engineering whereby the social unit grows and prospers by enhancing the gifts of each of its members. I suggest that one must look to the economy and to the inner temper and culture of the nation as a whole if one would find the roots of criminal activity. Much criminality is predicable and endemic; therefore it is only by rooting-out the social causes of these 'social crimes' that crime may be effectively diminished. Of course there will remain the hard-core of evil that will always thrive, finding its basis in greed, passion, and violence. Of course there is also the case of those mentally deranged persons who seem to have an inadequate sense of the humanity of others and a less than adequate conscience. These have left the social contract far behind and no other fate remains for them than to be exiled to a penal colony adapted to their own savage tastes."

"Surely you are being a bit of an idealist in reducing the majority of crimes to the social and economic causation, Holmes," interposed the Inspector.

"That may be," answered Holmes, "But what is the social order but an exercise in the ideal. This means that some prospect must exist for social advancement and democracy in the general populace. Poverty, squalor, and destitution create the desperation and despair that may lead many into a life of crime. If we are not to be considered as mere beasts requiring trainers, then we must make room for the ideal in humanity. I must return here to the teachings of the Catholic Church, which can have no illusions regarding human nature after the nearly two thousand years of its existence. The great cesspool of human depravity flows through the confessional in every church and chapel in the land and penances are imposed to reinstate the soul to some sense of its own dignity. The sin is judged so that the sinner may go free by being reinstated to sanctifying grace. How different is that of the judgment of a secular courtroom where the criminal is judged and often leaves in a spirit of pride and bitterness to serve his time in prison until he may again emerge and enact his hatred and revenge upon the social order that condemned him! Where is the hope of reformation in that process? The disease of criminality is further incubated in the artificial environment of the prison itself! What are prisons but a place of instruction in criminal methods and associations? Bah, the entire process is simply evidence of the simplemindedness and lack of will to address the underlying problems leading to crime and to probe that greatest of mysteries, the human heart, for a solution. If prisons must be maintained at all, they would be more effective if the prisoners were not locked away from the gaze of the society that must construct and manage them and must pay for their maintenance. Perhaps prisons should be run more like zoological exhibits, wherein convicted persons are separated by genus and species and gawked at by schoolchildren on holiday."

"My dear Holmes!" cried the Inspector. "Surely you are pulling my leg!"

"Oh yes," Holmes smiled, "I may at least be tugging on your leg a bit. But only reflect that if the goal is meant to punish criminals, then that punishment in order to be both effective and less costly to the rest of society should be the mildest and least brutal possible. No upright citizen should desire that proxies be appointed to exact a sadistic retribution that is done in the name and by the authority of the better members of society. Perhaps the most appropriate punishment then is to expose the criminal to the judgment and disapprobation of the social order that the criminal has violated and to be placed in the presence of the members of that society that has condemned him. This could be accompanied by being forced to confront those persons that the criminal has harmed."

Holmes continued, "Perhaps several months of watching through the bars as the public eats peanuts or toffee while gaping at him might cause a criminal to reflect upon his own lost dignity and to desire a change of life. He will see that by the crimes that he has freely chosen, he has made himself the rightful target for public opprobrium and has made himself ridiculous. What can be more embarrassing than to say that a man has made a spectacle of himself? Very well then, let a man be treated for a time as the beast most associated with his particular crime. Why imprison tigers and lions in zoos? What crime have they committed? Let them go free! Have we not sufficient murderers among us who are the real killers? Let them be fed raw meat in a cage. Have we no snakes among us: the forgers, the embezzlers, and the thieves? They shall be the exhibits in the realm of human herpetology! What of those who commit the supposedly clean crimes of fraud, of stock swindles, or of oppression of the poor such as vile landlords? What are they but the human version of jackals and hyenas? Let them bark and howl for the amusement of the crowd and drool from their gaping jaws. Surely to be human is a vocation to be a child of God and not a beast. Perhaps if a man is made to realize that he has made a beast of himself at once swiftly and effectively, then he may desire to reassume his human nature quickly and be released from custody to live a better life.”

Inspector Hopkins spoke up, “And if this way of reformation that you suggest fails, what then?”

“Well then we must return to the social contract. A point must be reached where it must be made clear that such a person cannot live in human society and a place must be devised where he can exist among persons of his own kind, but without guards.”

We still gaped at Holmes where he sat on the cushions of his railroad compartment seat with his chin resting upon his silver-topped hunting-crop. At last he spoke, “Ah well perhaps the whole scheme is fanciful after all, but surely no less absurd than the prison systems that already exist among us. But I see that we are drawing into the station at Boston where we can obtain a carriage to take us to Concord Village where we may at least find a place that was once the home of those great American apostles of individual freedom and virtue: Ralph Waldo Emerson and Henry David Thoreau.”

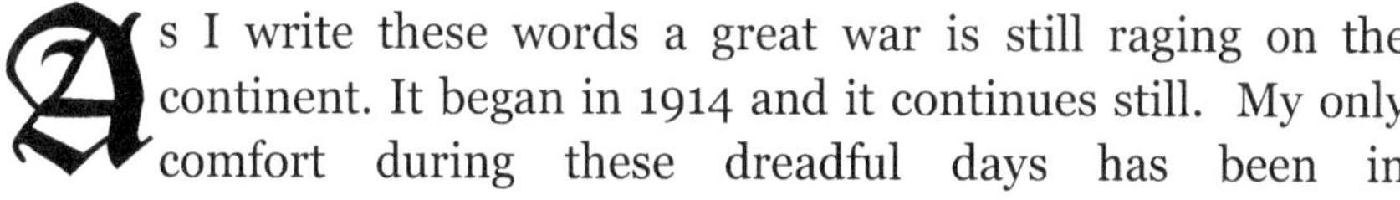

s I write these words a great war is still raging on the continent. It began in 1914 and it continues still. My only comfort during these dreadful days has been in reminiscence, to recall of the adventures of days now long gone by; that particular day now so long ago after we left Newport and those voices still echo in my mind as I write these words. America has always been a land that values superlatives and idealistic words that press the limits of the possible. Much of the charm of my friend Sherlock Holmes was his uncanny ability to discern what basic decency would counsel in any problematic situation. It was as though in his presence the cloudy became clear and the confused was reduced to clarity. In everything that I ever wrote regarding Sherlock Holmes I felt as though my pen was a conduit for his quiet strength and order in a world confused. Was this not precisely what the religions of the world promised? Was this not evident above all else in that most daring claim of all: that God (or an element thereof) would leave the celestial courts behind and descend from the joys of paradise and the honor of being the origin of moral perfection concentrated into one absolute being and embrace the human condition? Has anything more startling or improbable ever been proposed than these lines of the Apostle's Creed:

> *I believe in God the Father Almighty*
> *Creator of heaven and earth*
> *And in Jesus Christ His only Son, Our Lord,*
> *Who was conceived of the Holy Spirit,*
> *Born of the Virgin Mary*
> *Suffered under Pontius Pilate,*
> *Was crucified, died and was buried;*
> *He descended into hell;*
> *On the third day he rose again from the dead;*
> *He ascended into heaven,*
> *And is seated at the right hand of God,*
> *The Father almighty; from there He will come to judge*
> *The living and the dead...*

Everything else in Christianity is a matter of discerning who are the living and who are to be included among the dead. St

Paul assures us that sin brought death into the world. In other words everything that we see about us is a secondary phenomenon, a fall-back position held in reserve by God in case things did not turn out well after creation, just in case evil and its inevitable consequence death came into the world. Religion, and Christianity in particular, cannot imagine what such a world would have been like; all that is revealed to us is the lengths to which God has been willing to go in order to correct an intolerable situation.

But intolerable to who; that is the ultimate question? To those who are willing to freely embrace evil, death is an ally and a friend because they take no greater joy than in killing. Their one desire is to prevail longer than their foes. It is said that the devil is a liar and a murderer from the beginning and that every lie murders the truth. What is criminality then but the privatization of what nations and empires command everyday and call it virtue and patriotism. The deaths of those whom we fear or envy are considered to be a blessing to us and this is why Jesus dared to command us to love our enemies.

The truth of Christianity is not due to its innate appeal but rather to the extremity of the demands that it places upon us. Soren Kierkegaard, the great Danish philosopher was correct, that to be a Christian ought to be so difficult that we might well spend a lifetime and even a work such as I am now writing in order to clarify the greatness of the task. Fortunately God does not wait for us to approach Him; God takes the initiative and approaches us, so that no crevice of the human mind is immune from the demand that God must exist and a God precisely as portrayed by the humble figure of Jesus of Nazareth, someone from nowhere important, of questionable parentage, and one who failed during his lifetime to achieve his aims.

For God everything is deferred until after death and for us as well. We are not able to think or to manage ourselves out of the human situation. We are in the problem before we can foresee the problem and beg God to spare us the burden of existing at all! But having come so far we have no alternative but to continue to the end. That insight alone has kept me writing, years after the events recorded here and long after Sherlock Holmes left Baker Street behind to employ in an international setting those skills that he had honed during his long apprenticeship with me at his side at 221B Baker Street. I pray that I may live to complete this tale of how that immense transformation took place, but until then I can only continue this account by placing each successive event in order as the chronicler of his exploits.

Book Thirteen

The Tide Begins to Turn

Dr. Watson's Narrative Continues

My life like that of most other people has occurred in various episodes that must appear in retrospect to be too diverse to be part of a single narrative. I have been successively a soldier, a doctor, a sort of adjunct detective, a writer, a married man, a widower, and now a diplomat and companion on an international mission. I have not felt that I was the primary agent in any of these roles; instead life's exigencies and pure chance seemed to dictate my responses. The wheel of fate turned and I was caught up within it. There can be little doubt that whatever human situation we find ourselves in will eventually appear to us to be quite normal and we will judge others from that particular viewpoint. For this reason alone religious and political unanimity are an unlikely occurrence.

For instance, having lived among the patients with leprosy in Carville and among former slaves in the farms nearby, I found myself thinking and feeling that these were my people after all. Of course to a doctor all human bodies eventually appear quite the same. Illness and death bring all people to a common level. Still, there is little doubt that we absorb something from our surroundings so that after spending a summer surrounded by such elegance in Newport had exerted its own effect upon me, like one who has scaled Mount Olympus and then descended to live among mere mortals once again. While living at Land's End I had become accustomed to ring for a servant for any little need that I had and to leave on my plate any little delicacy that might have grown cold during the discussion at table. It began to feel as though I was one of the people among whom I was living rather than a guest, and a mere associate of Sherlock Holmes.

I did not feel such social difference in London and Holmes never referred to his roots at the elegant estate at Sigerside, the family home in Yorkshire. Holmes had trained himself to adjust to and to enact whatever was expected of him, just as a chameleon adjusts and changes color according to its surroundings. He could enter an opium den and assume the mien of a hopeless addict or stand toe to toe with a Duke or an Earl with no feeling of inferiority based upon the superior title of the other. He was neither disrespectful nor obsequious but only courteous and matter-of-fact in his bearing.

For me though such rapid transformation was not as easy. I felt in many ways as though I was betraying my most ardently held convictions by even being present among the ultra-rich denizens of Newport, yet I would not have missed the opportunity of enjoying such a lovely place for the summer and could not help feeling a pang of regret at leaving and resuming my ordinary manner of life. I tried to learn something from the experience though and through the acquaintance that I made there to discover some insight into how power manages to affect so many people, while its possessors remain aloof and unaware of the influences that their actions have on people that they will never meet. People are fired, evicted, or even thrown into destitution by policies and actions in the firms and trusts that these people own and not a ripple or a breeze filters up from the squalid cities to the people summering at Newport before returning in the fall to New York or Philadelphia or Savannah. Yet these people were courteous and well-spoken and I could not find it in my heart to condemn them for being spoiled by a lifetime of splendor when I began to weaken after a single summer of comfort and amenities. The search for equity and social justice was more difficult than I had imagined and I resolved to examine the structures of government with an equal curiosity whenever we arrived in Washington, D.C.

ur journey from Rhode Island and into Massachusetts was a short one. We disembarked at the crowded station and were soon fleeing from the crowded city of Boston by carriage into the lovely Massachusetts countryside on our way to Concord. My melancholy had lifted. During Holmes' discourse on prisons in the train he would now and again look over at me with a twinkle in his eye. As I had often noted before, Holmes had his own unique approach to things. I could see that Holmes enjoyed playing with an idea to see how far it might lead to a sensible outcome, no matter how outrageous it first appeared to be. He had learned that dictum well, which he often applied that order is found quite often within the absurd and that a man without humor will never comprehend the human situation.

As our carriage passed along the narrow highway leading to Concord, I could not suppress a feeling of excitement knowing that I would soon be in a place with so many historical and literary associations. I had always been an admirer of Henry David Thoreau. His detestation of the institution of slavery matched my own and I could not but admire his uncompromising sense of individual responsibility for the conditions that might prevail at any given time in society. At the same time he did not give up the longings of his own heart to thoroughly adapt to a locality and to use his literary gift to see and then to record the significance that lies within the simplicity of life. My own retreat in Cornwall was for me an English adaptation of Thoreau's cabin on Walden Pond. It was there that he laid out a vision for the freedoms promised to the individual by the great Constitution of America, a document of world significance particularly when it is combined with the American *Declaration of Independence.* This statement of principles is less of a juridical statement than it is an explanation of a new philosophy for human life.

The original charter for Americans was to be one of equality, opportunity, and of a collective witness to the rights of man. So daring was this experiment in government that it should not have come to me as a surprise as I witnessed the luxury of the

Newport mansions of the gilded age that the original experiment did not survive its first century. I could see that my melancholy in my final days in Newport had come from the clarity of this realization of American failure to actualize its first principles in the moment of the exhilaration at its victory in the war against Spain.

Instead of a gallant society of noble and independent yeomen farmers and independent craftsmen freed from the last legacy of the feudal guilds of Europe, the average American was now a prisoner of the iron-clad rule of the great trusts and corporations. The administration of William McKinley seemed dedicated to the growth of the behemoth that had replaced the original colonies with a great western empire gained by the extirpation of the Indian Nations that lay before it. That same national greed had led inevitably to a war with Spain, but not a war to free the Cubans as claimed but to remove any foreign colonial influence over lands that America would then be free to dominate with its various plantations: sugar, bananas, rum, and tobacco. The loyalty to the domination of industry had turned the once great and idealistic Republican Party that had once been one of sacrifice for the rights of man into the organ of American expansionism and greed. I knew that it was only by visiting again the home of America's greatest prophets that I might recover the roots from which the nation had strayed.

How appropriate that Massachusetts should have been home to the literary prophets of the old and true America: Emerson, Thoreau, Hawthorne, and Melville. These four men with the addition of America's eternal poet laureate, Walt Whitman, define America for me. Their lives spanned successive generations that witnessed the loss of the early vision and the descent into a fratricidal war. The early optimism of Emerson and Thoreau was replaced by the progressive disillusionment and darkness present in the writings of Nathaniel Hawthorne and Herman Melville. This devolution was the inevitable path from innocence to experience as the irrevocable darkness of the human heart finally emerges. All Pelagian dreams finally expose human nature revealed at last in the somber garments of its primordial sin.

Perhaps that sour minister, Jonathan Edwards, was right after all, not in his theology, but in his grim assessment of the national temper. The slide towards the rigors of Calvinism is a natural response in anyone who sees and evaluates the human condition over time. But Calvinism is in many ways its apparent opposite, Pelagianism, but in disguise. The true Calvinist never stops working in order to prove that he is one of the elect of God. Who was it but the English Puritans who dreamed of leaving the sin of the old world behind and building a new society, a new Geneva in the Arcadian forests of America?

Mere distance in space however does not preserve one from the infection that we all carry within us, of original sin. One of the greatest beauties of Roman Catholicism is that it has resisted any impulse to escape to a new land by changing the site of Papal governance except for the one disastrous experiment of the Avignon Popes. The Popes have remained ever since in Rome and built the universal Church in the very stronghold of the ancient Romans who crucified Christ and martyred St. Peter and St. Paul. The center of the Church exists where brutality and vice so long reigned and where the blood of the early Christian martyrs was shed. The Church does not seek to escape sin by running from it, but by the confrontation with the Cross of Christ extended even to martyrdom and thus to do penance and to bear witness throughout all ages to come.

How historically different had been the fate of America! The nation began as abstemious Puritan colonies and ended by becoming the very center of materialism and the domination of mammon as symbolized by the American dollar, which may someday become the dominant currency of the entire world. What was the fate of the laboring class under late 19th Century industrialism but as an appendage, a useful commodity, an element on a balance sheet? Did it matter if the laborer expired over a loom in Lowell on the Atlantic Seaboard or if he died in the silver mines of Colorado or Nevada or even in a lumber camp in Oregon? His fate was predetermined in 1898 by powers no longer his own. He would never know the freedom of even Thoreau's simple cabin on Walden Pond.

To assume that the only means of oppression of citizens lay in the existence of the titled nobility of Europe was to miss the fact that any concentration of power in the hands of the few is equally deadly to open markets and to democracy. The fundamental idea of America had once been to allow scope for self-determination based upon independent ownership of land. Taxation was to be limited by the scope allowed to a government of limited and enumerated powers. The concept of restricted and enumerated powers was in turn designed to allow for the free play of individual initiative, but at the same time to provide for a commonwealth of public resources in a common ownership of forests, grazing lands, and mineral rights. The primary function of law in a democracy was to preserve the structures that guarantee equal opportunity between and among generations, among families, and among individuals. This overarching policy would prevent the blockages to free-trade that stem from monopolies. When the law becomes the servant of the few, these ideas lose all civil support. A new plutocracy is then created to feed on the corpse of the former Republic. The railroad, oil, steel, and banking interests had by the year 1898 taken their models from the Medici and the Borgia families in their contempt for the common good. It was the wolf-like and rapacious ones who now came at last to rule and the people were left to shift for themselves and to divide the ever smaller remnant of the nation's once seemingly limitless bounty.

Walt Whitman still spoke of the pulsing organism of democracy, but it was not the conscious individual of whom he spoke; that imaginary individual was no more. Now there were only masses of men and women straining to create the megaliths of the new Babylon. The democracy that he once celebrated was corporate America and not the human cells that composed that massive body recently at war with Spain. Whitman's verse of vast expansionism was increasingly overblown and his optimism had a strain of hysteria about it. His orchestra was all brass. Thus idealism often celebrates what has already ceased to be.

The true poetry of America now requires a string section

for reflection and even lamentation. Such new poets will no doubt be quoted for years and their cymbals will clash and their drums will beat, but their clamor will only serve to cover the retreat of America from its original vision to the prosaic and grim realities of trade and the vast accumulation of wealth by the very few. Who may say when that process of wealth consolidation will be completed? Perhaps when America makes its claim upon the entire world and with fire and sword holds the nations in fear of the vortex of its ambitions?

How strange it is that a nation the humble beginnings of which were at the quiet bridge in Concord with musket fire directed by yeoman farmers would only a bare one hundred years later be engaging battleships in Manila Bay in the distant isles of the Philippines. Spain that at the time of the American Revolution was no friend of England was now an enemy of America, while England was a friend.

The former servant of yesteryear seeks servants of his own, with his own bondage a distant memory. Against this need to use the labor of others for personal enrichment Thoreau held up as a model for the new Americans the man who performs a simple but direct and honest service for another to earn his daily bread. This contract is individual and complete and bodes no relation of subservience in those matters that lie outside of the service to be rendered. Thoreau was a land surveyor by occupation and a naturalist and writer by avocation. He considered that the best part of a man's labors in this life may be for those tasks for which he will not be paid. To be in advance of one's age is to render services for a need that the mass of men has yet to recognize as essential. In this he acts like the honeybees that in providing for their hives provide also the food of all mankind by the process of cross-pollination.

The labors of the common folk are so customary and placid that we do not think to honor them. We reserve our historical accolades for generals and statesmen who for the most part have done all within their power to destroy the lives of entire populations through their absurd ambitions. The worst is this:

that the laws which should resist their hubris tend to aid them in their impious tasks. The law becomes then more than the last resource to solve conflicts and arrange affairs; its competence grows and grows until no area of human life but is permeated by the law, until the citizen finds that he is floating in a great sea of statutes and precedents. Law is a great beast that grows ever larger as it is fed. It gnaws into the vitals of nations as does the equal growth of fortunes made by the aid of the vast structures of trusts and corporations, which are mere fictions made of paper that soon enslave the individual citizen. The Creator limited the harm that the worst of men may do by providing for their death, but creatures of the law exist beyond the mortal life-span. The result is that capital grows until it becomes a mindless force sweeping the freedoms of men before it. In the end it comes to own even the government. In this manner the creations of mankind finally come to rule men and women and to deprive them of freedom, all in the name of some vast collective units of society which now demand allegiance to serve what are merely abstract constructions of the law, always under the aegis of achieving national glory by force of arms.

Seen from this point of view the function of American law as it is presently constituted is to allow the methods governing market capital growth to proceed unhindered by making them seem rational and just to those who are in an unequal bargaining position so that they will not band together to insert more equable elements in the system by political means. By restricting access to the vote and by relying on chicanery and demagoguery the citizens with wealth and power have recreated the very stratified class system that many Americans fled Europe in order to escape and to start a new life. By assuring the masses that they are "free" the new oligarchs immunize themselves from outrage and from retribution.

The remaining hope for an individual requires focus and a refusal to be seduced into such servitude. The American Constitution is remarkable, not for the powers that it grants, but for those that it withholds. The Ninth Amendment was meant to be a constant reminder that the majority of the rights of free citizens did not need to be enumerated because freedom presumes the right not to be annexed to the purposes of either government or of commerce. Each man exists, separate and entire, and may only be coerced when his own freedom impinges upon others. The existence of a private realm is the very stronghold of democracy and keeps it from being the mass-rule of the mob or the slavish capitulation to the wealthy. What the Ninth Amendment guaranteed to the individual, a realm of individual sovereignty, the Tenth Amendment guaranteed to the states as well. The States were conceived as the primary units which, because smaller and more easily policed for excesses by a vigilant populace, might see that the Federal government served the people and did not become an end unto itself.

Those safeguards against tyranny exist no more. The condition of America in 1898 and ever since has been governed by an all powerful Presidency, so that even Thomas Brackett Reed as the Speaker of the House of Representatives was unable to convince his countrymen that war would spell the end of peaceful existence for America. Instead America elected to join the struggles of the imperial nations of Europe and to join in that unending battle for supremacy that so many American citizens had fled in order to seek solace in a land protected by two great oceans. As America reached backwards across those oceans and built the navy that would enable it to assert its power beyond its own borders it inevitably exchanged the freedom of its citizens for the ability to project national power abroad. The center of concern at home migrated to the circumference just as it had before the fall of the Roman Empire. The fate of America was to be bled at home in order to feed the force of arms abroad.

How could it be otherwise, for thus it was with Rome and thus it was with France in the time of Napoleon? So it will be with America. The War between the American States was not between two powers, one which supported slavery and one that did not, it was a war to decide which form of slavery was to prevail, the racially based agrarian servitude of the south or the industrial servitude of the north. Each of the states had forgotten in its own way that freedom is measured by the number of citizens who actually possess it. Freedom was the faculty that could only be impaired in extremity as the constitution had promised. The presumption must always lie in the fact that a man may possess a sphere of time, property, and means of support that are the fruit and promise of individual dignity and isolation. The scope of government coercion is seen and its degree of imposition can be evaluated by observing the limitations imposed on the size of that sovereign sphere reserved to the individual. The promise of America, that each man might determine his own path to happiness within only a minimal web of laws to sustain the larger community of the State and the Nation was more than simply revolutionary, it implied a new concept of the purpose for human life in that it assumed that the basic unit of society was the individual person.

No other nation in history up to that time had shared this view. Even Kings and Queens were from birth constrained by the need to enhance the royal dominions by their choice of a spouse and thereafter by royal protocols such as being anointed by God to serve their subjects. Their subjects in turn existed to serve their monarch, to adhere to the restrictions of class or guild, and to serve the feudal lord or baron of the district to whom they were vassals or serfs.

In China and Japan a similar rule of tribute and subordination dictated one's social place and duty. Nowhere might the individual propose that he should be an end-in-himself and not be born in servitude to some larger structure. It was the presence of a frontier in America that made this bold assertion possible. The prospect of free land that any man might take up by musket and plough changed everything. The presence of frontier regions to be conquered and settled was a prerequisite to the entire American concept of government. When America reached its limits and the prospect of new frontiers was exhausted everything changed. The defeat of the rights of the states in the American Civil War was the prelude to empire. Thereafter the great centralization and consolidation of power of the industrial state and the great capital interests began.

What shall be the fate of America, I wondered as our carriage sped along the quiet country roads? As the war with Spain proved, America would soon need to confront and to accept what the other nations of the world have already learned, that man is free in this alone: he may choose the form of his servitude.

Americans traditionally fear nothing more than to encounter limitations. When they are constrained they form a force of arms to add to their territory. This makes them a martial people, a people to be feared. They are rather like the Mongolian hoards that swept over Asia in this respect. When the world is well-populated and no so-called savage regions remain, then the conqueror's vistas will cease. There will be no more men like Cortez of Spain, Pizarro of Peru, or Andrew Jackson of America. Perhaps only then will a world peace be possible for the good of all nations.

As I thought about these things I had bent over and touched the old wound on my leg. Holmes noticed this and spoke up. "Still ruminating upon war old fellow? You need not look up at me in surprise. We are going to the site of Concord Bridge where the American Revolution is said to have begun. We will visit Walden Pond and Hawthorne's Old Manse as well. I know the fascination that you have always had with America. It was one of the reasons for this journey of ours. But I beg you not to be so melancholy. We have exciting days ahead! It is autumn in New England; the leaves are turning slowly to old gold. We will soon see the lovely Lakes of New Hampshire and New York. We shall stand by the great Falls at Niagara. There will be time for melancholy when we see the coal regions of West Virginia on our way Washington. There we will spend the winter. It is there that we will make our final effort to steer public events. We will see if it is possible to affect important policies in what may become someday the dominant nation of the world. We will play our little role in history, Watson. I only hope that we may not regret the impertinence of the attempt!"

I suddenly realized that one of the purposes of this trip to America was to secure my own well being. I was touched by the fact that Holmes, if his condition worsened, was ready even to face dying as an exile from England so long as he might share the last months of his life at my side in my beloved America. He knew that I had long harbored the desire to explore the land that I had made the scene of two of my longest written accounts, *"A Study in Scarlet"* and a book unpublished at that time entitled, *"The Valley of Fear."* It was partially to allow me to see the sites of these twin narratives that he had risen from his sickbed and risked his life in one last trip with me as a companion.

I could also see that this quest of ours served a private purpose of Holmes as well. His career had been spent fighting tiny skirmishes with evil in the cases brought before him. Except in the case of the Bruce-Partington Plans, the affair with the French government that had brought him the Legion of Honor, and the business with the Vatican Cameos, Holmes had played a primarily domestic role. The one great exception had been the decade long battle with Professor Moriarty. But even that affair was more metaphysical in nature. Holmes had yet to strike into the very core of history, to attempt to see how far a man of good intentions might alter the destiny of nations. I know that he had long dreaded the actions that the Maupertuis affair now made essential. He had hoped for a last few quiet cases to fill out the years remaining to him before his retirement. Instead, he had been forced to undergo greater physical demands than any made upon him since the years of 1891 to 1894. I could not but admire such a gallant a gesture by an ailing man.

I also began to realize that Inspector Hopkins' long leave of absence was a gesture of respect for Holmes from Scotland Yard, for the man who had so often aided the official police. They would spare even one of their most esteemed inspectors to see that Holmes and I were guarded from any attacks that might come our way from Baron Maupertuis and his minions. We had been invisible in the retreat of Newport. We would not be so in

Washington. The papers in New York, after a long delay, had finally broken the story that Sherlock Holmes was in America. It was claimed that he was at a tuberculosis asylum in Asheville, North Carolina several states away from our actual retreat in Newport, Rhode Island. Holmes had heard by telegram that inquiries had been made in the region and we could not doubt that the Baron was on our trail. I knew that he would eventually trace us to Newport. There could be no doubt about that. If he did so, we were determined to lead his servants a merry chase. Besides, Inspector Stanley Hopkins was once again at our side and I could see that he was alert for any sign of a strange or menacing figure during the challenging days that lay ahead for us all.

Our first destination was all that I could have expected. Walden Pond presented a quiet beauty over which the spirit of Thoreau seemed still to hover. We walked its shores in quiet discourse. We then visited the grey and somewhat haunted former domicile of Nathaniel Hawthorne whose elegant prose and sense of romance could never hide his own dark broodings about the human condition. An autumn thunderstorm broke out as we gazed at the house and the wrath of the storm forced us to seek retreat in our covered carriage where we were forced to remain for some time. We could see across the fields where the furor of revolution had once broken out at the bridge spanning the quiet stream that wound through the meadows. The crash of thunder might have been the sound of cannon and musket fire. The wreaths of rain might have been witches flying to their dark Sabbats. We imagined that perhaps Hawthorne's ghost still walked those quiet fields seeking the peace that he never found in life. I had enjoyed his wonderful prose for many years and my bookshelf in Baker Street had several leather-bound volumes of his works. Beneath his mellifluous prose lay an intuition of the darkness of the human heart that few writers before him had ever dared to probe. His vision was essentially the vision of the great 17th Century English writers. These men of preindustrial England lived before the dream that technical progress could ameliorate the human condition; Hawthorne was of one mind with men like John Donne, Robert Burton, and Thomas Browne. His tone of grim destiny would not be met again until the writings of Thomas Hardy.

There is a certain comfort to be obtained in the grim visions of writers who will not turn aside from the horrors of life, in those who see beyond appearances into the great vacuum at the heart of things that only the vision of God may ever fill. Men like this know that if there is no God, then also there can be nothing really human. Only the fool believes that he may maintain the fruits of morality without an anchor in something beyond morality itself. If we are the origin of our ideas of good and of evil, then they have no absolute sanction and become only an expediency reached by various struggling factions of people. Everything becomes flux and fashion, mere migrating constellations of un-tethered moral assurance in infinite space and time. Men like Hawthorne remind us of what we are and of how deep the darkness beyond the flickering fires of civilization truly is.

Hawthorne's dark vision is a corrective agent to a man like Ralph Waldo Emerson who took nature as his God. What is Transcendentalism finally, but the old heresy of Spinoza in new garb; the heresy that God is the sum total of all phenomena and that man achieves his true stature by abstracting from the uniquely human and joining the all, willing the all, becoming the all.

Transcendentalism teaches that men become God by transcending their condition by entering into some ill-defined Over-soul, some collective will that represents the species at its highest point and by looking at the best representatives of the human race. This is not to say that we may not learn from the example of great men and women, but even they do not approach divinity. The life of the soul is not imitation but indwelling, and not of an Over-soul but one's own unique and individual soul under the tutelage of grace. Since grace belongs to God and does not have its origin in man, it is an act of arrogation to assume that we are the source of our own moral progress. How may we even define progress if we have no preexistent end in view from which to measure our advances?

Christianity in contrast to Transcendentalism places God beyond the sum total of existence as its source and origin. It is God who enters history by assuming its limitations and transforming the particular by giving it lasting significance. The concrete becomes Holy because God wills to honor it by assuming it to Himself in the Incarnation. How different are all forms of thought that seek to create an upwelling of spirit out of matter! Many have been thus seduced from Baruch Spinoza to Georg Hegel.

This heady brew of imagination which assumes that the course of history is progress towards the creation of God is taught by Hegel. To seek to escape from essences and to make time the measure of all things is to preclude the possibility of the eternal to which time is a mere dimension, a mode of measurement of limited existence. What we often laud as bravery and innovation in dialectical materialism or the equally absurd radical philosophical idealism is actually a retreat into primitive animism and pantheism.

To accept these jejune views is to light a candle before a hurricane! What are the achievements of even our own startling age but nothingness in the face of infinite time and infinite space? To presume so much on own efforts, if that presumption proceeds only from within our own aspirations, is for a worm to wear a top hat and cravat. The great English writers of the 17th Century knew this well. They knew that the burst of enthusiasm of Bacon's *"New Organon"* and of Rene Descartes' enthronement of reason as the measure of all things, must finally yield to the fatal eclipse of our individual deaths.

Death and decay do not deny the dignity of man and woman but only restore presumptuous humanity to its proper place in nature. In Sir Thomas Browne's words drawn from his majestic essay, *"Urn-burial,"* we hear this clearly where he states that "it cannot be long until we lie down in darkness and have our light in ashes."

The mind of man is raised to God when our limitations are

felt most acutely. The glory of Christ is never clearer than when he cries from the cross these words, "My God, my God, why have you forsaken me?" It was then that the crowd waited to see if Elias, as God's representative, would come to save Him. But Jesus died without rescue; that is the proper measure of man and simultaneously proof of the incarnation's reality! If Jesus as God was to leave death unplumbed of what good would have been all the rest of the incarnation but a masquerade? The miracles, the healings become mere empty signs worked from above and not from within human nature, but not by ourselves but by Jesus as God who is simultaneously one of us!

Christianity is more than mere admonitions to moral conduct. If that was all then to be a Christian would be to join the religious writings of the Hindu Vedas, or the sayings of the Buddha or Lao Tsu; but for God to enter into human life by becoming one of us is astonishing! Jesus must die or the incarnation is not complete. For this reason the only places where literature echoes Christianity is in those bitter writers who refuse to paper-over the darkness of human experience with a bland stoicism or a Rabelaisian carnival. For this reason men like Hawthorne, Poe, Lautreamont, and Baudelaire are closer to the vision of Christianity than optimistic but misguided men like Hegel, Spinoza and Emerson.

Of course American culture is still in its adolescence. Its full nobility will only appear when it comes to know age and decline. Virtue is shown by how we accept the human condition, knowing that no exception will been made for us. But currently America views itself as exceptional. Its arrogant optimism is based on the will to conquer. Its tragedy will come when it finds its limits and must turn in tatters and look at itself as a nation as Spain did in its defeat of 1898. The sun was already setting on the great empire of Spain that was once the glory of the world. Gold and silver had been drained from the continent to flood Madrid with treasures from the New World, while in exchange Spain paid for these gifts with brutality, slavery, and disease. The Spain of 1898 was paying the price of conquest in its own flesh. Could America's time be far behind? I thought at the time, if America was to supplant Spain by taking its robes and the scepter of domination upon itself that a similar fate would soon follow. The glories of Europe were already failing when the first American settlements were being formed. It is the foremost dream of humanity to leave its history behind and to make a new beginning, an aspiration that has yet to be achieved.

Such were my thoughts as the thunderstorm raged about us that day when our carriage stood parked before the Old Manse. As the storm passed the purple haze lifted and the landscape assumed again its customary green. We were able then to return to our inn for the night. The storm had cleared away my melancholy as only a vision of darkness may when followed by renewed faith. I felt again an uplifted sense of life within me, one not based upon progress or conquest, but upon the bare hope that is the foundation of the Christian life, the hope in the resurrection and of a new creation at the end of time. How frail and yet how solid are the foundations of Christian belief, but they are strengthened by the vanity of progress and any worldly optimism that would build the Kingdom of God on this side of the only gate to eternity. That gate is death: narrow, grim, ineluctable. The cross lies there before us still and though we may pray that that cup may pass us by, it shall not do so. But there is one who has gone before us, to prepare a place for us, that where He is there we shall also someday be, and that is always our comfort and our only hope.

Events had moved swiftly since our coming to America. We had stumbled upon an America in the throes of change. These factors had a decided influence upon our chosen method to use America to weaken the iron grip of Baron Maupertuis upon many European affairs. His influence could be discerned everywhere, but he was not alone. Our desire to weaken his grip on events had involved us in events of still larger scope. Whether we could succeed in our mission was still highly uncertain, so we adopted a policy of learning as much as we could of the character of the new nation that promised to follow England as the premier global power in world affairs.

My longing to return to my own inconsequential life was balanced against a dawning need to gain a comprehension of the forces that determine history and to discern if I might how the workings of providence might still be visible in worldly affairs. As I write these words in the middle of the Great European War that began in 1914, I am trying to recall how the new world that we all inhabit first became manifest after the extended period of peace that lasted, in Europe at least, during most of what may now be called, the Victorian Age.

Although the desire for general disarmament persisted in some quarters that desire was matched by increasing nationalism as the years passed as well as increased competition for new markets and for raw materials to feed the hungry factories. Industrialism had proven to be a mixed blessing. Consumers could now look to a wider variety of cheaper goods and the cost of housing had declined. The quality of living had improved for more people and diseases like cholera and typhoid were coming under control. But human life was still largely uncertain and many children still perished from small pox, scarlet fever, measles, and diphtheria. The agrarian regions were as oppressive as the cities in the north and in the midlands. The frivolity of London and New York existed side-by-side with appalling human misery.

As a doctor I had seen all of this and when I acted as Holmes *aide-de-camp* I witnessed the impact of crime and violence in human life. If I sought relief in the sea tales of Clark Russell or in the ghostly tales of the great Irish writer, Sheridan Le Fanu, it was because literature will always have a place in making life more tolerable and predictable. Religion serves a similar purpose, but I am not one who believes that religion and prayer are only part of a fictitious anodyne or elixir for the masses. There can be no doubt though that many use religion in precisely this way and some resist any inquiry into religion as a social institution for fear of upsetting beliefs that are in no way well-founded and buttressed against critical inquiry. Sherlock Holmes was not one of those for whom religion is merely cultural; he dared to believe, but simultaneously to question his beliefs. I could see in reading his journal the price he was willing to pay in order to sustain his faith. For my part I only know that part of my life, that period holding my best years, has already crossed the border between worlds.

While on this subject, I knew then and I know now many people among whom is a man that I value highly who has played a unique role by serving as my literary agent, even publishing many of my tales under his name at my request. He is also a doctor by the name of Sir Arthur Conan Doyle. The good doctor is a profound believer in spiritualism. However, I cannot join him in this belief, because for whatever reason I believe that the souls who have passed along the path of life into eternity cannot explain to us what we must undergo ourselves in order to enter heaven after death. I find it sufficient that I feel those whom I have lost to remain close to me and I entrust them to the mercy of God without reservations.

The Catholic Church condemns attempting to directly contact the dead, or necromancy as it is called. The reasons for this prohibition are many, beginning with a general suspicion of the occult as being aligned with sorcery and witchcraft. Prayer to God is considered adequate to meet all of our needs and even petitions for the saints to intercede with God in our behalf should not imply that God is too busy or indifferent to hear our prayers directly. The doctrine of the Communion of Saints reminds us that the dead are not indifferent to our troubles and we in turn are asked to pray to ease their passage to heaven with our support. Our solidarity with the dead however does not imply that they can be used by us to obtain secret knowledge. To seek to do so can place us at risk of opening ourselves to influence from the realm of darkness and such contacts once made are not easily broken. Curiosity and control are two sides of the same coin and when applied to whatever will greet us after death show a mistrust of God's providence and an unwillingness to place our eternal fate unwaveringly into His hands.

As this volume of my reminiscences closes I would like to

comment on the idea of what we leave behind us when we die. These remnants are referred to as our estate. English law anticipates the many modes by which possessions, particularly land, can pass at death. Various provisions are made that allow the testator some residual control after his or her death dependent upon various future contingencies. Wills, trusts, and various future estates allow the living hand to plan for events that as a dead testator he or she will never live to witness. A similar function can be obtained by the use of trusts. But the title of this volume referring to "the estates of Sherlock Holmes" was meant to call to mind the fact that my friend came from a very different social class than mine. His independence of mind could always be at least partially attributed to financial independence. Without the aid provided from time to time from Sigerside, the family estate, his early years of practice and his gradual fame as a detective would have been impossible.

His profound independence of mind was often on display when dealing with men far more powerful than Holmes. He would tolerate neither a brusque manner nor inordinate demands even from highly placed persons. Holmes made no apologies for humble lodgings or peculiar habits. Like Henry David Thoreau he asked permission from no one to live as he chose and to follow his conscience. During the years when I thought that he had perished at the Falls of Reichenbach I was surprised when Mycroft revealed how close to the mark he had always lived. His estate, had it been liquidated would have been small and mostly confined to various curios and personal items. He had set aside a bit for a retirement that later enabled him to purchase his cottage in Devonshire, but as further volumes will reveal he only grew busier as the years passed.

His sympathies always lay with the common folk who must labor for a living. He knew that many possessed secret talents that might have been developed had they the same or equal opportunities enjoyed by the favored classes. I never observed him to scorn a man because of ignoble birth or even acquired infirmities. His impatience was reserved for the arrogant and the self-important. For cads and bullies he felt not only contempt but a ready willingness to intervene, physically if necessary, to right a wrong or to rescue anyone in distress. It was this chivalric attitude that was particularly evident when the client was a woman, plus the fact that Holmes often noted that ordinary life contains more mysteries than the lamentable predictability of what are called "great affairs of state" that led to my choice of cases to be submitted for publication in The Strand Magazine.

His respect for beauty, particularly in music and in the arts was unbounded because these gifts above all others make life tolerable and elevate the mind and the spirit. Beyond this his tastes were simple but his enjoyment of what life offers was fastidious but profound. The estates of Sherlock Holmes were less physical therefore but rather they were moral and aesthetic in nature and he allowed me to share them for many years. The course of this narrative now demands that I return to those most critical sections where only the extended and intimate journal kept by Sherlock Holmes can provide a reliable narrative.

Since the reader by now has advanced to an advanced state of comprehension that can embrace those ultimate mysteries to be discussed in the course of the penultimate meeting of Sherlock Holmes and Professor Moriarty contained in the sixth and seventh volumes of this extended work, I will recede for a time before meeting my patient readers in the next volume after that supreme battle of wits agreed to in the shadow of the Falls of Reichenbach where these two formidable foes reached an agreement to wager their most ardently held convictions against each other in a debate where mind encounters mind, but with far more at stake than is usual in such confrontations; here God was the subject and the stakes were not an earthly victory alone but the question of eternal life.

From the Journal of Sherlock Holmes

June 21, 1893
I Move into My New Home

Today was my day of housewarming as I left Baskerville Hall to assume residence in my new abode. I chose the summer solstice as being most auspicious for such a new beginning. It is a day of celebration from of old here on the moors. Fires are lit today just as they are at Lammas or Lughnassa on the first of August. Dr. Mortimer, my pagan friend is in his glory on this day of the summer solstice. He no doubt left out a double measure of cream and cakes for the fairies on his doorstep last night. This gesture of friendship or appeasement is said to aid the fairy revels in their grottos below the hillsides of Devon. No doubt Puck and his chums will feast well tonight beneath the oak circles and fairy mounds of Grimpen. Dr. Mortimer's peculiar faith, which seems so at variance with his precise and methodical mind, must serve to lighten the burdens imposed by his usual prosaic scientific views.

To view all things with scientific detachment confines one to the observable and the measureable. The need for replication of experimental results can blind one to the unique aspects presented by the world of phenomena. Wonder in contrast opens the heart and it is but a short step from the experience of wonder to faith. In my recent travels I often noticed the impact of locality upon the spirit of the inhabitants. No place, not even the most austere, is without its unique beauty. Maps tend to distance us from the reality of landscape. When one finally arrives at regions that were formerly only names to us we are surprised to find that they actually exist. I can imagine a way of life spent in constant motion where each day would open another vista to the ever-seeking eye. All of the earth is a vast zoological and botanical garden. What child's catalogue of insects and leaves can indicate how many strata of life surround us as adults? If we were all as busy as children, exploring the earth with our extended means and faculties, then each day would bring a surfeit of surprises so that like children we would dread to fall asleep because we would be already anticipating the discoveries of the morrow. Routine and familiarity dull our perceptions and the hunger for the distant horizon that beckons beyond our natal gardens tends in many to fade with age.

This exhaustion grown out of an excess of familiarity is not to be found in me. Even my travels of recent years have not exhausted my passion to explore someday the tropical green plateaus of Venezuela, the Buddhist Temples of Siam, or the remote islands off the coast of Madagascar. The northern territories of Canada have rivers and vast timberlands that excite the imagination to frenzy, to walk where only wolves and reindeer dwell. There are islands in French Polynesia where white sand and clear waters reveal the incongruous denizens of reefs and tidal pools. What are these but visions as fantastic as even fairyland is said to be. Shall I live long enough to see them? Instead of casting off my cables once again and resuming my travels, I am tied to earth and to Moriarty and I have become an island in this green and brown sea of rugged moors.

However stability has its own pleasures. I spent the day with my friends engaged in pleasant conversation. It was a delight to me to play the host by treating the company to a feast in my new home that included a brace of pheasants, some trout from a nearby stream, and a fine rum pudding. The day had gone by without incident and we were in the main room of my cottage when one of the guests brought up the summer solstice festivities and the talk of the company began to focus upon the strange and the fantastic once again. Each of my guests had his or her story to tell of goblins, of the will-o-the-wisp, and of the dark forces said to haunt the moors. I looked over at once to Sir Henry and Lady Beryl. I could see that he was making an effort to enjoy the festive mood, but Lady Beryl looked a bit pale. I realized that the couple still felt the former dread and fear which was a legacy of the time when I had first made their acquaintance. I could not but remark the courage that they showed in staying in a region that had its share of unhappy memories, but like my brother Sherringford they felt an obligation to serve the people of the district and to carry on the tradition of Baskerville occupancy of the old manor house on the estate.

At last the local Anglican Vicar of Grimpen spoke up. "Well, my story may not partake of the fantastic, but it is strange none the less. Since Mr. Holmes is among us he may favor us with a solution to this mystery. I myself can make nothing of it. It involves a man named Isadora Persano whose nerve I would have sworn to be one of the steadiest in England. He is a well-known duelist and is said to have killed many an opponent in his own native land of Nicaragua. He is a man whom I should not care under any circumstances to offend. He has traveled extensively and is known as an international journalist. He is often consulted by heads-of-state and by businesses seeking to relocate into new areas of the world. He has often been able to make very valuable introductions and has been well-paid for his trouble and advice. He is then, or rather was, for his nature has now changed utterly as you will hear, the very type of sensible and resourceful man who might be expected to weather any shock to his nervous system. Yet this very man was found just last year stark, staring mad in his lodgings in Plymouth, a condition from which he has yet to recover."

He looked about our circle and rubbed his hands in gratification as he saw that I, the famous London specialist, was looking at him with intense interest. I noticed though that Lady Beryl seemed oddly distracted or discomfited at the mention of

Nicaragua, a nation that lies in close proximity to her own native Costa Rica.

The Vicar continued, "Isadora Persano is reputedly a Catholic and not of my own faith, but as a clergyman my duty is to minister to all of God's children so I decided to visit him at the local hospital to see if I might be of some spiritual comfort to him. Alas, the poor man was utterly unable to communicate in any sensible fashion. Upon my inquiring if I might be of any use to him, materially or spiritually, he looked up and merely said, in an accent of terror which I shall never forget, 'It is the worm; the worm that shall become the moth....' Then after a pause he grabbed at my cassock and pulling me close to him whispered as if granting to me a secret confidence, 'The devil lives!' I could get no more out of him so I turned to his nurse who only shook her head. Apparently that was always the extent of his discourse. He never strayed from that single topic, as though his mind had frozen upon it. The beginning of his affliction I was told was when he was found in his demented condition by his housekeeper, seated before a table with a box that had been delivered from an unknown address which contained only a peculiar worm in a specimen jar. The authorities who were immediately called in to investigate tried naturally to have the worm identified by experts in the field since the poor man seemed to attach so much importance to it, but beyond remarking that it had certain similarities with species found in Central America, the specimen at issue was quite unknown to science. Since the worm was dead there was no way of knowing what type of moth may have developed from it, but judging from its size it would have been a large one. The nearest relative of the worm in question, I betray my ignorance of course in calling it a worm and not a larva, is the great black moth known as Carnivora Diabolus."

The company looked suitably appalled at this revelation, which appeared to please the normally quite sedate clergyman who seemed to enjoy the sensation he was creating by this recounting this strange tale before the flickering fire. As he continued I could sense a growing unease in the gathering of my friends.

"This unusual moth is said to prefer carrion as food rather than vegetation. Perhaps, that is why the poor fellow kept muttering, that the devil lives. I must say that it makes my blood run cold even now to recall the tone of his voice with its attendant surprise and loathing. I left that day last year however with my mission unaccomplished. His attendants were able to make him eat a sort of gruel after days of abstention, but the expression of shock I was told at the time never leaves his face and he seems quite unable to attend to even his most basic needs without aid. I took an interest in his case thereafter and I am kept advised periodically as to his progress, which I am sad to say has been minimal thus far, although he has apparently graduated to solid food. I fear though that his reason is permanently lost and, a most sad affair and ... dear me Lady Beryl, are you quite alright?"

The attention of the company shifted instantly from the fascinating tale of the speaker to Lady Beryl who had suddenly collapsed upon the floor. Only Sir Henry's quick action of reaching for her at the last moment and catching her in his arms had prevented a serious injury. He proceeded to scoop her up and carried her over to the couch. I called at once for a cold cloth and by rubbing her wrists with brandy and the application of the cold cloth to her forehead she was soon brought round to consciousness. Her eyes though were at first glazed with terror, but we reassured her that she was quite safe and among friends. At this she seemed to rally but Sir Henry quite rightly took her home at once. I was sorry to see the evening end with such an unfortunate incident although its meaning and import will definitely require an investigation.

I shall certainly make inquiries to ascertain the reason for her extreme reaction whenever I judge that Lady Beryl may tolerate any questions. I blame myself severely for allowing the discussion to take such a turn and I know that the Vicar was quite mortified as well. Clearly some thread of familiarity may account for the reactions of two strong natures to a similar event. Can any creature be so horrifying as to create such an extreme response? Or is it perhaps some association to a superstition peculiar to this region of Central America? Or could it be that some other association of a more personal nature that accounts for the fear and loathing both manifest and not the worm at all? I must make some attempt to resolve the matter as soon as possible.

June 22, 1893
Baskerville Hall

I walked over to the hall this morning and asked if I might question Lady Beryl. She had spent a fitful night and Sir Henry said that he felt that any questioning would be premature as it might bring on brain fever. He had made his own attempt and received only tears and a shaking of her head as a response. Whether this betokens incomprehension on the part of Lady Beryl as to the reason for her response or a refusal to convey intelligence about a secret or painful matter cannot be ascertained. The issue I fear must remain an open one for now, but a new problem has been laid at my door at a time when I had thought that I might direct all of my energies towards the issues raised by the case of Professor Moriarty. I can of course attempt to interview this man Isadora Persano in person by traveling down to Plymouth. If Lady Beryl will not speak of the matter by the end of the week, I shall surely make the trip. Sir Henry remains troubled and I would gladly relieve his distress.

I have yet to hear anything from Professor Moriarty. Perhaps he is playing a game of nerves with me. Undoubtedly he would like his initial assault upon my citadel of belief to take root and to fester. His presumption of course is that doubt is the natural state of man and not belief. The one who poses the terms of the problem may often determine the result. If faith is seen as a mere addendum to life, as though life might proceed perfectly well without it, then the search for faith may be portrayed as a mere anodyne for those unable to accept the facts of life, a sop for those weak souls who need the comfort of futurity because they cannot accept the normal span of a human life or because they require some outer sanction in order to accept individual moral responsibility for their actions.

This technique allows a man like Moriarty to pose as a more courageous individual by accepting a Godless universe. He will then claim to be more honest because he frankly admits his decisions to be entirely his own and in pursuit of his own ends. He may claim to be more courageous because he requires no reward for any good actions that he may undertake, but he also scorns to be punished for any crime that he may commit. For such a man there is simply no outward source to which he must look for the confirmation of his opinions and actions. He simply acts as he does and defies the world to stop him. He scorns its censure as well as its praise. They are both of no use to him because he claims to be the sole and absolute source from which his own life springs. He is at once proud and humble: proud in that he stands completely alone, humble in that he knows that his efforts will come finally to nothing, for any awareness of his actions will terminate with his death. He feels no need to see how the universe absorbs his brief span as a causal agent. For him the vast brew of events will soon dissolve his individual impacts into the solution of history and the molten lava of change.

He is in spite of outward appearances, the epitome of the Dionysian man. Though a man of science, he scorns his own conclusions as a temporary pronouncement upon the nature of the inscrutable. Even scientific comprehension is repellant to his rejoicing in flux. It would make no difference to him if the valance of the universe were to change tomorrow to add to the chaos, for is not the present already chaotic? What are the dynamics of the asteroids but temporary diversions caused by bodies in motion?

Faith for men such as he becomes the search of weak souls for an outer order, static and serene, set up by a divine father or a nurturing mother, with a pantheon of saints to render aid through their intercession. Of what use are all of these to a man who desires to scorn all things and to stand alone as long as his consciousness persists. If he wakes to the day, all well and good, the same if he perishes in the sleep of night. He asks nothing of life and death and accepts nothing. By placing the source of all direction within, as regards both ends as well as means, he feels a vast sense of freedom, the Dionysian man, with every impulse there opens new universes of possibility to define the universe anew. Why would he exchange infinity for the strictures of a mere faith in God? Why should he kneel with charwomen and cabdrivers on a Sunday in the equal light of God's love for them or match his wits with a grammar-school teacher when he might be the great Professor Moriarty!

What have I to oppose this view but the search and witness of the historical structure of the Catholic Church, a church that believes itself to be holy because it is nourished from within by Divine Grace and called to teach an absolute truth? How absurd must this confidence appear to a man who will trot out the many dark periods of Church history to prove that it is quite human after all?

No doubt he will look to the origin of the Catholic Church in an obscure event in Palestine and mock its flimsy assembly of doctrines regarding what may never be known with scientific accuracy. He will point to the many similar cults that emerged from the first century mélange of Judaism, Zoroastrianism, and the goddess cults such as those of Isis, Astarte, and Diana. He will point out that upon these obscure origins is piled a history of deductions that may claim no greater substance and permanence than their base, which rests upon such shifting alluvial soil. To him the present day Catholic Church is a sagging structure that just proclaimed the doctrine of Papal Infallibility at precisely the lowest point in its institutional fortunes, when the Italian people, weary of the Holy Pontiffs of Rome, proclaimed a Kingdom of Italy and abolished the Papal States.

To Professor Moriarty the recent Popes are only pompous madmen who wave their crosiers about at this hour of most humiliating defeat. No Christian nation came to the aid of Pope Pius IX at the time of the Italian revolution and his lands were then stripped away for secular use. Still the Popes claim jurisdiction over the invisible realm. They may have lost lands in Italy, but they are able to claim, since the Vatican Council, that they alone may under certain conditions infallibly determine the truth about mankind and the rules that govern our origin and destiny by authoritatively interpreting and defining faith, morals, and the natural law. No doubt in precisely this manner Moriarty will mock me.

I believe that a thread of gold, the guidance of the Holy Spirit, leads from the Chair of Peter to Christ and from Christ to the one who sent Him. I exist within the Catholic Church as one who has already abandoned himself to the larger Body of Christ, which is the Church. My own being is caught up in the collective fate of all who have similarly surrendered their lives to that great unity. Charity comes naturally to one who sees that all lives are essentially his own and his own life is in all other lives. I trust to the merits of the saints to remedy my deficiencies. Where Moriarty would wish to see chaos, I see an imperfect realm calling out for the mercy of God. The hidden order of the universe under providence subsists forever. But the final and complete order, the dynamic inherent in all things, exceeds our ability to grasp.

It is not imperative that we do so. It is enough that I participate in the life of the Church which by the will of God receives all that it requires in due season, just as a day of rain is sufficient to the soil in my growing garden. At this stage of my life I require no proofs. I trust the God who waits behind the veil of historicity, completing redemption slowly through the incremental works of our charity. I am nourished daily by the Holy Sacrifice of the Mass, which is more than word and gesture.

The Mass is God acting among men and women in solidarity with our condition. In the very simplicity of the Mass is its power. To come to it is to draw close to the heart of the universe, the sap within the Tree of Life. To come to Mass is to open the gate to Eden, opened again at Christ's death, when from His side both blood and water flowed. These are the waters of Baptism and the Blood of remission for our sins. All that is required has been bestowed upon us. Our salvation is complete.

The Sacrifice of Christ at his crucifixion is the one definitive act of history. It is the beginning and the end, an absolute in itself.

It breaks time itself asunder and lets eternity in. The cave of Plato is no more. The Magi need seek no further. The Cross is all in all. To the man whose last breath is the name of Jesus, who dies embracing the Cross of Christ, whose final comfort is the Holy Oils of Extreme Unction, the seed of his life will break forth to enjoy the primal intention of God for every man and for every woman. Only then we will we know, even as we are now known, love as we are loved, and share in what only God is. We receive finally as gift what we once desired to steal in Eden, because the Trinitarian God wills it so.

June 24, 1893
Baskerville Hall

Today I was employed in getting caught up with my correspondence. I received an interesting letter from Mycroft that I will include on a page here in my journal without comment for future reference.

Dear Sherlock,

I am writing to acknowledge my obligation to you for coming to London to report on your on-the-spot observations of the situation in the Sudan. I must confess that during all the time that you were gone my nerves were strained and as a result my girth widened proportionately. You can little imagine how stressful my position is at times. International relations are largely based upon perceptions and these can be manipulated so as to achieve various strategic ends. Even governments are like a magic-lantern show projected out upon a screen. My position resembles that of a director of a play. I am not the author nor the actor, but only the intermediary agency that keeps the whole endeavor from destruction. The audience unfortunately is not purely domestic; the choicest box-seats are occupied by people who I will never meet because they work behind the scenes in foreign governments. Some players in the game are not statesmen at all but leaders of industry or commentators with a large following in newspapers or even in the universities.

Theory is always retrospective, whereas decisions in politics as in war must be made in the heat of battle. Secrecy and obfuscation are my primary tools. Force whenever it is used must often be clothed in suggestion rather than in actual deployment. The only real advantage that I possess is superiority in the most recent intelligence reports combined with an ability to weigh each factor in any situation for its relative significance. Beyond this there are only my three fundamental dicta:

> *1. Never forget in analyzing a problem that you are playing a game; but be sure you know what game you are playing.*

> *2. Be sure you keep track of who the other players in the game are before making any move or change in your position.*

> *3. Know when to leave the game and when to announce or to conceal (if that is possible) from the other players that you have left the game.*

These dicta may not make immediate sense to you, but I assure you that employing them has avoided many a diplomatic catastrophe for our country and kept me as your brother out of hot-water. In any case I am happy that you are home and await with interest the results of your work on what I prefer to call "the Moriarty Problem." It may be smaller than you suppose or more weighty than I realize at the present moment. I agree with your own policy of never reaching a conclusion without sufficient data; so please keep me informed as events unfold.

> *Be assured of my regard dear brother, Mycroft*

June 25, 1893
Baskerville Hall

Today I have taken Mycroft's three dicta that he offered me in his letter but without any detailed explanation of where and when they can be applied and attempted to use them as an aid to resolve my own preoccupations.

Regarding the first of these dicta I asked myself whether

the pursuit of salvation can be characterized as a game. Does the Church act as a channeling device to sort souls for God by applying various stress-tests to see which souls hold up well and which collapse in on themselves and need to be placed in the refuse pile? Is moral perfection not simply the better course but the mandatory course in order to meet the specified criteria of acceptability? Is Jesus the equivalent of a quality-control specialist in a factory maintained by His Father? Or is the Church more like a great infirmary where sinful souls are healed or where flawed parts are salvaged so that they can be of some use to a higher collective purpose?

Perhaps when seen from the demands of perfect sainthood the rejection rate of souls is over 90%, but what is that to the factory owner when souls are essentially a cheap and constantly replenished raw material? Who can enter the East End of London and see the ravaged souls there and still retain an exalted image of humankind as made in the image and likeness of God? If Jesus is in truth the savior of all of humanity the question remains regarding just how effective that saving action actually is? Mycroft's dictum enjoins us to be sure we know what game we are playing. Is the game of salvation one where many people win or only a few? If the rules cannot be adapted to our demonstrated capacities, then are we as theologians ready to admit that the game of salvation appears to be as cruel as Darwin's image of nature, red in tooth and claw?

The second dictum is to identify the players in the game or in other words to determine the parameters of play. In many games the rules are not sufficiently specific to curtail moves that may bestow an unfair advantage and many games exist where outside interests can interfere with play. An example is the supposed war between labor and management in capitalism, which fails to account for outside threats from other companies or even from other industries that can swiftly re-engineer a factory to be an unsuspected source of competition. In this case labor and management are best advised to work together rather than to oppose each other if both are to survive and prosper. Perhaps saints and sinners must learn to work together so that the most basic needs of human beings can be provided for without turning to God and expecting His miraculous intervention on every occasion to remedy our deficiencies.

Regarding the third dictum is it ever possible to leave the gaming table if, as the each religion claims, each is the only path to salvation. Is it ever an actual option to quit the game and not have God and perhaps the other players as well know that you are doing so? Is public worship the equivalent of an inspection in order to ascertain if anyone has attempted to escape over the wall of the prison to freedom overnight? Does religion force us into duplicity before God as a virtual requirement ever since Adam and Eve first discovered that they were naked?

These are hard questions to be sure, but the history of application of the various faiths to the actuality of human existence is not encouraging. Moral improvement is less evident than one might expect after so much effort expended on the part of an all-powerful God to redeem us, unless that failure was always calibrated and included in the design specifications for the human race as a whole. Perhaps this life was supposed to be filled with misery and slaughter as useful determinants of just who gets to heaven and who goes to hell after passing tests wherein some people have hard questions to answer and others easy questions. Absent some factor that balances chances evenly the game of salvation would appear to be the most brutal of all since the results are not correctable by further play or a new game after the final scores are added up.

I am not sure that I like Mycroft's three dicta because they raise theological questions that I would prefer not to entertain, even if they force themselves upon me from time to time. They raise the thought that if given a choice between two such mutually exclusive alternatives for eternity the wiser choice would have been never to be born at all and thus be spared the rigors of the game.

June 26, 1893
Baskerville Hall

Lady Beryl is no better, nor will she speak to Sir Henry or to me as to the source of her present affliction. Clearly the story of the vicar contained for her some secret meaning. Therefore, I am resolved to go to Plymouth to meet with this mad gentleman, Isadora Persano and to see if in finding the source of his madness I may relieve Lady Beryl's distress. Sir Henry will remain behind to support and comfort her. Dr. Mortimer has given me his own unique opinion of the case, but will not accompany me. He has a theory that the man has been as he calls it, "pixilated" or visited by the fairies. I can only humor him in his peculiar beliefs. Although I would enjoy his company, his manner might be a distraction to the patient and interfere with a rational investigation of the matter.

I spent time with Sir Henry today to reassure him that an answer will be found. He has been naturally upset by the whole affair and I in turn have been appalled that the origin of this perplexing reaction of Lady Beryl should have happened within the walls of my new home. The vicar has been even more mortified that his casual reference should have caused such distress. He is a gentle and discreet sort of clergyman and the very last man to wish to give offence. He apologized profusely at the time, but the damage had already been done.

Sir Henry was compelled to take Lady Beryl home. I ask myself what possible association there might be between a cold-blooded duelist and a noble woman who has lost already a husband and a father and a brother. She has born all of this with courage and resignation. Such women as Lady Beryl are not the sort of individuals who are subject to nervous indispositions. Whatever the link may be then must have some basis in fact.

Among the books that I have assembled on my new bookshelves is a complete set of the British Encyclopedia. I spent several hours yesterday in research and I may have picked up some clues. I researched Costa Rica and Nicaragua and did some cross-reference checks into the Mayan civilization and into the slave religion of Voodoo. While I found nothing conclusive, there were at least indications.

I hesitate to question Lady Beryl directly as to the basis of her fears since I might inadvertently trigger a general collapse. Certainly, she can see that her reaction has upset Sir Henry to the last degree and if she could speak to that distress she would have already done so voluntarily. She has said nothing, which indicates that she is either mystified by her own response or that for some reason of her own she prefers to remain silent, perhaps to protect her husband. If then I am to comprehend this affair, I must seek my evidence in Plymouth by interviewing this madman, Persano.

Dr. Mortimer meanwhile, in spite of his fantastic opinions, was of some assistance to me since, as a medical man, he is acquainted with various aberrant mental states. He advises that we try to administer scopolamine, a drug which may open the patient to our questions by lessening any inhibitions of the higher faculties. If we may once glimpse the truth through the fog of his delusions, we may proceed further to the entire truth. I must confess to feeling again something of the old excitement of the chase by having a concrete problem such as this to solve at last. I am only sorry that Dr. Watson is not here to record it. I shall certainly share the facts with him when we meet again upon his return from America.

I hope soon to make some progress with Professor Moriarty as well. If he does not contact me, I will take the matter in hand and simply proceed on to Kings Pyland on my own initiative. The Professor intimated that I might do so and there is always the danger that he may presume that his own arguments at our first meeting told upon me more than they did if I should wait too long before seeing him. I do not intend to play the mouse to his cat. It will not be easy to find some point of common-ground to serve as a base from which to build since Moriarty has already announced that he deplores axioms, even in his own field of mathematics. At least I seem to have recovered from my recent lung symptoms and feel quite able now to bear-up in whatever struggle lies ahead.

June 27, 1893
Plymouth

It has been a most extraordinary day. I believe that I may have in my hands the data that will yield a solution to the matter at hand in this matter of Isadora Persano. I traveled down to Cornwall today by the early train from Coombe Tracey through Launceston to Plymouth. I was met there by the Doctor who is in charge of the case, a man named Dr. Blackwell. The Vicar of Grimpen had already wired him on my behalf and he welcomed me most graciously upon my arrival. The asylum in which Mr. Persano is currently confined is a private one with its own grounds and a view over the sea. Our journey was a short one from the station. During it the good doctor was able to give me a brief outline of the case.

"The patient in question is hearty and sturdy of build, Mr. Holmes; just the sort of individual who one would think would be the last to lose his reason over an event so trivial. I have made an inquiry about the man's prior habits and way of life, but his servant at the time of his first attack could or would say nothing. I could see though that she was afraid of something. She is no longer available though for any inquiry that you might care to make, so I fear that you will need to be satisfied with my own impressions. She absconded to an unknown destination shortly after my first interview with him. It is a pity, because it has left only the patient himself for you to observe today. I see him once a week for therapy sessions, but he only sits in his chair, staring before him as though he had only just discovered the worm that was the instigating force of his malady. You may inspect that object of course; we have retained it. It is well preserved, but we have not been able to type it by genus or species, though we know that it is from a family of moths that have a rather grim reputation in their native Central America. They are no threat to man of course, but it is possible that seeing it has stimulated a series of associations in the mind of my patient. I fear that he will not speak directly to the matter however, so any direct questions put to him by you are likely to be useless."

"Have you tried scopolamine?" I inquired, thinking of Dr. Mortimer's advice to me before I left home.

"We have hesitated to do so for fear of sinking the patient deeper into his malaise. He is at least able to eat and drink and we have no desire to induce any further withdrawal. But, if you believe it to be a necessity, we might try a small dose. As his doctor, I cannot content myself by simply doing nothing. It may be worth undertaking some risk to shock him out of his present state, for I assure you that during the past months he has made no improvement. It would indeed be a pity if so vital a gentleman were to remain indefinitely incapacitated."

Our carriage had passed out of the old city and proceeded along a cheerful lane of modern villas with hedges that bordered the drives. We passed beyond these and came at last to a larger brick structure whose windows presented a rather bleak aspect by being barred. The grounds of the asylum are extensive and consist of lawns threaded with scenic paths into the woods. There are benches placed at frequent intervals where those patients with grounds privileges may rest or read.

On an upper hillside there is a small graveyard where some of the patients, having succumbed to life's last necessity without regaining their sanity, have been laid to rest. A small stream trickles through the grounds and a cleverly designed millwheel serves to provide power for a small gristmill. The stream is also a source of irrigation for several garden plots where strawberries and other delicacies are raised by some of the more industrious patients. All-in-all the place seems quiet progressive and civilized. While to lose one's liberty seems among the most to be dreaded of human fates, there must be compensations if one may spend his convalescence in such a place.

The establishment forms a sort of rural community. There are caring people to listen with interest to the description of one's symptoms. Medical care is readily available for any physical ills that may develop as a consequence of such close confinement. The doctor took pains to point out that there were no chains, cold baths, or other intrusions upon the dignity of the patients, though such things are common in most publicly financed asylums.

"We select our patients carefully," said Dr. Blackwell. "The more violent ones we must of course send away. Our clientele is also confined to those who can afford our facilities. We have no outside source of funds, but only our patients' fees to look to for support. Our mode of therapy is mostly confined to providing good food, rest, and a sympathetic ear for their troubles. We do not allow any experimentation by various medical zealots seeking cure of the mind. We provide the means to draw or to write letters. We have an excellent library and you see that we maintain gardens for those who wish to follow that favorite pastime of the English. The view over the sea from the rear of the building is excellent. There are no cliffs, but rather a gentle hillside and a beach. Some of our patients are allowed to go bathing on summer afternoons and we have many picnics. We try to allow them all the latitude that a prudent care for them will allow."

"Does Mr. Persano ever go out onto the grounds," I inquired.

"Ah his is a sad case. His powers of locomotion are intact and he is remarkably cooperative in every respect but one. He has a perfect horror of ever leaving the building. Whenever the matter is brought up he becomes severely agitated and on one occasion we found it necessary to sedate him."

I noted this at once. "Has he ever said anything about the nature of his fear?"

"Only once about a month ago did he give any indication, Mr. Holmes. I had asked him directly at that time if he would explain to me the nature of his fear, pointing out to him that the grounds were quite private and secure. He seemed more willing to speak of his affliction on that day for some reason. Even the most ill of our patients have periods when their malady seems to interfere less with their normal faculties. It was such a day for Mr.

Persano. I remember that he looked up at me and in a tone half of terror and half of scorn at my ignorance of the reasons for his precautions said simply, 'You do not know the man; he will stop at nothing!'"

The point struck me at once that Mr. Persano had a fear, not of a moth, but of a man. I thought for a moment before asking, "He said nothing else? Ah, that is a pity. But surely what he said is most indicative. We may assume that it is not the worm that he fears then but its source. Was it ever ascertained how he came into the possession of this remarkable worm?"

"It was sent to his door by a messenger who promptly vanished. There was no return address. No letter accompanied the box. There was nothing but the box and its strange contents," answered Doctor Blackwell.

"Then it must have some private or symbolic meaning to him that we may be able to discover. We will approach the investigation with that assumption. We must come to the matter slowly. Will he respond to my questions?" I asked.

"He is hardly voluble at the best of times, but he makes every effort to cooperate with reasonable requests, particularly since he has a dread of being transferred to another establishment. It would of course require him to be out of doors for a short time here and on the journey to the new asylum."

"Quite so, well Doctor, I think we may go up at once and see your remarkable patient."

We left the carriage which had traveled along a circular drive and had pulled up before the front portico. After climbing a series of steps, we entered the building. There was a nursing station and a drawing room on the first floor for the reception of guests as well as a dining room with views out and over the sea. In many respects the building resembled a guest house, such as those found at Brighton. Several nurses greeted the doctor who had shifted from his former genial presence and assumed a stern air of command upon entering. I remarked at this and the doctor smiled as we ascended the stairs to the wards above.

"A mental facility is rather like a ship sir. One must maintain proper order and command. Sanity is largely a matter of accepting and recognizing limits. We do not talk about the pursuit of happiness here for instance, but of the restoration of responsibility. Responsibility seldom brings happiness, but it may, if it is properly exercised bring one to a state of peace of mind. Most of our patients are here because in the pursuit of happiness they went quite mad."

We walked down the hall and turned at a bend in the corridor. We were now in one of the end wings and our guide chose the third door on the right. He explained, "Private rooms are maintained for those with sufficient funds. These end rooms include small parlors. We try and sustain an air proper to a British gentleman in any patient who requires the minimum of supervision. At the same time we reserve the right to enter the rooms at any time for the good of the patient."

"Mr. Persano was quite well-off at the time of his entry here and possesses adequate capital to pay for many years here should his stay be an extended one. His room is in demand by others similarly afflicted however, so we do not encourage any malingering. We trust that keeping up a man's sense of his own dignity may speed his recovery, so we encourage hobbies, reading, and keeping abreast of affairs in the world outside. Mr. Persano for instance subscribes to several news dailies, which he reads avidly as well as certain zoological journals and scientific papers. As a former journalist it is only proper that he should wish to keep abreast of affairs. He was at one time a contributing editor for the Times of London in matters dealing with Central America. Though Italian by birth he spent his early years in Nicaragua and Costa Rica. He left the latter country after the revolution that unseated the former dictator of Costa Rica, a man named Don Juan Murillo, who was a tyrant by all accounts. But let us enter and he can personally explain any point that you may consider pertinent to the case."

Dr. Blackwell knocked firmly on the door and after a

momentary pause entered.”

“Good Day, Mr. Persano,” I heard him say. “I have brought a friend down from Devon to meet you. He is something of a journalist himself and has recently returned from travels in Asia. I thought that you might care to make his acquaintance. Mr. Sherlock Holmes, this is Mr. Isadora Persano.”

At the mention of my name the man before me started and turned to me a look of surprise and hope, which was the more remarkable, for my first vision of the man had conveyed the impression of a man who was in the last degree of desolation and despair. He was sitting in a chair by the window that was turned towards the door as if he had anticipated our entry. His eyes alone had turned towards us as we entered, while his shoulders had remained hunched forward. He was a man who had clearly been an athletic fellow at one time, but he had clearly shrunken in some manner during his recent period of confinement. He seemed to be one of those men of whom acquaintances would remark after a long absence, that he was but a shadow of his former self. His very clothes seemed to hang upon him.

His face was a remarkable one. It betokened a man of high passions, of quick anger, and a readiness to take offense at any slight. But there was also an air of intelligence as well about the fellow, as though for all of his impulsiveness he knew when to delay seeking retribution or to seem to forgive a wrong until the tide of events might favor him. He was a man who would swiftly rise in any assembly of his peers. Men of power and importance always seem able to sense strength of purpose in another of their sort. Such men live by invidious comparisons. For them hierarchy is the first prerequisite of existence. They cannot live upon an inner world but only upon a world of great affairs, of conquest and acquisition. To stand still for them is to die. Yet here was such a man immobilized in an obscure retreat and living in apprehension if not in terror.

It is one of my maxims in the art of detection that any decided variation from the norm is the surest indicator of some proportionate extraordinary cause that is roughly proportional to its effect. True surprises in life are rare. Things remain as they are unless acted upon by an outside force. In the case at hand I found a man who appeared impervious to the fears that might beset a lesser fellow but who was now terrified. If the cause was proportional to its effect, it must be formidable indeed. I had already concluded as much in the first instant of my entry. In the conversation that ensued, I was to conclude far more.

We both sat down facing Mr. Persano who had not taken his eyes off of me since I had entered. He seemed to be engaged in some internal appraisal of me. At last he spoke, much to the surprise of Dr. Blackwell who was no doubt accustomed to a need to make a variety of sorties in order to get his usually depressed patient to speak.

"Mr. Sherlock Holmes of Baker Street, I have heard of you of course sir. Forgive my not standing when you entered, but I am somewhat sedated for my nerves." He lifted his hand and I could see a decided tremor. "You would not guess it sir, but I could formerly hold a pistol in this very hand and invariably hit my mark at fifty feet. I doubt that I could even maintain a grip upon a dueling pistol at this point, or even raise it to eye level. You see a man before you who is in his last decline."

"Oh come now, Mr. Persano," interrupted the doctor, "You must not take so grim a view of your situation. Indeed, I hope in a month to see you walking about the grounds, quite yourself again."

The man before us started. "Never Doctor, it would be as much as my life is worth to do so." His voice grew hushed as he turned to me an appealing glance, "It is the worm you see, the worm of the devil!"

He said this in a pleading and confiding voice. My first thought upon hearing his extraordinary expostulation was of the description of hell in the gospels, the place where their worm dies not, speaking of course of the damned. I have always regarded this phrase as indicative of the endless remorse of conscience of the damned soul, a remorse not bred of humility and penitence for having offended God, but rather a remorse stemming from a refined self-interest that would have the reward of heaven without first acquiring the necessary dispositions to obtain them. The worm that dies not is none other than the realization of one's actual status before God if final penitence should prove impossible. The vision of one's own iniquity would then be insupportable. It would gnaw forever at the vitals of the unrepentant sinner.

The one who does not love God finally comes to loathe even himself. His becomes the living contradiction that the more he desires for himself, the less he possesses. His very nature, made as it is for God, is nauseated by the foods that he himself has chosen in preference to the vision of God. Therefore such a lost soul learns to mock its own pain and only heaps upon itself greater pains in consequence, so as to prove its indifference to its own loss. The lost soul becomes at once persecutor and victim.

Such must be the fate of the damned; but what was significant in this case was whatever meaning Mr. Persano attached to the worm.

"What is this worm of which you speak?" I enquired blandly.

The grim voice continued as though he was speaking to himself and not to us, "He collects them. He pins them and they move no more. His collection is a vast one. I doubt that any will escape. He has pinned me at last, for here I am and here I shall remain." After which enigmatic utterance he sank into a profoundly deep and even catatonic state for a few minutes. His face during that interval wore a dreadful grimace and I could not doubt that he had seen the devil somewhere or sometime in the course of his days.

I have often thought how dreadful it must be to feel one's life cascading down about one's head, the dreadful shower of events, with so many empty of any response to the initiatives of grace. To be a barren fig tree in the garden of eternity, or worse to be brambles and thorns, or to be the clinging ivy that finally kills the tree of one's own life is a terrible fate. If even the saints recoiled at a vision of their sins, how much must a man dread who has given no thought to God over a long and seamy career. His very greatness in the eyes of the world must become to him a source of bitter reproach, his fearlessness before evil be counted only as intemperance, and his pride signify only the boasting of a hollow man.

The soul that perceives no need for God is well along the way to this final denial. For this reason, life's sufferings and humiliations may be counted as a blessing. They help us to recall that we in due season must bring our nothingness and our need for the Holy Spirit before God. The unforgiveable sin against the Holy Spirit is the final distrust and denial of the only life that God may ever offer us, His own. God can only give love for God is love. The man or woman seeks for God in vain who does not first seek the Holy Spirit within himself and if that spirit is not present to ask for this gift from God in penitential prayer. All of life it seems to me lies in making petitions, for we have nothing that is ours alone, once God is excluded.

Doctor Blackwell broke into my thoughts by silently beckoning to me. We both backed quietly out of the room unnoticed by the patient. When the door was closed, the doctor spoke, "You need not be concerned that our withdrawal was rude. I have seen Mr. Persano in this state before. He becomes quite oblivious of his surroundings. I have never been able to penetrate his reserve at such times. It is as though he has gone back to some prior existence. When he comes to himself, he is the most pliable and cooperative of patients. At times he seems almost sane, but these spells return as you have just seen where he is as immobile and inaccessible as the most catatonic of our patients. To attempt to reach the center of his particular maze at such a time might be to lose him forever."

"Still," I interposed, "If this state is not probed, he may never return to his former life, which I understand was one of pleasure and of travel."

"Indeed Mr. Holmes," answered the doctor. "Isadora Persano was a man who frequented the highest circles of society. He was even on familiar terms with the Prince of Wales. They share an expert's love of horseracing. Mr. Persano was, among his other accomplishments, something of what is termed a sport. He belongs to some of the most exclusive clubs in London. He has a love of gambling and is a charter member of the Baldwin and of the Bagatelle Card Clubs. It is indeed a shame that such a man should become so incapacitated, but we must try and hold him on the ledge to which he is clinging and not risk a further plunge into irreparable madness. If you will descend with me I will offer you some port and we may discuss his case further."

We descended the stairs and passed through an elegant carpeted hallway where we entered Dr. Blackwell's private office. He offered me a comfortable chair by the French windows overlooking the sea and poured me a glass of port and one for himself before rejoining me and saying proudly, "The view from this room is marvelous is it not, Mr. Holmes? I sometimes think that many a man in London would be willing to go mad in order to escape the greater madness of living in the metropolis and to ensconce himself here in our little retreat. Of course true madness is nothing about which to jest. Madness is often spoken of as a sovereign land created by the mind itself where refuge might be found from the trials and travails of life, but it is more often a diminution of the essential faculties. The world is filtered through the particular web of delusions that are unique to each madman."

"Madness may also at times cause a great heightening of certain faculties. The senses may become hyper-acute so that the slightest stimulation of them is an agony to the patient. We have a case in this very facility that manifests a perfect terror of going to sleep so terrible are his visions when in that somnolent state. What greater solitude does man ever know than sleep? It is then that the mind is alone with its memories and may people a universe with the play of fancy, all beyond the conscious control of the waking mind. Who would ever wish to be encased within his dreams as in a prison?"

"In my more fanciful moments I have imagined that God created the universe to keep Himself awake. What are prayers but those night messages read avidly by God lest he fall into some eternal slumber from which he might not wake. It is said somewhere that God sustains the being of all that is. If God should ever sleep then would not all things disappear? Or is it not that God is already asleep and this vast universe in which we live is really only the dyspeptic creation of a celestial dream from which God will someday awaken with a vow to curb whatever overindulgence has precipitated such a great absurdity? I can see, Mr. Holmes, from your expression that you are surprised at these arcane speculations, but then I live among madmen and I may have acquired some strange influences from living in such close and extended proximity with them. The result is that to speak with one like yourself who has seen something of the outer world is a rare pleasure for me. Pray how do you find the port? Ah, thank you. Please allow me to pour you another glass then. There now. As I was saying madness is quite an individual pursuit. I have learned to treat each patient as though he alone inhabited the universe. I learn to see the world though his eyes. If I am lucky my patient speaks freely to me, but if not then I seek only the silent sympathy of souls and read what I may from that silence."

As the doctor poured me another glass of port I reflected that I found his methods to be rather unique even for an alienist, but I believe in allowing each man his own special competence so I decided to keep an open mind and to learn whatever I might from his discourse.

"Then what is your theory about Mr. Persano's private world?" I inquired

The doctor thought deeply before responding. "It is clearly a matter of association. This unique worm perhaps reminds him of some train of events in his past associated with just such a worm. Associations are often a matter of accidental events joined together by few obvious links," he replied.

I probed him further, "But what of the man's words, can you make nothing of them specifically? He spoke of a collector and of himself as a specimen. Is it not possible that your patient has drawn a parallel between the worm and himself? If so, then it is not the worm that he fears but rather the collector. This would indicate, would it not, that if we may identify the collector of whom he speaks, then we might also identify the source of Mr. Persano's particular terror?"

Dr. Blackwell considered my supposition, "That may be, but Mr. Persano will allow no questioning upon the subject. His reaction is invariably to retreat into a state like that which you have just witnessed."

"Then we may need to press him further." I insisted.

"That, my dear sir, is in my opinion most inadvisable. As it is, he is quite pliable; indeed he is a model patient. I should not care to stimulate those dark passions that once made him one of the most excellent duelists in Europe."

"But to abandon so talented and formidable a man to his own despair is to condemn him to a death in life. Is that not an ethical choice which must be faced?" I protested. "But let us leave that point for the present. Has it occurred to you that the man may actually be shamming? I have written a small treatise upon the art of malingering. It is just possible it seems to me that the man in question has sought out custodial care for the security that it provides rather than in search of medical care. Let us suppose that this collector is a real living man, but one so fearsome that even a man like Isadora Persano would gladly surrender his liberty rather than to face him. I have known several such men in my life, men who leave a trail of destruction behind them. They have always shared one primary characteristic: they are all collectors of a sort. For that matter what is the devil but a collector of souls? Some evil men collect women. They leave a trail of broken hearts and abandoned children behind them. Other men collect businesses, money, or power. The worst of them though are like the devil in that they collect souls. Even power for such men is only a means or stepping stone to absolute control, the sort of control that might make a man pin a human being down like a worm to a board and then forget about it. Such men are bored as only God would be bored if He had no love. Such a god would play with the world, would pierce it through merely to see it squirm at the end of a pin."

The doctor spoke thoughtfully, "I should have thought that

arbitrariness was the entire point of being God; the god that you describe is the very god that rules this troubled world. For this reason, I am not a believer. I have never seen any reason to create creatures that are only bound to offend the deity by their very nature. On the other hand, I have yet to meet a man or woman who was worthy to keep eternal company with God, if God is as holy as He is reputed to be. And as for God's supposed love for mankind, while hating sin; why keep a dog if one dislikes fleas?"

Dr. Blackwell seemed quite pleased with his witticism, but I felt a need to respond, "But man and woman are said to be created in the image and likeness of God and as such to be capable of determining their own destiny. Your theory implies that human beings are incapable of improvement. I must quote a line here from *The Rubaiyat of Omar Khayyam,* that elegant poem dedicated to Epicureanism:

'I sent my soul through the invisible, some letter of that After-life to spell: and by and by my soul returned to me and answered, I myself am heaven and hell.'

"God does not prevent our freedom, but rather warns us of its consequences by His commands. In the last analysis God is not offended but rather wounded by our sins, since he takes them upon Himself. The offence is always ours, but God does not treat it as such; nor does God collect souls by force but only invites them by His nurturance. God's mode of action is always invitation and not compulsion or entrapment. The Absolute may only be claimed by a choice that is itself of an absolute character. God's jealousy is a function of a nature that cannot be other than as it is. To embrace God is to foreswear all that is not God, finding in God all that the soul requires. This world that we see about us is subject to contingency. Everything, including the evil that seems so dominant, is only a vast rehearsal for a choice that lies beyond all time and place when the soul shall contain itself entire and may make one final determination that will determine its fate forever."

"I have not heard theism put in just that way before," answered the doctor. "You are an interesting man, Mr. Holmes. I did not expect from you a discourse in theology but merely of the principles of identification and detection.”

“But that is what theology is, Doctor Blackwell. Theology is the exploration and clarification of our ideas of God through ever more accurate approximations so that the mind may contemplate Him clearly while detecting the obstacles that we erect to interfere with embracing His gifts.”

“But let us return to your remarkable patient. What I propose to do is to utter a single name and to see how Mr. Persano responds. If there is no recognition, well and good and in that case I must simply leave here perplexed; but if he shows some sign of recognition, then our knowledge of the case will be substantially advanced.”

“Well, I do not see that a single name will work any harm. Shall we ascend then, for I know that you must return to your duties at home? You have come down here only as a consultant after all and must do as you think best in the time that you have with my patient.”

We both rose and returned by the way that we had followed a short half-hour ago and soon found ourselves outside the room of Mr. Isadora Persano. We knocked and entered the room as before. His attitude was much as it had been when we had left him. He seemed sunk in a meditative melancholy. He looked up when we entered without interest but alert and I thought once again that the man might in fact be quite sane, so I addressed him as such.

“Mr. Persano, your doctor and I have been discussing your case and I have prevailed upon him to try a certain experiment, which if you are willing we shall now essay to attempt.”

I do not think that it was only my imagination when I saw a note of terror appear in the man’s eyes. He spoke up at once, “I think not gentlemen.”

“Oh come now, Mr. Persano,” interjected the doctor. “Mr. Holmes has come a great way to give us his aid. We owe him some degree of cooperation.”

“My case is quite hopeless. I shall remain here,” said the

patient with a pleading tone in his voice.

"It is quite simple," I interposed. "I shall merely state a single name and we will then withdraw. Surely you will not refuse us so meager a request."

"Very well," he answered reluctantly. "But I ask that after that, you will leave me alone."

"Agreed, now then Mr. Persano, former duelist and resident of Central America ... it is lovely there is it not, the banana plantations, and the great railroad across Costa Rica, the ..."

The man had risen in his seat and I could see how his every muscle was strained and his nerves appeared to be at a fever pitch.

I continued, "I see that my words are calling forth old associations. But let us not waste time on preliminaries. The name that I would like to place before you is the name of one whom you long thought you had eluded."

I paused before saying in a suggestive whisper, "Rodger Baskerville."

Our man rose slowly to his feet before pitching forward with a strangled cry upon the floor. Dr. Blackwell and I came at once to our feet as well and I stood back in order to allow the doctor to examine his patient. He took some smelling salts from his pocket and through a vigorous application of them soon brought the patient round again. We both helped him to his feet and over again to his chair where he sat mopping his forehead with a handkerchief for some time before speaking.

At last he said in a choked voice. "Wherever could you have heard that name, that odious name? Even I had thought that I had left it behind forever in Costa Rica, that beautiful but cursed land."

"Never mind how I know the name," I answered. "I beg you to place the case before me and we will see if perhaps we may lighten your self-imposed sentence, for I at least am of the opinion that you are not mad. If this man is such a threat to you, then you must trust us to act in your behalf if we may do so in conscience after hearing your complete story. I can promise nothing, but if you are indeed a man of honor, you must prove so now to us. Surely a man who has faced death many times with eternity in the offing may do so once again."

Mr. Persano looked up fiercely for a moment before hanging his head again. "You are right Mr. Holmes; I am not mad, although I deserve to be. You see gentlemen to what a sad state association with that man has brought me. I tell you he is a devil! There was a time though when I counted the man who bore that name as a friend and a compatriot. Together as partners we intended to make a fortune by developing a virgin country. We had the protection of Don Juan Murillo, who was a dull, savage, brute of a man, but one highly placed in the military. When he came to supreme power he had neither the wit nor the civility to procure investment money from the north. I was known as a traveler and a journalist, so it was I who went north into America to meet with the great business interests there, while Rodger Baskerville remained in Costa Rica to supervise the project of the railroad and the mines and plantations to be established there. We were granted concessions by the government in exchange for bribes. That is how things are done down there and no two men could ever hope to change the pattern. I told myself that all would come right in the end. The country would prosper with the railroad, which would unite the two oceans and make the two major ports of Costa Rica grow. I spent years in America, all the while hearing from Baskerville glowing reports at home of happy natives and satisfied workers. Production was always on schedule and the reports that I received showed every sign of the enhanced production of gold, silver, bananas, yams, and cacao from the garden-like region."

"The investors in the north were growing restive though as time passed, because the costs always seemed to be greater than any receipts sent north to pay dividends to the stockholders. There was always some new setback, a mine cave-in, or a flood. At last I was sent down to investigate the matter in order to prevent mutiny among the investors. I did not realize until I returned after seven years that the entire country had become a penal colony and that the profits were being diverted into the hands of Don Juan Murillo and his henchman Lopez, with the remnant remaining going into the hands of Rodger Baskerville."

"He met me at the boat full of tales of progress and as usual quite enthusiastic about his collection of butterflies and moths. His strange boyish enthusiasms covered his black heart. He had prevailed upon one of the noblest men of the country to surrender his daughter to him in marriage. She was a great beauty named Beryl Garcia. He had deluded her as he had so many others. His enthusiasms allowed him to paint great vistas of possibilities and dreams. He could make anything seem possible. He was a man born for great endeavors, but it was always results that mattered never the means of obtaining them. He had no patience with any human needs beyond his own. He would no sooner take up a cause than he would tire of it. Figures bored him. He had hired a team of brutal foremen and cost accountants to build that blasted railroad. Every mile of track was built upon the bodies of those who died like flies of yellow fever, malaria, and dysentery. He had advertised in Italian journals for more workers when the supply of extorted native labor failed. The native Indians melted into the surrounding jungles rather than be pressed into his work gangs. But the Italians who came died even faster than the natives, so he tried Chinese coolies and it was they who finished the railroad at last."

"I was two days returned to the country before I began to realize the full extent of what had occurred there in my absence. The workers were buried there in mass-graves, which were soon overgrown with jungle and forgotten. It was only the frightened and hostile eyes of the village people along the rows of plantations that alerted me to what had occurred. When I met the dictator Murillo and saw how his splendor and display had grown over the years I began to glimpse the truth. His mansion was a virtual castle in the jungle. Guards were everywhere, all in uniforms with gold braid. The meals were served on silver plates. The entire wealth of the country had been siphoned off to fuel a small oligarchy of the man and his cronies. Baskerville was a sort of technical advisor. He was awarded a high salary, but was not himself a great landowner. He was too restless to remain anywhere for very long. His method was to stay in one place until it became too hot to hold him and then to begin again somewhere else.   His capacity for re-invention of his personality was boundless. He could master the technical jargon of a field almost overnight. It was astonishing. At last I began to ask guarded questions and what were at first dark suspicions based on rumors soon became certainties.”

“When at last I confronted the man, he only laughed at me. ‘But these creatures are nothing,’ said he. ‘These jungles are as old as the hemisphere and as unchanged. There is no history here. Time simply passes. It takes effort to create history and effort must be imposed. The lives lost here have built a great railroad where before there was only a tangle of vines. Now their lives have significance. Before, they were nothing, now they are a railroad.’”

Isadora Persano paused in his narrative and wiped his brow again before continuing, “I was aghast, gentlemen. I tried him then by asking about the dictator, Murillo. Again Baskerville surprised me by showing an equal contempt for the most powerful man in the country.   I recall his words well, ‘That dull-witted baboon is another nothing! Murillo is the vacuum at the center of a storm of activity. He is a great low-pressure area that gathers about him only a throng of other non-entities. He is the most common of human types. They grow like mushrooms when the soil is rich. It only remains for someone to come by and kick the mushroom over since it has no roots. Murillo is little more than a potted plant. Even now there are men here who plan to kill him at the first opportunity.’”

“I asked him what then would become of his own position in the country, which was dependent upon to the patronage of the dictator. He answered me at once, ‘Oh I will strike at the proper moment and then follow the example of the Indians and simply fade away. I have plans to return to England.’”

“All of this was you understand some years ago, gentlemen. Well, all occurred just as he had predicted.   Murillo was overthrown and Baskerville managed to get his hands on much of the money at the time, since he had recently ascended to the position of the Secretary of Treasury; not that Murillo trusted him of course, but he trusted his countrymen even less. Baskerville managed to leave Costa Rica even before Murillo with what must have been a tidy sum. In any case the country was by then nearly bankrupt. Murillo and Lopez took the rest and absconded for parts unknown. I was left to face the indignation of the few honest men in the country who eventually managed to restore a semblance of order and justice. I was given a trial of course and given a five year sentence in a beastly prison for my part in the affair, but I was not hanged as I might have been."

"Upon my release I headed north. My own fortune, such as it was, was still in the United States. So after leaving the country I went north to claim it. It had been in stock and managed by a reputable firm. During my years in prison the railroad began to prosper and my stock holdings rose accordingly. They were immediately sold and I made some contributions to certain relief agencies of a missionary order operating in Central America to ease my conscience and then took myself off to England to start my life anew."

"I moved to London when I arrived seeking to lose myself in its vast millions. I never wished to see a colonial nation again. I lived in my clubs. Years passed and I imagined that I had put the nightmare of my past behind me when suddenly this box was delivered to me, without name or return address. It was carrying a worm, a larva actually, which I soon ascertained to be quite unique and unknown to science, at least in England. I could not doubt who had sent it to me. It was Rodger Baskerville's own peculiar calling card. Baskerville was attempting to lure me once again into his ambit. I fled at once in horror as you may imagine. Nothing would tempt me to join with him again, whatever that fellow's fantastic enterprises now are or to loan him money. I could not doubt that he was penniless once again if he was desperate enough to contact me. He was no doubt coming to me as his only contact in England, presuming upon our old acquaintance. I had had enough of his devil's bargains. But I fear him more than I despise him. I tell you that the man is a devil incarnate!"

He paused for breath before concluding, "So it is that I have sought refuge here and I beg you to allow me to remain in this sanctuary from his importuning and his revenge should I refuse him."

This was the strange tale that was laid before us. I answered him after looking over at Dr. Blackwell, "Your future of course remains with Dr. Blackwell, not with me. It may interest you though to hear that I have encountered Rodger Baskerville before in the course of my professional career. The man is just as you describe him, cunning and resourceful. Many people even now suppose him to be dead. Even I believed that he had perished some years ago. But I have always been troubled by the manner of his supposed death since the body could not be recovered. It is for that reason that I have come down to look into your own case, to see how strong the evidence might be for his survival. I will certainly warn the parties concerned in that prior case to keep on their guard from now on. For the rest, I fear that we must await events. I doubt he can be traced until he shows his hand or chooses to reveal himself. Until then you are as safe here as anywhere and if Doctor Blackwell will consent, it will be my recommendation that he retain you for as long as you wish to remain here and can afford the costs of your maintenance, since I do not doubt that you do indeed possess a nervous indisposition as your very constitution bears witness."

We both then turned to the doctor. "Well, it is not our function to be a police establishment, nor do I wish to place our other patients in danger or to put my staff at risk, but since Mr. Holmes approves ... if you consent to being removed to a separate but secure cottage upon the grounds, I believe that we may continue to accommodate you here, if that will be agreeable to you, Mr. Persano."

Mr. Persano agreed at once to the terms stipulated and I interposed before leaving that I would appreciate any further insights which Mr. Persano might give me via letter that might help in my own investigation. If Rodger Baskerville still lives, then I cannot doubt that either Sir Henry or I will encounter him again.

He has no hope, now that his identity and murder of Sir Charles is known of ever inheriting the Baskerville fortune. English law is quite clear upon the point that an heir may not profit from his own criminal activity. Sir Henry in any case has superior title to the estate by primogeniture. The murder breaks the chain of the legacy within the direct blood heirs. Even if Sir Henry should die from natural causes Lady Beryl would inherit by marriage since her former husband is presumed dead and he dare not appear to dispute that fact for fear of arrest. As a Catholic and to put her conscience at rest, Lady Beryl might conditionally have the prior marriage annulled under ecclesiastical law if she hears privately through me that her former husband still lives. Alternatively, Sir Henry might bypass the marital relation entirely as a method of inheritance and simply place the Baskerville Estate in trust for the benefit of Lady Beryl as beneficiary and thereafter to her assigns since no other Baskerville exists to maintain a claim and the estate is not entailed in any way. I shall advise Sir Henry to take the required steps upon my return home.

I could think of little more that could be done at the time but to ask Mr. Persano for a written statement that might be used at a later date, which he promised to forward to me in Grimpen. Thus was my day's investigation concluded; I have decided to spend the night here in Plymouth. I have spent the evening writing up these extensive notes while they are fresh in my mind. I intend to return to Grimpen tomorrow and to alert Sir Henry of the remarkable possibility that his great foe and cousin, Rodger Baskerville, may still be alive.

June 28, 1893
Grimpen

I returned by the morning train from Plymouth and am now at home in my own lodgings. Dr. Blackwell took me personally to the station and informed me that he would keep me informed of any changes in his unusual patient. My journey through the moors allowed me to reflect upon the strange synchronicities of life. All things are connected in ways that we may not imagine. A thousand plays are running simultaneously in even the smaller towns so we should not be surprised when a single actor may play roles in plays that intersect even across continents. The chains of circumstance are many. Synchronicity must then be inevitable in more cases of life than we imagine. The options of mankind are limited by human nature. To know the story of one is to some degree to know the story of all.

During my career in pursuit of solutions to the mysteries laid before me I have concentrated upon the solution to the problem and only secondarily upon the criminal. In many of my cases there was doubt if indeed a crime had even been committed. I have always considered the criminal codes of the various nations as not equivalent to moral strictures. I will even go so far as to say that many criminal codes are themselves criminal if viewed from the higher perspective of a true morality. Who is the greater criminal in *Les Miserables*, Jean Valjean or Inspector Javert?

It has always seemed to me that the business of courts is sordid in the extreme. The most unconscionable results are sanctioned as long as the forms are followed, while manifest injustices are often left without any remedy at law. Guilt after all is not easy to ascertain. Human actions are so conditioned by the abilities and predispositions of the criminal agent that no two human actions may have the same internal meaning and guilt. Society cares little for these distinctions however and applies a gross calculus that attempts to reach some sort of outer gage for the degree of understanding, reflection, and commitment of the will that attaches to the completed criminal act. It further erects a set of barriers to the truth by establishing rules of evidence and then choosing from among the populace, not those of fine judgment and discretion, but a mongrel assortment of supposed peers to decide as to guilt or innocence. This system then relies upon a judge to apply what matters most, the punishment of the convicted felon.

The sentence to a term in prison usually ensures the perpetuation of a resentful criminal class that guarantees that society will not advance or be spared from the commission of further crimes. Resentment takes the place of contrition and amendment, let alone the chimera of rehabilitation. The guilty man or woman feels unlucky in being selected from the class of criminals that surround them each day who do little more than thank their good fortune that they have been spared to continue to pursue their usual criminal pursuits until they in turn are apprehended and punished.

The net result of this legal system is that society does not evolve but only assembles over time a vast literature of human dismay and despair in the reported decisions of our courts of law. I have often wished to spare my conscience the burden of adding my own efforts to stirring this noxious societal brew. I have often given a malefactor a chance to escape the law so as to amend his life. The only exceptions to this preference or bias of mine towards mercy have been when I have been convinced that the malefactor posed a great risk to the general order of society due to a persistent love of evil for its own sake.

I do not consider the criminal as being different from the madman, since it is not the business of the social order to probe the soul, but only to prevent social harm. Punishment and the threat of punishment usually deter only those who would not think of committing crimes in the first place. In fact punishment imposes further costs upon the social order by mandating that the prisoner be fed, clothed, and sheltered at public expense. The subjective suffering of the criminal through hard labor imposed or by confinement is out of sight and hence out of mind of even our most vindictive citizens. Prisons only add to the strange and evil dance because those who guard the criminals are often of the same brutal and abrasive disposition of mind and heart as those that they guard and supervise.

It is a commonplace that the world of our everyday experience, even in Christian countries, is based upon a brutal struggle for survival or in pursuit of prosperity. Only the few, through membership in various Christian societies, do anything to directly impact the disproportion of accident, illness, and natal abilities among the population of these isles. It is as though practical Christianity can be relegated to the mere exercise of worship, while in the daily hubbub and maelstrom of life we remain animals and not human beings at all. If society is so fractured and divided, can we expect more of its members?

For this reason I am not without sympathy with those anarchists who advocate an abolition of the laws and the property arrangements that the rule of law sanctions, which are on their face unequal. Nature has yet to frame a more perfect example of stupidity, hard-heartedness, and duplicity than many who assume positions of power even in nominal democracies. For this reason I reserve the right to dispense mercy when I please and reserve the full rigor of the legal establishment for truly dangerous or evil men.

I have known three such dangerous men in the course of my career: the first of these is Professor Moriarty, the second is the man who was my opponent in the case of the Red-headed League, a young man of noble extraction, but of vicious ways whose real name I shall omit here, so as to spare grief to his family, and last of all and perhaps the only one that I view as evil without principle is the third man on my list, Rodger Baskerville. I will note in passing that there was also the bitter and vengeful Jonas Oldacre, but his dullness of wit only advances him to the position of a thug and keeps him from my list of infamy. The third named individual though, Rodger Baskerville, manifests that peculiar manner and degree of moral insanity that makes one doubt if he has quite reached the stage of being a member of the human species. He seems rather to be a sort of hybrid creature as allied to the beasts of prey as to humanity. Crime for him is less a passion than it is a matter of indifference or at most a matter of simple convenience.

The great task is simply to avoid such people. They partake of the nature of a calculable risk. To be in their proximity is to risk contracting the disease they carry. They are the cliff along which civilization walks. They are vipers coiled along the trail awaiting the unwary footstep. Outer charm is no warrant for their inner disposition. Indeed, it is best to suspect their presence when all else seems to augur trustworthiness and virtue. Often they reach great heights of honor and social esteem. They hide their contempt of those who bestow the titles that they enjoy behind a mask of humility and geniality. Rodger Baskerville is true to the type. I had always suspected that he might have escaped the clutches of the Grimpen Mire. Such men cannot conceive of their own extinction and are often ingenious in assuring their own survival. It would be only too natural for such a man to have long since made a plan for his escape should he fail in his design to kill Sir Henry, his cousin.

Now, I am in possession of reliable evidence that Rodger Baskerville still lives and might be in need of money. The sign of the worm with its carnivorous associations that could only be recognized by a man who had been in Costa Rica where the moth abounds was ingenious. It was an advance warning that the man himself would soon appear. His intent was no doubt to reach the one man in England who had known him in the days of his former power in Costa Rica and to use the fear that his mere presence could even now instill in Isadora Persano to demand money or other concessions.

I asked Mr. Persano if he possessed anything that might be of use to me in my investigation before I left the asylum. After deep reflection, the patient could think of nothing. He said that he would gladly pay to remove the source of his disquiet, but he knew that once in the grasp of the villain, no amount of money would purchase his freedom and he would always be subject to further demands. This sounded to me at first like mere blackmail, but I have come to the conclusion that Persano has an almost superstitious dread of Rodger Baskerville.

Therefore he has chosen to run from the man into hiding and to seek a refuge of comfort and security that his still ample means can supply, even if his liberty must suffer in consequence. At least his retirement ensures his safety for now and his survival would seem to be secure.

But why would such a formerly bold man seek refuge in a rest home for the mentally afflicted if the threat posed to him was not a great one? I have agreed with the wisdom of his choice and assured him that I will inform him at once if I should be able to apprehend the man who is the source of his fear. I must now inform Sir Henry of my suspicions and risk upsetting his peace of mind in order to warn him that this devil may be still alive and hovering somewhere near. In any case I shall be living nearby to Sir Henry and Lady Beryl and shall keep a weather-eye peeled for any sign of the man formerly known as Stapleton who proved to be actually Rodger Baskerville, an heir to the Baskerville estate after Sir Henry. If I may lay Rodger Baskerville up by the heels I shall account it a signal moment in my career.

July 1, 1893
My Cottage on the Moor

y meeting with Isadora Persano has set in motion a strange train of thoughts, which I must attempt to put down here. I am still trying to account for the man's strange terror. The return of the past is a thing that haunts us all. Which of us would not gladly rid ourselves of those phantoms of our past actions and associations and create ourselves anew? I have often thought that the peculiar joy of children stems from the fact that they have as yet nothing to regret. The world is for them a blank slate, an unsoiled canvass. Infinity lies before them like a beach on a sunny morning when the tides are breaking on a pristine shore. By evening those same bright sands will contain what the day has flung upon the strand, the foul sea-wrack of kelp, dead shells, driftwood and the chill night wind will blow the sands along to mock the aspirations of the dawn with ages yet to be, of which these now aged ones, grown old in the space of a day, will have no part.

Who does not regret with Shakespeare's Hamlet the shocks that flesh is heir to, the many humiliations that one needed to endure to avoid a greater harm, the love scorned, the best of efforts misunderstood, the drifting apart of old friends, the upstart preening himself in office, the swift loss of innocence, and the sad abuse of the elders among us. Each generation is allotted but a short vista of history. History itself is but a tiny respite between the glacial ages of the earth. How can we assume that we have any significance at all in the face of the brevity of our custody of the world? Are we not all then like Isadora Persano, seeking a retreat from the vague dangers that beset us among the muttering denizens of a madhouse? Are not our various loyalties merely an attempt to give our lives significance and meaning? We endure the prison of this world rather than to risk another. But who can contemplate eternity without terror? Would any of us wish infinity upon ourselves and to span the great abysses of time and space? If as Wordsworth said, "This world is too much with us late and soon," then how much more insupportable would be eternity without the help of God to endure it?

Blessed is the man who knows the dimensions of his cell in this great prison of a world. Open the gates to freedom and he would summon his warden with his cries to remain a prisoner. Which sane man would ever be content to assume that his particular vision should be dispositive for the universe? Let the mad ones find a few others and form some sect of mutual affirmation. Perhaps the religions of mankind are only asylums for those upon a trek too soon ended. Therefore they are not appalled with the vast expanse of the untold deserts of eternity that lie ahead.

We die in the wasteland of our various religious opinions with only the sound of the wailing from the inmates of adjoining cells to soothe our own nightmare mutterings. The vision of a ruined mind in the case of Isadora Persano has brought forth all my own fears and doubts once again. This is no state in which to face Moriarty for our next encounter. I feel once again my entire inadequacy for the task that lies ahead; yet I must proceed, for Moriarty has threatened to make good his threat and has placed the outcome of events upon me. He will destroy the British Empire, such is his boast. Certainly such a threat would be madness if claimed by another, but I believe that Professor Moriarty has the wherewithal to accomplish just such an end, though what his means might be I have no clue.

Let me look to the motive of evil for a solution. The great question that must always be posed to evil is why does it even bother to assault the good? The usual answer given is that true evil realizes its own vacuity. It is drawn to the good, for only goodness possesses being. The vacuum of evil abhors both its own evil and the goodness of which it is deprived. It is drawn to that which it despises. So much is clear, but what of my initial objection: if evil chooses itself in opposition to God, why should not its own pride cause it to refuse to meddle with the good? Is it not a confession of defeat for the devil to wish to tempt us? What is it to the devil if men and women are destroyed? Does it not clutter the ebony halls of Satan's kingdom to have ruined souls lying about? Does not true evil desire solitude above all else? Once having swept the universe of God, why then should the devil stake a claim upon God's creatures? True contempt of God should foreswear even vengeance? Or is it that the angelic nature, made for love, still asserts itself, so that the devil longs for what it may possess no longer, its former status as loved by God?

Thus everything evil manifests self-division. Perfect evil is impossible, for only goodness admits of perfection. Thus the devil's quest fails *ab initio*! The whole thing is pointless and we are thrown back upon the great why of evil from which no rational thought may escape. All human efforts to resolve the manifold contradictions of radical evil only further complicate the snarl of metaphysical string that lies before us. We assume that there are two ends to the string and we follow the string for a time in either direction, but the ends never appear. Perhaps good and evil must remain forever adjectives and not nouns!

So limited are we in our speculation about such meta-values that neither principle may be grasped in its entirety. Both our sins and our virtues are wholly inadequate as a basis for an eternal destiny. Surely the mercy of God must realize this and in some manner make an accounting and elevation of our faculties at the moment of death in preparation for eternity... If there are many souls unworthy of heaven then surely there are many, even grave sinners, who are unworthy of hell! Is Moriarty one of these? Is Stapleton? Or is it only heaven that sets the narrow standard so that hell is always the default assumption and destination when one considers mankind? Is this what is meant by the narrow gate, that most will fail? Yet in contrast to this view, how wide are the dimensions of the virtue of hope?

From these questions arise the fear and trembling that must beset even the religious soul. On these questions Christianity has been divided as each branch attempts to resolve the width of the gates of heaven to see who will be excluded and who will finally enter the Kingdom of God. The task of the Catholic Church has always been, not to explain the many paths to hell, but to chart the narrow and most sure path to heaven. So humble is its mission that only the homely metaphor of the sheepfold proves adequate to its highest conceptions of its own nature.

Perhaps true Christianity should remain a stranger to metaphysics. If one must be like a little child to enter the Kingdom of Heaven, then perhaps all of the speculations and arguments with which I would confront Professor Moriarty are really beside the point. Was the sacrifice of Jesus a final admission by God that in the face of evil, no arguments are adequate and that evil must be allowed to take its own course, even if that means to accept even evil acted upon the Beloved Son of God Jesus, the awaited one who is also the rejected one, yet the messiah we hope and pray will come again at the end of time?

But to return for a moment to metaphysics if evil is always seen in relation to God, for it defines its position in opposition to God, then the nature of evil must always be seen in relation to love. It is love's denial that defines evil. Since the nature of God is the one great constant among a sea of variables in creation, God persists and consists of love, not only as His defining characteristic, but as His very essence. What such a love might be is only hinted at by the imperfect loves that we know in our lives. Certainly the willing sacrifice of Christ is the unique event manifest in history that spills over into the living waters of the Holy Mass that is celebrated each day throughout the world.   But even the

Crucifixion of Jesus as Savior of the World is by its historicity only a sign and example of the love of God the Father who creates the entire universe for and through the Beloved Son. This means that Divine Love, like light, only appears when reflected off of an object. What Divine Love is, as shared within the Triune Godhead, must remain a mystery.

We may only imagine the higher degree of the penetration and comprehension of that mystery of love as revealed to the intellectual comprehension of the devil and those other angelic natures that chose to share its chosen fate in hell. But this much is clear; if evil could exist at peace with God, then it would still enjoy some measure of God's love, which would create a wedge into that very denial of love that must inevitably destroy that very inversion of love that is the fruit of the primal rebellion. For this reason, angelic sin must preclude all later appeals for mercy. Angelic evil is by its own choice final and irrevocable, for no further evidence will ever be admitted to change the devil's mind!

By presuming to judge God and to condemn His love, the principle of evil that we call the devil has made the entire matter as it were *res judicata*. The devil has no option thereafter to choose to enter through mere degrees of evil into hell for to do so would make hell less odious, made less bleak and final by moments of "diabolic compassion." The only hope for the devil then is our own contingent choices which stem from our freedom. Perhaps the devil's only practical illusion is the hope that it may still triumph over God through sustained resistance. If that is so, then complete defeat may open a tiny window of opportunity for even the devil to repent at last. Paradoxically then, defeat is the devil's only hope!

For this reason the Catholic Church calls the devil, the enemy of our human nature insofar as our human nature still bears the imprint of its origin as created in the image and likeness of God. Human nature was created in the image of love. All that denies love then denies human nature. Sin then is profoundly unnatural to man and woman. Our gorge rises in nausea at the very sins that we commit and that we so easily condemn in others.

367

Only the partial blindness of our pride or our sheer desperation may hide for a time the strong acidic after-taste of sin.

A final point ... many human actions although evil are not sins. True sin only exists when the will is complete and when moral clarity exists. It is sad but true that many human beings are too debased by habitual vice and too ignorant of their true nature to really sin. It is due to this fact that many souls may be spared eternal condemnation. It may be the case that few souls have the unparalleled clarity and maturity that allows for complete moral choices to be made. The majority of humankind blunder about in what might be called pseudo-sin or venial sin, not because the evils that they do are minor or lacking in what is called serious matter, but because their full humanity is so impaired by prior moral choices or by the fallen nature of man that no definitive choice for good or for evil exists as dispositive of their entire being.

In the Garden of Gethsemane, Jesus warned his disciples to pray that they would not undergo the test. What was that test? The test is the final rejection of the very principle of love made manifest in Christ. To deny Christ as the definitive Word of God to mankind but only in full knowledge that one is doing so, which may only be possible within the mystery of death is *ipso facto* to go the way of the devil and his angels.

Clearly even the sin of St. Peter, his three-fold denial of Jesus, was not an absolute choice, although it required a three-fold reaffirmation of love before Peter was restored as the rock of the Church, one affirmation for each denial in the courtyard of the Sanhedrin. The Doctrine of the Sacred Heart of Jesus gives to the Catholic Church a place of refuge that dwelling constantly before the love of God made manifest we may be prevented from sin brought about through a gradual erosion of faith, hope, or charity.

The function of prayer is to induce a habit of mind and heart that cuts through the many distractions that would replace the eternal good of our souls with a desperate desire to find our complete happiness apart from God. Most sins are acts of desperation rather than gratuitous malice. It takes leisure and reflection to be a great sinner. It takes the beginnings of love in the soul to make it possible to reject that love. Since so many people feel the vast abyss of lovelessness in this world, most cannot appreciate God's love for them; and if God is not contemplated in some way, He may not be completely rejected in Himself.

This means that most of what we call sin is indicative, but not dispositive. It is no less evil of course for all of that, but it cannot absent more and deeper knowledge of God, determine the final destination of the soul. The task of the man or woman of good will then is to weed the garden of his or her soul on a daily basis through constant penance and to nurture the virtues so as to enhance the final realization of the cardinal virtue of hope, which promises eternal salvation to those who believe.

The Catholic Church exists to aid us in this personal effort through the ministrations of the Sacraments and the Sacramentals, the prayer of the Divine Office, and the intercession of the Saints and the Holy Souls in Purgatory. It is the mandate of Christ to the Church that it may forgive sins. What sins it may not forgive are retained, not through some willfulness or failure of charity in the Church, but as a sign of Christ's unity with the Mystical Body of the Church. No sin will be retained arbitrarily as a mere manifestation of the power entrusted to the Church as a judicial tribunal. The Church is not a court of law. Retained sins are retained simply because forgiveness is the healing without which the soul remains in its orientation away from God and thus at risk of making an eternal choice contrary to love. Hope for the conversion of even great sinners is nourished by the knowledge that it is the will of God that none shall be eternally lost.

It is the Church in its highest calling that is given this full power of God to remit sins. The command is to the Church as a whole that it must manifest the charity of Christ. If during any period of history members of the Church even within the highest orders of the clergy have failed to adhere to this duty, then it is the very person of Jesus who is the life of the Church who will exercise in His own person the acts of mercy denied to the sinner due to the sins and negligence of the ones entrusted with the powers to bind and to loose from sin. The final judgment of all souls remains only with God.

It is said that the soul thirsts for God even when it is unaware of doing so. This is due to the profound inadequacy of human life as a self-contained entity. In every act of perception we are directed outward to a world of objects, but even more than this we are directed outward to a world of other subjectivities. It is only in communication that we may discover ourselves. Prayer in this sense is the ultimate in communication because it is a reaching out to the ultimate subjectivity, the one that embraces all things, the all-comprehending mind of God.

To pray therefore is to dare to risk a reaching out into what is not immediately perceptible, because as ultimate subjectivity it cannot be reduced to an easily discernible object of consciousness. God does not stand over against us as something that we can pick up and turn over in our hands as it were. A better analogy for the communication with God that occurs in prayer is to enter into what already encompasses us. We exist within God in a manner so pervasive and intimate that it precludes all objectification whatsoever. It is deeper than even what we do when we engage in a silent dialogue with ourselves.

For this reason the prayer of silence is as adequate as petition and awareness of sin is as complete as verbal assertions of repentance. Conversion of heart is far deeper than simply making a resolution to do better; it is a coming together of past, present, and future in one single moment of surrender to that which is grace, the grace that must act within us rather than ourselves relying upon our unaided determination to do better; it is an act of silent trust, a turning over of our lives to God.

There are many ways to express this reality and many methodologies have been devised to aid us to pray, but the fundamental insight of faith is that God comes to meet us before we go out to meet God. God forgives us before we even think to ask for forgiveness. It is a mistake to attempt to instigate a dialogue in prayer. The greatest mystics agree that prayer is always a preparation rather than a pursuit. God is not an object of our intentions; we are a subject of God's intentions for us and how those intentions are to be accomplished is only revealed to us at God's discretion.

 he origin and distinguishing feature of Christianity is said to be in the revelation of God through His Divine Word. The primary aspect of anthropology as of religion is the fact of communication. Without that communication the idea that what human beings call meaning is of any relevance to the world that we pretend to comprehend will immediately become evident: we must posit some manner of consciousness to be present among inanimate things or in a deity or we would be plunged back into an intolerable contradiction between our search for meaning and its lack of any basis in any consciousness but our own. The book of the universe would remain unwritten and unread unless we assume that the mere existence of objects is already a type of language speaking to us. The undeniable fact of our own consciousness immediately presumes a need for communication. The inherent social nature of human beings likewise makes some sort of religion inevitable, because our inherent sense of meaning must be grounded in something besides our own sensations and reflections.

The resistance to our desires and constructions put up by objects is our best guarantee that our consciousness does not create reality but is molded and formed by our encounter with the world. Part of that encounter is our sense that some things simply should not be, because they are evil. This intuitive grasp of evil arises from our sense of the uncanny, the false, the disproportionate, or the terrible in the world that we encounter. Evil in turn does not merely resist us; it stands over against us as a disturbing and alien force, even when it erupts from within us. It is this fundamental contrast between what is and what should be that creates morality, a sense of obligation or duty, a sense of guilt, and those higher aspirations that we call holiness.

If knowledge was confined to sensation alone it would be impossible for the mind to form concepts and comparisons and reason would falter into insignificance. Language in turn would be unimaginably primitive and confined to grunts and groans with no purpose to seek aid or arouse sympathy from our fellow human beings, let alone from God. Our solitude under such conditions would be intolerable. Christian theology in the doctrine of the Holy Trinity implies that not even God can tolerate absolute solitude. Words cannot exist in a vacuum and for this reason composition is the natural result of thought. The universal presence of language in even the most primitive societies is testimony to the central and indeed essential role of communication in human consciousness and therefore the essential element of human bonding without which we would dissolve into ashes and succumb to despair.

I thought it would be proper to review in this brief summary my understanding of evil before attempting to deal with the two souls that I have mentioned above whose manifest evils threaten us at this time. If I am to prevail with Professor Moriarty and to thwart the possible designs of Rodger Baskerville, I must have some knowledge of the moral temper of their souls. I pray that I possess the requisite degree of knowledge and fortitude for the task that lies before me.

Only prayer may sustain me in such a formidable task. It is always dangerous to do battle with the devils of this earth. To encounter evil is always to risk contagion by the very thing that we oppose. This was why Jesus asked us to seek to love our enemies and to do good things to those who persecute us. It is a good thing to always remember that to walk in the footsteps of the devil may lead one to the same destination. The way of Jesus Christ in contrast remains the path that says, "Forgive them Father for they know not what they do."

June 30, 1893
Word from Mycroft

I received a most interesting missive from Mycroft today that may help me in my efforts to confront Professor Moriarty on this question of the fate of the British Empire. At the time of our wager it became clear to me that Professor Moriarty had grown to view his criminal organization like any other business venture, as a source for capital accumulation. For all of our social pretence that the higher intellectual disciplines of philosophy, theology, and even science somehow rule the world, the fact remains that those who make the larger decisions in human history are not scholars but men of action. The academy will always be the slave of the moneyed interests and of the military that pushes forward the borders of trade and colonization.

At the time of our meeting at the Falls of Reichenbach Professor Moriarty made it clear to me that crime had served its purpose, that he had become a wealthy man, that he was ready to have his organization (having served its purpose) dismantled lest it prove a hindrance to the new life that the Professor envisioned for himself, and finally that I had become rather boring to him and having also served my purpose I was about to be furloughed to wander the world in pursuit of eternal truths. I even detected a certain degree of affection for me that had grown up over the years; just as a child favors a special toy even after he tires of it, but still retains it as a stimulus to memory of times gone by.

Having exhausted the amusement that I could provide, Professor Moriarty was now ready to take on a greater challenge, that of world affairs. Placed squarely in his way of course was the one man, who more than even members of the British Cabinet and the leaders of Parliament could grasp just where the currents of the world were tending, that is to say my brother Mycroft. I had presumed from the beginning that our battle would be primarily waged on the higher plains of the intellect, while it was more than probable that the Professor would point out the utter irrelevance of philosophy except as window-dressing for decisions that might cost the lives of millions to ensure national supremacy with its trade and military advantages. I read as much in the letter from Mycroft that I will now include as an appendage to my journal entry as follows:

My Dear Sherlock,

 I take it from your silence that you have yet to hear from our former stable boy, James Moriarty. You will forgive me if I speak slightingly of a man that you seem to respect as your former chief adversary. Perhaps I do so because I feel in regard to him a secret fear. His threat that during your absence he would devise a plot to destroy the British Empire seemed at the time to be so much bluster and I would prefer to continue to view it in that light. However, I must admit that underneath our thriving empire certain troubling aspects exist that might betoken just that sort of weakness that could play into the hand of a cunning villain like Moriarty. It is a treat for me to share my thoughts with the one man whose mind and mental capacities are a parallel with my own; that man is you Sherlock. So let me begin...

First I would like you to note that we are being driven into various potentially costly alliances in order to protect the eastern part of the British Empire. The future of the world will always depend upon who can dominate central Asia. Europe proper, continental Europe, if viewed strictly geographically, is a peninsula and the British Isles are islands off of that peninsula. Is it probable then that a mere island can long succeed in an Asiatic struggle for power in world affairs? The question immediately suggests the answer; the answer is a resounding no! The British Empire for all of its colonial scope cannot hope to triumph in Asia; at best we may continue to dominate the Mediterranean and trade with India by protecting the Suez Canal and by maintaining an outpost in Egypt for another century. Eventually the British Empire must falter and fail even without the machinations of Professor Moriarty and any man that he chooses as an associate. Yes, Sherlock, there are already rumors afoot, but I will not speak of them now.

Let me continue by saying that we are being drawn into an alliance with France and with Russia that may lead to our undoing. A western war in Europe will only be an adjunct to a wider eastern war that may require over a century to emerge in clarity and the key to that resolution is the fate of the Russian Empire. The contenders in that great struggle will be four in number: Russia, China, India, and Persia and the goal will be to dominate central Asia in what may be referred to by its usual title "the Great Game." The task of England to my way of thinking is to avoid being drawn into a sideshow, a war between France and Germany. We are not a land power; we are a great naval power and our natural ally is America. We will have enough to do keeping our colonies in Africa and even that will not be possible to maintain indefinitely. All of our interests lie in other words in the west. We are a western nation and Russia is part of the orient. The Russians are not and never will be European.

So taking that statement as my primary hypothetical let me continue. I foresee the next century, and perhaps even the following century as well, to be centered on the question of the fate of the Russian people and their tendency to submit to autocratic government. Added to this is the ancient rivalry in Christendom between Rome and Constantinople, with Moscow as a contender to be "the third Rome," and you have a deadly religious broth only lightly seasoned by Protestantism to add spice to the brew. Then to complicate matters there is the religious empire of Islam reaching from the Arab lands to Indonesia. Shake it all up and you have the probable course of history that lies before us.

Granted your own religious preoccupations you may point out that the Holy Land may play a role in unfolding events. I am in contact with a man named Theodor Herzl who is quietly dreaming; as such men always do, of a restoration of Jewish rule in Palestine. In my view that is for God to accomplish on the last day and not before and certainly not with our aid. The eastern Mediterranean is a pie with too many hands reaching for a piece.

My position in the government does not allow me to share my views with more optimistic men; therefore I share them only with you and perhaps someday with Sherringford who has already taken note that the British aristocracy is going down by the bow. Taxation has forced the great landlords to sell-off the huge estates and with them the way of life of the tenancy that sustained an agrarian mode of existence. The result is that

Englishmen are flooding the cities in the industrial regions of the north and the midlands to the degradation of morals and the erosion of a way of life befitting an heir of the British Empire. Compared to these concerns what threat is posed by Professor Moriarty. Still he may have something in the works that I cannot foresee, so I ask you to exert all of your efforts to oppose him in that contest that you have been pleased to refer to as "a wager," that private affair between the two of you reached above the seething waters of Reichenbach Falls. You have my support and encouragement. Your much beleaguered brother,
Mycroft

July 2, 1893
Baskerville Hall

went over today to Baskerville Hall to see Sir Henry and to enquire after the health of Lady Beryl. I met him in the library. He entered with a distracted air about him, not his usual decisive and cheerful demeanor. I could see the wear upon his nerves of the events of the past week. His aspect was of one haunted and pursued by some ineluctable fate. He demanded that I be quite truthful in relating any suspicions that I might entertain as to the cause of Lady Beryl's malaise after my investigation in Plymouth. I knew that the news that I had to bring him would come as a shock, but I could do no less than to comply with his wishes.

"Sir Henry," said I, "It is one of my dicta that the keys to the present lie in the past. I have asked myself when it was that Lady Beryl was exposed to worm larvae in her past, since her reaction seems to be oddly similar to that of this man Persano whom I have just met. Was not her former husband, the man called Stapleton, a collector of butterflies and moths? Was it not a passion in his life so that his name was even associated with several species that he was the first to describe?"

"Surely that is a mere coincidence Holmes," objected Sir Henry.

"I have learned that in this world with its many strange connections and relationships that true coincidences are rarer than one might suppose," I replied. "My first thought was that the comments of the vicar had merely brought on a series of unpleasant associations in Mr. Persano, but how then to account for the lasting nature of his affliction. Then there is the case of your wife, how was it that she shared the same associations and extreme reaction? No, there must be something more I told myself, more than a mere dread of a rare carnivorous moth, thus my trip to Plymouth. I met there with the patient. He remains in a highly nervous state, but he is not mad in the strict sense."

"Then what is wrong with the man?" inquired Sir Henry. "Please tell me. I cannot bear to see Beryl suffering in this fashion."

"Well, let us consider his words as reported to us by the vicar. His words were if I recall correctly 'It is the worm, the worm that will become the moth.' This phrase of course tells us nothing, but the last words may tell us more for he affirms in so many words that 'the devil lives.'"

"But these are surely merely the ravings of a lunatic. I am surprised that you assign any meaning to them at all," expostulated Sir Henry.

"Bear with me a minute Sir Henry," I pleaded. "It is another of my dicta that one should never assume unreason when there is still a possible rational explanation for events. Who was this devil? Was it the moth? Surely that would be a gross exaggeration. No matter how disgusting its habits might be, it was surely not a devil. Was it the real devil then to which he referred? I could not imagine one skipping from a mere insect to the dark force of a rational but elevated angelic mind. But what if the phrase was a metaphor for an evil man? This seemed to me to be the most likely solution. Persano was saying that the man who had sent the moth was a veritable devil."

"By Jove," cried Sir Henry. "I believe you are right, but who is that fellow?"

"My interview with the Persano may have answered that question. He believes that a man that he once knew in Costa Rica is on his trail, perhaps seeking money. For this reason Mr. Persano has gone to ground in Plymouth and I have agreed to keep his refuge there a secret. This will mean that the "devil" in question must eventually seek some other means to obtain funds. I have reason to believe that he is still in England. He may after all not have the means to leave."

"I begin to glimpse what you are hinting at, Holmes," said Sir Henry quietly. "This man is from the same region as the moth which is native to Costa Rica. This man..."

I interrupted him, "I must I fear tell you that Lady Beryl's fear is quite well founded. If all else fails he may apply to her for aid because of her father's former position as a leader of the resistance to Don Juan Murillo."

Sir Henry answered, "Well what of that? She would be happy to aid a fellow refugee in his distress. I would even be willing to...."

I was silent and Sir Henry looked at me with increasing alarm in his face and voice.

"Holmes? There is something you are not telling me. Who is this man?" asked Sir Henry, with a most dreadful look. "Was he some assistant of the man Stapleton, for I may still not bear to refer to my late cousin by any other name? He is quite unworthy of the name of Baskerville!"

"I fear not, Sir Henry," I said quietly. "I am afraid that the man with the moth is the man himself."

Sir Henry leaped to his feet with a startled cry, "But Stapleton is dead! He lies a mere mile distant in the depths of the Great Grimpen Mire! He lies where I have long since consigned his mortal body and his soul to hell. Do you tell me that the devil still lives?"

I said quietly, "Your own words match those of Isadora Persano. I can see by your reaction that you are convinced already of the truth, so I will not explain more of the details through which I have reached my conclusion. You must be on your guard, Sir

Henry, from now on, both day and night."

"But surely we may spare Lady Beryl this knowledge," He began, but ceased to expostulate when he observed that I was shaking my head.

"I do not think that would be wise, Sir Henry. A vague apprehension is often worse than a confirmed dread; your wife is the key to this mystery. Only she knows this man, insofar as his evil nature may ever be comprehended. We must use her particular knowledge about her former husband to mount our defense against him. I know that you have preferred to avoid all awkward questions about her past. The time has come though when further reticence can only aid your enemy. It is time that we heard Lady Beryl's complete story from her own lips."

Sir Henry stood with his back to me gazing out upon the desolate moor. I could see that he was engaged in a deep interior struggle. His every instinct as a gentleman had been to avoid causing pain or embarrassment to Lady Beryl by inquiring about her former relations with her husband. The natural dignity of her person had seemed to forbid all inquiry upon the subject. She had preferred to begin life once again as if she were still the lovely girl she had once been in Costa Rica when she might still believe that men were like the cavaliers and knights of old.

She had once viewed Rodger Baskerville as a rising force in the nation. His youthful enthusiasms were such that he might have hidden his dark side from her. One might only imagine the long path of her subjugation and degradation at his hands after her marriage. Such things leave a trail of damage, particularly in women. In the effort to deny the truth many women create a strange world in which they are still married to their initial idea of their husband, long after that man, if he ever existed at all, has died being supplanted by the man that he in fact always was. The more brutal the man, the more cruel and persistent is this tendency toward self-deception. It is in the nature of women that they wish to believe that their husband is noble and themselves beloved long after the basis for such faith has been removed. After deep reflection Sir Henry turned to face me decisively. "Come

Holmes, you are right. It is time that we both face the truth of this devil, Rodger Baskerville.”

With that we ascended the great Baskerville staircase and entered the presence of Lady Beryl who was now wedded to a second Baskerville, if a far different type of man from that of her first husband.   Yet both were from that same accursed line that had known so much sorrow since the time of the rake Sir Hugo of infamous memory.   Curses are lasting affairs, particularly those that afflict families.   The fortunes of individual lives are partially pre-determined by how our progenitors have lived their own lives and we in turn leave traces behind that may linger for generations to come.

Lady Beryl rose to her feet as we entered, while her maid who had opened the door for us quietly withdrew from the room at a sign from Sir Henry.   Sir Henry went to his wife’s side and embraced her and then taking a seat beside her on the couch held her hand in his own.   She looked up at me with her clear green eyes, which told me that she knew already what I had discovered. I nodded my head and watched as those magnificent eyes clouded over and filled with tears of pain.

She dropped her head and Sir Henry reached over to kiss her hair briefly and tightened the grip that he retained upon her hand.   Already, I could see she was far from us, lost in a time now vanished, a time when she was again the young woman she had been so many years ago in Costa Rica.   Quietly, as if speaking to herself, she began her tale with no request having been made by either of us.

“What you are telling me by your manner has long been my fear, Mr. Holmes.   The devil lives! I feel it to be true! You cannot know what it is to have lived with one whom you have both loved and feared as I did him.   In my own country I have seen great brutes like Don Juan Murillo be mesmerized by my former husband. So great was his cunning that he became for these men whatever they needed him to be.   Always he had an answer for their difficulties.   He could show them the way to retain power over the people and to pose as a savior for them. There is always a desire of the people that their leaders should be noble and good. The more disappointed they are by the actual facts of their lives, the greater is that need. Rodger Baskerville showed the leaders of my country, who with the exception of my father and brother, were feeding upon the people's substance and growing fat, how to deflect the people's outrage. There was always some enemy in the traditional fears and prejudices of the people who could be made to bear the blame. Every remedy of sacrifice imposed on the people only tightened the grip of this oligarchy upon the economy of the nation until at last the people were so weary and bewildered that they would even believe lies that would be contradicted upon the morrow and still the people believed lest all their sufferings should have been in vain."

"All of this could be traced to my husband's peculiar genius for affairs. Even I had wished to believe him. How could I not? I had married him. Only my father saw him at last for the fiend that he was. I told my father that he was wrong, that my husband's plans had been spoiled by the man whose business it was to execute those plans through his contacts in America, Mr. Isadora Persano. My father was quiet when he saw my pain and hesitation. At last though even I began to doubt my husband's sincerity, but that was near the end when even our supine and afflicted people had had enough."

"There was a revolution and in the chaos that followed we escaped to England. Even then I wished to believe in my first husband, perhaps I always shall. You cannot know a woman's heart, Mr. Holmes. Once she gives it away in love with her whole being and before the witnesses of her family and blessed by the solemnities of the Church she cannot imagine that she could have been wrong in her assessment of her husband's true nature all along. A woman has few powers in this world, but one she holds most dear that she may make her husband live up to her dreams of what he can be. He is her hope; she has after all placed her entire future into his hands."

Lady Beryl paused for a moment in the grip of deep

emotion and I could see Sir Henry again tighten his grip upon her hand. At last with an effort she continued, "When I saw him with the boys at the school he founded, sharing their sports and enthusiasms, and explaining to them the science of insects that he knew so well, I dreamed that my wishes had come true and that he had found his proper place at last. I had not been able to have children and here was a large family ready-made for us. When sickness came to the school I saw my husband work to try and save the boys who were ill, but he would not bring in outside help. He had concocted his own remedies in his laboratory. Even now I cannot say if they merely failed or if they poisoned the children, but all at once I began to realize that the entire school was simply a laboratory for him and that the boys were no more than white mice to my husband."

Lady Beryl shivered before continuing, "So terrible was this thought that I could not bring it forth. I have kept it in my heart until now when I tell it to you. In the uproar that followed the epidemic, the school was closed and my husband fled before the wrath of the community. We changed our name to Stapleton from Vandeleur and fled from Yorkshire to Devonshire. At first my husband had hopes of applying to his uncle for money as a distant kinsman. We had invested our all in the school. But we settled down here in a simple cottage and waited, for the name of Baskerville was now notorious in the North of England and we could not be sure that pursuit might not reach us even in Devon. We established ourselves in the quiet society of Grimpen where no one asks questions of his neighbor, each is as solitary as the moors themselves. We grew to know Sir Charles who never suspected that his friend, Rodger Stapleton, was in fact his nephew. Then came the business of the hound of which beast my husband claimed to be as much afraid as all of the people hereabouts, the more so because he was also a Baskerville and as such under the family curse."

"The rest of the story you know already. You know how Sir Charles met his end by that same hound and how even my dearest Henry was almost killed when his own time came. Never could I believe that my former husband had himself procured and nurtured that horrible beast who has so terrified this region that even now the sound of the baying of a hound causes people to board up their shutters in the village for fear of that spectral beast. Such is my tale and such is my guilt. I followed along at the very side of the devil, Rodger Baskerville, who blinded my eyes so that I could see in him only what I had so longed for and prayed might exist in him, a virtuous heart and a pure and noble soul."

She hung her head and burst into tears at the conclusion of her remarkable confession. Sir Henry held her until she grew quiet again, but even then she would not raise her head. I beckoned Sir Henry and we left the room.

"I do not think she can bear any more at present, Sir Henry. The new situation must be faced of course, but I do not wish to have her mind dwell upon what course to take when it is not clear even to me. We must wait until she is in a less excited state before going any further. You may of course go in to comfort her, but I advise against any speculations or confirmations that her husband is still in fact alive at this time. I will return to my home and will contact you soon. Until then, I advise you to speak to your staff and double any security measures that you may already have in place in case he surfaces and tries to contact her. Lady Beryl must cease her visitations upon the moors for the present. I am afraid that we shall have a long siege ahead of us. There, there old man, you must bear up. All will come right in the end." With these parting words I left him. As the doors of the great hall closed behind me I decided to take the extended sightseer path over the Baskerville Estate back to what was now my new home in order to review the facts of the case. It was at times like these that more than ever I missed the presence of Watson by my side.

The habit of marshalling my facts in preparation of placing them all before him had through the years become an essential element in the resolution of problems such as this one presented. Two foes now opposed me and at precisely the time when I suddenly felt an urge to live a private life, to grasp the hours and days that now seemed to flee past me like the wind that was rising as the slanting rays of the slowly setting sun brought out all the colors of the moors, the greens, browns, and reds of the heathers and gorse.

As I left the ornamental lime walk behind and entered the path to the high country beyond I began to climb. The granite tors that dotted the landscape, harsh and intrepid, seemed to represent the scattered elements that I had labored so hard to assemble into a coherent pattern in order to prove, not merely to Professor Moriarty, but to my own mind as well that this world for all of its harshness and inequity was still guided and guarded by a benevolent force. But the presence of evil could also never be put aside as the battle against it never ceases and even foes long since vanquished may rise again, just as Rodger Baskerville had done from his presumed final resting place in the depths of the Great Grimpen Mire.

Every now and again I came to a resting place where the path turned and a rustic seat had been provided from which various attractive vistas beckoned the eye of the wanderer. I resisted these however as I wanted to circle round home before darkness fell. The sounds of various songbirds rose with the gathering shadows as the moths rose and fluttered in the golden light.

How peaceful it all was. No hint of the dreadful baying of the beast that had once haunted this place so many years ago was to be heard, but only the sighing sound of the summer evening breeze and the trickling sound of the numerous water-courses that threaded their way down to the peat lands below. Occasional oak-tree copses, perhaps like those sites of ancient druid gatherings, appeared now and again as if deliberately placed there by design to break up the mono-chromatic scene before me.

Gradually as I walked my confidence began to return, perhaps not the untested confidence of youth, but something deeper and more rooted for having been sorely tested by the years and by my travels over the face of the earth in search of that quiet and inscrutable sensation that holier men than I have found in prayer and contemplation.

Just before the last rays of the setting sun vanished beneath the horizon with the falling night I returned to my own dwelling. I left the path to Baskerville Hall behind, opened my gate, and walked up my own gravel path to the door only to find that the long awaited missive from Professor Moriarty had been delivered in my absence and was awaiting me in the postbox carefully placed beside my entrance door.

I took the letter inside, sat down at my desk, and opened it by my still and silent hearth in the shadow-filled room. It was short and to the point. It said briefly but allusively:

To Sherlock Holmes—

I am debating entering a filly in this year's Wessex Cup Race. Come over at your convenience and we shall discuss horses and of course … other matters."

Professor James Moriarty

Note From the Author

As one who has always esteemed writers such as Graham Greene, Evelyn Waugh, and George Bernanos (each of whom was Catholic) it has been my hope that my own effort in The Confessions of Sherlock Holmes might be part of a venerable tradition. I would like to point out however that the position of a writer who incidentally is Catholic must be distinguished from that of a Catholic writer whose writings are meant precisely to reflect church teachings as such. There is a tension between these two positions that makes it difficult for a Catholic to be both true to his faith while remaining simultaneously true to the form and literary intent that must accompany any act of composition. It would be awkward and indeed impossible to write a cohesive narrative seeking to capture and comment upon human life and conflict if the writer had to simultaneously ensure that goodness and fidelity always emerged in clarity and triumph while its opposite was equally revealed in all of its inherent malice and folly. Fiction, even when dealing with theological reflection, as is the case with the present work, can never be a substitute for catechesis. The reader is therefore cautioned that in reading the present text no decisive conclusion be drawn that the positions of any of the characters reflect either the final views of the author or the official position of the Catholic Church. Literature embraces life according to its own limited perceptions as it is and even in its suggestions of a better world must always fall short, not only in displaying accurately whatever emerging forces may exist in human history, but in depicting all that has been revealed of a higher purpose and source to illumine us in our beleaguered world.

Thomas Mengert possesses a Masters Degree in English Literature with a special expertise in the complex works of the Irish author, James Joyce. His background in humanities and philosophy are combined in this probing novel. As a final Sherlockian synthesis, The Confessions of Sherlock Holmes is Mengert's attempt to understand the true depths of the best known detective in world literature, a hero to his many fans who find in his character and habits of mind an endless fascination.